DESCENT: LEGENDS *of the* DARK

Terrinoth: an ancient realm of forgotten greatness and faded legacies, of magic and monsters, heroes, and tyrants. Its cities were ruined and their secrets lost as terrifying dragons, undead armies, and demon-possessed hordes ravaged the land. Over centuries, the realm slipped into gloom…

Now, the world is reawakening – the Baronies of Daqan rebuild their domains, wizards master lapsed arts, and champions test their mettle. Banding together to explore the dangerous caves, ancient ruins, dark dungeons, and cursed forests of Terrinoth, they unearth priceless treasures and terrible foes.

Yet time is running out, for in the shadows a malevolent force has grown, preparing to spread evil across the world. Now, when the land needs them most, is the moment for its heroes to rise.

ALSO AVAILABLE IN DESCENT: LEGENDS OF THE DARK

*The Doom of Fallowhearth* by Robbie MacNiven
*The Shield of Daqan* by David Guymer
*The Gates of Thelgrim* by Robbie MacNiven
*Zachareth* by Robbie MacNiven
*The Raiders of Bloodwood* by Davide Mana

# *The* TOWER *of* NEREK

DAVID GUYMER

First published by Aconyte Books in 2022

ISBN 978 1 83908 174 3

Ebook ISBN 978 1 83908 175 0



Cover art by Asur Misoa.

Map by Francesca Baerald.

Distributed in North America by Simon & Schuster Inc, New York, USA

Printed in the United States of America

9 8 7 6 5 4 3 2 1

**ACONYTE BOOKS**

*An imprint of Asmodee Entertainment Ltd*

Mercury House, Shipstones Business Centre

North Gate, Nottingham NG7 7FN, UK

*aconytebooks.com // twitter.com/aconytebooks*

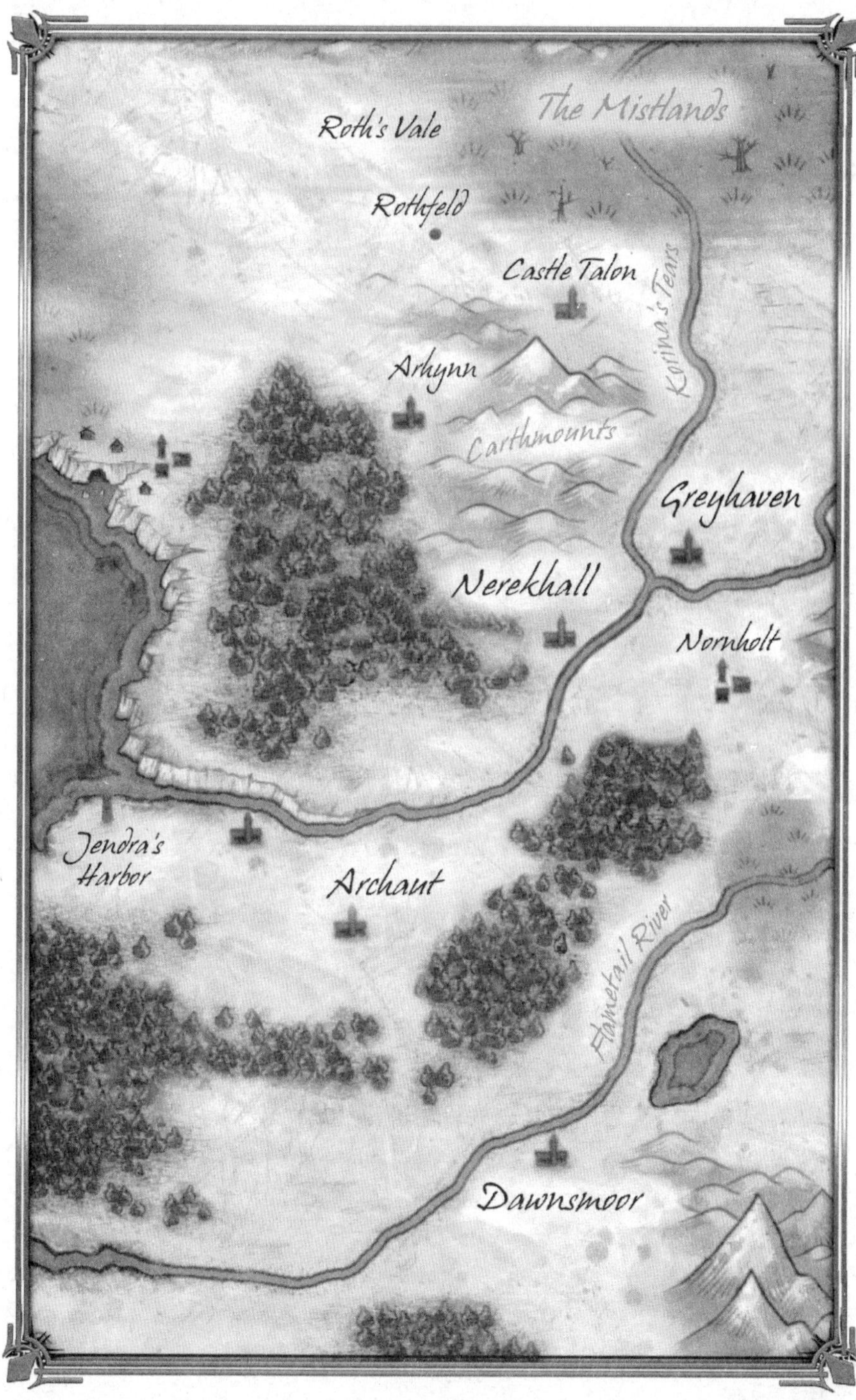

The Mistlands
Roth's Vale
Rothfeld
Castle Talon
Korina's Tears
Arhynn
Carthmounts
Greyhaven
Nerekhall
Nornholt
Jendra's Harbor
Archaut
Flametail River
Dawnsmoor

# CHAPTER ONE
## *Trenloe the Strong*

Trenloe hated running. He was too heavy for it, in armor or out, and he had no technique. There were few creatures in Terrinoth that were stupid enough to chase Trenloe, and he had never been the sort to run after someone who had already given up on the fight. When Trenloe ran, it was like a warhorse trying to get up a flight of stairs.

"Slow… down. By… Kellos." His armor clattered as he thundered down the narrow alley, arms and legs heaving up and down as though he was milling flour on a stone. "I'm not… going… to hurt you…"

He staggered on another ten yards before collapsing, red-faced and gasping, against the dark, timber frontage of the nearest house. The wood was so old it felt like bone. Thin ice, from the morning damp, tinkled onto the muddy lane. He gulped on a breath. The ripe, unfamiliar odors of people, woodsmoke, and open sewers made him regret it. He coughed it back up.

"All I want… is…" He looked up, watching as his coin purse, and the small girl who was currently holding onto it, disappeared down yet another unmarked alley. Trenloe pushed himself up off the wall with a groan. "My purse back."

Give him another demon lord to battle. Or a horde of Uthuk Y'llan to hold across a ford. Anything but more running.

With a resigned growl, he shook the sweat off his forehead and half-ran, half-stumbled after her into the alley.

Somewhere over Nerekhall the sun was shining.

Trenloe had glimpsed it briefly for himself when the guards had opened the South Cailn Bridge to traffic from the east roads. Whatever had become of it since, it didn't shine here. The buildings held each other close like partners in crime, upper stories bowed over the alleys, their roofs practically touching. Washing lines threaded the occasional gaps between the overhanging jetties, as though the only thing keeping the gloomy hovels upright was each other. Given the lingering chill of late Snowmelt and the continuing absence of sun, drying laundry had given way to thousands upon thousands of raucous city pigeons. The birds perched on the lines, pecking at the moths fluttering around the jaundiced glow from the city's ubiquitous yellow lamps.

In spite of the hour, the narrow lanes were already full.

Townsfolk in purples, blacks, and grays blended anonymously into the dark woods and deep shadows of the street. Whispering groups of them stood in close huddles over the broken cobblestones to gossip about the war in the east, the latest Guild scandal or unexplained disappearance. Children, cooped up through the long nighttime of winter's final months, ran and screamed about the alley.

Trenloe's own accursed runaway slipped through them all like a mouse across a taproom full of legs. He struggled to keep her in sight.

"Excuse me, miss." Without breaking stride, he scooped up an elderly lady who had chosen that moment to cross the street. His hands swallowed her stooped shoulders, immense biceps bulging as he deposited her as politely as possible on the opposite curb. "Make way."

A circle of older children was gathered around an oxbow in the gutter channel, fishing in the scummy water. They didn't move and Trenloe was forced into a swerve to avoid trampling them. "Coming through."

Two men carrying shoulder bags jangling with tools walked slowly ahead of him, dragging their feet as they argued about an unpaid debt to the river bailiff.

"Begging your pardon, sirs," he said, turning himself side-on and barging between them.

"Oi!" one of them yelled after him, but Trenloe was already through and several yards down the street and by then neither man, having had a proper look and a moment to consider, felt like pursuing the grievance any further.

The girl was just ahead.

She threw a sharp look over the shoulder, yelped at the sight of Trenloe the Strong bearing down in full armor, and veered into another branch in the alley.

Nerekhall was a maze of them. A sunless warren of winding alleys, blind-ends, double-backs, and crooked little lanes that got a person nowhere except lost. Trenloe had always had a terrible sense of direction. His father had despaired of it. But Nerekhall was something else. He had seen only one straight path in the entire city and that had been the road going in.

He chased the girl onto the branch, only to pull up when he found himself confronted by an unassailable wall of bustle.

Several of the crooked houses were fronted by simple

awnings in a variety of drab, sooty colors. The smell of baked loaves and barbecued meats filled the air, seeking to dislodge the less savory urban scents and not entirely succeeding. Men and women pushed carts and set up stalls, shooed stray urchins from their porch steps and hawked homespun wares.

Blowing steam into the cold air, Trenloe planted his hands on his hips and surveyed the unexpected crowd.

A maze. There was no other word for Nerekhall that fit.

He had only meant to leave his companions, Andira and Owl, at Bridge Market for a moment or two while he found directions to the Academy. Now, he was going to have to pay a guide just to retrace his steps.

"Damn that... girl."

She was nowhere to be seen.

Trenloe was not overly concerned about the money. He had made and given away more in a single day than he had just lost. The occasional clean bed or cooked meal notwithstanding, it was not as though he wanted for much. No. It was the fear of returning to Bridge Market and facing Andira Runehand's disapproval, having lost what was, after all, technically *her* money, that had kept him running across half of Nerekhall.

His friend terrified him the way no foe ever had.

"Has... anyone seen... a girl...?"

He looked hopefully around the shoppers and traders, but wherever he turned, folk glanced quickly away. *Nerekhall,* as Trenloe had been firmly informed by the black-masked captain of the watch before being admitted across the bridge, *is a law-abiding city.*

It minded its own business, and it saw no evil.

"Anyone?"

A middle-aged woman in a short dress of tattered fustian

who was setting out homemade pottery on her windowsill caught his eye. She pursed her lip briefly, then nodded towards a narrow lane that opened immediately across from her window. It was little more than a gap where two houses failed to fully meet, effectively hidden away by the clutter of street furniture.

*A maze.*

Trenloe would never even have noticed it was there.

He turned to thank the woman, but she had already disappeared, drawing the shutters over her shop window.

*It saw no evil.*

Taking a deep breath, Trenloe crossed to the alley.

It was so narrow he had to enter sideways. A pair of rats, fleeing the sound of metal armor scraping on old timber, scampered ahead, their panicked squeaks echoing from the high walls. They rose to three stories either side. The way ahead smelled of rotting trash and damp.

Had the girl really gone this way?

Could he have misinterpreted the potter's direction? Was there, even, a second alleyway she had been pointing to but which he had not seen? Or was everyone in Nerekhall a crook, petty or otherwise, and it had simply been the woman's intention to throw him off a fellow thief's chase? He shook his head, firmly berating himself for the unworthy thought. He did not mean to look for the worst in others, but he had grown up with the same stories of benighted Nerekhall as everyone and they were difficult to look past.

Nevertheless, he was still torn between turning back or trusting the woman and pressing on when a shaft of gray sunlight suddenly lit up the alley ahead.

It was not coming from above, but rather from a door that

had opened at the alley's blind-end, backlighting and framing the girl who had just thrown it open.

She was much younger than Trenloe had been expecting, no more than ten years old and strikingly, almost painfully thin. Her smock was undyed, the gray-brown color of sheep, her frightened face and dirty blonde hair streaked with mud.

Trenloe felt a stab of guilt. He was almost ready to give up the chase and let the poor child have his coin.

"Fortuna's luck," the girl spat. "What does it take to get rid of you?"

She slipped through the open door and pulled it shut behind her.

Trenloe sighed, and scraped doggedly along the tight passage.

A few seconds behind the girl, he made it to the door. He tried the latch.

The door rattled. Bolted from the other side.

He hated himself for it, but this girl was beginning to annoy him.

"Gods forgive me. This coin's supposed to be spent in a good cause."

With absolutely no effort on his part, he threw his shoulder through the door.

It crashed onto the neat, yellow-stained flagstones that lay on the other side and Trenloe blinked as he staggered through into the unexpected brilliance of direct sunlight. He had been expecting the backroom of some pickpockets' den, but found himself instead in what appeared to be a narrow backyard.

A-shaped wooden frames filled the available space between the walls. Sheepskins, apparently intended for book bindings judging by their size and shape, were stretched taut across them, creaking contentedly as they cured in the dim sunlight.

A dwarf in a stiff leather apron and gloves turned towards him, bloodshot eyes peering out over a thick woolen mask.

"Girl?" Trenloe managed to pant out.

The dwarf raised a bushy eyebrow and glanced pointedly towards the door lying on the ground at Trenloe's feet.

"I'll pay for that," Trenloe added, reaching instinctively for the coin purse at his belt before remembering where it had gone. "I'll owe you. I promise. You can find me at the Ironbrick Inn. Ask for Andira Runehand."

The dwarf appeared to scowl, though it was difficult to be completely certain through the layers of protective clothing, and jabbed a thumb over his shoulder towards the building behind him. "Thank you," Trenloe said, but the dwarf had gone back to work as if the giant in his yard had already left.

Trenloe was halfway towards the tannery when a scream pierced the cold air. He halted mid-stride, head turning towards the sound as it bounced confusingly around the jumble of garrets, gables, and walls.

It sounded as though it had come from the next yard over.

He threw another look towards the tannery, indecisive only for the time it took him to turn away and size up the yard's stone wall.

He would make up the lost coin to Andira somehow. Some things were more important than gold.

The dwarf, he noticed, was studiously getting on with his work, refusing even to look up as a second scream rang out from the other side of the wall.

Trenloe would never understand this city.

He didn't even feel guilty this time as he punched through the wall.

The old, dry stone gave before his fists as it might have done to a battering ram. Two more punches and a shoulder charge and he was through, coughing on stone dust and taking in the even smaller, even grayer yard that lay on the other side.

It was a garden. A thin trickle of sunlight fell through the overhanging eaves, enough to keep a wall-scrambling holly, a few scrags of fruiting mistletoe, and several clay pots of young tomatoes alive and green. Postern doorways and derelict wooden stairs tumbled towards it from a number of neighboring buildings including, Trenloe noticed, the one he had just left behind.

And true enough, there was his thief. She must have entered the tannery and then double-backed down the outside stair to the adjoining garden to throw him off. If she hadn't stopped and cried out, Trenloe would never have caught her.

She was buried to her shoulders in mistletoe, Andira's purse clutched to her chest as though it was Fortuna's talisman and staring not at Trenloe but at what appeared to be a suit of armor standing on the opposite side of the small yard. It was seven feet tall, more massive even than Trenloe, and in black iron from the crest of its great helm to the toes of its boots. In its left hand, it was holding a rune-embossed shield. In its right, a monstrous glaive. A tabard bearing the purple and black bicolor flag of Nerekhall hung from its groin. The limp cloth bore a white heraldic rune that Trenloe didn't recognize. It was one of the ironbound. There had been one accompanying the guards on the South Cailn Bridge. But that one had not moved.

With a grinding of gears, the suit's great helm *clanked* around until it was staring at Trenloe. There was no visor. No slits for eyes. Its face was a smooth plate of black iron patterned with gold. And yet Trenloe felt the full weight of its attention on him. A sound, like that of a sniffing hound, echoed up from the hollow prison of its helm and Trenloe felt a shiver run through him. His every sense rejected the thing in front of him.

Unalive, and yet apparently aware. Cold, and yet profoundly malign.

Trenloe had seen at close quarters the animus that the magisters of Greyhaven had sent east to fight alongside the barony of Kell against the Uthuk Y'llan. They had been inert lumps of stone, lent a crude and temporary life at their master's command.

But this...

This...

It sniffed again, as though to make certain of something, and whatever it smelled was evidently not to its liking. Hot steam whistled out through the joints of its armor and runes began to glow. Its helmet clanked sharply back towards the girl cowering in the mistletoe, who took a deep breath and screamed again, and Trenloe did what he was famous for.

He acted without thinking.

His fist, still gray with dust from punching through the wall, smashed across the thing's face. The helmet gave a hollow clang, twisting a quarter turn to the side, but the armor didn't so much as stumble.

Trenloe, meanwhile, roared in pain, drawing his bruised knuckles to his chest.

It was like punching an anvil.

The ironbound's return blow came while he was still reeling from the shock, a steel-crumpling backhand that sent Trenloe crashing through the wall and back into the tanner's yard.

He coughed, face buried in the dust and rubble, and immediately needed to cough again.

*Walk it off, Trenloe,* his father had always used to say to him when he was down. *You're a big lad, so on your feet and walk it off.*

Unshipping his shield from his back, he planted its pointed base into the crack between two stones and propped his chest up off the ground.

He hung his head in near-despair as the ironbound stomped through what was left of the wall. It said nothing. It made no sound but for the grating of heavy armor and the *tick-tick-tick* of hidden gears. It was not quick, but it came on with a relentless indefatigability that was exhausting just to watch. At least it was coming for him now instead of the girl. From somewhere deep inside, he found the strength to curl his injured fingers around the handle of his axe and draw it from his belt.

From behind the advancing armor's back, he saw the girl's pale face peeking through the hole in the wall.

"Run," Trenloe hissed, as the ironbound built up a head of steam, smashing the flagstones between it and Trenloe under its heavy iron boots. It drew back its shield to strike. Trenloe's voice rose to become a yell. "Find Andira Runehand at Bridge Market and tell her–"

He never finished.

The armor issued a shuddering metallic howl, iron pushed to its breaking point, and its heavy shield stove into the side of Trenloe's head.

Trenloe hit the ground.

And fell silent.

## CHAPTER TWO
### *Andira Runehand*

*Bonggg.*

The dirge-like notes of the Academy bells rolled across the sleeping city, muted by the late hour, dulled by distance and by the thick stone walls that surrounded her. They were dark and laced with cobwebs.

*Bonggg.*

Andira reached out for an empty sconce to brush away the cobwebs. The rune of power drawn across her palm filled in the concavity with a pale blue light, shining so brightly against the lingering taint of the Ynfernael that she could make it out through the back of her hand. An incomplete circle, a vertical line just slightly off-center striking it through. A sword and a shield, that was how Andira had always seen it, traced with the light of the Empyrean and blurred by the intervening meat and bone of her hand.

*Bonggg.*

She drew back from the wall, her fingers sticky with old webs, her brow knotted in confusion. It occurred to her that she was unsure what had brought her to this hallway, this building, only that it was important to her, and that she had come a long, long way in order to get here.

*Bonggg.*

A long flight of spiral steps lay behind her like a trap. The darkness it harbored was deep, the breeze emerging from its rotten stone mouth hungry, and yet vastly patient. It was a whisper on the back of her neck, a rumor and a temptation, but a warning, too, a small and ephemeral hand tugging on her hair, urging her back.

She ignored it.

Andira never turned back.

*Bonggg.*

The corridor ahead of her was low and narrow. Close. The walls and ceiling were crumbling from untold years of neglect. At its far end, a small wooden door hung ajar, rotten on its hinges. The sight of it made Andira's breath catch. She did not fear death. The threat of pain or failure gave her no pause. And yet the aspect of that slightly open door set her heart hammering in her chest.

*Bonggg.*

The funereal bell shivered through her.

"*My beloved foe.*" The door seemed to breathe outward, creaking wider to release something that should have remained behind it for all time. "*My paramour.*"

A horned silhouette stood within the now-gaping door.

Andira blinked, taking the backward step she had sworn never to accept, towards the solace promised by the stairwell. When she next opened her eyes, the figure was gone.

*Bonggg.*

Breathing hard, she reached over her shoulder for the

poleaxe she always bore with her. It was not there. She looked up. The corridor before her had shortened, dragging the door towards her, or her to it. The figure stood over her, twelve feet of cold, hard ivory, a statue to the pitiless majesty of hate. It looked down on her with eyes that were hollow wells, smiled with a mouth that never moved.

Andira screamed.

*Bonggg.*

On the eighth and final bell, she woke up.

Andira jerked reflexively, gripping her thigh plate tightly and sitting up, drawing a deep breath and gasping at the cold that hit the back of her throat.

She was still in the Bridge Market, an open square filled with murmuring crowds and tented stalls, enclosed on one side by the slate-gray expanse of the Korina's Tears River, and on the other by the dark timber and brooding stonework of Nerekhall itself. From the top of a short flight of granite steps, she looked out across the river. The statue of some well-known local merchant loomed over her shoulder, her long blonde hair having thoroughly knotted itself into the grain of the stone where she had slept against it.

The warrior she knew as Owl sat three steps down from her with his arms resting over his knees. He held Andira's poleaxe loosely in one hand, its small flags and pennons beating in the cold breeze off the river. He was dark-haired and unshaven, bearing a closer resemblance to a sell-sword down on his luck than the nobleman that Andira knew him to be.

His hair had been allowed to grow so long that it obscured most of the heraldic symbols on his armor that might have identified him. He had had a name, too, once, and a past that went with it, but he recalled neither and Andira had sworn never to speak of them. He had the right to find his own path, wherever it led. Trenloe, with characteristically abundant good humor, was the one who had dubbed him Owl, for the gold blazon on his enameled breastplate, and for want of a better name, it had stuck.

She looked over her other shoulder. There was no one else there.

She turned back to Owl, concerned. "Where is Trenloe?"

Owl shook his head. His gray eyes looked sad.

Andira rubbed the last of the sleep from her eyes, pulling the clutter of the recurring dream from her thoughts. It was rare that she needed sleep. The rune provided her body with most of the rest and nourishment that it needed. To have simply dozed off where she had been sitting… it made the experience of waking all the more disconcerting.

"It was six o'clock when the guards opened the bridge. That means…" She frowned suddenly as her mind cleared enough to perform straightforward subtraction. "Trenloe has been gone for two hours. Flames of Kellos, he was only supposed to be asking for directions to the Academy. Why did you not wake me when he failed to return?"

"You needed rest," Owl replied, and unfolded one of his arms from across his knees to present her with a waxed paper bundle.

There was a cold meat pasty inside.

"You bought that for me while I was asleep?"

A nod.

"But Trenloe was holding all of the money."

Owl tucked his fingers in over the waxed parcel and turned his knuckles towards her. One of his fingers was missing a ring. Andira shook her head. He was as careless with his money as

Trenloe, but at least Owl had the excuse of being born noble. "You traded your ring for a pie?"

Owl shrugged, shuffling a short way along his step to show the empty wrapping he had been sitting on.

*Two pies.*

"That is kind, but I do not need rest."

"You do," Owl insisted.

"What I need is to be on our way. Where is Trenloe?"

But Owl had already turned away, distracted by the boats on the river.

Peasants punted their small craft under the stone double-arches of South Cailn Bridge while two dozen students in sleek black boats practiced for the boat race with Greyhaven. An annual event that even Andira had heard of, it took place on New Year's Day to mark the end of winter and the start of the new academic year. And settling, for the next thirteen months, whether it was to be the Nerekhall Academy or Greyhaven University with the right to call itself the most esteemed college of rune-lore and magic in Terrinoth.

They seemed to be living in another world to the one that Andira saw.

But then, eyes could adjust to shadows in time. Why not hearts and minds?

"You have not slept properly since the day you found me," said Owl, still watching the boats, and the flocks of Lorimor geese scudding belligerently amongst them. "And when you do, you..."

*Dream*, he did not quite say.

They had started about six months ago, almost immediately after the Battle of Furnace Gate and the defeat of the demon king, Baelziffar. Nightmares when she slept. Omens and portents when she did not. Visions of some rising evil, calling her somewhere she knew not, to perform some task she knew not.

She seldom recalled much of what transpired in her dreams when she awoke, only the unsettled feeling that remained when she did. They had only grown more vivid, and more frequent, as they traveled further west from Kell, until she could barely now close her eyes without seeing her nemesis, beckoning her towards some unspeakable goal. She knew when she was being drawn somewhere, but not why. She could be certain of only one fact, and that was that in coming to Nerekhall she was, if not in the place that she needed to be, then at least on the correct path.

She hoped to find something more resembling an answer in the Academy.

With a glare, because as much as she would sooner deny being as mortal as everyone else, she knew that Owl was right, she snatched the wax parcel from his hand. He smiled, as though pretending not to have noticed, and turned back towards the river.

Unpeeling the paper, she bit into Owl's pasty. The filling had turned stodgy as it had cooled, but it had a peppery warmth that was welcome against the cold morning. Chewing absently on the breakfast, she looked around the Bridge Market square.

This was part of the city that few visitors to Nerekhall ever saw beyond. It was all shops, coaching houses, and banks, tall buildings with grand, but foreboding frontages, catering to the merchants who came from all over Cailn to Nerekhall's markets and the tenant farmers who visited for the day from the surrounding fields. The boulevards were wide and open, as though the city's planners had been afraid that if darkness was allowed in, even for the few hours before dawn, then it would never leave. Or worse, that people might find that they liked it.

Tall, wrought-iron streetlamps stood on every corner, with similar lamps bolted to the towering half-timber facades of those buildings gathered around the market square. In spite of the sunrise, currently laying its red fingers across the rooftops, they were still lit, lending a sepia pallor to the crowded, quiet streets whilst drawing deeply shaded lines around the darkness.

As she watched the crowds, licking her finger for the last flakes of pastry, she felt a prickling down the back of her neck, a vague but familiar tingle from the rune in her hand. It was not the nightmare. Food and fresh air had rid her senses of that.

She was being watched.

Andira frowned for a moment, certain that she had seen a small child standing suspiciously still amidst the moving crowds, but before she could look again to be sure, Owl was tugging on her sleeve and directing her eyes elsewhere.

"Look."

A horse-drawn wain carrying a group of black-robed students was pushing its way slowly across the market. Bound for the Academy, no doubt, summoned by the bells to their morning classes.

"We could follow them," said Owl.

Andira sucked on her teeth as she considered, then reluctantly shook her head.

The thought of cutting Trenloe loose and continuing on without him did not trouble her. Indeed, it had a certain appeal. Her first meeting with Trenloe the Strong had been on the battlefield at Furnace Gate. Coming so soon after the loss of her pilgrim followers and the death of her champion, Sir Brodun, joining with a hero of such renown that even she, ten years in the wildernesses, had heard his name, had been comforting. The novelty had not long survived the westbound road. The man was like a performing bear, as innocent and as distractable as a child, but if anyone could look after himself in a strange city then it was him.

But, if Andira intended to learn why Baelziffar was sending her nightmares in spite of his apparent demise in Kell then the Academy was the place to find those answers. Trenloe claimed that an old friend of his now taught there. How a semi-literate Trastan farmhand had come into acquaintance with a Nerekhall rune-scholar was a mystery to Andira, but the man made friends everywhere. To a woman who had few friends anywhere it was a skill as baffling as any magic.

"No, we–"

She stopped, turning her head as though the itch down the nape of her neck was the claw of the Ynfernael tapping on her shoulder for attention. The child she had felt watching her from across Bridge Market had crossed between the stalls and was now standing at the bottom of the steps to the merchant's statue. She was a scruffy, feral-looking thing with a rattish haircut and nervous eyes, as though she, too, had been awake all night and would never sleep again for the things she had seen.

Owl smiled down at her.

Place a child in front of him, and her brooding protector became a stuffed toy.

Andira glowered. "You were watching us."

The girl swallowed. It was obvious that she wanted little more than to flee back into the crowds, but for some reason unbeknownst to Andira she chose instead to stand her ground.

"My name's Lidiya," she finally piped up. "And I'm not afraid of you."

Andira raised an eyebrow. She was more accustomed to monsters than people, and was more a stranger in Terrinoth's cities than Trenloe. Owl had been the parent, even if he did not remember it, not her – she had no idea how to talk to a child. "Good," she answered, stiffly. "I am not afraid of you either."

The girl looked unsure whether she was being teased or not. For reasons Andira did not quite understand, the possibility seemed to put her more at ease. "You're Andira Runehand, aren't you?"

"I am. Who sent you here to ask?"

The girl looked relieved. "Thank Fortuna. He said I'd find you here."

"Who?"

"Trenloe the Strong, of course. Who else?"

Andira closed her eyes and let out a long, resigned breath.

Of course. Who else, indeed?

"And what did he say?"

"Just to find you here. It was… It was all he got to say." The girl's lips moved nervously, as though uncertain which form of expression was the correct one for the words they had to say. "Before they took him away."

# CHAPTER THREE
## *Thaiden Mistspeak*

By mid-morning, half the city had heard that Trenloe the Strong, the renowned southern hero, had come to Nerekhall.

Rothbert Tierney, a Wick Lane laborer, had grumbled to his workmates of being run off the street by a giant in silver armor. One of those same workmates, purchasing two cuts of freshwater trout from the jetties later that morning, had opined that this must be the very same man who had charged into the dawn fair at Dillholme shouting about a thief. Several laughs later about the chances of blundering through Dillholme at any time of day or night and finding someone who was not a thief, it had been wondered whether it was the same man, too, who had wrecked the yard behind Olf Strengsson's bookbinders' shop.

According to Olf himself it most certainly was. He would be seeking Trenloe out, he said, and this Andira Runehand with whom the hero was supposedly lodging, at the Ironbrick Inn to claim the damages he was owed just as soon as his friends were fully mustered and armed.

Knowledge was the only currency worth anything in

Nerekhall. Over the counter, its merchants and its banks traded in the same crowns, stars, and pennies as their counterparts across Terrinoth, but they were merely the tools to pry the real treasure from its black soil. Information was the one thing that Nerekhall could truly be said to produce, its principal export, the thing that most who found their way within its borders came to find.

And in that, Thaiden Mistspeak was no different.

Nudging up the wide brim of his hat, a pair of brilliant red cardinal feathers sticking out of the band, he stood out in the coaching yard and looked up at the Ironbrick Inn.

It was reputed to be one of the oldest buildings in Nerekhall, having survived war, flood, a mysterious subsidence that had claimed three quarters of the city about a hundred years before, and fire. The Ironbrick had not always been its name, and nor had it started life as an inn, but it had earned the name that befit its sturdiness.

Some locals claimed that it was the Mason's Guild of Thelgrim who had built it. Others said that it had been raised from its foundations by Soulstone architects at the very height of that era's magical hubris. So far as Thaiden could tell, and he had a knack for sifting gossip from rumor, there was nothing to choose between the theories and no real basis for either. It was always easier to credit Soulstone magic or the dwarves than to put genuine thought into how such workmanship had been achieved and to wonder why it was not commonplace.

It was just a well-made building. And, perhaps, a lucky one.

Three brooding stories of stone and half timbers rose over the secluded yard. The walls were stained yellow, made somehow to appear menacing by the sickly guttering of its lamp fixtures and what little sunlight had proved able to pierce the clouds. Solid transoms jutted from the walls like fortifications, the windows' leaded glass naturally secretive and dark. A dull murmur of noise leaked through the rough joins between the little diamond-shaped panes and the wooden frames. And through the cracks around the heavy door.

It was not much, like listening to a conversation through a wall, but it stood in contrast to the general air of wariness that pervaded across Nerekhall. Even the Korina's Tears, some miles behind him now, remained as an audible babbling in the background of the city.

There was a pair of well-appointed coaches parked in the yard. They were darkly colored, the better to blend in with the subdued tones of their surroundings, and sparingly decorated with gilt. The box windows were curtained. Those curtains were drawn. The horses huffed and snorted, whickering to one another in the lowest of low voices and obscuring their intent behind clouds of vapor.

Terrinoth was an enormous country.

It was a sprawling realm of loosely aligned territories, each free city and barony with its own customs, laws, and vested interests, little pockets of civilization broken up from one another by deep forests, rugged mountains, half-forgotten ruins, unmapped rivers, and endless downs.

There were any number of ways that a person who wanted to disappear might ensure they were never found, but most invariably turned up in a predictable handful of places.

The truly desperate would often find their way to Last Berth in the mountainous north of Rhynn barony, or instead struck out east to Last Haven, across the civilized frontier and onto the Ru Steppes. Until the Uthuk Y'llan had swarmed up from the Darklands and razed it to the ground on their way through to Forthyn and Kell, of course. Bad business that, but none of his. The adventurous might flee to Isheim. The wealthy to Lorimor or Al-Kalim.

But for most, those without the means, the spirit, or simply a good enough map, the destination was always Nerekhall. It was a large city, overcrowded enough to disappear into, secretive enough to hide them, for a cost, cursed enough to keep them, if they were less than careful. Thaiden was not a native to Nerekhall, but given the nature of his work it was something of a second home. He could follow a beast or person across a mountain by the month-old tracks they had left in the grass, or find a lost treasure by the clues left in the shape of the earth, the behavior of the animals, or the nature of the foliage that had grown over it.

Removing his hat, Thaiden shook off the collected dew, stamped the mud and the wet from his boots on the front step, and then pushed in through the front door.

The Ironbrick Inn was the kind of establishment in which the opening of a door caused conversations to still and patrons to turn in their seats to appraise a newcomer. This was not out of any sense of hostility, though Thaiden nevertheless felt his collar growing hot under the regard, but because the Ironbrick's clientele tended to be people who were worthy of note. The minstrels on their stage, however, discreetly tucked away in the stout timber curve of the staircase, never stopped playing.

With a nod to the rich and powerful of central Terrinoth, Thaiden stumped his way to the bar. There, he pulled up a stool, unslung the light crossbow from his shoulder and propped it up against the side of the counter, set his hat on the polished wooden top and sat down.

"For your labors," said the man beside him as he got up to leave, pulling on a rich coat and sliding a silver half-star across the counter towards him.

Thaiden looked at the coin, perplexed. By the time it dawned on him that the man had obviously mistaken him for the inn's hostler he had already gathered up his two children and was halfway across the common room towards the door.

It took all Thaiden's willpower to not simply snatch that coin off the table and hurl it at the back of the man's head with a curse. No. More than that. He wanted to march back there, take the fool by the hair, throw him into the nearest table, then drag the man out by the scruff of his fine coat and have him empty his purse into the actual hostler's hands, because shoveling manure was as honest work as any in Nerekhall, and then roll him into the gutter to consider his life's choices.

He took a deep breath.

Thaiden was always angry. He could no longer remember a time when he had not been. With a smile as thinly worn as his boots, he slid the silver coin across the counter, summoning the prosperous-looking woman from the other side of the bar.

"A plateful of something hot and a tankard of something strong." When the innkeeper continued to regard him dubiously, he forced a "Please" to which she gave a resigned grunt and scraped the coin off the countertop into her apron.

She withdrew to the kitchens.

While he waited, Thaiden pivoted in his stool, lounging

back with his elbows on the bar and watched the room as a hawk would a field.

Any fool could secrete himself in a corner booth, smoking a pipe with his feet up on the table and his hat pulled down, looking about as inconspicuous as a dire wolf at a farmer's market, but the bar was where things happened. It was where the ale was poured and the gossip spilled.

The innkeeper returned with a bowl of beef hash, half a loaf of nutty bread, and a mug of spiced ale. Thaiden ignored her, and so she set the refreshments on the counter and left.

There were as many ways to find a person in Terrinoth as there was to lose one, but Thaiden had a knack for it. There had been the time he led his clan through the Crags of the Forgotten to find safety from Uthuk raiders. The rainstorm after the Stormtide Ceilidh in which he had rescued his wife-to-be from the Gray Wastes whilst half-sober himself. The time his sister had hidden their grandmother's lucky hairpin in a haystack, or even…

He stopped short, before he could think too long about those friends he had used to have, of how his talents had proved equally effective in tracking down their murderers and the things he had done to them once he had.

The rage that had driven him to it had never gone away. It had stayed with him. The way family should.

He didn't know how his talent worked. Mostly it was doggedness and the ability to pay attention. Amateurs asked questions. Thaiden just listened.

"First Kell and now Forthyn," Countess Mirabel was murmuring to her guards. "It will be Carthridge falling to the Locust Swarm next, and I do not plan on still being here when it does…"

"No, no, no," another lady, Vanja Hess, was insisting. "I have it on good authority that tangerine is to be the color that the ladies will be wearing for the Council of Barons this Highsummer. I have two shiploads of orpiment due into Jendra's Harbor from Al-Kalim next week and ready to be shipped upriver to Nerekhall..."

"And she told me she intended to marry him," Commander Bregen was growling to the man at his left. "I told her she's here to study, and she's only been in the city a week..."

If Thaiden has been interested in real gossip, then he would have gone to the Rat-Thing King's in the old city or the Wizard's Keys on Academy Lane. The wealthy rarely had anything interesting to talk about.

"Did you hear about the brawl in Dillholme Market this morning?"

With cool indifference, Thaiden swiveled back towards the counter. He leaned forwards, tearing a chunk of bread off his half loaf and dunking it idly in his steaming bowl.

The man who had spoken was sitting a few empty places down the bar from Thaiden. His name, Thaiden had gathered from listening in with half an ear, was Trence Hanlow. He was forty-eight years old and had three daughters, none of whom knew what he had done to become rich or would approve of if they did. His companion was a boatwoman, named Jadren, also a Hanlow, but an in-law, and burdened each day with lunch at the Ironbrick with Trence.

"Always someone getting hit over something in Dillholme," Jadren replied with a shrug.

Trence gave her an indulgent laugh.

Thaiden felt the softened breadcrust crumbling in his grip. He'd had an older brother once.

"You think I'd mention it if it were some ten-a-penny brawl?" said Trence, apparently offended by the accusation. "No. Some thoroughbred lump of Trastan farm boy, fresh over the South Cailn Bridge, only went and thought he could take on one of the ironbound."

Jadren stirred her soup. "We're getting a lot of dark sorcerers coming up from Artrast now, are we?"

"I wouldn't like to say. But I'm told he threw the first punch."

"Now I know you're yanking my chain."

"On Aris' coin, it's true."

"No one'd be that dumb. Not even a country Trastan."

"Good hit, too, or so I hear. Put a dent in it. Right here."

"Impossible!"

"It's true. I wonder if he's looking for work."

Jadren snorted. "Good luck. You won't be seeing him again."

Thaiden glanced their way, entirely casual, and nodded towards the pair. "Must've been a big man. To put a mark on an ironbound."

Jadren looked up, and then immediately back down, as though regretting even her passive role in this conversation thus far. A person could never be too careful about what they said. Or who they said it around. There were powerful people in Nerekhall, Thaiden knew, who viewed even idle gossip about the ironbound as a subversive act.

Trence gave him a cursory once-over. If the far northern accent, which Thaiden could shamelessly lean into or drop entirely, didn't present him as a harmless outsider then he was confident that his appearance would do the rest. His cloak was stiff and color-faded. His boots were cracked. Even the crossbow, though a good one, contributed to the desired effect. Only outsiders and soldiers in uniform bore arms so openly in Nerekhall.

It was a law-abiding city.

"Biggest you ever saw," Trence offered. "Some ogre blood in him, I'd say."

"Still got dragged along his half-ogre backside to the Tower though, didn't he?" said Jadren, as though speaking for an audience it was safest to assume was present.

Thaiden dutifully raised an eyebrow. "The Tower of Nerek?"

"Aye." Trence set his fork down beside his plate and looked thoughtful. "Waste of good talent, if you ask me. The river trade is always looking for strong men who aren't afraid of a little work."

"Good riddance, I say," Jadren added.

Thaiden frowned down into his bowl of hash.

*The Tower of Nerek.*

The place had a cursed reputation, even in Nerekhall where people knew more about curses than most. It was an elven ruin to the south of the city, turned later into a prison by the master of Nerekhall. Thaiden gave this new information due consideration. There was no place he could not get into, and no place he could not get something out of. He had been paid well, and in advance, to find this person and Thaiden prided himself on always finding what he set out to. He had something of a reputation, too. It was, arguably, all he had.

Carefully, as if wary of damaging the table, he set down what was left of his bread. He wiped a spot of beef gravy from the corner of his mouth.

"Are you finishing that?" said Trence.

Thaiden pushed the half-finished bowl of beef hash towards

him and left a pair of bronze pennies on the countertop. He picked up his hat and his crossbow.

He knew where he needed to go.

# CHAPTER FOUR
## *Andira Runehand*

"How much further to the Tower?" said Andira, the blued steel of her armored boots splashing in the water where it had pooled between the broken cobbles, the bladed ferrule of her poleaxe clacking rhythmically on the dark stones. Her gaze swept from side to side in time with her stride, as though the Tower of Nerek might be drawn from hiding by the challenge alone.

The streets, even in this most misbegotten quarter of a misbegotten city, were crowded, but wherever Andira set herself to walking they almost magically cleared. Whether human, elf, orc, or dwarf, there was something about her that made honest folk recoil and the dishonest flee outright. They avoided her, and always had done. She did not know if this was something to do *with her* or just another element of her rune's power that she did not yet fully understand. It was possible, of course, that it had something to do with both her *and* her rune. She had little time for other people, and so the magic of the rune took that wish and imposed it on those around her.

Andira shook the thought from her head. There was nothing more self-indulgent than a question with no answer.

"Not far," Lidiya called breathlessly from behind.

Lacking Andira's unconscious ability to part a crowd, the girl slipped nimbly through it, sidestepping a woman in a hooded shawl before being pulled out from the path of a laden barrow by Owl. It was heavy with winter greens and parsnips, clattering up a flight of steps to bash through the door into a cheap inn. The off-key strains of a lute tumbled into the street, a few bars of something maudlin to the clattering of wooden crockery, before the door *thunked* shut behind the disappearing barrow. Owl glared wordlessly after it, Lidiya dragging him away by the wrist.

"It's that..." The girl pointed out an alley, but Andira was already veering off from the main street, scattering urchins before she had the chance to add, "... *way*."

At this point, Andira felt as though she barely had need for a guide at all.

She had always, at least as far back as she could recall, possessed a deep sense for the Ynfernael. She could tell where the boundaries between the physical world and the lower plane lay close together, where the walls between them were in disrepair or had collapsed entirely. She could not put words to the feeling she had from Nerekhall but the usual barriers between the planes here were thin enough to be almost non-existent.

Everywhere she turned, she saw not a city of mortals, but a place where fear and suspicion had been allowed to fester and spread like damp across a plaster wall. She saw it in the untended cobbles and the leaking gutters, in the long shadows that no amount of artificial illumination could uproot. She saw it in the people, too, in the way they looked suspiciously at three strangers, and spoke in whispers for fear of who or what might listen and use an unguarded word against them. Where children played it was amongst the detritus of the failed generations that had preceded them. Andira could almost see the demons, shadows of the Ynfernael lying in wait for their innocence to die.

The further Lidiya took her from those regions frequented by merchants and students, the stronger her sense of descent became. It was as though she was going downhill, slipping a dozen paces through loose ground for every one she took by choice.

She could have found her way to the Tower blindfolded. She was not sure she could have chosen another destination if she had wanted to.

"I feel I should be able to see it already," she said, looking suspiciously up at the tall buildings hemming them in.

They stood three, four, at times five stories high, each tier overhanging a little further over the one beneath until they leant over the alley like tired giants. Leaded windows returned the streetlamps' smudged yellow glow. The small diamond-shaped panes made them look like the eyes of insects.

"You would," Lidiya answered, "if the houses weren't so high." With Owl still holding her firmly by the hand, she pointed to their right. Andira looked. There was nothing there but another tall, brooding house. "No one in Nerekhall is allowed to look at the Tower. There's a law. It's why the houses are so big, and so close together. And why all the windows face away from it."

Owl looked up at the house. His gaze tracked across it, then he turned and did the same with the building opposite.

"I hadn't noticed," he said, after a long moment's thought. "I knew there was something… *wrong* about them."

"It is not the windows," said Andira, with conviction.

"It is one way to find your way."

Andira shivered. *And not the only one.* Feeling as though something invisible was breathing on her neck, she turned sharply, eyes blazing silver-blue, and sent a perfectly innocent-seeming man in a winter coat reeling from her gaze. With a frown, she turned back, the power of her rune making a golden halo of her hair and her pale skin luminous. "What happened here, to leave Nerekhall this way?"

She had heard the stories, of course. Dark tales of ambitious mages and the slippery paths they took towards necromancy and disaster, but they were little more than fables, cautionary tales to warn later generations of the danger posed by powerful mages left unchecked. Even in Greyhaven, where scholars could be relied on to speak with relish on the unsavory reputation of their rival school, it was a subject that was rarely addressed. Suspicion of magic, and mages, cut both ways, she supposed.

"It was about a hundred years ago," said Owl, speaking with eyes glazed and face averted, as though reading from a text somewhere inside his mind. "A sorcerer called Gargan Mirklace destroyed half the city, though I do not know why or how. After his defeat, the Council of Thirteen met in Archaut to vote on purging what was left of the city and its surviving inhabitants, in order to be certain that whatever Mirklace had unleashed there was eradicated. One abstention was enough to spare it."

He said nothing more for a time, then shrugged to indicate that he was done.

It never ceased to amaze Andira that Owl could recall next to nothing of his former life and yet be so learned in geography, theology, history, and law. It was a similar phenomenon, she supposed, to her apparent knowledge of rune-lore. She had less memory even than Owl sometimes displayed, but the mystery had managed to become a part of her over the years.

"That's what I heard, too," said Lidiya, nodding. "But my parents didn't like it when I asked. The shadow has passed, they said."

"Where are your parents?" Andira asked.

The girl shut her mouth and looked away. Owl laid a hand on her shoulder and led her on.

Andira wondered if the Council's decision to spare Nerekhall, or rather their indecision about destroying it, had been the correct one. It had been the humane one, certainly, but Andira was not sure if it was the one she would have made in their place. The uncertainty troubled her.

When a person lied, Andira could always tell. The mere *intent* to deceive was an act of harm that scarred the veil in ways that few could see, but she could. And when a thousand people, ten thousand people, shaped their very existences in service to a lie until it *became* truth, then the scarring thickened until the firma dracem itself became weak.

*The shadow has passed: a lie.*

Andira marveled at the fact that nobody had noticed but her. She wondered if this could be why her visions had led her here.

"Do you know this city well, Lidiya?"

The girl nodded. "I've lived here my whole life."

"Do you know the way to the Academy?"

She gave Andira a look as though she had been asked if she had ever seen the color blue. "Of course."

"Once we are done here, could you take us there? I will be able to pay you, just as soon as we have retrieved Trenloe and my coin from the Tower of Nerek."

The girl colored and looked away again.

Andira wondered if she had offended some local sensibility by offering her payment. It would be something to bear in mind the next time she needed aid in Nerekhall. It did, however, raise the question of why she was so keen to help her release Trenloe, if not for the hope or promise of coin.

With a sigh, she took that thought and put it firmly away into the part of her mind that she had begun to label *Trenloe.* She put terror into some people, it was true, but to her mind they acted even more strangely around Trenloe. They tended to do things out of the sheer goodness of their heart.

Lidiya and Owl rounded a corner.

The girl screamed.

Owl pulled her back by the wrist, going to one knee and drawing her into the protection of his arms while Andira firmed her grip around her poleaxe and raised her glowing hand to whatever Lidiya had just seen.

The ironbound stepped over the last cobbles before the path they had been walking gave out to weed-choked common land. The dark iron of the armor's panels had been polished to a black shine, as though nothing less would have permitted the runes written into it to take. The arcane designs swirled around and through one another, often beginning in one plate and then carrying over the golden edge trim to merge into the patterns of the next. Andira's rune-lore was purely instinctive, but she mentally traced each design as she recognized it – a rune of vigor, of endurance, of anti-magic, of strength – and the many others that she could not make out in full or identify at all.

The craftsmanship was staggering. The wealth that had gone into it was beyond her comprehension.

With a hollow *TICK*, as though a clock had been sealed inside its iron chest, the helmet turned a fraction of an inch from center until it was facing towards her.

Lidiya gave a terrified cry, burying her face in the Owl's graying hair as the knight lifted her off the ground and took her into his arms.

Andira felt her heart thump as the rune-light from her hand guttered. The runes of anti-magic etched into the armor were dampening its powers. The hairs on the back of her neck stood on end. She felt almost faint as the rune's magic leached out of her. She had never felt so *ordinary.*

The armor looked at her impassively, as if it had never moved, and it was only her lack of sleep that had led her to imagine it.

Andira took a step back, feeling her pulse strengthen and power trickle back into her limbs as she put distance between herself and the armor. Tentatively, she lowered her hand, as if to show this sentinel that she meant it no harm.

"The ironbound were first built after Nerekhall was saved from Mirklace," said Owl, continuing to offer silent comfort to the girl in his arms. "The Council of Thirteen demanded a militia to whom they could entrust the safety of Terrinoth should the threat of dark magic arise in Nerekhall again. The ironbound are the soldiers the Artificers of Pollux provided."

Lidiya sniffed and lifted her face from Owl's chest. She flinched when she saw the ironbound, but it did not move again, and appeared to take a kind of courage from being so overlooked. "It was an ironbound that fought Trenloe."

"There is no one in Terrinoth more obviously *not* a dark mage than Trenloe the Strong," said Andira. "Why would one of Pollux's soldiers attack him?"

"He was protecting me."

Andira looked at her sternly.

The girl swallowed. "I… I don't know why it attacked me."

Andira could always tell when a person lied, but in this instance she did not even need to ask. If the girl had been an illicit blood witch, a worshipper of Ynfernael powers and acolyte of Llovar, then Andira was certain she would have discerned it by now. But evil magic came in many forms, forms with which she was less familiar and, perhaps, unable to sense so easily. Necromancy, for instance, or the harsher practices of elementalism performed by the priests of Nordros.

But she believed her. The girl was not lying.

And yet the ironbound *had* attacked her.

She turned her attention back to the ironbound. It had not moved again, either to track her movement or to return its head to a forward-facing position. For some reason, seeing it with its "head" askance sent a shiver down her spine. "Why does it not attack us now?"

Lidiya sniffed. Tears glistened in her eyes. "I don't know."

Making quieting sounds, Owl guided the girl's face back towards his shoulder and stroked her hair. Andira decided to drop the question for now. It seemed clear that Lidiya knew no more than she claimed. Perhaps Trenloe would know more.

Leaving the ironbound to its vigil, they crossed onto the common.

The Tower of Nerek rose from its center.

It stood alone, cut adrift from the city but for the occasional outline of a long-abandoned house or a length of rotten fencing. People had thought to try and dwell there once, but no longer, preferring the rank overcrowding and human menace of Nerekhall to the shadow of the Tower. And perhaps wisely.

The Tower of Nerek itself was a deceptively beautiful bastion of pale stone. Something in its decaying elegance and tapering height spoke to Andira of elven architecture. Andira had spent several years in Arlathan Forest and the Bloodwood, and knew the work of the Latari by sight, but she knew that Nerekhall was a long way north of the Latari elves' traditional Aymhelin heartlands. The Tower of Nerek could, perhaps, have been the work of one of the lesser elven clans, but most of those had been transient, gone far away from Terrinoth, or more enigmatic even than the Latari. Andira had names for fewer than half of them.

More recent attempts at restoration clad the elven ruin in crude wooden wall walks and mantlets. Timber palisades staked out large sections of a projecting gatehouse. A solitary flag, the purple and black bicolor of Nerekhall, flew from the pinnacle tower, tearing at its pole like a felon in the stocks.

It looked like a fortress.

"Trenloe is inside?" she asked.

Lidiya looked up, puffy-eyed from crying, and nodded.

"Are we breaking Nerekhall's laws now by looking at it?"

"The city ends at the edge of the common." Lidiya sniffed. "So my mother told me."

Owl pursed his lips, turning to take in the bleak wooden skyline that encircled the scrubland. Nerekhall had grown entirely around the Tower but, for whatever reason, had never quite claimed it. "So, we're technically standing in the Wildlands now?"

Lidiya shrugged, and they crossed the rest of the way in silence.

The Tower of Nerek seemed to demand it.

There were no paved roads across the common, but several well-worn trails linked the Tower at its center to the city surrounding it, each one made permanent by centuries of mailed boots and prison wagons laden with Nerekhall's unwanted.

The pennons affixed to Andira's poleaxe fluttered fiercely as she bore it onto the downs, and into the wind that tore across it unchallenged. The wind against her became blistering, and laden with a discord of what sounded like voices. Damning. Condemning. Cajoling. Welcoming her to their prison. She belonged there, and would have realized before now, had she not been so irredeemably damned. Whatever evil lived in Nerekhall, this here had to be its source.

Was *this* the origin of her visions?

Ignoring the sensation as best she could, she bowed her head and fought to keep pace with Owl.

There were few guards in evidence. Not nearly enough to defend a castle of the Tower's size. Three black-armored soldiers held positions along the gatehouse's wooden stockade. Andira caught them by the glint of the noon sunlight on the iron of their crossbows. The same number again were just about visible as black dots against the inner walls and turrets. Guards were expensive. The Tower's dread reputation presumably sufficed to keep trouble at bay, and the ironbound were capable of dealing with any trouble that was not so readily subdued. She could not help but admire the efficiency.

A second ironbound stood guard at the main gate. It was identical in every respect to the one they had just passed, except, perhaps, for a slight variation in the pattern of runes. That was so subtle a variation that Andira was not sure she could call it one. It would have been like trying to tell identical twins apart by looking at their fingerprints.

It did not move as Andira approached it. It did not move as she walked past. Nor did it react as Owl followed with Lidiya held close to his chest.

Again, she felt the ironbound's runic protections sapping the strength from her rune, and from her in turn, returning it all-too-slowly as she continued on to the gate. She leant into the haft of her poleaxe as though it were a walking staff, recalling how Sir Brodun had always chided her for her reliance on the power of her rune. For perhaps the first time in her life, she conceded that he might have been right.

Up to this moment, she had been of a mind to simply demand Trenloe's release, and remove him by force if she was denied. She was accustomed to dealing with provincial authorities, with frontier outposts and border forts where laws could be bent to suit, if one was forceful enough. The direct approach had served her well over the years.

It did not look as though it was going to do so here in Nerekhall.

She recalled seeing Trenloe punch through the brick wall of a farmhouse in western Kell in order to pull a young couple from a fire. At a ford in Dhernas, she had left him to single-handedly wrestle with a troll while she had tended to the life-threatening bite it had taken out of Owl's arm. But it seemed even Trenloe's legendary fortitude was not equal to that of an iron frame marked with a rune of strength. And if just one ironbound was the equal of Trenloe the Strong, then the Tower of Nerek might just be the most formidable stronghold in all of Terrinoth.

That the properties rendering it proof against the Ynfernael were the exact same ones making it unassailable to her had not escaped her notice. She did not appreciate the irony.

Her least favored option was the only one still available to her.

She would have to *ask nicely* for Trenloe's release.

The gate was ten feet high and solid, the darkened wood studded with metal rivets. It was closed, but the inset postern door was ajar. Andira ducked the head of her polearm and stepped through.

Inside was a guardroom with crumbling stone pillars, bare wooden beams for a ceiling and no roof so that it better resembled the courtyard of a castle ruin that someone had endeavored to make homely with a table and chairs.

A pair of human guards sat at the table playing dice. Both were identically dressed in a quilted doublet with long padded sleeves, worn under a vest of iron rings and a black surcoat that fell just short of the knees. This final, outer layer bore the heraldic ram of Nerekhall as its central charge with the sacred Flame of Kellos and Hammer of Pollux blazoned on either side. Both soldiers wore large shields across their backs with a halberd propped up against the side of the table and a short sword and several knives belted at their hips. What the Tower militia lacked in numbers, they made up for in armament.

The most striking item of raiment, however, was the black iron mask that obscured their faces. The soldier to Andira's left was wearing the likeness of a leering goblin, while the soldier to her right was wearing what appeared to be the face of a barghest, an undead wolf-creature common to the Mistlands. They were faces that did more than simply shield the wearer's identity. They were meant to impose obedience through terror.

Standing at the far end of the courtyard, a spectacularly large priest of Kellos tended to a stone hearth.

In spite of the late winter chill, his chest was bare, a long skirt of burnt samite squeezed in tight around his bulging middle with a thick golden chasuble that jangled with keys. The bare skin of his chest, back, arms, and face, was marbled with old whip scars and healed burns. Some looked more recent than others. The priesthood of Kellos worshipped fire. They viewed it as the bringer of light, solace, and redemption, as well as the bane of the undead whom Kellos had first arisen to oppose, and employed it in every ritual that Andira had ever seen. Even the most devout, however, took the stories of bodily and spiritual purification through flame to be metaphorical.

Most. But not all.

There had been times in her life when Andira had herself been considered holy, even divine, and had attracted a following of her own. Having the power to confront evil, and the determination to do so whatever the personal or collateral cost was a property more closely associated with the godly than the human.

Andira had never actively encouraged these ideas, but nor had she gone to great lengths to disabuse them. She respected the gods and those who put their faith in them, even the likes of the Nordros, Syraskil, and Marnn whose rituals were viewed with distrust across the more wealthy areas of Terrinoth. She did not pray herself, however, and held no single deity as being preeminent over all others.

True faith, the searing obedience to one god in a world that contained hundreds, had always baffled her.

Owl looked up, over Lidiya's bowed head, through the crisscrossing knotwork of wooden beams to the pale tower above them. "This must be where they hanged the Dread Prince Farrengol at the end of the Years of Grief. I had… I had imagined… something…" He trailed off, his mind finding itself in a conversational blind-alley it did not know how to back out of.

The priest, meanwhile, set down his poker and turned from the hearth. The roaring fire threw his belly half into shadow, like the pitted surface of a moon, but the smile on his face was disarmingly genial as he clapped his hands with a jangling of sacred icons and spread his arms in welcome.

"Visitors," he announced. "The Light of Kellos reveals no end of wonders." Grinning broadly, he gestured to the taciturn pair at the table. "Pray forgive these two. They are fine people, but ill-accustomed to welcoming those who come *willingly* to the Tower." He chuckled as if at a joke.

Andira waited impassively while his mirth settled. Trenloe had often scolded her for having no sense of humor. She suspected that that, in itself, had been his idea of a joke.

"There are no visitors to the Tower," said one of the guards.

With their faces covered and their bodies so well-armored it was impossible to be certain whether they were male or female. Even the voice did not make it clear. It rang hollowly from behind the black mask.

"I am not here to visit," said Andira. "I am here to retrieve a friend of mine."

"No one leaves the Tower," growled the other.

Andira's knuckles turned white around her weapon. She

remained painfully aware of the ironbound outside the gate.

"Now, now," said the priest. He looked amused as he patted the second guard on the shoulder. "My colleagues get carried away with their duties at times, but they forget that the flames of redemption are available to all who would walk through them. Indeed, what hope would there be for this world if the sinful were only to be condemned?"

He extended a hand to Andira. "My name is Brother Birkin Augost, Light of Kellos and Chaplain of the Tower." When Andira did not immediately accept his handshake, his face crinkled into a self-deprecating smile and he nodded towards the small banners fluttering at the head of Andira's poleaxe. They bore stylized renditions of her rune across a white field of fine Rothfeld cloth. It had been paid for, as had the rest of her armor and equipment, from the personal fortune of her first follower, Sir Brodun.

"And this would be the point, I presume, where you ask if we do not know who you are. I assure you…" The smile faded into the scarring lines of his face, a firmness appearing in the affable doughiness that, Andira suspected, was as much of a mask as the metal counterparts worn by his soldiers. "It does not matter here who you are. Not to Warden Daralyn, and not to Kellos."

"My name is Andira Runehand," she said, accepting his handshake. His hand was feverishly hot to the touch, his grip unexpectedly strong "At one time of Roth's Vale."

"I am afraid I do not know you."

"You will be more familiar, I am sure, with the friend I have come for. His name is Trenloe the Strong."

The guards shared a look across their table. Andira caught it even through their masks.

Augost raised an eyebrow. "The famous hero?"

"The same."

He looked at Andira, eyes twinkling with renewed appraisal. "Yes, I see it in you now." He glanced briefly aside to include Owl in his assessment. "Both of you." He sighed, as he returned his full attention to Andira. "Adventurers come to Nerekhall sometimes, lured by its reputation and the dark tales they have heard as children, but they seldom stay for long. Nerekhall is a law-abiding city."

"So I have been told."

"Its shadow is long passed."

From her position against Owl's chest, Lidiya dutifully echoed the refrain.

"Trenloe fought the Uthuk Y'llan in Kell. Almost single-handedly for a time. He is no criminal," Andira said.

"And yet he finds himself in a prison, so it logically follows that he must have committed a crime." Augost smiled as though to soften his words. "Kellos will illuminate the truth of the matter, I am sure. If he is innocent, or contrite, then he might be released. As I have said, the Flames of Kellos show no favor."

"You say he committed a crime *in* Nerekhall," said Owl, slowly, as though working up to speed. "But this is not Nerekhall, or so I am told. Common law holds here, and I do not believe that the nearest courts would be entirely ambivalent towards the imprisonment of a renowned hero without cause."

Augost's smile wavered, albeit for the barest moment, irritation reaching his eyes before clearing like so much smoke. "You are a learned man, I see. That is good. Education is the light that rids the mind and soul of darkness. But you are not the first learned man to find his way to the Tower. I have heard this plea before and expect you to have the same luck getting a favorable ruling from the justices in Arhynn." He chuckled as though they were debating nothing weightier than the minutiae of divine law.

"The Tower has served the Lord of Nerekhall, and more latterly its Council of Magistrates, for many centuries after all. But," he added, forestalling further argument, "I will agree to assess Trenloe now, and judge his case for myself." He offered his hand, and smiled. "You are welcome to accompany me." A nod to Lidiya and Owl. "You and your companions."

Again, the two guards shared looks.

If they had been made uncomfortable by the thought of holding Trenloe the Strong, then the idea of admitting three strangers, two of them armed, was clearly aggrieving them. Andira looked up at the great, dark spire of the Tower and shivered. She was not dreaming now, but to her great surprise she found that she was afraid.

She did not want to set one foot inside the Tower either.

"In exchange for a small donation to the Tower and reparations to the victims of his crimes," Augost went on smoothly. "Two gold crowns, let us say, that you may leave with my colleagues here." He gestured to the two soldiers who visibly relaxed into the backs of their chairs. This, apparently, was more like it. "Warden Daralyn will not even need to know that Trenloe the Strong was briefly in her dungeons at all. Her interest is purely in the protection of her city. Mine is rehabilitation. I am *sure* that once Trenloe has been made aware of his sin then you and he will be moving on like every other adventurer before you and none need be in any way inconvenienced by Kellos' show of munificence."

There was a smirk in his eyes as Augost crossed his arms over his chest.

Andira was not sure if it was because he suspected the outrageous sum of two gold crowns would be beyond her means and that she would now leave, or whether, on the contrary, it was just sum enough for a hero of Trenloe's renown.

"Trenloe had all of our money," she said.

Augost tutted, shaking his head in apparently genuine sorrow. Lidiya cleared her throat nervously. Andira looked around to see her in Owl's arms holding up a felt purse that looked weighty with coin.

It looked familiar.

Because it was *her* coin purse.

Her frown settled more firmly into the lines they had dug into her face over the years as she mentally retraced everything the girl had said since their departure from Bridge Market, piecing it together with this new information in mind, and finally realized how some Nerekhall stray had got herself mixed up with Trenloe the Strong.

"He was thrown into the Tower of Nerek for defending his own cutpurse, wasn't he?"

Lidiya's expression was pained. "Please don't be upset."

Andira gave a heavy sigh as she reached out to reclaim her purse.

What reason could she possibly have for being upset? It was the most *Trenloe* thing she had ever heard. Andira turned back to Brother Augost with two gold crowns. It was half of everything she had left.

She would have given or said almost anything to avoid discovering just what it was about the Tower that terrified her, but if it would hasten Trenloe's release then she would face it. She told herself she had confronted worse.

For some reason, she had trouble believing it.

# CHAPTER FIVE
## *Trenloe the Strong*

Nerekhall minded its own business.

But, by Kellos, when it chose not to, it was serious about it. That much, Trenloe had taken firmly on board.

If getting beaten half to death by a mechanical watchman hadn't made that message clear, then having his unconscious body dragged across town to the Tower of Nerek rather than the nearest House of Aris just about did it.

With several painful twinges and a grimace of effort, he lifted his hand up off the scuffed granite floor of his cell and rested his fingers ruefully against his chest.

The ironbound had put a dent the size of a horse's kick in his breastplate and left a matching bruise across his ribs. Just sitting his fingers against it made his head spin. He wondered if he might have broken a rib. Working tentatively through his muscles and joints, he catalogued his injuries.

His right hand looked like something that had been wrenched from the arm of a lobster. It hurt just to think about it. His head felt as though it had been kicked from Highmont to Haverford by an ogre. His left eye had swollen closed. The right one, after opening it briefly to take a look around his cell, he kept closed by choice. The lamplight flickering through the bars of his window was too bright. It went in between the eyelids and into his pounding head like a surgeon's needle. The last time he'd woken from a beating like this was after the Battle of Hernfar. He'd been the last survivor of the fight to hold the ford against the Uthuk Y'llan, and then fended off a demonic possession for good measure.

He shifted, determined to be upright. Anything less felt like a slight against those who'd been less fortunate. The bruises on his back rubbed painfully on the parched stonework as he tried to sit up against the wall.

There was a school of thought in adventuring circles that if you'd not spent some time in a dungeon, be it at the hands of some petty provincial reeve or a cackling Tanglewood necromancer, then you weren't doing it right. Trenloe's old companion, Dremmin, one of those lost at Hernfar, had boasted of having been incarcerated in each of the thirteen Daqan Baronies (the Mistlands proudly included) and that this had been before she had traded the life of a professional soldier for a too-brief stint as an adventurer. Trenloe had always politely disavowed that opinion. It'd been a point of pride for him that, however far from home the mercenary coin had led him, he had always been able to stay on the right side of whatever the local laws happened to be.

He sighed. Until now.

He sat for a moment with his back to the wall, waiting for his breath to come steady and the walls to stop spinning. Once they began to, he cracked open his one good eye and allowed himself a look at his accommodations.

The walls were of an old, crumbling stone. The window was a

mousetrap-sized square filled with bars. It was set into the wall at about eye level, facing out over a gloomy inner courtyard filled with lamplight and despairing howls. The door was a slab of dark oak. From somewhere on the other side, he could hear one of the priests of Kellos shuffling barefoot along the corridor, offering the flames of redemption to inmates who begged to receive it, if only it would bring them closer to their freedom. A single bunk with a mousy blanket and a flaccid straw pillow had been pushed up against the side wall.

It held Trenloe's solitary cellmate.

The elf was sleeping the sleep of the very, very drunk, his breathing intermittently broken by loud snores and a few repetitive bars of a broken tune. He had a sickly pallor that sleep had done little to diminish, and a brocade coat that might once have been called regal but which now looked like something on which a nobleman would wipe their boots. Clumps of sick glued his long blond hair to the collar. As was typical for an elf, his age was impossible to guess.

The walls sounded as though they were whispering, muttering, a weight of voices held by the sheer mass and age of the stones around him. But there was no one there but himself, the elf and the priest in the corridor outside.

Wincing, Trenloe raised his arm in order to scratch absently at his ear.

It was the cries from the neighboring cells. That was all. That, maybe, and a knock to the head. Trying to stifle the uneasy sense that he was being watched, he let his gaze drift towards the door.

It was solid oak. But he could take it.

The guards on the other side, he wasn't too sure about. Or the priests of Kellos. Not to mention the likelihood of another run-in with the ironbound. He dismissed the idea of escape for now.

The rough welcome aside, the Tower of Nerek wasn't nearly so bad as he was allowing his imagination to make it seem.

The cell was clean. It was dry. It was warm.

If anything, it was a little *too* warm.

The attention that the Church of Kellos showed towards the Tower's inmates was commendable, but Trenloe could feel the heat from their ritual flames through the floor. The smell coming off the sick bucket under the elf's bed was already about as much as Trenloe could bear.

This was all the consequence of a terrible misunderstanding, he was sure.

All he had done was what any decent person in his shoes would have done. He had only stepped in to defend a child from an out-of-control automata: nothing, surely that any civilized penal code would punish someone for. No, trying to escape now would only make things look worse than they already did. The best thing he could do was to sit where he was, give his body the chance to heal, and wait for common sense to prevail as it always would in the end.

He was, if nothing else, an optimist.

Gritting his teeth in effort, he folded in the fingers of his right hand until they were making a fist. The whole arm shook, but he looked at it proudly.

"I would be loath to see the other gentleman."

Trenloe looked up.

His elven cellmate who was, apparently, not so sound asleep after all, had both eyes drowsily half-open, but had not otherwise moved. With his aristocratic features and once-rich coat, he managed to convey the appearance of being rudely interrupted mid-nap, as opposed to being unearthed in stale clothes and soiled hair in a Nerekhall dungeon.

"Nobody was hurt but me, I assure you."

"Ahhhh." The elf propped himself up on his pillow. "I, too, may have taken out my frustrations on the occasional wall about this fair city." He sighed heavily. "It is not the place I once thought it was. Sometimes, I wonder… Would things really have turned out any worse if I had never come here in the first place?"

Trenloe did not know how to answer that. To a man in a dungeon cell, most paths untaken probably looked preferable. At least Trenloe could say with confidence that he would have done nothing differently.

"It wasn't a wall." Well, now he thought about it, he supposed there had been a wall as well. And a door. "It was one of those ironbound."

The elf narrowed one bloodshot eye. He spent a long and very serious moment appraising Trenloe through the slit. "A good joke. Very droll. I would steal it for myself, but I appear to have stumbled across free room and board and no longer need to perform for my keep. And–" he glanced at the door, and then back "–a word to the unwise, my friend, there are people here in Nerekhall who have what could only be called an *aversion* to that kind of humor."

"I'm not joking. It really was an ironbound."

"Well then…" The elf blew out through his lips, and looked up at the ceiling. "In that case you definitely don't want to be talking about it."

"But, I–"

"*Shh-hh-h.*" The elf pressed a grimy finger to his lips, glaring pointedly at Trenloe before forcefully adding another "*Shhh*" just in case he had been insufficiently clear. Plumping up his straw pillow under his balled fist, he hit the bunk and rolled over so that he was facing the wall with his back towards Trenloe. After a minute of silence, Trenloe thought the elf might have fallen back to sleep, until his fingers began idly plucking the notes of the melody he was humming along the wooden frame of his bed.

"Why can't I talk about it?"

The elf sighed into his pillow. "You have never been to Nerekhall before, have you?"

"What does that have to do with it?"

"I thought so."

"I haven't answered yet."

"Oh, you have."

Trenloe cleared his throat, still unsure what he was supposed to have said. "You can call me Trenloe, by the way."

"That's very kind of you," the elf countered.

Trenloe waited.

"Fine." The elf gave a sigh even deeper than the last. "For what it's worth to you, or to me for that matter, my name is Rendiel. Barfly. Raconteur. Eolam of the Latari and all-round cautionary tale. Firmly at your service. Bring me in a round of drinks at the Book Louse when we are free of this fair hostelry and I may tell you the rest of the story."

"What did you do to end up in here?"

Rendiel stared up at the crumbling stonework for a long time. "The last thing I remember is… Yes," he said with some finality. "Yes, it was probably that." Lifting his head from the pillow, he glanced over his shoulder, grimacing as he noticed the foul whiff rising off his sick bucket. "I have heard of you, actually." Trenloe shifted uncomfortably. He was less enamored of his own legend than he had been before Kell. He'd wanted to help people, but he'd led them badly. The world was better, as he saw it, with him by Andira's side. "Trenloe the Strong, am I right? The Giant of Artrast. The hero of Nordgard Castle and the Demon-Slayer of Furnace Gate."

"I was there, but it was a man named Owl who slew the demon."

"Modest, too. I see why they make songs about you. I was asked to compose one once." The elf frowned and shook his head. "You don't happen to have anything to drink on you, do you?"

"I'm afraid not."

The elf deflated back into his pillow. "Too much to expect, I know. So… you've taken to fighting ironbound, have you? Not enough demons in the east?"

"But, you just told me not to–"

Rendiel cut him off with a dismissive wave of the hand. "I'm a bard, my friend. We say a lot of things, most of it nonsense and the rest plain lies. But it holds up the roof over our heads."

"Well…" Trenloe frowned, flexing his fingers in thought, wincing at the pain it brought but doing it anyway. "I'd just had my purse lifted in Bridge Market, and–"

"Scoundrels," Rendiel muttered to himself. "Hanging is too good for them."

"I chased the girl who took it," Trenloe went on, ignoring the interruption. "Although to be honest, I would never have caught her if the ironbound hadn't cornered her first."

Trenloe thought back.

The way it had just been *standing* there in the garden, watching her, waiting, the way it had sniffed at them both before arriving at the decision to attack. Like an animal someone had put together from metal and gears. He could still hear the girl's screams.

He looked up to the corner where they seemed to be ringing from the stone.

There was nothing there.

"I hit it before it hit me, but…" He cleared his throat and shrugged ruefully. The black eye, bruised hand, and wheezing chest told a better story than he could. "I hope the girl was far away by the time it was done."

"She was never in any danger, you know," said Rendiel. "The ironbound are more than just mechanical watchmen. They were built on the Anvil of Pollux to oppose evil mages and hunt down sources of dark magic. They do not waylay petty thieves in dark alleys."

Trenloe thought back, recalling again how still the armor had seemed as he broke through the tanner's yard wall and found it there, standing over the girl. Could the elf be right? Had he simply acted without judging the situation properly? No. The menace he felt from the construct had been so real. And it *had* moved first.

Hadn't it?

It was so difficult to remember clearly now.

"This one… this one didn't seem to be acting like it was supposed to."

"And how sure are you that your little pickpocket isn't a young Uthuk blood witch?"

Trenloe gave the elf a look.

Rendiel shrugged against his pillow. "This is Nerekhall, my large friend."

"Could an ironbound… break somehow?"

Rendiel delivered a laugh so painfully melodramatic that he

had to cut it short to slap his hand to his forehead and sink back into his pillow with a groan. "Very good, Trenloe," he groaned, hoarsely. "Another hilarious joke. Quite excellent." He lowered his voice to a more comfortable register. "Were you not listening when I told you that the ironbound were *designed* to be infallible. By the priests of the Artificer god, no less. They are incorruptible, stronger than any warrior and impervious to magic. It is a crime in Nerekhall even to imply that they might be anything less than perfect, which is why, if you remember, I told you not to talk about it."

"But then you said–"

"*Shhh!*" Rendiel hissed. He raised his eyebrows warningly. "Nothing like that could ever happen again in Nerekhall."

"Did you say happen *again*?"

The elf's eyes darted back and forth between Trenloe and the door, as though backed into their sockets and cornered. "No…?" he said, unconvincingly, just as a clattering of rusting metal drew Trenloe's attention to the cell door.

It gave a rattling *clank* and the upper slot was drawn back.

A pair of faded gray eyes appeared in the narrow window.

"Trenloe?" they asked.

With a grunt of effort, Trenloe peeled a little more of himself off the floor. "Yes."

"You have a visitor."

Trenloe's relief was so great that his famed strength almost failed him and he slumped back into the wall, even as the window slot shut and keys clinked from the other side. He had known that this would all get cleared up, just as soon as he was able to speak with someone in authority. Warden Daralyn, perhaps. Or even one of the Artificers of Pollux.

"The shadow has passed," Rendiel hissed at him.

Trenloe turned to him.

"The shadow has passed," the elf repeated. "That's all they want to hear. Tell them you made a mistake. It was dark. You were tired, confused, a stranger in a strange city with a dark reputation. Tell them you are sorry and that you will never do anything of the sort again, and they will let you go."

Trenloe's brow furrowed. "But, if there's a problem with the ironbound then someone needs to be told."

The elf smiled. It looked as though it had been painted by an unhappy child onto a sickly-looking doll. "I've tried, Trenloe. By the gods, believe me that I've tried. So long as there are not demons on the streets, nobody wants to know."

Trenloe opened his mouth to ask just what his cellmate knew, but before he could do so, the cell door swung inwards with a creak and the elf rolled over to feign sleep once again.

Andira swept inside. In spite of everything, Trenloe smiled as though the sun outside his small window had just risen. There were times when Andira was simply too big for this world. She could not simply *walk* into a room. After losing everyone who had trusted him to lead them, falling in with Andira and Owl and playing sidekick for a change had been the best decision he had ever made. Nothing would ever take Andira Runehand that couldn't best Trenloe first.

"Thank the gods, you came," he said. "The girl… ?"

Andira clenched both hands into fists. She was, and with some considerable effort, resisting the urge to drag him out by the ankle. Trenloe looked at her quizzically. He had never seen her so agitated. The blued steel of her armor twitched and glittered, like dark water in the lamplight.

"She is outside with Owl. And safe. Thanks to you. We are also both substantially poorer. *Thanks to you.*" She took a calming breath, and a deliberate backward step, indicating as she did so the large man who had appeared behind her. He was so wide he filled the doorframe, face beaming as though in competition with his girth. There was something in his eyes though, not to mention the heavy mace hanging from his belt, that told Trenloe he wasn't to be dismissed out of hand.

"I have spoken with the Chaplain of the Tower here and you are free to go, provided you make fulsome and heartfelt apologies to Brother Augost. Honestly, Trenloe..." She pinched her eyes shut, turning for just a moment towards the same corner from which Trenloe had thought he'd heard the young pickpocket's scream, and appeared to shudder. "If I did not need your introduction to this friend at the Academy, then I would gladly leave you to Brother Augost, with my blessing."

"The Eternal Fires of Kellos burnt the hand of death itself when it sought to reach into Terrinoth's borders," said the brother amiably. "They will purge us all if we but allow them. And if not..." He shrugged, the ring of keys swinging from his golden belt-rope clinking against the meat of his thigh. "Well, they're eternal, aren't they? Andira Runehand is more than welcome to come back tomorrow."

"*Now* Trenloe. I have spent two gold crowns and the entire morning on you already. Repent, swear to obey Nerekhall's laws and to leave the moment our business is concluded, and we can go."

There was an edge to her words that Trenloe had never felt before.

She was in pain, he realized, and more than that: she was afraid. There was something about this place that terrified her, and he could not begin to imagine what it was. He did not think he had ever seen Andira with anything less than supreme self-confidence. It was like watching the sun rolling backwards, sinking beneath the horizon to bury its head in the east. It occurred to him that he was going to be leaving this cell one way or the other, and if Andira had to fight through a castle full of guards and a priest to drag him out by the ankle, then she would.

It looked as though he had no choice.

He couldn't have that on his conscience, not when he could prevent it with an apology he didn't mean and a promise he didn't want to have to keep.

"All right," he said. "I'll apologize." With a wince, he drew his head back up, like a weight at the end of his bruised neck, and gestured towards the elf pretending to be asleep on the bunk. "And how much for the release of my good friend here as well?"

He didn't hear what Andira said to that.

But it wasn't generous.

# CHAPTER SIX
## *Andira Runehand*

It had gotten late and it had started to rain. At Rendiel's suggestion, Andira had reluctantly agreed to delay their visit to the Academy for one more night.

The Book Louse was a tavern in a particularly destitute pocket of Nerekhall's southern outskirts that Rendiel had called the Snicks. It was a semi-derelict pile of fossilized woods and lichen-encrusted brickwork that, again according to Rendiel's telling, had been turned into one of the quarter's better taverns. Everything was tarnished. Everything was broken or slowly rotting. The ceiling was low and stained with damp. When Andira opened the door and set her weight on the floorboards, the staircase at the far end of the taproom creaked. Moths fluttered about the cheap, thickly smoking candles that dribbled over every table. Rats chittered from inside the walls. Dark stains on the walls indicated highwater marks. The floods of previous years had made it all the way to the first-floor landing.

The proprietress was a leathery-skinned orc in a tawny overcoat and mildewed sleeves. She was pointing a battered crossbow that looked old enough to have slain a dragon in the Third Darkness. The unfinished plank that doubled as the tavern's bar also trebled as the crossbow's mount. There was a bolt in the track, its dulled tip winking in the excess of candlelight.

Andira could strike a bolt from the air if it came to it, but with the unholy aura of *Nerekhall* burning under her skin like a fever, she was not confident that she would stop with the bolt if she did.

"Put it down," Andira said, firmly. Her feet ached, her eyes were tired, she was wet through. Her head hurt from the effort of ignoring the taint that she could see, hear, feel, taste, and smell all around her. The Book Louse was a long way from her quest to find Baelziffar but at this late hour she would settle for a dark room in which she could lie down and close her eyes. It was better than the Tower of Nerek.

"Put it down," she said again, with enough steel to cut across the dingy common room. "Before I break it."

The innkeeper blinked.

This was clearly not the expected response to an orc with a loaded crossbow. But then a loaded crossbow was far from the usual response to her walking into a tavern, so Andira considered them even.

With a warning growl, Owl made to draw his sword, dissuaded from doing so only when Rendiel pushed between them both like a tatty breeze, and declared the next round to be on Andira Runehand and Trenloe the Strong.

There were cheers at that, and some of the tension went out of the room.

"Rendiel the Bard." The innkeeper lowered her crossbow. "I thought you gone for good this time."

With every appearance of the prodigal son returned home, the elf took an unclaimed seat at the bar. "What manner of world is it, Sanna, when a bard can be imprisoned for the crime of singing."

"It's what you were singing though, isn't it? And outside the Church of Pollux, too…"

While Sanna and Rendiel insulted one another in the manner of reunited friends, Owl returned to Andira's side, turning to scowl suspiciously over the damp, overcrowded room. Its shady clientele steadfastly avoided his gaze. He had, at least, withdrawn his hand from his weapon. He should have known better than to think of drawing it in civilized lands, particularly in places as hostile to dark magic as Nerekhall. It had been a nobler weapon once, as he himself had been nobler, but the evil thing he had used that weapon to slay had changed all of that.

"A fine place," said Trenloe, limping inside with Lidiya in tow, bald head stooped to avoid adding to the collage of bashes on the ceiling beams.

Andira could never be sure if her companion was being deliberately polite, or was just willfully ignorant. "And a welcome as warm as a handshake from the Dread Prince."

With an apologetic grunt, Sanna pulled the bolt from her crossbow and released the tension from the limbs. She set the crossbow away behind the bar. "It's not often we see new faces in the Book Louse. Most of those bring troubles with them, and we've more than enough of those."

"What kind of trouble?" Trenloe asked, taking the seat next to Rendiel.

The stool creaked decrepitly under his weight.

"We could have been in the Ironbrick," said Andira, as

much to keep Trenloe from getting himself involved in another passing acquaintance's troubles than to air a genuine complaint. In truth, she did not care where in Nerekhall they slept for the night, so long as their stay was brief.

"We couldn't have afforded the Ironbrick," said Trenloe, with no obvious sign of an apology.

In the meantime, Sanna had brought out tankards and was lining them up along the bar. Andira took the seat on Rendiel's other side. Owl remained standing, turning his back and glaring threateningly over the room. With his one good hand and no apparent effort, Trenloe hoisted Lidiya onto the bar beside him. Starting with Rendiel, and to the elf's apparent misery, Sanna proceeded to pour a thin brown ale into their cups.

"Rendiel tells me how you got him out of the Tower. And what you did for…" Sanna's eyes gestured furtively towards Lidiya, as though someone might hear the thoughts behind her head even if she didn't speak them aloud. "You'll all room free here tonight."

"You see?" said Trenloe. "Now aren't you glad we helped them?"

Andira pushed her cup of ale down to Rendiel with a grimace.

He accepted it with a similar expression, but sipped it nonetheless. His own had already become empty.

She had borne hunger without complaint, and made do with lesser accommodations than those offered by the Book Louse. She was tired. That was all. The corruption of Nerekhall was a light she could not extinguish, a noise she could not shut out. It was taxing her strength, not to mention her patience, and she would be the first to admit she had never been particularly well endowed with the latter.

"Are we going to talk about it?"

Andira looked up, startled out of herself.

It was Trenloe who had spoken.

"About what?" she said.

"About you looking half-ready to kill that priest and fight your way out of the Tower if I hadn't agreed to leave with you."

Andira frowned, but did not dispute that she may have, or pretend that she had an answer to give him. All she knew for certain, looking back on it from a place of relative safety, was that she would have done almost anything to get away from the Tower of Nerek.

"A good man, Brother Augost," Rendiel mused over his ale. "It genuinely frustrates him that I keep finding my way back to the Tower."

"You just have to stop playing subversive songs outside the church," said Sanna. "It's not complicated."

"The muse takes me where it takes me, my friend."

"The muse is all right. It's the ale that keeps getting you into trouble with Augost."

"And yet, here we all sit." Rendiel gestured to the two empty cups in front of him.

The innkeeper grunted and refilled them. "Cheaper than paying you to sing, I suppose."

"What is an elven lord doing in a place like this?" said Andira. The elf had prattled on about Nerekhall and its history for much of their long walk from the Tower, but had spoken little about himself. He seemed genuine enough, but she had not yet formed an opinion on whether that was a good thing or not. Anyone who Trenloe had met in a dungeon and cost her her last gold crown warranted a certain level of suspicion.

"Place like what?" said Sanna, affronted.

"Who says I'm any kind of lord?" said Rendiel.

"You told Trenloe that you were Eolam. The word has a complicated meaning, as most Latari words do, but in essence it means noble."

"Just my luck. I get rescued by the one person in Nerekhall who speaks Latari."

"So what brought you here?" Trenloe asked.

The elf shook his head and drank.

"There is an evil at work in this city, Trenloe," Andira said after a minute, in a roundabout way answering the earlier question he had put to her about her behavior in the Tower. "Whether it is Baelziffar himself or something else, I do not know, but having been inside the Tower I am more certain of it than ever." She struck Rendiel on the arm with the backs of her fingers until he looked up again. "What is the story behind the Tower?"

"Why are you asking me?"

"Everyone seems to think you are some kind of bard, though I have yet to see much evidence of the fact."

The elf sighed. "Where to begin… The Tower was here long before the first humans crossed the Lothan River from the Ru Steppes and settled in Terrinoth, and was cursed even then. They say it is elven-made, but my own people in the Aymhelin never claimed it. The tale we tell is that it once belonged to the Daewyl who–"

"The fallen tribe?"

Rendiel looked surprised. "You know of the Daewyl?" He shrugged. "Of course you do. Then you know what it means."

Andira nodded.

The Daewyl were the eleventh and last tribe of elves, the so-called Twice-Fallen, who had purportedly succumbed to the corrupting whispers of the Ynfernael many centuries before the first kings of Terrinoth. Those who survived were scattered across the world, persecuted by their own kind and rightfully so. If the Tower of Nerek had belonged to the Daewyl during the age of their fall then it would explain much of what she had felt.

"I don't know what it means," said Trenloe. "Are we going back?"

Andira shook her head, quicker than she would have cared to acknowledge. "Perhaps, but not yet. We will go to the Academy, as planned."

Trenloe lay his injured hand gingerly across the bar, as though it was a wounded cat he had rescued from the street, and picked up his cup of ale.

He sniffed at it.

"I don't drink," he said. "My father always said I shouldn't."

"It's like medicine," said Sanna.

Relenting, Trenloe lowered the cup to his mouth and took a sip. "Gods," he swore, spitting out the mouthful and wiping his mouth on his bicep. "My father was right."

Rendiel patted the larger man remorsefully on the back, turning in his stool and raising his own cup in toast. "To Trenloe the Strong, my friends: vanquisher of Uthuk Y'llan and slayer of demons, savior of small girls and disconsolate elves."

The tavern raised their cups and muttered, "*Trenloe the Strong.*"

Andira sighed.

Just what he needed more of: encouragement.

"You're so set on getting to the Academy and finding your demon," said Trenloe, still wiping the taste of Sanna's ale on the questionably better one of his unwashed forearms. "If it had been you chasing a thief through Nerekhall instead of me, you would have left her to the ironbound, wouldn't you?"

Andira shook her head. Seat Aris beside Trenloe the Strong and the Goddess of Charity herself would start to look mean-spirited by comparison. How he had managed to hold onto that kind of good-heartedness whilst commanding a company of Trastan mercenaries was beyond her. It had been before they had met so she could only imagine. In many ways, he was a child still, believing that he could save the world one person at a time. But the world did not work that way. There were choices to be made. Sometimes there were sacrifices. Trenloe would never be the man to make them. It was why strangers in taverns would never cheer her name, and why she did not care.

She looked sadly across at the girl. Lidiya was staring down at the floor between her knees, determined not to be involved in any conversation about her.

"Of course not. But there is a war being fought here, Trenloe. It is only now starting to be felt again in the eastern baronies, but it has been raging in secret since the time of the Daewyl. There are innocents even in war and sometimes innocents get hurt. I am not heartless simply because I remember that there is a larger picture at stake."

Trenloe thumped his uninjured fist on the counter, spilling his beer and making Lidiya jump. "What picture is so large you'd ignore a child?"

"I would save a continent from the demon king who covets it," Andira countered. "Whatever Lidiya's guilt in the eyes of the ironbound, she seems to be an intelligent girl. Ask her yourself if she would give her life to spare everyone in this room, everyone in this city, from an eternity of slavery under Baelziffar?"

"She doesn't have to make that–"

"No," Andira interrupted, voice soft but without mercy. "She doesn't. And nor does she have to, because *I* am here to do it for her."

Sanna gave a conscientious cough. "You've done enough already. Really. Both of you. Folk'll sleep safer just knowing there are two heroes under the same roof."

"The shadow has passed," Rendiel muttered under his breath.

"There's something wrong with the ironbound," Trenloe insisted.

Andira frowned. Trenloe had raised the matter repeatedly since they had left Brother Augost and the Tower behind them. "According only to the child they attacked. The child that *robbed* you, Trenloe."

"I'm going to help her."

"You made a promise to a priest of Kellos not to interfere."

Trenloe grumbled under his breath but knew better than to argue.

From over her shoulder, Andira felt Owl silently disapproving. The two men rarely had cause to speak to one another. Trenloe was garrulous where Owl was reserved, but on any matter of contention they invariably agreed.

"Are you going to cause trouble, Trenloe?" Andira asked.

"No."

"Good. Now, it has been a long day and since there is nothing more to be done until tomorrow, I suggest we both get some rest."

As if on cue, Sanna leant across the bar with a rusty key

attached to a wooden block. "Rooms are up the stairs. And don't shift the chamber pot, it's there to catch the leak."

Andira took the key.

She reminded herself, again, that she had experienced worse.

"I'll put these four together in the room next door, shall I?"

"That will be fine." She glared steadily at Trenloe, who quickly looked away. "Just so long as they do nothing reckless between now and sunrise."

# CHAPTER SEVEN
## *Trenloe the Strong*

The ironbound couldn't see them. It stood to reason. It had no eyes. Moreover, he and Lidiya had found themselves a good hiding place behind the broken sill of a second-floor window overlooking the alley. Trenloe peered out through the punched-out panes in the glass. The street was lamplit and quiet, patiently waiting on a dawn still half an hour away. The only sounds were the thin, faraway honks of geese on the river and his own breathing.

Trenloe the Strong was not a quiet person. He breathed like a labored ox. His armor creaked with every shrinking and swelling of his barrel chest. Bits of broken glass and small pebbles popped under his shifting weight. He scratched absently, and even that had his fingernails sawing through the two-day stubble of his chin.

The ironbound didn't move.

The gilt patterning of runes across its black armor twinkled with the guttering of the streetlamps, like an oil lamp being opened and closed.

The Snicks were otherwise deserted. The stillness was absolute.

"It's not doing anything," he whispered.

"They can't all be charging around attacking people," Lidiya whispered back. She had draped herself in a cloak that Trenloe had insisted she let him buy for her, the hood pulled down over her anxious face, but still he saw her shivering. "Someone would've noticed."

"Good point."

Trenloe watched the ironbound do nothing for a while longer.

They had devised this plan to go out in search of malfunctioning ironbound after Andira had retired for the night, sneaking out of the Book Louse before dawn once Owl had dozed off and Rendiel had finally passed out from too much ale.

His mouth stretched around an escaping yawn.

The automata in the street below continued to stand idle, staring sightlessly at the slumped half-brick wall opposite.

Given the lack of eyes and ears, he wondered just how the ironbound perceived the world around them. He recalled hearing the ironbound sniff at him and Lidiya before making the decision to attack. Was their worldview based on smell? Trenloe closed his eyes and tried to picture what that might be like, putting himself inside the head of an ironbound, but it was too alien to imagine.

And even if he was right about the sense of smell, it seemed doubtful that a construct of metal and gears would pick up the same scents as Trenloe's nose. All he was picking up was the damp of the abandoned building, the stagnant reek of the sewers. In the dark, he might not have been able to see the ironbound at all had he not been looking for one, never mind smell it. Cold iron had no smell of its own. At least none that Trenloe had ever noticed before.

That wasn't to say it wasn't smelling him even then, smelling him and choosing to ignore him for incomprehensible reasons of its own.

His unwashed skin. The breath steaming from his mouth. The cold sweat beading across his brow. Perhaps even – the thought almost stopped his heart – the dark magic he had come across since leaving his home for the war in the east. That *was* what the ironbound had been built to do, wasn't it? He had once been briefly possessed by a demon lord, a lesser minion of Andira's nemesis, Baelziffar. What if Andira and Rendiel and Brother Augost were all correct and there was nothing wrong with the ironbound? What if it was him, and he had not fended off Prutorn's possession as completely as he thought he had?

What if *that* was what the ironbound had smelled on him?

He frowned. For all his many faults, Trenloe was very much a creature of the here and now. Circumspection didn't suit him.

"How many ironbound are there in Nerekhall?"

"I don't know." Lidiya shrugged. "Enough that they hardly need soldiers anymore."

Trenloe couldn't understand how fearful a city would have to be to effectively replace its militia with faceless automata. Mortal soldiers were fallible, he couldn't deny. He'd crossed more than his share of inept or downright corrupt officials in his travels. Even the fairest and most well-meaning could be bought or misled, or simply get out of bed on the wrong side. But weren't they also capable of compassion, of leniency, of judgment? Was simple *humanity* too degraded a quality in Nerekhall to be valued? In hindsight, it was unsurprising that his own small crime would have bought him an indefinite stay in the Tower of Nerek if not for Andira. If he was going to surrender the entire idea of justice to the Church of Pollux then he'd want to believe that they were infallible, too.

"What are the chances that we'll run across the one ironbound doing something it shouldn't?" he said.

"This is the Snicks," said Lidiya. "There're always more ironbound here than elsewhere."

"Why's that?"

"I don't know. You'd have to ask Rendiel."

"How does Rendiel know so much about Nerekhall? He doesn't give the impression he was born here."

"You'd have to ask him that, too." With a shake of the head, Lidiya dropped down from the broken sill. "Come on, this one's not doing anything. We should find another."

With a nod, Trenloe drew back from the window.

His armor grated loudly. The boards creaked.

Still, the ironbound didn't move.

They exited the house by the same means they'd entered, peeling back a loose board in the side wall and ducking through into the alley. Trenloe had felt guilty about it at first, but he'd come to the understanding, after Lidiya had explained it many times, that property and ownership didn't mean the same things in the Snicks as Trenloe was used to. If it opened and it led somewhere then congratulations, you had yourself a door. If it was unclaimed then it was yours. If it led somewhere it shouldn't, somewhere that didn't make sense or that didn't rightfully belong in Terrinoth at all, then you shut the door and walked on and pretended you never saw it.

Those were the rules as Trenloe understood them.

Somewhere faraway, the Academy's bells tolled their seventh hour.

It was still dark, the sun creeping furtively over the high rooftops and staining the ridges pink. The Snicks greeted it like a rodent with bad memories of the day before, cracking open shutters to air overcrowded rooms, inching out onto porch steps and sniffing warily at the morning.

Trenloe and Lidiya walked on, peeking through windows they found ajar and down deeply shadowed alleys, ears alert for what Trenloe could not even imagine might constitute a suspicious noise in the Snicks. If there were a hundred ironbound in all of Nerekhall and half of them were to be found in the Snicks then Trenloe could still walk all day without encountering more than a handful.

The Snicks accounted for a more substantial area of the city than Trenloe would have imagined, appearing to comprise everything from the city's southern extents to the banks of the river. It encompassed such a surfeit of geography that even Lidiya soon confessed to being thoroughly lost. Local knowledge extended to the end of the street and no further. Those from further beyond were strangers, as baffled as any Trastan adventurer by its bewildering maze of blind-ends, deadfalls, and chaotic architecture.

This had had all the makings of a better plan when he had first proposed it in the candlelit warmth of the Book Louse. But after months following Andira on her relentless march west, leaving behind so many who might have used their help, he would probably have suggested it anyway. It was the right thing to do.

Trenloe didn't know much, but he'd always known that. Standing in front of what looked like it had once been some kind of public library – going by the crumbling Penacor-era columns and the armless, noseless statue of a woman holding a book – there was another ironbound. Its gargantuan shield hung a fraction of an inch above the split cobbles. Its glaive was a four-inch-thick compass needle pointing to the streaks of cloud clawing their way across the sky and just beginning to come into color.

How different would Terrinoth look now if there had been a regiment of these at Castle Kellar? Trenloe couldn't help but wonder. But then, if he wouldn't want the ironbound administering justice in the Free Cities, why should he be more accepting of them battling the Uthuk Y'llan on the eastern frontier? Did that make him hypocritical, or simply no more or less human than the magistrates of Nerekhall?

He passed his hand slowly back and forth across the armor's blank helm. When it did nothing, Lidiya stuck out her tongue and made a face at it. The *tick-tick-tick* of slumbering mechanisms echoed dully from its metal shell, but so subtly as to be overtaken by the cautious susurrus of the awakening neighborhood.

They left it behind them.

With a creeping sense of unease working its way up the back of his neck, Trenloe glanced back over his shoulder.

It was still there.

He suppressed a shiver. The ironbound were having him jump at shadows. "We should think about trying to retrace our steps," he said, his voice low in unconscious imitation of the city around them. As though the ironbound were merely sleeping and too loud or sudden a noise might rouse them. "Andira will be up soon, and wondering what trouble we've got ourselves into."

"Anyone in the Book Louse could show her the way to the Academy. She could take Rendiel."

"I'm not sure that she likes Rendiel very much."

"Well, I don't like *her* very much."

Trenloe resisted the smile he felt coming. "She's not all bad."

"She wanted me killed by an ironbound!"

"Now, she didn't say that. She only said that she–"

"Didn't care?"

Spoken as baldly as that, it did sound like a terrible thing to have said. Trenloe found he had nothing to say in his friend's defense. It was an accurate summary of Andira's argument.

"Please, Trenloe," she said. "Just a little longer."

Trenloe smiled at her sadly. He'd never learnt the trick of saying *no*.

"I made her a promise."

"Like the one you made to Brother Augost?"

Trenloe frowned. As he saw it, taking an early morning walk around the Snicks wasn't breaking any promises. He wasn't spreading any unfounded rumors about erratic ironbound and he'd be leaving the city as soon as Andira was done with it.

"And like I made to you," he said. "That we'd search the Snicks together until–"

Something from further down the street had caught Lidiya's eye. She pulled suddenly on his arm, not nearly hard enough to make him move but enough to draw him from the middle of the street and into the shaded portico of the tenement opposite the old library. He turned to see what the girl had spotted, just catching the ironbound as it exited the alley ahead of them and clanked heavily across the street as it made for the one opposite. The handful of people out and about averted their eyes, as though looking directly upon an ironbound would communicate their guilt, swerving out of their way to avoid it.

Aside from that, however, and a marked dent in its helmet, the only feature out of the ordinary about it was that it happened to be moving.

The only feature…

The only…

His mouth fell open.

By all the gods, that dent in the helmet: it was the dent that *he'd* put into it.

He wasn't accustomed to coming out of a fight second best, even against a seven-foot-tall automaton of runic iron, and finding that it hadn't walked away entirely unscathed either was a balm to his bruised pride. It was the very armor he'd fought the day before, and if there was one ironbound in all of Nerekhall that he could say with certainty was acting awry, then it would be that one.

"Not the ironbound," Lidiya hissed, and pointed.

There, creeping after the receding ironbound, a dash of faded reds and frayed brocade with a battered Aymhelin lute strapped across his narrow shoulders, was Rendiel.

"I thought we left him sound asleep on the bar," said Trenloe.

"We did."

"So what's he doing sneaking around after our ironbound?"

Lidiya's eyes shone with excitement. "Let's follow him and find out."

# CHAPTER EIGHT
## *Andira Runehand*

The light stole in through the small window, sifted through the dust on the cabinets, admired its image in the small dresser mirror in its tarnished frame, but left the shadows where they lay. The room had no curtains, but the soot and grime caking the glass on both sides served almost as well.

Andira stiffened for a moment, experiencing the fleeting tension of one waking to her first glimpse of an unfamiliar place, before the memories of the previous day came creeping over her as furtively as the morning.

She was in one of the upstairs rooms of the Book Louse. Her lips tightened as she recalled why.

"Trenloe," she muttered aloud and drew herself straight.

She had been so tired that she had fallen asleep in the wooden armchair by the door without ever endangering the bed. The rune throbbed against her palm like an infected wound. It was trying to rouse her, and failing. Nerekhall was a simmering fever that she could not shake. It was under her skin, in her thoughts. The dream had come to her again in the night, as it had done every night, and most days when the lack of real sleep became too much even for her.

She had walked up the crumbling stone stairs of the Tower – and it was the Tower, she was sure of that now – felt her dreaming heart quicken at the sight of that door ajar, heard the voice of Baelziffar from beyond, though she could not recall what had been said. He had sounded urgent, needful. The demon king had *wanted* something from her. She had rebuffed him, walked towards the door, put her hand on the knob, and then–

The knock on the very real door of her room startled her.

"Miss Andira," came the hesitant-sounding voice from the other side of the wood. "Sanna said you wanted waking at dawn."

"Yes," Andira replied, with more bark than she had intended, and deliberately attempted to soften it with a, "Thank you." Gripping the chair's creaking armrests, she rose stiffly to her feet.

She had slept in her armor.

That had partly been down to sheer exhaustion. Dressing and armoring herself was a time-consuming exercise and she could sleep perfectly comfortably in a suit of full plate. More than that, however, there was something about Nerekhall that she simply did not trust. She did not trust Rendiel. *How convenient that Trenloe should make such a helpful friend in his short spell of incarceration*. She did not trust Sanna. *Far too welcoming of three strangers.* She did not trust Lidiya. *The ironbound do not attack without cause, and that cause is invariably the taint of the Ynfernael.* Then again, maybe all of that was just Nerekhall, burning in her thoughts and darkening her perceptions of everyone within it. It was what Trenloe would tell her, were he here to confide in.

Whatever the reason, she would not go a night without her armor fastened and her weapon close by.

Her armor had been hand-crafted to her measurements by the finest armorer in Castle Talon. Crafted from Forge steel, and employing a cabal of Nerekhall rune-mages for every stage of its creation, it had all but bankrupted Sir Hamma Brodun to commission. It did not rust. It did not wear. No blade or arrow had yet breached it. Unlike Trenloe's well-loved plate which creaked when he sat down, or even Owl's priceless but battered heirloom, her armor made barely a whisper of sound through any range of motion.

Already dressed and wearing most of what she owned, she crossed to where her poleaxe was propped against the wall. Considerably taller than the height of the ceiling, it rested at a low angle. The crisp, bright colors of its bannerol flew like an occupying host's standard over the peeling gray wall.

As she picked it up, she took a quick glance at herself in the dressing table mirror.

Her blue eyes were brighter than the smudge of sunlight in the window, sharp enough to pierce the cloudy image in the mirror's glass. Her pale face was almost luminous, her hair a tangled mess that it would take more hands than the Book Louse could command to make right. She wondered if her unkempt appearance was going to be suitable for the Academy, but dismissed the concern with a thin smile. If half the things she had heard about the Academy were true, then she suspected that the magisters would cope.

Weapon in hand, she exited the room onto a creaking landing. The servant who had woken her had already fled downstairs. Andira went to the next door along and tried the latch. It was unlocked. She opened it without knocking.

The room was larger than hers with three single beds and a place laid out on the floor with blankets, presumably for Lidiya. They all looked entirely unslept in. Daydreaming columns of dust twirled through the obscure patterns of light, fashioned for it by the small window and its uneven coverage of grime.

"Trenloe..." She scowled, leaving the door open as she descended the stairs to the common room.

It looked different by day than by candlelight.

The room was shabbier, sadder, but less ominous for it, appearing less like an enclave of some other, malevolent, world than another sorry pocket of this one.

A handful of patrons whom Andira vaguely recognized from the night before were still there, sleeping it off over their tables. Owl was one of them, which accounted for at least one of the unused beds. There was no sign of Trenloe or Rendiel.

The Kellar knight was leaning back in his stool, elbows propped up on the counter and his head resting against a post. He was facing the door, one hand around the grip of his demon-cursed sword, as if prepared for whatever danger seemed likely to come bursting through it. Andira glanced up. The door was still barred for curfew, and further bolstered with several stout metal locks. It looked sturdier than the wall around it. If something were to hit that door in an attempt to get inside, then Andira suspected it would be the rest of the tavern that came down.

Making her way to the bar, Andira paused to unwrap Owl's fingers from his sword.

The knight startled awake. He blinked quickly as he sat himself up straight and wiped a line of drool from his chin, looking around the taproom before his eyes alighted finally on her. Whatever thoughts troubled him at moments such as those, the sight of Andira invariably managed to silence them.

He gave her a tentative smile as she continued on to the bar.

Sanna was quietly occupied behind the counter. She was wearing the same suspicious frown and the same damp coat as the night before. There was no sign that she had yet been to bed. An air of world-weariness stooped her shoulders as she worked at the countertop with a spirit-soaked rag.

"Where is Trenloe?" Andira asked, without preamble.

"Gone," Sanna replied, no less curt, flicking her gaze briefly up to her before returning to the beer stains on the counter.

Andira's grip tightened around the edge of the bar. That accounted for the second unused bed.

"Gone where? And when?"

A shrug. "Last night. Told him about the curfew, but he wouldn't listen to me..."

"*Where* did he go?"

"Didn't say. At least not to me. But he took that young girl, Lidiya, with him."

Andira scowled. More likely, it was Lidiya who had taken him. Turning from the counter, she looked over the common room's inhabitants.

"I don't see the elven bard either."

"Rendiel? He's always come and gone as he fancies." Sanna snorted, putting her elbow into her work. "But he always comes back."

Andira turned to Owl, silently debating with herself what they should do now.

They could go on to the Academy without Trenloe, risk his supposed friend refusing to help on a strange woman's say-so, or wait for him here, potentially losing another full day to Trenloe's folly and risking the ire of Brother Augost at the same time. Owl looked back and offered no opinion. Andira did not mind. Sometimes, just going through the motions of a dialogue helped her to think.

"I almost forgot." Sanna cursed herself, fishing around in her apron for a small piece of paper. "He left you this." The innkeeper presented her with it.

It had one jagged edge and looked as though it had been torn out of an old book. A block of handwriting filled one side and it had been neatly folded along the middle.

Andira turned it over and opened it. She read what had been written inside.

It was one word. A name.

*RAYVAYLA.*

"Trenloe..." she muttered as though she could make the word a curse, folding the note again and pocketing it.

Say this for Nerekhall: it was literate.

But while Lidiya could clearly dictate, she could do nothing for the fact that Trenloe was unable to spell.

"What is it?" Owl asked.

"The name of his contact at the Academy. He is as good as telling us to go without him."

"Can I fix either of you with a breakfast?" Sanna asked, her attempt at congeniality wilting under the frostiness of Andira's mood.

"Who out of this roomful of drunks would you trust to see Owl and myself to the Academy?"

The innkeeper puffed out her cheeks as she surveyed her unlikely candidates.

"I'll take her."

A man in a long, moss-green traveling coat and feathered hat looked up from his corner snug. He had his feet up on the table and had been smoking on a pipe up until the moment he had spoken. Neither hat nor coat marked him as out of place, not in this company, and not in an alehouse so predisposed to leaks and chills, but the light alley-piece crossbow sat beside him certainly did, as did the fact he was sitting alone. Andira did not recall seeing him the night before, although given that the door had been barred since sunset, he must have been there.

Sanna, however, appeared equally puzzled by him.

She scratched her head. "I'm afraid I… I don't know this fellow."

The stranger removed his hat with a flourish, pulling his feet back off the table in order to affect a bow. He had a short red beard and neatly combed hair at odds with his worn apparel, and had a sunless pallor to match his far-northern accent.

"My name is Thaiden Mistspeak. I'm not from Nerekhall originally, true, but this city and I are no strangers." He smiled and set his hat back straight on his head. "I can find my way out of the Snicks, and see you to the Academy. I've affairs of my own to settle at the North Gate. Partners come a long way from Carthridge to discuss business, and I've no objection to having you and your friend for part of my way."

No one enquired as to what his business might be.

Nerekhall was not that kind of city. The Book Louse was not that kind of inn. But that he was not native to Nerekhall and a stranger to Sanna were marks in his favor as far as Andira was concerned.

Owl chose that moment to stir. "I think I will have breakfast."

Andira smiled at him sadly, warning Sanna off with a glare.

They could eat on the way.

# CHAPTER NINE
## *Trenloe the Strong*

The alley was scarcely lit, relying on the leftover glow from the street behind them. Buildings rose tiredly to either side, slumped into their timber frames like old men stuck in their chairs. The air was a haze of dust and middle-aged creaks.

Trenloe crunched down under a crooked beam that had buckled outwards into the alley under the weight of its wall and knelt amidst the accumulated rubbish. His armor's knee joint squeaked as it bent, and he grimaced. He was as subtle as an ox drawing a plough.

But the ironbound didn't turn at the sound.

It didn't react at all.

Its complete lack of interest gave Trenloe a moment's consternation as to whether this was really the same ironbound, but no, he was sure. The pattern of runes was familiar. The dent in its helmet was as distinctive as a birthmark, a perfect match for his own bruised knuckles. There could be no doubt. So why was it not responding to them as it had yesterday?

Trenloe peered into the wood-scented haze.

The ironbound had halted about forty yards down the alley,

the arcane glow of its inner workings haloing it in concentric rings of pink and purple dust. Its back was turned to him, its head bowed. The faint glimmers of external light scattered across it to craft a black silhouette twinkling with embedded gold. Its attention was fixed on a patch of ground immediately ahead of it. Trenloe could see nothing there.

Nor was there any sign of Rendiel. The elf appeared to have vanished.

"Finally," said the gloom immediately beside his left shoulder. "You both made it."

Lidiya covered her open mouth with her hand to prevent herself from crying out. Trenloe turned. Rendiel was crouched in the rubble, his red coat sprinkled with dust, although not nearly liberally enough to conceal him as completely as he had been. Trenloe hadn't seen him there at all.

"How did you do that?"

"What are you doing here?" Lidiya cut in before the elf could answer.

Rendiel looked at them both as though they were stupid. "Following *you*, of course."

"I thought you wanted nothing to do with this," said Trenloe.

"I want *nothing* to do with it," Rendiel said, with feeling. "But I don't want to see the two of you earning a one-way trip back to the Tower either."

"He's lying, Trenloe," Lidiya hissed. "I don't know why, but he is." She glared suspiciously at the elf. "I'm from Nerekhall. We can always tell."

"My friend," said Rendiel, with a heavy sigh, ignoring Lidiya altogether to address Trenloe. "You didn't have the good fortune of seeing what you looked like when the guards dragged you into my cell. Why? Because you were *unconscious*, and given how far they had to drag you to get you there from Bridge Market you were unconscious for a *long* time. I don't think that this one–" he bowed courteously towards Lidiya "–is going to tilt the rematch in your favor."

Trenloe looked at his hand in the dark.

The swelling had reduced overnight, even without the benefit of Andira's healing, and the redness was almost gone. He could make a fist with it, grip an axe, but he didn't want to be punching any more suits of armor today if he could avoid it. The ironbound were incredibly strong, but Trenloe was reassured to see that he'd caused this one some damage, even if it was just a little. If it could be hurt, then it could be hurt enough to be stopped. His mistake had been to try and fight it as though he was fighting a soldier in armor. Now, he knew better. Working silently, he loosened the cord holding his axe at his thigh.

"You won't be able to pierce its armor with that," said Rendiel.

"It'll pierce it with me swinging it."

"You're just going to break a perfectly good axe."

"See?" said Lidiya. "He's only here to scare us off."

Rendiel put his hands up. "Just trying to help."

"Ironbound are strong, and once they've got you, they don't ever give up, but they're slow, and they're not bright." Lidiya turned confident eyes onto Trenloe. "Keep it moving and you can beat it."

"I'm not exactly the quickest either. Or the brightest…"

Trenloe turned to Rendiel, fully expecting the bard to have something to say, but the elf was frowning into the drifting sawdust haze.

"What is it?"

"The ironbound," Rendiel murmured, as though reluctant to acknowledge he even knew what an ironbound was. "It's doing something."

It had not moved, its attention still fixed on the empty square of alley floor in front of it, but it seemed to be powering down as they watched, becoming inert again as its inner furnace cooled and its halo faded. Were Trenloe to have come across it only now that it was stationary, then he would have probably passed it by as he had the others, not even noticing the dented helm in the dark.

Trenloe allowed himself to relax a little.

"What's it doing?"

"I don't know," said Rendiel. "I suspect that it was searching for an opening. That's what the ironbound are sent into the Snicks to do."

"An opening?"

Rendiel sighed quietly. "Nerekhall exists on sufferance, you see, on the rest of Terrinoth being perennially reassured it's not the hotbed of demon-worshipping cults and despotic rune-mages it deep-down believes we are." He gestured to the sagging wall and moldering timber beams around them. "The Snicks wasn't always like this, though there aren't many humans left in Nerekhall that remember. This is the part of the city that bore the brunt of Mirklace's calamity. The north, west, and eastern quarters of the city have recovered to some extent, although most outsiders would still call them cursed, but the Snicks are broken. Anyone who's lived here long enough could give you a story of alleyways that lead not onto brick walls but into pocket dimensions of the Ynfernael, or of doors that no amount of force will open but where a desperate man can crouch by the keyhole and have his appeals heard by demons."

"It's true," said Lidiya. "When my parents were alive, we had this wardrobe where–"

"It's nonsense," said Rendiel, shaking his head.

"You sound very sure of that," said Trenloe.

The elf tapped his forehead and gave him a knowing smile. "Because Mirklace wasn't trying to get into the Ynfernael. And why would he?" He shuddered dramatically. "Even mad mages have that much sense. No, he was trying to access a region of the Aenlong called the Black Realm. That's where all the unopenable doors, blind alleys and magic wardrobes in the Snicks will take you."

Trenloe's brow wrinkled in thought. Andira had explained the hierarchy of the planes of power to him but he had never understood it.

"What is–?" he began, but Rendiel pre-empted him.

He lifted a hand up high. "The Empyrean." Brought it down low. "The Ynfernael." Raised it to hover in between, at chest level. "The firma dracem. Us." Threw it about in vague, formless circles all around him as though swatting at a fly. "The Aenlong." He brought his hand down again. "The Black Realm belongs to the Aenlong, but lies very close to the boundaries of the Ynfernael."

"So… the ironbound go into the Snicks to find and close these portals?"

Rendiel nodded. "Though obviously, it didn't find anything."

"What makes you say that?"

"Because if there was a portal to the Black Realm here, we'd be–"

"What?"

Still in his crouch, the elf inched a little further down the alley. "Oh no. Oh no, no, no, no."

"*What*?" said Lidiya. "And don't try to scare us."

"Don't you smell that?"

Trenloe lifted his nose and sniffed. He smelled old wood and sewage.

Rendiel turned back to them, his long face harrowed by sudden worry. Trenloe had never seen the elf looking so deadly serious. "Run," he hissed, speaking to Lidiya. "Head to the Book Louse and whatever you see or hear behind you, don't stop."

"I'm not leaving Trenloe–"

"Go!"

Lidiya threw a glance at Trenloe, who nodded.

He'd always anticipated having to leave the girl behind sooner or later. He'd imagined that it would be so he could tackle a rogue ironbound, but the armor they had followed here had not moved and appeared to be completely powered down. What had unnerved Rendiel so completely, he could not say.

While Lidiya picked her way back up the alley, the elf drew his sword. The tarnished bronze handle with its gaping sockets, where precious stones had presumably been scraped out of the hilt and sold, was not the most reassuring sight to have on a sword beside you.

And then all of a sudden, Trenloe found that he *did* smell something.

It was wheat rotting in the field after two weeks of rain, a barn full of cattle wasting with the sickness, the smell of human goodness and pure evil separating from one another like curds and whey and turning rotten without the balancing action of the other to keep them fresh.

A thin slit, like a cat's eye, had appeared in the air in front of the static ironbound, an old and haggard sort of light leaking through the breach and throwing the armor's shadow wildly across the sides of the alley. The dust in the air shivered, a foul gust brushing down the street as though the opening had just taken its first breath.

Trenloe felt ill.

He wanted to be sick, but his body refused.

"A black rift," Rendiel breathed, as a clawed paw ventured through the opening.

Unthinking, Trenloe drew his axe.

And still, the ironbound did not move.

# CHAPTER TEN
## *Andira Runehand*

The Academy. Finally.

After six months on the pitiless roads of the northern baronies and Trenloe's eleventh hour distractions, Nerekhall's infamous seat of learning stood before her as something of an anticlimax. A storm-troubled castle brooding over the freezing waters of the Korina's Tears, shunned by the city that harbored it and hidden away behind higher walls would have been closer in keeping to its reputation.

Rows of nondescript shops surrounded the modest, timber-framed manor, huddled under their bleak awnings like mourners in the rain. They made discreet offerings of rare tomes and tailored gowns, glass and silverware, tonics that were almost certainly illegal but sold with the promise to fortify the memory and strengthen the mind.

Of the tens of thousands who called Nerekhall home, most would never come close to a runestone, and yet unwittingly drew their livelihoods from the practice of magic, nonetheless. They traded in paper and in candles and the ingredients of simple potions. Merchants from further afield brought in silver from the Carthmounts, the latest periodicals from the copy houses of Greyhaven, and luxuries from Nornholt, Tamalir, Forge, and beyond, that only a tenured magister could afford. They left their coin in Nerekhall's inns and carried Nerekhall's produce home with them when they left.

By a centuries-old decree, Nerekhall was governed by a council of magistrates elected from the city's professional guilds. Interference from the Academy was strictly forbidden.

As was so often the case, reality was the hard soil in which good intentions withered.

The Academy *was* Nerekhall.

"This is where I leave you."

Thaiden Mistspeak doffed his feathered hat, a smile for any occasion on his face, and bid them farewell. Owl watched his every step until he dissolved into the sober crowds of shoppers. Andira thought that she liked him. He was quiet. The walk across Nerekhall had taken most of the morning and taught her no more about him than his name. After a season on the road with Trenloe, she had heard so many stories that she could have passed convincingly as a Trastan native.

Seeing no guards at the Academy's rather ordinary-looking front door, she walked inside.

A small foyer welcomed her. The walls were paneled in bronzed teak. The air smelled of aged wood and polish. Stepping across the thick-bristled mat that lay in front of the door, she continued into a long corridor. Tapestries and shelves crammed with curios from across the known world obscured the wainscotting of the walls. Freestanding glass cabinets gleamed like treasure chests, discouraging haste through the corridors. A few of the artefacts on display bore labels, citing lands that Andira had never heard of, intrepid scholars lost to the niches of history, and magical properties that had never been tested. For the most part, however, Andira was left to wonder.

She wondered again at the lack of guards. Perhaps the warning from the guard captain when he had admitted them to the city had had some truth to it after all: Nerekhall really was a law-abiding city.

After several minutes spent wandering museum corridors without spotting hide nor hair of a student, she chanced upon a young dwarf in a pinafore dusting a wall of books.

"Good morning," said Andira.

The dwarf looked startled to see another soul at large. Andira walked to her, taking the note that Trenloe had left for her from her pocket and showing it to her. The dwarf squinted at the writing, sounding the word aloud before understanding flickered in her eyes.

"Ahh, it says *Ravaella*. You're looking for Mistress Lightfoot."

Shaking off her feather duster, the dwarf led Andira and Owl a short way back down the corridor to an anonymous oak door almost hidden amidst the shelves. She raised a hand to knock, only to think better of it and turn back to Andira. "I sit in on Mistress Lightfoot's lectures sometimes. They're always... interesting."

"Interesting how?"

"They..." A smile crept across the young dwarf's face, but she left the explanation unfinished and bobbed a courtesy. "Well, you'll see."

Andira turned a raised eyebrow towards Owl as the maid returned to her books.

He shrugged back at her.

Andira wondered if this Ravaella Lightfoot was really a

friend of Trenloe's at all. Trenloe never forgot a name, or a face, and had the infuriating habit of referring to everyone he had just met as his *friend*. Uncertain what to expect, she knocked on the door.

She waited.

There was no answer.

She knocked again, harder, and when there was still no answer, she tested the latch, finding it unlocked, and pushed her head inside.

The small room looked like a private study that some senior academic had claimed to store the overspill from their bookshelves. Every shelf, side table, tiny chair and the one low-slung desk was stacked with open books, half-rolled manuscripts and random assortments of papers. A white ragdoll cat lay in a repose of supreme boredom across an illuminated text that had been left in the sunshine on the windowsill. It blinked drowsily at her. Andira ignored it. She had never understood the need of some people to keep pets.

A gnome, about three feet in height with ankle-length red hair in a ponytail and pointed ears, sat at the epicenter of the clutter. She was peering over her shoulder at the open door with an expression of annoyance, her long ring-heavy fingers fidgeting with a quill pen.

"I knocked," Andira said, accusingly, pushing in the rest of the way.

The gnome lowered her pen to the desk. "You can see me?" When Andira simply frowned at her, she sprang out of her chair and waved her hand in front of her own face. "How vexatious." The motions of her hand across her face conjured into being a gold-framed mirror that floated, partially transparent, in the air in front of her. She peered into it, turning her head to one side and brushing away her hair. "Definitely invisible." With a roll of her fingers, the mirror turned back into air. She pursed her lips and looked up at Andira. "You have some explaining to do, young lady." The gnome raised one hand, thumb poised against middle finger. "How about–"

She snapped her finger.

*"–now?"*

Andira blinked, taken aback.

The gnome was gone.

*"Fascinating."*

Andira whirled to see the gnome now in the corridor behind her, circling around Owl, pulling at his armor and peering at the scuffed heraldry as though he was a new artefact brought in for display.

"You're from Kell, yes? The owl." She reached up on tiptoes to tap the breastplate device. "Dead giveaway. A knight of some kind, or a lord. Yes, I know I've seen this heraldry somewhere before–"

Andira cleared her throat.

The gnome looked up and frowned, as though she had not been expecting to find that Andira was still there.

"Who are you? Did I ask that already? Did you say?"

Andira thought that she understood what the maid had been trying to tell her.

"We are friends of Trenloe."

"Trenloe…" the gnome muttered to herself, drumming her fingers together in thought. "Trenloe… Trenloe… I don't know any Trenloe."

Andira turned her face to the ceiling. She should have known.

Before she could speak again, an awkwardly tall young

man in plain black student's robes appeared at the end of the corridor.

"Mistress Lightfoot," he called out, in a sullen voice. "I–"

"Not now, Cabdal!" she snapped, and leant in close, forcing Andira to stoop to hear her whisper. "This is why I spend my time invisible. Come in, come in, quickly, before any more turn up." She ushered them both back into her study and shut the door behind them.

A second gnome was already there waiting for them. She was wearing a pair of thick-framed reading glasses and carrying an open book with the title *The Subordinate Elements*. Her hair was a more orangey shade of red and the trinkets about her neck lay in a slightly different pattern, but in every other respect she was identical. The first crossed to her and took the book.

"I need you to read chapter eight for me by lunchtime," said the second gnome. "For some reason, one of us agreed to give a lecture on it this afternoon."

"Yes, Ravaella," said Ravaella.

"I'll handle this," said Ravaella again, the second one, making an arcane pass of her hands that caused the first to vanish, book and all.

The ragdoll on the windowsill yawned as though it had seen it all before.

"A simulacrum spell," Ravaella explained, in response to the stunned expression on Andira's face. "Unlike certain so-called institutions of learning, the Academy turns no one away. Anyone with the interest and the talent is welcome to study here. Laudable as that is, it does become a tremendous drain on one person's time." She smiled brightly and gestured to the mess around her. "So, I learned to delegate. Whoever heard of a gnomish sorcerer? Right? I have to do more than everyone else and I have to do it better, so why not do it all myself?"

She took up the seat that her banished double had left vacant and with a straightforward gesture conjured two human-sized chairs from amidst the mountains of books. "So, you're friends of Trenloe, are you? How is he? I've not seen him since he was a boy no taller than me and I was performing self-taught conjuring tricks at village fayres."

Andira stared at her open-mouthed.

She did not know if it was the gnome's off-hand displays of magic or her breathless manner of speech that left her stunned.

"You are a sorcerer," she said.

To most of Terrinoth, words like *mage, wizard, runemaster,* and *sorcerer* were synonymous. To the untrained eye, their magic was identical, but rune-magic, the common form of magic in Terrinoth, the form that Andira intuitively practiced, was a skill that anyone could learn and that a few might find the aptitude to master. Sorcery was something different. It was the innate gift to draw upon the limitless energies of the Turning. Requiring no rune to shape the effect they wished to produce, their abilities were limited only by their imagination. They were rare.

Andira could count on one hand the sorcerers she had heard of.

Now, she had met her first.

Ravaella grinned immodestly. "And still Greyhaven turned me away. A conjurer and a trickster, they called me. Laughed at me. Told me gnomes have no talent for magic." She scoffed. "As though you need *talent* for the magic they teach in Greyhaven."

Satisfied that her chair was solid, Andira sat down. It creaked as it adjusted to her weight exactly as a real chair would. She marveled at it. She did not think much of Trenloe's usual choice of friends, but power she could admire.

Owl crossed his arms and remained standing.

"He doesn't say much, does he?" said Ravaella.

"He lost his memories."

"Fascinating..." said Ravaella, hopping back out of her chair as though there was a spring under the cushion. "How did it happen?"

Owl looked down at her, puzzled. He thought for a moment. "I don't remember."

"Fascinating."

"It happened before I met him," said Andira, hoping that would close the matter.

It was no lie. The man he was now had not existed before the sword he bore had been used to slay Baelziffar. That man had earned his rest. The man he had since become deserved his own chance of a life.

"It would be a simple trick, you know," said Ravaella.

"What would?" asked Andira.

The gnome looked up, surprised, again, to find her thoughts in an external dialogue. Her long fingers gestured vaguely towards Owl. "To turn him back. To restore his memories. Aren't you both just *burning* to solve the mystery of who this knight of Kell really is?"

"You... could do that?" said Owl.

The gnome shrugged. "What is the mind but an engine of illusion? It tells us what to see, what to think, who to be, and like a gullible audience we fall for it every time. It would be quite simple, as I say, to pull the trick on *it* for a change."

Owl looked confused, uncertain how to respond, and

visibly startled when Ravaella suddenly clapped her hands and swung back towards Andira.

"So, how do you know Trenloe?"

Andira took a moment before answering. It was difficult to match the gnome's pace. She was still thinking through the ramifications of her unexpected offer to Owl when Ravaella changed the subject.

"We met in Kell," she said. "We traveled there separately, but both fought in the battle at Furnace Gate."

"Which explains you." Ravaella winked at Owl. "What brings you all the way to Nerekhall?"

Andira took a deep breath and proceeded to describe her vision. The stair. The corridor. The beckoning of the open door. The taunting apparition that could only have been Baelziffar, whom she did not name.

When she was done with the telling, her heart was thumping, her palms clammy as though in spite of the comfortable chair and the cool daylight, she had not simply retold it but relived it.

"Fascinating," Ravaella mumbled to herself. "And what are you hoping I can do?"

Andira shrugged. "Give me some answers."

"You've been traveling for months across half of Terrinoth. You've already passed Greyhaven – not that I blame you, mind – so why here?"

"This is not my first vision. They have guided me as long as I can recall. Nerekhall was not our original destination on departing Kell, we were simply heading west into Forthyn on the trail of the blood sister, Ne'Krul, but the further we traveled in this direction the more vivid the visions became and the more frequent. It was only after passing Greyhaven and entering Cailn that Trenloe mentioned you, said you were a friend and knew more about this sort of magic than anyone else."

"Ahh, Trenloe. Always so easily impressed." Ravaella studied her with an intensity of focus that she had not shown until then. Andira tried to read what she was thinking, but the gnome's face was so open it performed the trick of giving away nothing of what passed beneath. "Hmmmmmm." The gnome beckoned for Andira's hands. "I do know a little divination, as it goes. Give me your hands."

Andira opened her palms.

With a gasp of surprise, Ravaella snatched up her left hand in both of hers, her long fingers tracing the pale blue outline of the rune in her palm.

"Marvelous," she murmured, as she poked and prodded, turning the hand over to examine it from both sides, then back again. "The transfer of a rune from its stone onto a discrete object, a sword for example, is relatively straightforward. Commonplace even. But the first recorded instance of a runestone bound to living flesh is in the works of Dalmar the Great. He describes setting a rune of mental quickening into the head of his youngest son and the procedure was, by his own account, a resounding success. Paraplegia and premature death notwithstanding, of course. I know of only one other living specimen and Baron Zachareth is, as you might imagine, not a terrifically willing subject of study."

Andira found herself, again, speechless.

She had no memory of her discovery of the rune, or the life she had led before it. She had wondered at the higher purpose that had brought her this power many times, but it had never occurred to her to think that there could be others. It hit her harder than she would have ever thought, and left her feeling cold. The rune, and the destiny it pointed her towards, were all she had. If she shared one or either, did that not lessen her?

"He is rumored to have bound a rune of strengthening to himself whilst concluding his magical studies here in Nerekhall," Ravaella went on, oblivious. "No one knows how he did it, or has managed to successfully repeat it since. And not for want of trial and error, I assure you. It's the one period in my entire tenure that you couldn't find a single rat anywhere in the Academy's grounds."

Andira folded her fingers back over the rune and drew her hand gently but firmly into her lap.

"My vision," she said.

Ravaella looked as though she would insist on seeing the rune again, but the impulse passed. She retreated to her chair and fell back into it, steepling her fingers under her chin.

"Magic is forbidden in Nerekhall, you know. That surprises most people, but only the Academy has a license to practice and teach it, and only so long as it stays within these grounds. That said, though… mages with darker intentions have always found their way to Nerekhall. Maybe it's the promise of a free education at the Academy that draws them here. Or it could simply be power. No one can deny that there's power here, if you're not too troubled about where it comes from."

Andira nodded. Nerekhall was a town on a precipice, teetering only until the dark power over which it had been built finally gave way and allowed the Ynfernael to swallow it whole. Until that day came, however, power, the very darkest essence of it, was the air that Nerekhall breathed.

"I'll help you if I can," said Ravaella. "But not for Trenloe. And not for you either."

Andira sank back into her chair.

She had been waiting for this.

Trenloe seemed to believe that everyone would offer their help to him out of simple generosity because that was what he would do. But not even Trenloe could generate enough good will to sustain an unconditional friendship over a decade of absence.

The gnome smiled and pointed a ring-heavy finger at Owl. "Him."

"Me?" said Owl.

"I cannot just *give* you Owl."

"I don't mean…" Ravaella wrung her hands apologetically. "I'm running away with myself. I don't want to *keep* him or anything. I want to help him. I'm just curious, aren't you, to look inside that head?"

Andira looked at Owl.

The man was torn. But then, he did not know the horrors that his current state had allowed him to forget.

"Can we speak with Trenloe and consider it?"

"Of course, of course. Let me come to you later this evening. It will take some time to compile what rumor and hearsay I have for you in any case. Where can I find you?"

"We have rooms at an inn called the Book Louse."

Ravaella made a face.

"You know it?"

"Only by the reputation of some of its clientele, but that's another story. If that's where you are then I'll find you. And don't worry." She gave her a wink. "I'd like to see the guard that can catch me breaking curfew."

Andira offered her hand and Ravaella shook it. The rune in her hand *ached* before the immensity of power that that child-sized appendage contained. She could not help but wonder which of them, if the cause should arise, would be the greater.

Letting go of the gnome's hand, she turned to Owl and made ready to leave.

With any luck, Trenloe was having a less interesting day.

## CHAPTER ELEVEN
### *Trenloe the Strong*

The beast of the Black Realm resembled a monster that someone had squashed together from off-cuts of clay, someone who had never seen a living creature and thought nothing of assembling one with a corkscrew spine, lumpen skull, and five limbs of differing length. Walking on its knuckles it pushed through the black rift and into the alley. The resulting tremor brought bricks tumbling from the walls to either side, cracking harmlessly across the slabbed cartilage armoring its back and bursting into powder. It towered over the unmoving ironbound in front of it. The demon's lips twitched as though it was uncertain what they were for, perturbed by the nullifying aura that shrouded the ironbound even while it was inert.

While the armor had all of its attention, Trenloe struck.

His axe hacked into the monster's shoulder. Lumpy gray juices sluiced down its flank. It bellowed in pain, rolling its shoulder and swinging the arm to throw him off.

Trenloe wrenched his axe free from the cartilage even as the arm came up. He ducked the swing, the arm thumping across his head as he stepped inside and delivered a punch to the gut with his shield boss. The up-angled blow bludgeoned its gray flesh and broke whatever it had underneath, lifting the enormous beast off the ground and slamming it against the wall behind.

Brickwork and timber splintered around its outline and the thing flopped to the floor, bonelessly squirming like a fish tricked onto rocks.

It looked like it was dying, but Trenloe couldn't be sure.

Nothing alive could possibly die like that.

"You were right," he managed to get out around the convulsions of his chest. The stench was appalling and getting worse by the second. He was genuinely concerned that he might yet throw up. "The ironbound was doing what it was meant to all along. It came here to stop the rift."

"That's not how ironbound work," Rendiel shot back, shifting his weight anxiously from foot to foot in the dust, sword-point raised in the classic duelist's guard. "They react to dark magic and destroy it. They don't pre-empt. They can't. Creating an ironbound that could find a black rift before it opens would be like… like…" He shook his head as though even with the deep lore and broad vocabulary of an Aymhelin bard he was lost for a parallel.

"It would be like finding the last resting place of King Daqan. Or following the tail of the Chaos Serpent to the edge of the world. It would be to the Artificers of Pollux what finding a note from the creation-song of the First would be to the Latari. It's a veritable sacred grail," Rendiel eventually said.

"But the rift is right here!"

"And your perfectly normal ironbound is just *sitting* there."

Trenloe didn't have an answer. The elf made an excellent point.

"Then what–?"

"Look out!" Rendiel yelled, swinging his guard towards the downed beast.

Its death-throes thrashed it out of the wall, pulling it back upright even as broken bones were re-knitted together and slathered in glossy white flesh. Like watching wet dough being rolled out under a pin.

Before Trenloe had even begun to accept that horror, a fresh gust of stomach-turning foulness emanated from the widened rift. A second set of claws began tearing at its edges. The resistance of the firma dracem was weaker this time. Trenloe had no idea how to kill a beast he had already thought dead, and the idea of having to fight two of them did not appeal.

Acting faster than Trenloe could think, Rendiel lunged across, slashing his beggared rapier across the second monster's knuckles.

A muted bellow reverberated up from the deeper plane of its origin, gray blood-ooze trickling down its fingers and sizzling where it splashed the alley floor. But the thing held on, determined to be born. It wedged a spiked shoulder into the tear, then a head, more malformed and corrupted than its twin before it.

Trenloe had seen for himself how the powers of the lower planes could reshape the natural creatures of the Charg'r Wastes and Ru Steppes. He had seen, too, the ruinous true forms that the denizens of the Ynfernael could assume when given access to this plane, but even they paled in comparison to this.

The beasts of the Black Realm were all the more monstrous for not knowing what, exactly, they wanted to be.

Jaw locked lest he cry out in horror, Trenloe smashed

his shield through the monster's grotesque face and sent it howling back into the Black Realm.

The elder twin, meanwhile, having rebuilt itself with an over-muscled upper body and huge slabs of thickened cartilage armoring its breastbone and shoulders, shrugged off the wreckage of the building that Trenloe had thrown it into and snapped at Rendiel. The bard veered onto the back foot to avoid having his head ripped clear of his shoulders.

"We should run, too," Rendiel suggested, with a pointed jerk of the head in the direction Lidiya had fled.

"We can't!"

Just as Trenloe spoke, the rift spasmed and a hand large enough to swallow both of his burst from it, catching his axe-hand by the forearm. He grunted, pulling back against its grip, but its strength was horrendous. He braced himself, boot heels dragging across the alley floor as the monster pulled him in, using Trenloe's own opposing strength as the leverage to haul itself back up and through the rift.

The beast roared in Trenloe's face, showering him in hissing gobbets of spittle.

Trenloe slammed the rim of his shield down across the monster's wrist, and then again. He heard the bones split, felt the grip on his forearm loosen, and then rammed the monster back again with his shoulder.

Breathing hard, he turned to Rendiel.

The elf was a blur of red brocade and dirty metal as he kept himself one step ahead of the beast's rampage. He must have been quite something once. Not for the first time, Trenloe found himself wondering how Rendiel had ended up singing cheap songs in exchange for free lodgings and all the ale he could stomach.

When this was over and he was sure that Lidiya was back safe, he intended to find out.

"We can't leave," Trenloe called back. "This ironbound is the proof Andira needs that Nerekhall's in danger. And that Lidiya's no blood witch."

"In the next five minutes, every ironbound within a mile of here is going to come down on this alley like the hammer of Pollux himself. If you think this alley looks bad now, you don't want to see what it's going to look like after they've got here."

The beast's jaws dislocated, opening wide, saliva the consistency and color of treacle coating its heinous array of teeth. The elf stood his ground, reacting at the last possible second before being snatched off his feet and swallowed whole to ram his sword into the soft palate of the demon's mouth.

"Sword of Emorial," the elf sang in a high, clear voice, steam billowing through the monster's wedged lips and scorching some of the grime from his sleeve. "Thy heavenly guide, to a fallen pride, Purgatory's end, is golden send." The beast yowled as Rendiel ripped the now-blazing sword from its throat. It reeled backwards, head thrashing from side to side as though to smother the burning in its mouth.

Trenloe stared in wonder at the bard.

What was that – magic?

He wondered how he had managed to work it at such close quarters to the ironbound. Was it possible that bardic magic, and perhaps the divine powers practiced by the priests of Kellos and Pollux, too, were unaffected by ironbound nullifying runes? Andira might have an explanation, if Trenloe lived long enough to ask her.

"Ungh." Rendiel shook himself off, dry-retching as though

he had just licked the back of a horse. "I need a drink after that."

"What did you just do?"

The beast's younger twin bellowed from the other side of the rift. Trenloe saw it thrash, and thrust his arm into the breach to push the struggling demon back down. Muscles knotted and bulged along the length of his forearm. Trenloe gritted his teeth. It was like trying to kill a giant by holding his head underwater.

"Just a little verse I learned before leaving the Aymhelin. It's been a while though, I wasn't sure I could still hit the right notes," Rendiel said.

"For what it's worth, I'd say you can."

"An appreciative audience makes all the difference."

With his foe belching up smoke, the bard hurried to the unmoving ironbound. Trenloe felt himself tense, ready to abandon the rift and charge to his aid if needed, but even now the automaton stood immobile. With the tip of his sword, Rendiel traced out one of the runes on its back.

"What is it?" Trenloe asked.

The elf looked up. "These runes," he admitted, rapping his sword once against the ironbound's armor. "They're what grant the ironbound their properties: strength, endurance, immunity to magic. But there are also runes created by the Artificers that tell them what to do and how to act. And there is something..." He withdrew his sword, puzzled. "Something *different* about this rune here."

"One of the control runes?"

Rendiel nodded and bent in for a closer look.

"For Kellos' sake, could you do it any faster?"

With a grunt of effort, every muscle in his upper body taut

and straining, Trenloe forced the beast in his grip back into the Black Realm. He couldn't see the demon through the planar barrier, couldn't begin to imagine what part of it he was holding onto from feel alone, but he could feel its desperation getting the better of its efforts.

The black rift was failing, the edges sucking in around his bicep and trapping the beast on the other side. It was like watching a wound heal in accelerated time, the foul reek of the Black Realm leaving the air with every gulp of it he swallowed. At the last second before he lost all sense from his fingers, he pulled his arm from the closing rift. The beast lunged the moment it was free, but Trenloe had timed his moment right, and its claws ripped futilely at the walls of the Aenlong.

Its shriek sent an existential shiver down Trenloe's spine, but the beast was gone.

The black rift was closed.

Trenloe wriggled his fingers to assure himself that the hand at the end of the arm was his own and not some meat puppet of the Aenlong, and breathed a sigh of relief that it seemed to be so.

The elder beast, recovered now from its scalding but trapped in the firma dracem, gave a shuddering howl, its body mutating again even as it launched itself at Rendiel. The elf threw himself to the wall but the demon ignored him entirely, trampling bricks and debris on its way towards the faint yellow square of light and murmuring of voices that promised escape.

"It's running for the street," said Rendiel.

"Stay here with the ironbound!"

"I will, I will." Rendiel leant against the wall and trembled like an old man who'd been made to run ten miles. He waved Trenloe off towards the street. "Get on with you. Go."

Leaving the elf to mind the captive machine, Trenloe charged after the beast.

He only had to follow the screams.

Bursting back onto the street that he and Lidiya had been walking down a few minutes earlier, he found its handful of occupants fleeing in terror. A young couple who'd been caught out in the open screamed, frozen in place, as the enraged demon stampeded towards them.

"Over here!" Trenloe yelled, and threw his axe in desperation.

The weapon wasn't weighted for throwing, and Trenloe was a poor shot in any case. Anything more than spear-length away, and he'd be the first to admit that he was useless. The blade's flat skittered across the demon's armored shoulder and flew clear. It landed somewhere up the street. Trenloe didn't see where.

Drooling, growling, eyes alight with the fear of a beast that knew it didn't belong, the monster stomped round to face him. With a frenzied jerk, it wrenched a streetlamp from its iron base, taking it in two of its three forepaws like a morning star. Trenloe smiled grimly as he saw the trapped couple help each other up and flee, quickly raising his shield as the demon stove it in with its lamppost. The bulb shattered, cool yellow fire rolling across Trenloe's shield and splashing the cobbles, the massive impact beating him to the ground. With a clatter of plate and a grunt, he got back to his feet, rolling the feeling back into his shoulder and raising his shield again.

The demon snarled at its broken lamppost, and tossed it aside.

Trenloe looked quickly left and right, making sure that the people of Nerekhall had all managed to get clear. A part of him was surprised that no one else was trying to fight back. There was almost always someone ready to step up and be a hero, at least to protect what was theirs. Perhaps it was for the best they didn't. Trenloe had seen enough examples of what happened when ordinary folk took up arms against monsters.

A ferocious, high-pitched scream rose above the abandoned street. Trenloe turned his head towards it, and quickly came to an understanding of why everyone had been so quick to get clear. Rendiel had tried to warn him.

It wasn't the beasts of the Black Realm they were running from.

The ironbound he'd seen outside the old Penacor library came thundering up the street like a runaway carriage, rune-heated steam blasting through every joint in its body as it built up speed and power. The demon turned towards it and recoiled, visibly weakened by the runes seared in sword-slash lines of white-gold across its black plate.

But, unlike the ironbound it had encountered in the alley this one wasn't going to just stand there.

The long, spiked point of its glaive punched through the monster's breastbone, the ironbound's huge mass and unstoppable momentum seeing it run the beast straight through and skewering it to the road. The demon squirmed under the combined injury of anti-magic runes and impalement and Trenloe was not sure which was the most grievous. It clawed at its attacker's armor but found itself too weak to leave a mark against the rune-hardened black iron.

The ironbound raised a boot to stamp down on the demon's head, just as a second construct came charging in.

It was the one that he and Lidiya had been spying on from the derelict tenement, he was sure of it, and coming by the most direct route available to it which just happened to mean ploughing straight through the building opposite Trenloe. The entire facade came crashing down over it, along with most of the roof, brick and stone slanging harmlessly off the ironbound's shoulders as it strode through the deluge, joints shrieking out aggression with every step, to join in the murder.

Trenloe watched, appalled by the extraordinary degree of violence but unable to look away, as the two ironbound hacked the demon's twitching body into the road.

He had wondered, after striking the beast for the first time, how to finish such a monster.

This was how.

When it was done, and all life had been expunged from the demon's remains to the ironbounds' satisfaction, heat began whistling off them as their runes cooled and the two automata powered down.

The ironbound that had come from the library turned on its heel and clanked back towards its former post. The armor from the alley wrenched its shield out of the gray slurry that was now spreading slowly through the gaps between the cobbles, straightened its glaive and assumed a new position where it was, knee-deep in the wreckage of the building it had just demolished and squarely in the middle of the main street.

Trenloe felt almost as rigid as the ironbound across from him.

The fighting was over, but he couldn't look away. His hand simply refused to let go of his shield. How often did something like this happen here? Did anyone even know? Was there an Artificer of Pollux somewhere, or a senior magistrate on the city's council whose responsibility it was to be informed of every Ynfernael attack on their city? Or, when it came to erasing the evidence of Nerekhall's shame, did the ironbound have complete impunity to act?

And if someone had found a way to corrupt them…

As Trenloe stood there, still watching, people began emerging from their hovels to poke through the rubble and tut to one another, as though it had just rained unseasonably or a neighbor had thrown rubbish onto their yard, unwilling to criticize the ironbound even then.

Crossing the street to reclaim his axe, he headed back into the alley to find Rendiel.

The elf was exactly where he'd left him.

He looked up at Trenloe apologetically.

The ironbound was nowhere to be seen.

Trenloe looked up and down the alley, as if an ironbound might be hidden under a heap of wood dust. "What…?" he mumbled, more thoroughly exhausted by the fight with the demon than he'd realized, and more disturbed by the response of the ironbound than he could explain. "Where is it?"

"I'm afraid it got away."

"Got away?" Trenloe asked, incredulously. "How?"

Rendiel shrugged, as though he was the last person Trenloe should be asking this question, but then grinned broadly and brandished a piece of paper with what appeared to be a charcoal rubbing of a rune on it. "But I did manage to get this."

Trenloe squinted at it. "What is it?"

"It's the altered control rune, of course. We don't need to hold the ironbound when we have this."

That was, or so it felt to Trenloe's aching muscles at that moment, a far better idea than dragging a rogue ironbound back with them to the Book Louse.

He was so enamored by it that it did not occur to him until much, much later that Rendiel never had explained just how the ironbound had gotten away.

# CHAPTER TWELVE
## *The First Flame*

The Cult of the Rising Flame met in secret, in a room that did not exist.

The First had conjured it herself to resemble the grand forum of the city magistrates, a chamber that she had visited only once, years ago, but had recalled with envy ever since.

Even looking on it like this, made her angry.

By what authority, intellectual or moral, had any of *them* thought they possessed to pass judgment on *her*.

That was the problem with Nerekhall. It was a city that existed, quite literally, on the threshold of unlimited potential, but it had hobbled itself with rules, and with the legion of dry fools it needed to record, amend, and enforce them.

The dead were stirring in the Mistlands, worrying at the borders of Carthridge and Rhynn like a newly arisen ferrox at a bloodied sleeve. The north-eastern baronies no longer existed. Terrinoth was crumbling, and soon Nerekhall would find itself at the vertex of its disintegration. Refugees flooded in and no one noticed. The inns were full and no one cared. The wars of the age were on their doorstep and who did

Nerekhall have to lead it into the Fourth Darkness? The sorts of men and women who could bear scrutiny with equanimity, whose lives were small enough to tolerate an inquisition from the magistrates and the Church of Pollux.

The centerpiece of the space was a large, circular table of white Carthmount stone. It had a golden rim with the flowing inscription: *one land, one people, united against the darkness by one law*. The quote was attributed to Arcus Penacor, the first king of the confederation of baronies that would become Terrinoth. The rest of the chamber was indistinct as she had poured considerably less attention into creating it. There were suggestions of hanging tapestries and whispering courtiers, hidden within a roaring wall of flame. The table was the only part of the forum that was currently playing a function.

Four anthropomorphic avatars floated over the chairs set around it.

To her left was a coiled boa with bright pink scales and half-lidded eyes. Opposite from her was a burning candle with lines of scripture written in gold foil around the wax body of the stick. To her right, an enormous human skull. Beside her, a reaper's scythe gave off a pungent green smoke that, even in this unreal meeting place, made her eyes sting.

Of them all, Scythe was the only one here who knew her true identity.

He had served the Burning Lord when he still lived, and had devoted the eight centuries since to seeking his undying shade in the Aenlong. He had founded the organization known as the Dread, with the goal of restoring the Burning Lord to the firma dracem and, when it had fallen to infighting and failure, had nurtured the Cult of the Rising Flame in Nerekhall as its natural heir. But Scythe existed to serve. Those had been his words. So long as the First led capably, he was content to cede the throne-in-hiding to his protégé.

Boa, Candlestick, and Skull were others that she had recruited over the years since. Initially, she had kept their identities from one another to protect herself from their ambitions. As the cult had spread its roots, however, the reason for continuing to do so was that most of her allies would refuse to work together if they knew. Lines became blurred in Nerekhall. That was its special power. Warlocks. Fanatics. Necromancers. Rune-mages with ambitions beyond their talents. They all found their way to Nerekhall in the end, and the oppression they all suffered under the Church of Pollux made unlikely alliances possible. It amused her to think of this as the natural end result of the city's obsession with law and order.

How was that for an unintended consequence?

But everyone had a line they wouldn't cross and, like any true thing, it was the lines that defined them.

"I heard about the opening of the Black Rift in Wicker Lane," said Candlestick, his voice similarly disguised so that it sounded like the hiss and sputter of melted tallow. "I assume that is why you called us here."

"It is. One of my ironbound pre-empted the rift by several minutes and was able to lead one of our agents to it before it opened."

"At last," Boa hissed. "Progress."

"The alterations you have been making to the ironbound have started to be noticed," said Candlestick. "Two guards were attacked last night. They had nothing on them but a gold coin apiece. That is harder for me to dismiss than the occasional disappearance of a peasant. The incident with

Rylan and Tristayne is not so long ago that everyone has forgotten. The chief artificer came to the Tower of Nerek to examine the ironbound personally."

"And?" said Boa.

"And I made sure the construct in question was elsewhere, or do you take me for a complete fool?"

Boa considered answering that, but turned instead to the First. "What of the rift?"

"My agent could not get close," Scythe answered, his guise making his voice sound like metal vibrating under the blow of a hammer. "Another had tracked the construct and was there before us."

"You should have killed them," said Boa.

Killing tended to be his first and last recourse. He was, as the First had come to learn, unnaturally gifted at it.

"And expose us? For a mere test? With my lord close enough to touch from beyond the veil? No." Scythe gave a hiss, like a blunt edge drawn across a stone. "This Trenloe seems quite capable. My agent could not have done that deed."

"Then do it yourself," said Boa, forked tongue flickering across his lips. "Or give it to me and I will."

"Trenloe the Strong," Candlestick sputtered. "He…" The First watched him pick his next words with care. The others were occasionally careless with what they revealed of themselves, but Candlestick, unlike the rest of them, was still very much a creature of rules. "He was in the Tower of Nerek just yesterday."

The skull stirred. "If it is too overt an act for our friend Scythe to simply kill him then could this Trenloe not have been held forever in the Tower? Is that not within your power? If not, then why did the First Flame privilege you with a position around this table in the first place?"

"Perhaps it is," Candlestick answered cagily. "But the last thing the Rising Flame needs is a hero of his reputation at the center of things when we are finally ready."

"He is a great hero then, this Trenloe the Strong?" Skull asked.

"Even in my land, we have heard of him," said Boa.

Scythe dipped his blade. A nod.

"Yes," the First reluctantly agreed. "Yes, I believe he may be."

"Well, Vorakesh has never heard of him."

Hidden behind her own disguise, a stalk of golden wheat swaying in an imagined breeze, the First winced. Skull's tendency to boast in the third person made a mockery of her attempts to obfuscate. She had no doubt that Boa, and possibly Scythe, too, knew exactly who their partner was and had come to terms with it. She was fortunate that Lord Vorakesh's reign of terror was deep enough in the past and, to be blunt, too insignificant in the grand sweep of Terrinoth's brushes with darkness, to be widely remembered. If Candlestick were to ever become curious and research the name in a library then he would likely never answer a summons again, and would probably burn half of Nerekhall to the ground in order to uproot them all.

Approaching a man of his position had been dangerous, she knew, but he had rewarded her gamble thrice over. His knowledge of the Tower of Nerek, and its bloody past, had brought them closer to their mutual goal than either Skull or Scythe had come in centuries.

"Vorakesh was a contemporary of Timmoran Lokander," Skull went on. "He walked in the company of Waiqar Sumarion, who would become the Undying King, and shared a battlefield with Triamvalor, high king of all the elves, and

Falladir Penacor. He has faced the assassins of the Qaro'Fen sent to claim the head of his master, and crossed spells with the great devil of the Charg'r, Llovar, himself. He has known real heroes and is unimpressed with this Trenloe the Strong."

The First chose not to mention that Skull knew none of the current century's heroes because he spent his time sequestered with books and corpses and lived in a tomb. He had taken little interest in the living since the living had slain him, scattered his runes to the corners of the world, and ended his own quest to restore the Burning Lord to his power.

He was mighty in himself, the First conceded, but contributed little these days beyond the occasional rant and bluster.

She should have dealt with him some time ago, before she had approached Candlestick, but Scythe had counselled her against it. Creatures like Vorakesh did not disappear quietly, or even die permanently. And she suspected that Scythe had his own inhuman sense of honor regarding such matters.

*Soon,* she thought, impatient for the day. *Soon, we will announce ourselves to the world and all of Nerekhall will see who I am. What I can do.*

"Our friend, Candlestick, made the correct decision in releasing Trenloe," she said. "Although not for the reasons he believed at the time. "I have made a discovery of my own and believe that Trenloe might hold the last piece of the puzzle. The missing key that has thwarted all previous efforts to restore the Burning Lord to life."

"A genuine relic of Margath," Scythe breathed. "Trenloe holds one?"

The First nodded. "We have learned of the door through which the Black Realm can be entered. We have engineered the means to find it and proven its success. All that we lacked was the means to summon the Burning Lord's wandering spirit from the far reaches of the Aenlong… until now."

Boa uncoiled from his seat and hissed. "All of Nerekhall whispers that the great hero stays in the Ironbrick Inn."

"You are talking about the most prestigious inn in Nerekhall," said Candlestick. "It is too well guarded. We cannot make an attack like that until we are certain we are ready."

"A rising flame lifts all wings," said the First, placatingly. "For once Nerekhall's whispers are out of date. Our city has already done what it does best and emptied the adventurers' purses of coin, forcing them to trade down. I know where they are."

She surveyed the hovering avatars.

Boa. Candlestick. Skull. Scythe.

And she knew just who to send.

# CHAPTER THIRTEEN
## *Andira Runehand*

The sun was lowering its head into the dark clouds of the Snicks' jumbled skyline when Andira and Owl found themselves before the Book Louse's rotted front door and sagging eaves.

A mist of drizzle pattered across the roof slates, dirty water gushing from a broken gutter. Two ironbound loomed over the narrow lane that led to it. One of the pair tracked its helmet to follow Andira as she passed, a slow grind of iron over iron. The second audibly tightened its grip around its glaive. Andira turned to look at them. One was still looking down at her, but neither was noticeably moving. She shook her head and turned back around.

Owl watched them both, backing after Andira with his hand on the hilt of his sword, until the door creaked shut behind them.

It was almost wetter under the Louse's ceiling than it had been in the rain. The merry flicker of candlelight and the fog put out by an unlimited supply of cheap tallow kept the cold at bay, but did nothing for the damp. Surly locals, all of them coated and booted as though expecting a storm to land at any moment sat drinking around tables.

Andira spotted Rendiel by his tired red coat. He was sitting at one end of a communal table with his legs half-crossed, one foot up on a stool while he adjusted the strings of a painfully out-of-tune Aymhelin lute. Trenloe was hunched over the table with Lidiya and, it seemed, half the tavern's clientele gathered around him. They were engrossed in the piece of paper he was holding, something drawn on it that he was describing with his finger.

Trenloe smiled broadly as Andira crossed the crowded common room towards him.

She looked over the small gathering. "What is this?"

Trenloe looked confused for a moment, then gestured to the heavily bearded man beside him. "This is Tuschels. He's a sewerman. They explore the old sewers, tracking dangerous monsters and scavenging for Penacor relics." While Tuschels raised an embarrassed hand in greeting, Trenloe gestured to the woman on from him. "And that there's Anya…" The group looked decidedly uncomfortable at having names and life stories they had probably not even shared with each other before Trenloe had come along freely bandied around in front of a stranger.

Anonymity, once given away, could never be taken back. But Trenloe had a way of turning acquaintances into friends, and setting the most steadfastly suspicious at their ease.

"Lidiya was right," he went on. "There *is* something up with the ironbound."

Andira's expression darkened. "What did you do?"

"I kept my promise, I assure you." Trenloe slid the piece of paper that his impromptu co-conspirators had been studying across the table.

She looked down at it. It was a rune of some kind, a spiral pattern intersected by dots and lines, far more convoluted than the usual patterns that rune-mages employed. It jogged nothing in her subconscious. If it was a rune, then it was an unusual one. She wished she could say for certain, but her knowledge was instinctive rather than learned. She had no idea what its limits were. "I have never seen a design quite like it," she admitted.

"Did you go to see Ravaella?" Trenloe asked, pulling her from her contemplation of the rune.

"She will be joining us later, and then perhaps we can return to the real reason we are here." Andira lifted the piece of paper from the bar, holding the charcoal rubbing to the candlelight. "My first inclination would be to call it a forgery. Every city in Terrinoth has at least one charlatan with a little artistic talent and enough rune-lore to create *runebound objects* for a small fee. This design is far too complicated for a mage to use. Where did you find it?"

"On an ironbound."

Andira lowered the paper to the bar. If the rune belonged to the ironbound then it was no surprise that she did not recognize it. It was likely that the Church of Pollux employed many runes of their own design. "You promised Brother Augost that you would not interfere."

"I didn't do anything," Trenloe protested, raising his hands to show innocence. "I only went out to watch, and I was actually on my way back when, well…" He turned back and waved for the bard's attention. "Tell her, Rendiel."

The elf continued to pluck at his strings. "This is obviously an argument between the two of you and I would rather not get involved."

"Rendiel thinks it's a sabotaged control rune," Trenloe said anyway, tapping emphatically on the drawing and smudging charcoal on his fingertip.

Lidiya propped herself up on her stool to whisper something in Trenloe's ear. She was, apparently, not speaking with Andira anymore. That stung more than Andira would have expected. She wondered if, perhaps, she owed the girl an apology for what she had said last night. Whatever Lidiya had to say, however, earned her a shake of the head from Trenloe.

"He's been different since then. I think he just needed to see the proof for himself."

Lidiya huffed, unconvinced, but too enamored by the legend of Trenloe to disagree. Andira had seen people of greater stature than Lidiya swoon under that charisma before.

"You should've seen Rendiel fight, Andira," said Trenloe. "If you'd seen him fend off a beast of the Black Realm then you'd be as glad to have him with us as I am."

Andira raised an eyebrow, startled. "A beast of the *what?*"

Trenloe gave a nervous cough. "I was… about to mention–"

"It wasn't Trenloe's fault," Lidiya muttered, without looking up from the table. "Black Rifts open all the time in Nerekhall. Especially around the Snicks. Trenloe was just in the right place to help."

"Somehow, he always is."

The Black Realm was a hinterland of the Aenlong, and well known amongst scholars of all branches of the arcane as a realm awesome in potential and power. The Aenlong was an amorphous realm, infinitely vast, but there were regions that bordered the other planes which, lacking any firm characteristics of its own, assumed something of its neighbors' properties.

The Black Realm was believed to lay across one such border with the Ynfernael and was viewed by scholars with an unhealthy taste in the illicit as a gray area, where mages could dabble without technically overstepping any boundaries. The Aenlong was also held by many to be the plane of existence that the recently dead needed to traverse in order to attain their afterlives, and where those restless spirits who had lost their way, or whose ties to the firma dracem were too great, lingered on as wraiths and spirits.

In other words, no one of any pure intent had any interest in the Black Realm.

"Apparently this sorcerer, Mirklace, tried to move all of Nerekhall there or… or something." Trenloe scratched his head. "Rendiel explained it to me…"

The elf clutched his lute and turned his face to the ceiling. "Heavens above and Tears falling," he declared. "It's like listening to a makhim perform the Lives of Emorial. Nerekhall has been a doorway to the Black Realm for thousands of years. The Latari certainly knew of it. But it was Mirklace, being the equal in recklessness to Malcorne of the Daewyl but so very much the greater in ignorance, who sought to throw it wide."

"I don't understand why anyone would want to cast a city into the Black Realm," said Trenloe. "Wasn't he in it?"

"It makes no sense to you because you are not a deranged mage intent on despoiling the firma dracem," said Andira with a smile.

Trenloe smiled back. It was probably the kindest thing she had said since her nightmares had stopped her from sleeping.

"Your illusionist friend told me that mages like Mirklace are often drawn to Nerekhall," she went on. "I have felt the same pull. It would not surprise me to discover that a cult in thrall to Baelziffar has been able to establish itself here."

"Wouldn't the ironbound root them out?" said Trenloe.

A few of the locals around their table scoffed.

"If mages are going to gather outside the Academy, then it would be somewhere the ironbound are unable to tread," Rendiel elaborated.

"There are such places in Nerekhall?" said Andira.

"Sadly, yes. Or fortunately, depending on your point of view. They're barred from entering the Academy, for obvious reasons. And if you go far enough beyond the city's original limits, or deep enough into the old sewers, then they'll eventually give up and turn back."

"How do you know this?"

The elf spread his arms. "I wasn't always the reputable bard you see before you now."

Andira snorted.

"I knew it!" said Trenloe. "I knew you were some kind of hero."

Rendiel sighed. "A long time ago." He nodded towards Andira. "If it's a cult you're looking for then my money, such as it is, would be on those sewers. Easy to run to, if need be, and they go everywhere."

"A lot of sewers though," said Trenloe, unconvinced. "A lot of innocent people living in them, too."

Rendiel nodded.

"Regardless, we will wait for your friend to join us," said Andira. "She should be here soon, and she may have more information to share with us."

"And we would like to show her this." Trenloe tapped again on the charcoal drawing of the rune.

"We?"

Trenloe indicated Lidiya and himself. Andira was not sure whether to feel offended, or amused. Only Trenloe could replace her with a ten year-old girl who, just one day earlier, had been picking his pocket.

"So, *now* you want to go to the Academy?"

Trenloe shrugged. "Maybe, instead of looking for signs and omens, you could just look up and see what's there in front of you. If I was a spirit of the Empyrean, or whoever it is that hands out visions and destinies, I'd want to make it good and obvious."

"For you, my friend, it would need to be," Rendiel joked, and Andira, in spite of herself, felt a smile pulling on her lips.

She started to laugh and Trenloe, after watching her in disbelief for a second or two, was soon laughing, too. Once he was at it there was no hope left for anyone. The entire table burst into laughter, tears streaming down their faces though Andira doubted they could explain what was so funny. Even Owl smiled.

Andira decided that Rendiel had some talent as a bard after all.

She wiped a tear from her eye as Trenloe took a deep breath and turned to Owl.

"What do you think, Owl? Do you think we should pursue the ironbound and help Lidiya, or chase Andira's cult?"

Owl's smile faltered as though the question baffled him. "I follow Andira."

"I just thought someone should ask you what you wanted," Trenloe said.

That seemed to rattle the knight even more. "I… follow Andira."

Andira cleared her throat. She had not even gotten around yet to the price Ravaella had demanded for her help. Thanks to Rendiel's clearing of the air, this seemed like the best time to raise it.

The door behind her creaked open.

It was a rare enough occurrence that every head in the room turned to see Thaiden Mistspeak stepping inside and shaking the rain off his coat. He took off his hat, forced a smile onto everyone that had not yet gone back to their own business, and nodded towards Andira.

"Just the woman I was hoping to find."

"I thought you had business in the north," said Andira.

"I did, but now it brings me back to the Snicks."

"Just what *is* your business, exactly?" said Rendiel.

"I find people."

Thaiden crossed the room to their table and there was something different about the way he walked, as though he'd taken off a cloak she had not realized he was wearing and replaced it with another. He stood a little straighter. His eyes were a little colder. He did not smile. For all her ability to spot a bald-faced lie, subtext had always evaded her. She could not read a person the way Trenloe could.

The northman shrugged off his crossbow's shoulder strap and took the weapon in both hands. Owl tensed, hand floating towards his sword grip as Thaiden's crossbow passed through his hands and went down on the table. The man reached into his coat, withdrew a crisp white envelope with a wax seal, gave a smile that earlier in the day would have creased his face with false merriment, but which now avoided his eyes like guilty men around a guardsman's door, and offered it to her.

Curious, she took it from his fingers.

"What is it?" Trenloe asked.

"In the name of all the gods, Trenloe. I have not even looked at it yet."

"Read it," he urged her.

There was nothing written on the envelope. She turned it over to examine the seal.

Her heart skipped a beat.

The Brodun family seal. She recognized it immediately, but had never thought to see it again after Sir Hamma Brodun had fallen to the bandits of Kell's Whispering Forest. Was it a letter from Sir Brodun himself, sent before his death? Impossible, surely. She did not know whether she wanted to tear it open or preserve it like a relic of her former mentor. In the end she did neither. She just held it, staring at the seal as though it might speak.

"Open it."

"Shut up, Trenloe." She lowered the envelope and looked hard at Thaiden. "Who are you really?"

"Thaiden Mistspeak," he said. His face was impassive, but there was something in his eyes that almost begged Andira to be upset. To be angry. To do something about it. "Really."

"And what are you doing in Nerekhall?"

"Finding you."

"Why?"

He shrugged. "Because finding people like you is what I'm–"

Andira had one hand around the man's throat before he could raise his arms to defend himself or choke out in alarm. With a surge of rune-powered strength, she lifted him off the floor, and then slammed him onto the table, shattering a dozen glasses and showering everyone around it in brown ale. Owl's fingers had not moved a half-inch closer to his sword. Trenloe and Lidiya were still seated, blinking in surprise. Rendiel whistled and looked very pointedly away.

Thaiden groaned.

"Are you an assassin of the Uthuk Y'llan? Who wants me dead?"

Thaiden's eyes gestured to the letter in her other hand. "Do… the Uthuk… write letters?"

"He has a point there," Sanna, the innkeeper, called nervously from behind the bar.

Andira held him down a moment, then growled and released her grip on his throat. Thaiden gasped for breath.

"Was that really necessary?" Trenloe chided her.

"Time will tell."

"One of these days, you and I are going to have that arm-wrestle."

Andira rolled her eyes.

Thaiden sat slowly, his coat unsticking from the tabletop, rubbing at his bruised throat. His smile, this time, seemed quite genuine. As though he had enjoyed that. "Just read the letter. I was only told to find you, and then once I had, to deliver that." With the hand that was not currently rubbing the life back into his neck, he gestured towards the letter. "I find things. I'm not an assassin."

"Sundown," Sanna barked. Over the course of Andira's altercation with Thaiden, she had crossed to the front door. "Anyone's who's not paying for beds for the night can get lost now." A few grumbling patrons finished their drinks and got up. Most stayed where they were. When the last leavers had finally left, she closed the door behind them, shouldering it forcefully into its frame, and barred it.

Andira took another look at the letter.

She was tempted to know what was written inside, but that part of her life had died with Hamma. It had no part to play in her destiny. That it also brought a pain she did not want to touch was, she told herself, irrelevant.

She threw the letter back towards Thaiden who made no attempt to catch it. It sycamored towards the floor.

"You're not even going to read it?" said Trenloe, aghast.

"No."

"But… you don't know what it says."

"It does not matter."

"Can *I* open it?"

"You can't read."

Thaiden shrugged. "It's yours now. Do what you want with it. I was only paid to put it in your hand." Sliding himself off the table, he tugged the crease from his collar and picked up his crossbow.

"Wait," said Andira, as he got up to leave. "If your work in Nerekhall is done, maybe you could help find something for me."

Thaiden smiled as he massaged the reddened skin of his throat. "I can find anything, for a fee."

"We've no money," said Trenloe.

Andira turned to glare back at him. Not after freeing Trenloe and Rendiel, at least. "And you ask if I am glad we kept the bard."

"The bard is sitting right here," said Rendiel.

"In that case," said Thaiden, offering another doff of his hat, "I'll be back about my own business."

"So what do we do now?" Trenloe murmured, as the northerner walked over to the bar to confer with Sanna, presumably about purchasing a room now that night had fallen. Trenloe's eyes wandered to the unopened letter on the floor.

Andira sighed and picked it up. She stuffed it into her breastplate. She would read it before she went to bed, if only to keep Trenloe from pestering her about it.

"We will wait for your friend to join us. We will listen to what she has to say, and then Owl and I will be acting on it, one way or another. There is no reason to wait until morning."

"Except… dinner? And sleep?"

"You are fighting a losing battle there, Trenloe," said Owl.

The knight was not smiling, but Andira could sense the jest trying to be seen.

"You may join me, or you, the girl, and your bard, can go your own way. I have no hold over you, or whether you choose to follow me or not."

Trenloe opened and closed his mouth, uncertain what to say in reply. "Are you telling me to–"

The thump on the door interrupted him.

A drizzle of years-old soot and accumulated mold came down from the ceiling. Several of those sat nearest cast the door uneasy looks.

Nothing good went abroad in Nerekhall after dusk.

"We're closed," Sanna barked, back behind the bar now, picking up her heavy crossbow from its hiding place and cocking it. She aimed at the door. "Head yourself back home before the guards spot you out at night."

"And what if we are the guards?" came the voice from outside.

Andira and Trenloe shared a look.

"Was that . . . ?" Trenloe began.

"Augost," Andira hissed back at him.

If Trenloe's foolery with the ironbound had drawn Augost to the Book Louse and jeopardized her meeting with Ravaella then she would let the Brother hang him from the Tower.

"We keep our doors locked and our candles lit," Sanna shouted back, her crossbow still leveled at the door. "And guards don't dare come this far into the Snicks."

With a grunt, Trenloe pushed his stool back from the table.

"Stay where you are, Trenloe," said Andira. "You are not here to solve everyone's problems."

Trenloe looked up at her, puzzled. "Maybe that's how the big problems you're after get to be big. No one dealt with them while they were small."

"I am only looking for one person," Augost called in. "No one else needs to be involved."

"Anyone coming through this door before sunrise is getting shot," Sanna retorted.

"Sanna–" Trenloe began.

Augost's laughter rang through the sodden wood. "I was hoping you would say that."

A fist the size of the spiked head of a mace smashed through the door.

"A rising flame lifts all wings!"

# CHAPTER FOURTEEN
## *Trenloe the Strong*

Sanna loosed. Her iron-tipped bolt flew on blunted wings through the chaos of the common room, perfectly skewering the hole left in the front door by their assailant's fist. A moment later, realizing what she had just shot, she dropped the crossbow with a strangled cry and stumbled back from the bar with her hands in the air.

The ironbound kicked in what was left of the door, iron bolt protruding from its breastplate, scattering the Book Louse's inhabitants to the back of the room. It stood framed by the wreckage of the doorway, seven feet tall and all of it metal. The smooth plate of its face ground from right to left as it surveyed the room.

Lidiya screamed as the thing's blank stare passed their table and stopped. Trenloe heard it sniff and felt his insides empty, as though its hollowness was somehow drawing his strength and courage to it, sucking it in through the gaps around the neck that served for nostrils to feed the collection of cogs and gears that cumulatively stood in for its soul.

"There's no magic in the Book Louse," Sanna yelled. "Whatever you've come for, you can–"

With a blast of steam that sent those still trying to get away to their knees with hands over their ears, it lifted its shield, leveled its glaive, and charged.

It was pounding straight for the bar.

"Out!" Trenloe roared at those clamoring for the exits and shrugged into his own shield. The entire table rang with the sound of unsheathed metal. Rendiel drew his rapier, Owl a long knife. Lidiya, Tuschels, Anya, and all the others pulled improvised alley pieces from an array of concealed locations.

Thaiden Mistspeak, standing in front of the bar, put a second bolt right alongside Sanna's.

It did not even slow the ironbound down. The northman cursed and loaded another.

"Everybody down!" Andira yelled, slamming her poleaxe to the floor as though to anchor herself to a moving world. "Cover your eyes and ears!"

With a roar of concentration, she punched the air with her open hand.

The ensuing flash blew out every candle in the room and drove a deep crack into the boards beneath her feet. The building groaned. Sparks wheeled like drunks across Trenloe's eyes. His ears popped. A ball of massively compressed tavern air and crackling rune power rolled towards the oncoming ironbound, only to dissipate against its armor like a wave choosing to sink back into the sea rather than strike at the land. Trenloe, his eyes still open wide, gawped at the result. He had never seen Andira rendered so ineffectual.

By then, Lidiya and the others had cleared the table and so, before he had time to think about it, Trenloe took it in one hand and threw it onto its side. It was fourteen feet long and made of oak and weighed as much as a large horse. Half-finished drinks and used crockery slid to the floor just in time to hit the ironbound's charge.

Trenloe dropped down and threw his shoulder into the table's underside to brace it against the impact, letting out a groan as the collision speared through him. It was like trying to stop a bull by stepping in front of it.

A hundred different cracks split through the table's finish, but by some miracle it held.

He peered over the top of the table as Andira looped her poleaxe overhead. Once. Twice. Thrice. Spinning power from speed in the old-fashioned way given that she no longer had the strength of her rune. The blade chopped into the joint between helmet and bevor with the precision of a headsman's swing. The ironbound staggered under what must have been a colossal blow, and sank onto the opposing knee. Mechanisms buried deep inside the armor ticked louder, faster, steam whistling from the partially severed neck around Andira's blade. She struggled to hold onto her weapon, snarling in frustration as the entire construct began to shudder with the build-up of internal pressure.

With a screech of metal joints, the ironbound surged back to its feet, pulling its neck free of Andira's blade and casually throwing the woman clear.

"Andira!" Owl cried, caught between dragging Lidiya back from Trenloe's barricade and charging to his companion's aid.

Thaiden shot another bolt through the ironbound's helmet. Sanna, pure fury written across her tusked, leathery face, picked up her crossbow and joined him from the other side of the bar.

The ironbound looked like a training dummy that someone had gone berserk on, dented, battered, riddled with bolts, but coming on still. The runes across its armor burned brightly enough to sear their lines into the backs of Trenloe's eyes. It raised its glaive high, and clove through the upended table just as Trenloe threw himself clear.

The heavier bolt from Sanna's larger crossbow smacked into it. It staggered under the impact, but proceeded to barge through the wreckage of Trenloe's barricade.

Trenloe hurriedly gave ground.

How did you fight something that couldn't even be hurt?

Just as he was desperately considering that, two more strode unhurriedly into the common room.

The first took what was left of the door, but the second came in through the wall. A portion of the roof collapsed over it in a cataract of broken slate and rain. The Book Louse groaned and shifted, as though accounting for the injury with the strength of its three remaining walls and just about managing to remain upright.

"Now we're having a party!" Thaiden screamed, spittle flying from his mouth, and shot one of the newcomers to no avail. He whooped, as though he had scored an incomparable hit, and proceeded to rack another.

At the door, meanwhile, a mob of Book Louse patrons armed with lead-bottomed tankards and chairs rushed the two constructs while Rendiel shouted encouragement from the rear. The improvised weapons were doing little actual damage to the ironbound but, remarkably, the mob did seem to be slowing them down. The two ironbound paused to consider every individual fighter in their way, lifting them bodily out of the melee to sniff at them before shoving them aside as forcefully as they could without causing injury. They were engines of law-enforcement, Trenloe realized, not war. Whatever changes had been made to their control runes, they did not seem to have overridden the fundamental edict against indiscriminate murder.

"Are you convinced now?" he yelled, as Andira charged back in.

She did not answer, focusing all her energies on a swing to the elbow that the ironbound blocked with the long metal haft of its glaive. While she recovered from the ringing parry, Trenloe struck from the other side. The ironbound adjusted its grip to sweep the pole upwards into a block that beat Trenloe's axe aside and immediately bled into a torrent of blows. Trenloe fell back under the onslaught.

He was coming to realize that the greatest strength of the ironbound was not their physical durability and power. It was not even their resistance to magic. It was the fact that they could fight without feeling. There was no respite between blows, no lull while they recovered from a particularly vicious exchange. They simply attacked, attacked, attacked, until whatever they had been commanded to pacify was on the ground, submissive or dead.

Standing side by side with Andira was the only way, thus far, he had come close to battling one to a standstill.

"You need to destroy the rune shielding it from my magic," said Andira, back on the offensive, her poleaxe and the ironbound's glaive showering the damp rushes with sparks while Trenloe worked life back into his hands. "It is too strong to defeat otherwise."

Trenloe gripped his axe and looked over the scrawling pattern of runes that decorated the ironbound.

"How?"

"Leave it to me!" Thaiden snarled, launching himself from the bar with his crossbow held back-to-front like a club and smashing it across the ironbound's shoulder. The weapon broke apart in his hands, but cracks splintered through the construct's pauldron, breaking the intricate lines of the rune depicted thereon.

Andira produced a grin fiercer than Deepwinter. Tracing the rune in her palm with the little finger of the same hand, she muttered something under her breath and made a fist.

The ironbound's upper torso imploded.

Internal gears creaked and muttered, then stalled. A breastplate crushed down to the size of a dead knight's beaten helmet found itself no longer able to support the weight of its own arms. The thing tottered for a moment, still struggling to lift its glaive and fight, before finally succumbing to the damage and falling, crashing to the floor in a heap of lifeless iron and scattered gears.

Trenloe slumped against the bar, exhausted. While the ironbound had been alive, he had somehow convinced his body to carry on, but it was spent. Taking a shuddering breath, he looked around the ransacked common room.

The Book Louse's regulars were still holding the other two ironbound at the door. Rendiel had withdrawn to an even safer position at the top of the stairs where he sat with his half-strung lute across one knee, playing the heroic ballad, *Brothers Over the Devide*. Trenloe wasn't sure if there was any real magic in the bard's playing, but it made him think of golden summers in Artrast, of feast days and saint's days and every occasion where bards played *Brothers Over the Devide* to cheer the two thousand year-old backs-to-the-wall triumph of Terrinoth and its allies over the Locust Swarm of Llovar. He almost felt his strength returning.

Further from the main fighting, Owl had finally managed to pry Lidiya out from the wreckage of the table. She had been trying to recover a coin purse that had fallen with the rest of the table's detritus when Trenloe had flipped it to stall the ironbound. It was Andira's old purse. There had been so little money left in it that Andira had reluctantly agreed to let Lidiya keep it. As Owl dragged her away, her fingers brushed one of the drawstrings, opening the purse and spilling a derisory handful of silver and copper coins over the barroom floor.

The two ironbound at the door reacted as though a demon of the Ynfernael had just risen up from between the floorboards. Both of their heads snapped towards the girl.

The one nearest shuddered, shrieking like a kettle about to explode as it drew power from runes that burned red in turn. It stomped towards Lidiya, crushing a man's leg in the process, no longer caring who it injured now it had scented its quarry.

And suddenly, Trenloe understood what they were after.

It was Andira.

Whatever power she drew on, fought against, and communed with through her nightmares, it had obviously affected her somehow, tainting her and the coins she had carried with her across Terrinoth.

That was why they had attacked Lidiya.

Owl pulled the screaming girl out of harm's way, just as the ironbound trampled over the scattered coins and continued on a beeline towards Andira herself.

Trenloe pushed himself off from the bar and into its path, but he was wearier than Rendiel's playing had allowed him to feel. He was still lifting his axe as the ironbound beat him aside on its shield. He crashed through the wooden plank of the bar and into the drinks cabinet behind it. His bald head smashed in the glass front and went through its bottom shelf.

The building gave another fraught groan as Trenloe pulled his head out of the wall and shook it off. He boxed the sides of his head to quiet the ringing in his ears, and turned back.

The melee at the door had been broken. The survivors were fleeing for the back door and the kitchens. Owl had Lidiya over his shoulder and was bound for the stairs where Rendiel had stopped playing and was beckoning him to hurry. Something was burning. A loose spark from Andira and Trenloe's duel with the ironbound perhaps, or a knocked-over candle.

Whatever had started it, and in spite of the drizzle slanting in through the hole in the roof, it had caught and spread with unnatural speed. Already, it had roared to consume the entirety of the front wall, sweeping across the ironbound and herding the most stubborn of the remaining combatants, Sanna and Thaiden included, towards the rear of the inn.

Only Andira was left, her skin red, ankle-deep in flame, facing off against two armored constructs that were glowing in the heat.

Before Trenloe could raise so much as a cough, he heard a *crack*, like wooden beams disintegrating in a fire, as one of the two struck a blow to the woman's temple. The fight immediately went out of her. She fell lifelessly into the arms of the second construct which proceeded to drag her out through the flames.

"Andira!" Owl cried, choked with grief, abandoning Lidiya on the bottom step in spite of the flames lapping at the old staircase, and ripping his accursed sword from its scabbard.

The single rune stamped into the flat edge of his sword

flared, line by line, like a demon called into being from across the veil and savoring its taste of freedom. It was horned and evil, like no common rune Trenloe had ever seen. How a man like Owl, in the company of someone like Andira, had come to keep such a ruinous weapon, he did not know and, in not wanting to know, had never asked. All he knew was that Andira had always forbidden him from drawing it.

With a howl of fury, the knight charged into the fire after the two ironbound and his fallen mistress.

Trenloe looked from Andira to Lidiya, lying unconscious on the stair as it burned.

It was happening again.

However strong he thought he was, however bravely he fought, people around him got hurt. He had thought that having Andira beside him would end that cycle, and for a time it had, but here he found himself again, the last man standing while everything around him burned.

Andira thought that he couldn't make these decisions, but he could. He made them every day and, unlike Andira, he got them right more often than not.

Andira had Owl. They could both look after themselves.

With a howl of despair, the grief in his chest burning more fiercely than the smoke coming down his throat, he shielded his face from the flames and fled towards the stairs.

# CHAPTER FIFTEEN
## *Owl*

Owl charged headlong into the fire as though, if he ran fast enough, it wouldn't burn.

In his mind's eye it was a great hearth, roaring in a stone hall. He heard minstrels playing *Brothers Over the Devide,* imagined a beautiful woman with dark skin sitting in a chair just beyond the flame, tapping her heel to the tune in spite of the thinly veiled disdain on her face.

*Beggars and priests made music,* Renata had used to say, *nobles make war*. Owl added his own wordless scream to that of the burning tavern. Who was Renata? Did he want to know? The fire in his mind spread to encompass a horizon made jagged by snow-capped mountains and decades of hardship. He smelled the smoke of burnt-out villages and ravaged fields and screamed again. He was staring down the nostrils of a green dragon as an ember struck in the back of its throat, hemmed in by knights and horses emblazoned with the same owl he wore on his armor. The dragon exhaled. Owl raised a heater shield he no longer held, and howled his defiance.

The ironbound that had stolen Andira from him was

marching out of sight through a wall of cinders. The one left behind turned to face him.

Owl set his jaw and focused on that, firming his grip not on an imagined shield but on a sword. The weapon was meant to be wielded alongside a shield from horseback, as it had been in the memory, but he took it two-handed, the way the berserkers from across the Lothan wielded theirs. It had been a prince amongst swords. Somewhere in his fractured recollections, he remembered that. Now, it barely even resembled a sword. It had been scorched black, its blade melted, the single draconic sign on its spine glaring redly from the deformed metal, given sharper edges and crueler intentions by the magic it had been used to smite.

Andira had warned him never to draw it, not even in defense of his own life. Only in defense of their goal.

The sword struck the ironbound's arm as though he was sawing a wedge of soft Pelgate cheese from the wheel. The arm fell away in a shower of sparks and a cascade of gears. The sword trembled in unsatisfied hunger, emitting a keening note as the rune pulsed a longer, deeper red, and Owl pulled his arm back for another blow.

There was an irony, or so Andira had observed, that the blooding of a demon king had turned his sword into this, corrupting the runestone so totally that only the slaughter of demonkind could sate it.

Rather than die, the ironbound emitted a furious wail. Its armored frame shuddered as runes heated up across its body. It was as though, as dissatisfied as the sword had been with its cold skin and oily blood, its very existence drove the ironbound to fury.

Owl ran the sword through the construct's chest. While the

ironbound flailed he twisted the hilt and ripped the blade free, stepping smartly to one side as the maneuver unbalanced his gigantic assailant and brought it crashing to the floor.

In his more lucid moments, Owl recalled being an exceptional swordsman. Better than either Trenloe or Andira who relied on other, mightier, gifts. He remembered battles with dragons and demons and Uthuk zealots, and daily bouts with a man named Highgarde that he had won as often as he had lost.

He coughed in the dust and cinders raised by the ironbound's fall, drawing up the hem of his cloak to cover his nose and mouth, and peered through narrowed eyes into the blaze.

There was no sign of Andira. He turned around. There was no sign of Trenloe or Lidiya behind him, nor of Rendiel, or the stairs. He whirled again, no longer certain which was the direction he had been heading in and which was back.

The fire had taken everything.

"Andira!" he yelled.

Though he usually kept them to himself, Owl did have thoughts of his own. They were often confusing, disturbing him sometimes with hints at the man he had been before. But Andira gave him direction. She gave him certitude. The cart did not need to doubt the horse and he had never once resented being the man who followed where she led.

He took a deep breath to scream her name again, doubling up with a lungful of smoke and a fit of coughing.

"Well, well, well," the fire mocked him, seething and rippling with a voice as deep as the Korina's Tears. "The lawyer."

The flames drew apart like the curtain from a theatre stage, leaving behind a corridor with a low carpet of flame through which Brother Augost strode barefoot, kicking up sparks. The marbled skin of his naked chest glistened white in the ferocious heat and light of the burning inn. A ring of heavy keys and religious icons clanked from his golden belt. The mace that he wielded two-handed reflected such a brilliance that it seemed to be on fire itself.

"You are not in the Wildlands now," he snarled, and delivered an overhead swing towards Owl's forehead.

Owl slid onto his back foot and raised his sword to parry.

The intricate lettering etched into the mace's head inflamed on impact, searing Owl's eyes with their brilliance and showering his face with sparks. He stumbled back from it, riposting blindly with his sword but, where the priest had been, he struck through only a resurgent wall of flame.

"The priests of Kellos are warriors first and holy men second, defenders of the living and scourges of the unclean and the undead. What are you without your hero friends? The silent one. A broken man with a broken sword."

Owl spun on his heel, hacking through the flames with a bark of anger and seeing them part cleanly before his downstroke.

"The ironbound do Kellos' work for us this day. Praise Pollux. Praise the Rising Flame of the Burning Lord! I pray that my cousins in faith might be deemed worthy of redemption when the fires of Margath Resurrected sweep this land of its evils."

Owl swung back, sword raised, as Brother Augost erupted from the flames. The inferno died to a simmer where he trod, as though frightened back into the cracks in the wood from which they had emerged by his presence. In the fleeting stillness he brought, Owl caught a glimpse of the wrecked doorway, orienting himself towards it and locking it in his memory as Augost's mace crashed against his sword, dousing him in hot sparks and stealing it from view again.

He was more than just a mute follower, and he would prove it.

"I gave you all the chance to leave, and like the godless fools I see every day you spurned it," Augost hissed, his words as hot as the embers flying from the head of his mace. "Perhaps it is for the best. Redemption will not be for Nerekhall alone, but for all of Terrinoth in time. Better to face the judgment of Margath now than to live with the fear of what it must be."

Owl parried the priest's hammering blows as skillfully as he could, but he could barely see for the flames, defending himself purely on instinct. The priest was as skilled with his weapon as he boasted and the flames, as though alert to the shift in their master's fortunes, returned to bite at his heels. Owl could spare no effort to counter-attack. Avoiding death then and there was the most that he could manage.

Another man might have countered with words, bought himself time and advantage by parrying the priest's rhetoric as well as the swings of his mace, but Owl had nothing to say.

His every thought was fixed upon Andira, his nerves suffering under an almost physical burden of pain for every moment that Augost prevented him from recovering her.

He swept up his sword to block an overhead blow, only to scream in pain as the third and final ironbound, returned to the fray without Andira, caught his wrist from behind. He looked up at it, his face a snarl, and pulled on his arm. It did not move. Almost contemptuously, the ironbound tightened its grip.

Owl gasped as his vambrace crumpled under the pressure and crushed his arm. His fingers sprang loose from around the grip of his sword and the blade clattered to the ground. No sooner had he been separated from his sword than the ironbound lost all interest in him. Owl staggered like a puppet that had been left to walk on its own, clutching his wrist to his chest. The ironbound, meanwhile, bent to collect Owl's fallen sword, and immediately threw its strength into snapping the blade in two.

By the time its slow, rune-controlled intelligence had come to the realization that the accursed sword was quite indestructible, it was too late.

Augost thumped Owl in the gut with the flat top of his mace, forcing the wind from his lungs and driving him onto all fours. The flames swelled as though at a command from their master, breathing heat into his face, baking his eyeballs, cracking his lips, circling him as he attempted to straighten and spitting, barking. With an outstretched toe, Augost prodded at the sword that the ironbound had, as its final recourse, thrown away to be retrieved later and confined.

He tutted. "A blade of Ynfernael power. You make this too easy for me, Sir Owl. Is it not enough that you advertise your whereabouts and intentions? Must you rob me of the need of a convincing excuse for confining you and your companions as well?"

At a gesture, the flames currently consuming the Book Louse died away without disappearing altogether. The tavern creaked like a body that had been pulled, alive but only barely, from a fire. At that point, it seemed like it was only centuries of ingrained damp that was holding the building upright.

At the priest's summons, however, scores of human, elven, and dwarven soldiers stepped gingerly through the ruined doorframe into the suppressed flames seething over the floorboards. Their faces were hidden behind masks of black iron, but Owl heard several of them shiver in ecstasy as their feet sank ankle-deep into the unnatural flame. Owl had assumed them to be soldiers, but as they spread through the burning common room, he began to doubt it. Despite their masks and wargear, most wore prisoners' garb. Manacles still hung from their wrists and fetters dragged about their feet. The brand of Kellos' redemption stood proud of the bare skin on the backs of their hands or the tops of their feet.

"I believe in second chances," Augost said over Owl's bowed head as his followers spread out to secure what was left of the building and those within it. "I believe the pain that Kellos provides can redeem even the worst amongst us. That is why, after several years spent bringing illumination to the restless dead in the villages of northern Carthridge, I asked the Archpriest at Vynelvale that my reward be this small church in the Tower of Nerek." He rested the spiked head of his mace on Owl's head and smiled beneficently down. Owl struggled to get up, but he could not pull enough breath into his chest.

"Seize him," he ordered his soldiers. "Secure the weapon and deal with Andira Runehand, see them both to the Tower."

He turned his beatific smile towards the ceiling, just as the entire building began to groan alarmingly around them all.

"And someone bring me Trenloe the Strong."

## CHAPTER SIXTEEN
### *Trenloe the Strong*

Trenloe grasped at the coarse sackcloth sheet that had been laid across his chest, expecting to find himself buried under the wreckage of the Book Louse and oddly panicked at finding himself instead on a straw mattress looking up at a shadow-infested ceiling. Every joint was stiff. Every muscle ached. He remembered the moment the building had collapsed, trying to throw Lidiya across to Rendiel before the floor gave, and then... He shook his head slowly. It felt as though it had been broken on a rock.

"Where–?"

A hand smothered his mouth. It smelled like burning alehouses.

"It's all right, Trenloe," said a voice he recognized, and which belonged to someone that clearly recognized him, but his head was not yet fully awake and would not draw the name to put to it.

His body, meanwhile, reacted to the unwelcome fact of the hand over his mouth by instinct. With his left hand filled with sackcloth, he took the wrist of the offending hand in his right and squeezed down tight.

"Arrrgh. Trenloe!"

Drawing the figure in by the wrist, he threw them.

There was a heavy *thud* as they hit a wall, then another as they landed on some item of furniture, followed by a self-pitying curse.

The approach of hurried footsteps brought a creak from the floorboards.

A door opened.

Trenloe blinked in the insipid candlelight from the other room.

A bearded man with a wooden crutch under one arm and a cheap porcelain chamberstick stood in the doorway. Trenloe looked away. The effect of the candlelight was like being punched in the face by his own eyes.

He had no memory of how he had gotten here.

"You promised to keep him quiet."

It was Tuschels, The sewerman from the Book Louse.

With a muffled groan, the figure that Trenloe had thrown into the dresser picked themselves up, unhappily testing out the range of motion in their bruised wrist.

"Rendiel?" said Trenloe. "I'm sorry, did I do that?"

"Of course not, Trenloe. It was the other dolt in bed with you."

Trenloe rolled his head on the straw pillow.

There was no one there.

"Trenloe, I swear by the four spheres of the Empyrean that you're the most literal-minded man I ever met."

"Can you both keep it down?" Tuschels lowered the chamberstick, his hand so unsteady that gobbets of semi-hard wax were lapping at the rim of the bowl, and limped towards the window.

With the room illuminated, Trenloe finally got a sense of *where* he was, even if he still had little idea how he had got there or why.

He was lying in what appeared to be Tuschels' bedroom. The mattress filled most of the floor. A dark wardrobe leant up against one corner like an old guard stealing a nap. A dressing table that didn't quite match stood under the window frame. The window itself was high up the wall, allowing only a narrow view of the armored boots tramping by outside. The sewerman's house was at least partly below the ground level of the street.

"Damn it," Tuschels whispered. "I think they heard." With the light inside and the darkness out Trenloe couldn't make out much of what was going on. From the way the rough glass trembled he suspected there were a lot of people outside. "Looking for you, I'm thinking," Tuschels went on in a low voice. "Looking for *us*. Three ironbound went into the Book Louse for you and your friends and only one came out. That gets noticed. That gets all the wrong sort of notice."

Trenloe sat up against the wall behind him and closed his eyes. The guttering of Tuschels' candle was only worsening his headache.

One of these days he was going to wake at dawn without a fresh injury, or even with one that he remembered taking, and wouldn't know what to do with himself.

"Where are we, and how did we get here? The last thing I remember is–"

"*Shhhh*," Tuschels hissed, forehead pressed to the lowest pane of the window, looking up, misting the glass as he murmured, "You helped me out of there when the ironbound broke my leg. Do you remember?" Trenloe shook his head.

He didn't at all. "Well, when I saw the roof come down with you still inside, I went back for you. Anyone would've done the same."

"I'm not sure that they would," said Rendiel.

"*You* were there."

The elf smiled as though he was hiding something that hurt. "Old habits really do die hard, I suppose."

"You must have a head made of Dunwarr stone," said Tuschels, turning back to Trenloe.

Trenloe rubbed the back of his head, ruefully. "I wish I did." He thought back to the last thing he remembered. "What happened to Lidiya?" He glanced up at Rendiel, who looked deeply uncomfortable. "She was with you, wasn't she?"

"I'm afraid I… lost her."

Trenloe felt an unfamiliar flash of anger. "You lost the rogue ironbound in the alley. You lost Lidiya. How do you manage it?"

"I was distracted," Rendiel answered, suddenly defensive. "The inn fell down. It could happen to anyone."

"She's most likely been taken to the Tower," said Tuschels. "I heard Brother Augost say that's where he was sending Andira. Owl, too, I think."

Trenloe recalled how disturbed Andira had been by the Tower of Nerek. She had been frightened and, up until then, he would not have believed that anything in Terrinoth could do that to Andira Runehand. The thought of her waking up there, injured, afraid, and alone, upset him more than he could express in words. It hurt him even more than the idea of an innocent child being locked away alongside her. This was all his fault. Tuschels would not have had his leg broken, Sanna would not have lost her inn, Lidiya would not be imprisoned in the Tower, if he had not come into their lives. The knowledge that far worse might well have happened without him did not make him feel any better.

He started to get up, only for Rendiel to hurry back to his side to ease him back down.

"Augost's men and the soldiers of the Tower are everywhere, rounding up everyone who escaped from the Book Louse," he said. "They're still looking for the rest of us."

"Should we be keeping that light so close to the window?" Trenloe asked, nodding towards Tuschels.

The sewerman looked down at the candle in his hand and then back to the window. He shook his head, distracted. "It'd be more suspicious if we didn't. No light means nobody home, means someone's out breaking curfew."

"Brother Augost…" said Rendiel. "I still can't believe he's involved in something like…" He trailed off, wafting one hand vaguely through the air. "Whatever *this* is." He gestured towards Trenloe. "You say the ironbound have been tampered with, and I believe you. Andira is convinced that her demon king has some design on the city, and I believe her, too." He stilled both hands by stuffing them in his jacket pockets and gave a snort. "Because this is Nerekhall. But what does any of it have to do with a priest of Kellos?"

"I heard him say something to Owl about Margath," said Trenloe. "About Margath Resurrected. Redeeming Terrinoth in fire."

The elf turned pale. "Are you sure he said *Margath*?"

Trenloe nodded. He had the feeling that Augost had wanted the whole city to hear it, as though he had been ecstatic about no longer having to hide it. "Why do you look so worried?"

Rendiel tutted, but couldn't mask his nervousness, fingers

tapping out a few short bars of an incomplete melody across the hilt of his sword. All of a sudden, it felt as though the shadows were paying attention, Tuschels' small candle doing little more than making them curious.

"How did you manage to travel through Kell and not learn everything about Margath the Unkind?" Rendiel asked. "He's the villain of every other song up there. This kind of ignorance is what comes of remunerating bards so poorly. Margath was the mightiest Dragonlord who ever flew south from the Molten Heath. It was Margath who razed Tamalir and ended the line of the Elder Kings. And it was Margath, or so it's said, who began the Dragon War in the first place, and the Queen of the Heath who ended it once it came to her attention."

"But Margath was killed, wasn't he?"

"By Roland of Kell at the Battle of Weeping Basin, but neither his body nor Margath's body were ever found. The battle is believed to have been fought somewhere in the Mountains of Morshan, but no one knows exactly where. There is no *Weeping Basin* in the maps of Arendor Keep. Every year or so a historian from Vynelvale Cathedral will lead an expedition into the mountains, certain that they've located Roland's resting place or the Dragonlord's remains, but always come back empty-handed."

"What's the Cathedral's interest in Margath?"

Rendiel shrugged. "Fire. There's always been an extreme fringe in the Church that sees the dragons not as the terrors of the Third Darkness but as the vessels of their sacred fire. They don't deny that Margath burned Terrinoth to the ground eight hundred years ago, but they'd argue it was because there was something about Terrinoth that needed burning."

"And you think Augost could be one of them?"

The elf sighed. "Honestly, Trenloe, I don't know what to think anymore."

Trenloe thought for a moment.

He'd seen a dragon once, at Hernfar, and though it hadn't deigned to participate in the battle for the Lothan ford itself, he'd seen the burnt-out shell it had left of Nordgard Castle afterwards. Anyone who would pray for the Dragonlords' return and hold them as sacred had not stood as close to their fire as he had.

"If Augost has Andira and the others then we need to get to them now. Who knows what he intends to do with them?" He started again to rise.

Rendiel tried again, and this time failed, to hold him down. It was like shrugging off a determined blanket.

"Keep it down, both of you," Tuschels growled from the window.

"What are you going to do, Trenloe?" Rendiel argued. "After just about killing yourself against three ironbound, do you really feel ready to take on ten? And what about the hundreds of guards between you and the Tower of Nerek?"

"Andira talked them into letting me go. Maybe they'd agree to the same for me."

"Don't forget that it was Augost who let you out, and for reasons of his own, no doubt. Probably in the hopes of getting you and Andira far away from Nerekhall before whatever move he's been planning was ready. Believe me, there's nothing more unwelcome than a pair of meddlesome heroes when you're planning on purging Terrinoth in fire."

Trenloe worked his jaw in frustration.

The elf made a good point.

"I have to try."

"All these guards about might be a good thing for your friends," said Tuschels, nodding towards the dark glass of the window. "They can't all be Augost's."

Trenloe startled as Rendiel snapped his fingers. "That's right! You just destroyed two ironbound and burnt down a tavern. The Chief Artificer and the Magistrates Council will want to know what happened and Warden Daralyn will want to be sure she has answers for them by the time they wake."

Trenloe tried to look on it as Tuschels and Rendiel were, but he found it hard to think of any of this as good news. Laws on the just treatment of prisoners varied from barony to barony but, compared to what someone running afoul of a local martial in the provinces might expect, the Free Cities tended to be relatively humane. If what Rendiel was saying was correct, however, then the Warden of the Tower was probably questioning Andira even now. If this Daralyn felt pressed for results, then who knew what she might resort to?

"It's all right, Trenloe." Rendiel gave his shoulder a reassuring pat. "Andira and the others are as safe as they can be while we think of something."

Trenloe straightened. The elf had just given him the beginnings of an idea.

"I should give myself up."

"What?" Rendiel blinked as though Trenloe had just woken him by snapping his fingers over his eyes. "No. That's a terrible idea."

"It's just like you say. Augost won't be able to touch me while the Chief Artificer and the Warden are taking an interest. I could speak with them both and get all of this sorted out tonight. Do you still have the rubbing you took of the ironbound's control rune?"

"No," Rendiel said, covering his breast pocket with one hand.

"Give it to me."

"Trenloe..."

"The last words Andira and I shared were angry ones. She told me I was welcome to leave and I didn't get to tell her that I never would. I'm certainly not leaving her in the Tower of Nerek."

"Don't let him do it, Rendiel," said Tuschels.

"Does it look like I'm letting him do it?" Rendiel snapped, batting away Trenloe's hands from his pocket.

"You're not bringing the guard to my house!"

"It'll be all right," said Trenloe. "You can hide here. Only Rendiel and I need to go to the Tower."

Rendiel snorted. "You want me to go with you?"

"You've been before."

"For drunkenness and being a public nuisance! Not for destroying ironbound."

"*Please,* keep it down," said Tuschels.

"Give me the rune," said Trenloe.

"No," said Rendiel, backing away. "I don't do that sort of thing anymore."

Trenloe made a grab for the elf's jacket.

Rendiel darted out of reach and backed into the dresser. He swore, rubbing at the back of his trousers, as the unit thumped against the wall, then side-stepped as Trenloe came for him again, rattling the dresser further and knocking Tuschels' arm. Candlelight flashed across the window pane. Tuschels and Rendiel both froze. Trenloe hesitated, fists half-raised, and turned towards the window.

The lane outside had fallen silent.

"Maybe they've moved on," Rendiel suggested, hopefully.

There was a bang on the front door, hard enough to shake the furniture in the back room. Tuschels closed his eyes and moaned.

"City watch. Open the door."

"Is there another way out?" Rendiel asked.

Tuschels shook his head. He looked ill.

"You two stay here," said Trenloe. "I'll talk to them."

He walked from the bedroom and into what appeared, by the light of the single candle, to be a small kitchen and living area, musty with damp clothes and muck-splattered tools. There was no other way out. There wasn't even an upstairs.

The knock on the door sounded again.

"No, Trenloe," said Rendiel.

The elf grabbed hold of his left arm. Tuschels took his right. Trenloe dragged them along behind him as he walked to the front door. They were powerless to stop his progress and soon relinquished their grip. Trenloe allowed them a moment to hide amongst the living room's meagre furniture as he opened the door.

A pair of human guards were standing on the stoop. Both were similarly clad in a dark, quilted doublet with long sleeves and a vest of black iron. Their faces were hidden behind black masks that reminded Trenloe unpleasantly of the ironbound. The only feature that remained visible was the eyes, and Trenloe saw both sets glaze over as they took him in. For some reason, both guards lowered their eyes to a spot roughly corresponding to Trenloe's collar.

"Sorry to wake you at this hour, miss," said the guard on the right.

Trenloe frowned, somewhat taken aback by that. "But, I–"

"We're looking for anyone who might have fled the disturbance at the Book Louse," said the one on the left.

Trenloe looked between the two, wondering what was going on. "Yes, in fact–"

"Very good, miss. Sorry again to have disturbed you."

Trenloe stared after them as the two guards turned and walked back up the steps, ducking their heads as they felt the rain.

"What in the name of Latariana's Gift was that about?" said Rendiel, behind him.

Trenloe didn't answer. He was still watching the two soldiers leave, which was surely the only reason he failed to notice the gnome woman already standing on the bottom step of the stoop. She pulled off her hood, spattering the sheltered area under Tuschels' gable with droplets of rain, to reveal a thick bushel of reddish-brown hair and a familiar impish smile.

"I wasn't at all sure that that was going to work," she confided, as though they were all good friends, introduced years ago. "You have no idea how challenging it is to create an illusion that talks, and then cloak a real person with it. Practically impossible. I should have known I could do it!" She smiled up at him. She had a long way to smile. "Trenloe the Strong, I assume?"

Recognition came like a messenger in the night.

"Ravaella?"

He had not seen the gnome since she had left Trast to seek her fortune in Greyhaven, when he had been an impressionable boy and she had been much, much younger. Recognizing her finally, all he wanted to do was drop to his knees and embrace her. He was afraid that if he did, he might crush her, and there was also the nagging worry that being picked up and hugged might be beneath the dignity of an Academy mage.

He settled for a broad smile.

Ravaella returned it with one of her own, and then frowned at something over his shoulder. Trenloe glanced back. Rendiel was standing behind him with his sword out.

"Ravaella," he hissed.

"Rendiel?"

"You … know each other?" Trenloe asked.

"A long story," Ravaella replied, bristling like an animal confronted by a rival in its territory.

"You never told me that *she* was the mage you'd come all this way to see," said Rendiel. "If you had, I would have tried harder to make you forget it."

"Put that old thing away, Rendiel," said Ravaella. "You know you wouldn't be able to hit me with it anyway."

"Oh, won't I?"

The elf leveled his sword at her.

Ravaella smiled, the tip of the rapier inches from her nose.

Trenloe gasped as, suddenly, the sword was no longer there.

Rendiel swore floridly, drawing his hand to his face, staring into the open palm as he waved it back and forth across his eyes. "What did you … ? Give it back!"

"Have you checked in your scabbard?"

The elf's hand dropped to his hip where, lo and behold, his sword was scabbarded as though it had never been drawn at all.

"You were always so forgetful," Ravaella tutted, as Rendiel drew the sword a second time and held it at guard. "Always half a mind on that song you were trying to find." She turned to Trenloe, a mischievous glint in her eye that had him chuckling despite himself. She was older than he remembered her, cloaked somberly in black, but in that look he saw the same Ravaella who had once turned Farmer Taufik's prize bull into a life-sized wooden replica and '*borrowed*' the grain mill for a week.

"Come on." She glanced at Rendiel, blew a flat raspberry, and then turned back to Trenloe. "Both of you. The guards are looking for you and you can tell me all about it on the way to the Academy." She drew her hood back up over her head and spun away, skipping towards the street as though in no conceivable plane of existence could Trenloe have questions.

"Wait," said Trenloe. "What about the soldiers?"

Ravaella turned back, green eyes twinkling from under their hood.

"As I mentioned to Andira already, I have my own ways of avoiding curfew."

# CHAPTER SEVENTEEN
## *Andira Runehand*

Andira drifted in and out of consciousness. In those fleeting moments that she spent awake she was aware of being dragged. She would open her eyes to swift stabbings of yellow light, high buildings looming over her in silhouette like the morbid crowds she had become accustomed to in Pelgate and Kell, as eager to see Andira Runehand as they were terrified of her. She would hear the tramp of feet, the jangle of armor, cruel chatter muffled by the dark iron of monstrous helms, and then her eyes would flutter closed and she would dream again.

There, she found herself walking the stone corridor that had become so familiar, her feet moving no more willingly than the body that the guards were dragging across the streets of Nerekhall. The small, raggedy wooden door at the corridor's end yawned silently open, both an invitation and a threat. Andira's heart thumped. She felt it shifting in her chest, as though to pull the rest of her back, but she walked on, one foot in front of the other. As though she was being pulled in.

*Bonggg.*

The Academy's bell tolled one.

*"Beloved."*

A shadow breathed its voice through the gap around the opening door.

Andira's breath caught in her mouth, but her feet continued to pull her towards it.

*"What a beautiful, fragile ornament you are. A shield made of glass. How easily you break. How wantonly. I tried to warn you, foolish mortal. The closer you came to this accursed abode, the louder I shouted, but you would not heed me. You hold all creatures of the Ynfernael as equally worthy of your contempt and confuse your denial with wisdom."*

She got her lips to move. "Baelziffar?"

A second disembodied voice chuckled up from the stairs behind her. The stairwell was bottomless and dark and, unlike the ambivalence of the door she was being pushed towards, promised nothing but damnation.

*"Darkness, pain, hunger, and death," it said, its voice the self-satisfied whisper of a knife across a throat. "These are but four of the many spheres of the Ynfernael. Each with its own lords and its king above them and, some say, a king above them, as well as all of those who could be, once were, or will one day become kings themselves. The one you have wasted your life pursuing is but one sovereign amongst many, and neither the cruelest nor the most mighty."*

"*Do not heed him,*" said the first voice.

*"She will heed only me."*

"Are you Augost's master? Are you the Rising Flame?"

The voice from the stairwell laughed.

And she woke again.

She felt hands on her face, peeling her eyelids open between forefinger and thumb. There was pain as the light hit her eyes, and she jerked, attempting to draw back from it but getting no further than the clank of heavy chains would allow.

Brother Augost's unpleasant features swam through the glowing spots in her vision. There was a redness in the priest's skin, like a candle that had been extinguished but which still had its glow and which might easily ignite again if one were to breathe unwisely. He was surrounded by soldiers in black mail and wearing the faces of monsters. He looked exultant.

"I am not the Rising Flame," he said. "You will know its light soon enough."

Andira stared at him, trying to summon her hatred, to use the pain of his fingernails against her cheek to fight off unconsciousness for a moment longer. His leer stretched. His face hardened and became woody, purpling, spreading outwards like a diseased tree to fill her vision until he was as old, crooked, and malignant as the buildings of Nerekhall. It was as if they were all lesser, human-made copies of this.

"*You are mine now, Andira*," said the second voice.

"I will never be yours."

Augost looked at her quizzically, his face his own again, and broke into a wide grin. "The Tower of Nerek breaks some people. They hear voices. It drives them insane. Even the soldiers, sometimes. The only humane course is to lock them away forever."

He leant in close to her ear.

"*Forever*," the demon whispered to her through his lips.

Andira flinched, but the chains held her fast.

"And what about you, Augost?" she said. "Did you hear voices? Is that why you are doing this?"

The mirth fell from the priest's eyes. "The ironbound took you because you are clearly tarnished by the Ynfernael." He looked down disdainfully, the smile returning like a fire reintroduced to dry fuel. "But it was never you that the Rising Flame sought. I delivered them your friend, and now you get to rot in the Tower of Nerek where you belong."

"*Forever.*"

Andira struggled once more, her vision already fading, surrendering Brother Augost to the other monsters around him. Without any noticeable transition she found herself dreaming again.

She reached for the wall in front of her, grabbing at a sconce filled with dust and dried-out cobwebs and holding on. The dim light of her rune painted the stonework blue.

*"I could offer you anything. I have that power."*

"*Do not heed him.*" The voice of Baelziffar sounded weaker now, the squeaking of keys in distant locks, the fury of evil things sealed away and made impotent by closed doors and their gaoler's laughter.

*"What is your desire, Andira? The strength to purge this realm of its evils? Eternal life with which to wield it? I can give either, both, more."*

Andira tried to shut the voice out and think of nothing.

This was a dream. It was her dream.

"I desire nothing."

"*Everyone desires something. Even you. I ask for so little in exchange.*"

"There is nothing you could offer that I would accept."

The voice in her head chuckled. "*Nothing that I could give? But Andira, you have not even asked me my name.*"

A clash of iron brought her back around.

She opened her eyes to find herself inside a stone cell even smaller and more miserably furnished than the one from which she had rescued Trenloe. There was a bucket, a bit of straw on the ground for bedding, but no actual bed and no window. There would not have been the room for more. Augost laughed at her from the other side of the door as his key turned inside the lock, but Andira could not focus on it.

There was laughter all around her. Voices. They screamed and cursed and pleaded, the living and the never quite dying forced to share in one another's purgatory by the millennia-old leakage of the Aenlong into the Tower of Nerek. She felt delirious and feverishly weak, sitting up against the wall of her cell and shivering in the heat.

Whatever power the Daewyl had sought to reach out to here, it was close.

And it had a name.

*"Ask it of me, Andira. Ask it, and I will tell you. What could be the harm? Are you not curious to know?"*

With a tremendous effort of willpower, she raised her hand to blast through the door with her rune power. She could not recall seeing an ironbound outside her door, and so at the very least she could get to the end of the corridor and maybe even find a way to recover her weapons and armor before something arrived to stop her. Her wrist moved half a foot and then clanked to a halt. She looked down. It had been manacled to her ankle on a short chain. She wanted to cry out in frustration. It was only with an effort that she did not. Augost had known what he was doing.

Rune magic obeyed the laws of directional motion, of action and reaction. If she wanted to deliver a force then she needed to be able to summon and direct that force. Short of cutting off her hand, Augost had ensured that she was incapable of doing so. She was helpless.

Squeezing her eyes shut, she glared at the locked door in front of her as though she could *hate* it to smithereens.

She was not helpless, and Augost would suffer for thinking it. Whatever Augost planned, he would regret bringing her here. Andira Runehand was more than just the power she had been given.

*"Ask me for my name, Andira."*

Andira had to bite her tongue to stop herself from blurting out the question.

*"Ask."*

*"Ask."*

*"Ask."*

"No!"

*"I am patient. And we have forever."*

Andira turned her fever-wet face from the door, opened her mouth wide and screamed until she was hoarse. She loathed herself even more than the demon in that moment, but the panic needed to come out and would not be stopped. A part of her welcomed it. It felt good to drown out the voice and its promises. When it was done and she was sat gasping against the wall, the smug amusement of the voice was still there, waiting for her.

*"It is a name, Andira. Only a name."*

"A first step is always followed by a second, and a second by a third." She thought back to the bottomless staircase that had lain behind her in her visions, the sense of menace she had always felt from it, and shuddered. "And you do not even know how deep they go until you can no longer see the light above you."

*"Then perhaps I will just tell you."*

Andira instinctively raised her hands to block her ears. The right hand came up. The left clanked at the end of its chain.

The voice laughed.

*"Oh, what fun we are going to have between now and the end of eternity."*

She worked her lips as though to ask the question, screwing her eyes tight shut and forcing herself to think of something else.

Anything else.

Trenloe would come for her.

Whatever words had been said, whatever their disagreements, the First themselves could not convince her that he would not come.

*"Shall we play a game while we wait? I will go first…"*

Andira closed her eyes.

She could hold on until he did.

## CHAPTER EIGHTEEN
### *Trenloe the Strong*

Trenloe reached into the cranny at the top of the bookshelf and made reassuring noises. It was as much for his own benefit as for the large, fluffy white cat that hissed at him and batted at his fingers. Ravaella had brought him and Rendiel to her study and promised to return soon. That had been almost an hour ago. He was starting to worry.

"Leave the cat alone," Rendiel snapped, equally on edge. "It's probably bewitched."

"It's not bewitched."

"It's *acting* bewitched."

"It's probably just hungry."

Trenloe turned to the small side table between the trio of plush armchairs where refreshments had been set for them. There were jams, breads, cured meats, nuts, bowls of dried and pickled fruits and clotted creams, and a steaming pot of rose tea that came with a complicated apparatus that Trenloe was unsure how to operate.

The platter had been brought in by a thin man in plain

black robes and dead eyes who had glared balefully at him and Rendiel as if to say that he had not attended the Academy in order to be a servant.

Trenloe dipped his finger in the cream and offered it to the cat.

The animal looked at his finger as though it might prefer it over the cream, but emerged from its corner for neither.

"Bewitched," Rendiel muttered to himself. He was perched on the edge of Ravaella's desk with his back to the darkened window, flicking idly through the papers cluttering his impromptu seat. The elf threw the papers back across the desk with a disgusted sigh.

"You can't trust her, Trenloe." Rendiel cast a glance towards the closed door. Satisfied that their host was not yet back, he leant forwards and hissed, "I know you say you knew her before, but either you didn't know her well or she's changed since then. Believe me. People do change."

Giving up on the cat, Trenloe licked the cream off his own finger. "You still haven't told me how you know her."

Rendiel drummed his fingers on the desk. The thin muscles of his jaw twitched, as though with the unpleasant aftertaste of a memory. "We met here in Nerekhall. At the public hanging of a necromancer named Tristayne Olliven." He gave a bitter laugh. "It turned into quite the spectacle after the condemned man went on to reanimate himself right there at the end of his rope. It convinced a few magistrates who had been unsure of his guilt until then, let me tell you. The ironbound seemed bizarrely uninterested, despite rogue necromancers being exactly the sort of thing they were built to stop and, as you've seen for yourself, without the ironbound there isn't a lot that the Nerekhall militia has going for it. So Ravaella, me–" a smile graced his face with a fleeting visit "–Tinashi the Wanderer, Orkell the Swift; we did what we could.

"Events conspired to hold us together after that. Nerekhall has a way of foiling the good-intentioned, but we did some good things in spite of that. Not that anyone ever acknowledged what we did, of course. Not the Magistrates. Not the Artificers. And definitely not Ravaella." He cast another sour look around the study. "Not while she values any of the status she has bartered her silence into since."

He leant forward suddenly, with such intensity that Trenloe felt compelled to step back.

"Ravaella didn't go traipsing through the sewers into the lair of the Rat-Thing King, or delve into the heart of the Black Realm itself, because she wanted to do good. She did it because she thought she had this tremendous point that needed proving to the world. She did it because it was *fascinating* to her. All of this ..." He gestured disinterestedly at the bowing shelves and the piles of manuscripts. "All of this is what she truly wanted. Power and prestige and the recognition of everyone around her. And when the newly appointed Chief Artificer and the surviving Magistrates wanted us to keep our mouths shut and go away, Orkell and Tinashi moved on, I as good as sank into the Snicks, but Ravaella was only too happy to oblige and pretend everything we did never happened."

Trenloe had never seen him so animated. For a bard, he was unusually reticent about his own story. He thought back to the Ravaella he had known. It was impossible to reconcile the mischief-making entertainer he remembered with the ambitious mage that Rendiel wanted him to see.

"Why didn't you leave, too?" he asked.

Rendiel pursed his lips. He turned towards the window, as

though searching for a glimpse of his past self in the reflection. "I didn't leave my home in the Aymhelin out of a burning desire to do good either. No more than Ravaella. I was wealthy, and bored, and one day came up with the amusing notion of traveling the human realms in search of the lyrics to a song I'd overheard from a merchant in Summersong. After everything we went through, everything we did and saw and then not even being able to speak about it afterwards… It all seemed so trivial." He shrugged, turning his back on his faint reflection. "I had no better place to go, no good reason to leave, so I stayed, and I met Sanna, and I drank and… well, you know the rest."

Trenloe didn't know what to say. He had left his own home on a whim no grander than Rendiel's. He had daydreamed about being some kind of hero, of finding adventure in faraway lands with names like *Isheim* and *Zanaga* and battling the fantastical creatures that dwelled there. But, if he was being truly honest, it had been his friend, Dremmin, who had talked him into it, and she had been motivated solely by turning his growing reputation into gold. If she hadn't, then he would probably be a contented, middle-ranking officer in Baron Rault's army today.

Now he thought about it, perhaps there was something to be said for Andira's single-minded attitude towards her quest. She never doubted herself, had never once woken without a sense of purpose, and for as long as she had been with him, neither had Trenloe.

He saw with sudden clarity how easy it would be to wake up one day and find that he was no different to Rendiel: waiting for the next adventure to find him, without realizing that the world had moved on without him.

Ravaella's return spared him the need to explore that uncomfortable thought further.

The gnome bustled in through the opened door like a midwinter gust, unsettling loose pages and sending a chill up Trenloe's back before kicking it shut behind her.

She had changed her attire at least once since their rescue from Tuschels' home, rustling into the room in a gown so densely embroidered with arcane sigils it was more golden than black. Her unruly abundance of hair had been restrained by several loops of black cloth and lay across one shoulder. A wand of purple beechwood had been tucked into the belt. There was not a trace of tiredness on her that Trenloe could see, not a single crease or shadow under the eyes to attest to the fact that she had been up all night.

"Sorry to keep you," she said. "It might be the middle of the night, but the whole institute is in uproar. Two ironbound destroyed. Another missing somewhere in the Snicks. Talk of two guards being beaten near to death in the Tower of Nerek." She grinned wickedly. "Suffice it to say, half my fellow magisters are secretly delighted by the whole affair while the other half are packing their bags and arranging for fast horses to Jendra's Harbor." She paused long enough to breathe. "I see you've met Belt."

The cat raised its head and blinked at the mention of its name, but remained more than happy to stay where it was.

Ravaella smiled at Trenloe. "And animals always seemed to love you."

"Never mind the cat," Rendiel snapped. "I take no more pleasure in being here than you do from having me. Not after the unpleasantness of last time."

"Oh, Rendiel." Ravaella made as though to go to the

desk where he was sat, but then hesitated. After a moment's indecision, she took one of the chairs and sat down. The large armchair shrank to her dimensions as she lowered herself into it. "You could have come to see me at any time. You know that."

"Oh, you would have *liked* that, wouldn't you?"

"Please," Trenloe interrupted. "We need to do something about Andira and the others. Brother Augost has fallen in with some extreme cult that wants to bring Margath the Unkind back from the Aenlong and has modified some of the ironbound to help him do it. He has our friends in the Tower and there's no telling what he plans to do next."

Ravaella thought for a moment. "Perhaps I should summon Cabdal to bring us some more food." She smiled brightly at him. "Would you like some more tea? Or something colder? Hotter? I forget how large the human stomach can be."

"Latariana's shining tears." Rendiel gestured impatiently towards Trenloe. "Show her the rune already, Trenloe, before she talks both our ears off and turns them into marigolds."

"I'm not hungry," Trenloe said, pulling Rendiel's charcoal drawing from his sleeve. "But thank you."

All the same, Ravaella helped herself to the pot of rose tea, pouring a fresh cup with a slice of the preserved fruit and a stir of honey.

Trenloe coughed awkwardly. He hoped it wasn't too obvious that he'd eaten the preserves, used the honeypot to dunk the bread, and taken the tea mixed with cream. Ravaella sipped at the hot, sweetened rosewater, cocking her head sideways to examine the drawing from every angle.

"It's not a particularly good drawing."

"I'd like to see you do better from the back of an ironbound," said Rendiel.

"When it comes to rune magic, details are crucial. Put one line an inch to the left, or a fraction shorter, and suddenly your simple illumination spell is a fireball."

"Andira was convinced it was fake," said Trenloe.

The gnome frowned. "I wouldn't necessarily say that."

"Then what exactly would you say?" said Rendiel.

Ignoring her erstwhile companion's exasperation, Ravaella took another long sip of tea and brandished the charcoal sketch in his direction. "Does it remind you of Rylan's work at all?"

The elf leant forward and gave it a cursory frown. "A little," he conceded. "I suppose." He leant back. "But then you'd be the expert."

"Say what you like about Rylan's motives, there was nothing to fault with his genius. Without any involvement from the Academy, or Greyhaven University, he managed to propose and craft four entirely new rune combinations. Even eight hundred years ago, when the first scholars were piecing things together to master the magic that the dragons had left behind, that would have been exceptional. But today? In this age? It's unheard of."

"Yes, yes, the *knowledge on its own isn't evil* excuse. I believe it was Tristayne himself who said it before we saw his corpse hanged a second time."

"If you think differently then why come to me for help?"

"*I* didn't *come to you.*"

"Do you still sing songs about Waiqar from before he became the Undying King?" Ravaella snapped, springing out of her chair. "You used to, I remember. There are people in Rhynn and Carthridge, even here in Nerekhall, who would call that dangerous. And that pretty historian Orkell took a shine to, Celia: you and he were both very interested in the stories she had to tell us about Mirklace and the Black Realm. If the Magistrates had had their way, then she would have disappeared along with her stories."

"And they got it," Rendiel muttered darkly. "Thanks to you."

Trenloe cleared his throat angrily. He didn't understand what had come between the two of them, but they had more important things to do than re-hash old grievances now. "Who's Rylan?"

"Rylan *Olliven*," said Rendiel, without tearing his gaze from Ravaella. "Tristayne was his younger brother, and it was Rylan himself who turned him over to the authorities, and who called so vociferously for his hanging."

"Although, of course," Ravaella added, the mischievous smirk returning to her face as though it had never left. "Rylan knew full well that a hanging would only be a temporary inconvenience to Tristayne and that, for a while at least afterwards, long enough, he would be quite beyond reproach."

"It helped that he was the Chief Artificer of Pollux," said Rendiel.

Ravaella nodded. "He and Tristayne had conspired together to realize Gargan Mirklace's ambition, to sink Nerekhall into the Black Realm and share its raw potential between them. By the time we were able to piece it all together it was almost too late. Rylan had even managed to subvert the city's ironbound, reworking their control runes to make them loyal to him and Tristayne." She held up Rendiel's drawing and smiled. "Sound familiar?"

Trenloe thought about his thankfully brief glimpse into the Black Realm, and his encounter with the creatures that had emerged from it. "Why would anyone want to go into the Black Realm?"

"There is power in the Aenlong, and potential. Things are possible there that a more fully realized plane would never allow a person to attempt."

"Who else could do what Rylan did?" said Rendiel.

"Rylan was a genius," said Ravaella. "It would be impossible."

"Unless…"

"Unless?" said Trenloe, starting to feel a little left behind. Rendiel and Ravaella might not have been friends anymore but they had a short-hand that Trenloe struggled to follow. He was just waiting to hear how any of it pertained to Augost or Andira.

"Rylan died when he failed to open his rift." Rendiel turned to Trenloe. Whatever he was thinking was making him deeply unhappy. "But Tristayne… He failed to stay dead once before."

Ravaella seemed to perk up at that. Her face seemed to want to smile, but then she shook her head, looking as discomforted by the whole suggestion as Rendiel appeared to be. "No. Impossible! We disposed of the body so as to ensure he could never rise again."

"It has to be him." Rendiel jumped from the desk and began pacing, animated now. "You said it yourself. No one else could command the ironbound the way he did."

"Augost is a priest of Kellos," Trenloe reminded them both, hoping to draw them back to familiar territory, and when Rendiel waved it off as irrelevant, he continued, "Even if he's extreme, he would have to *loathe* the undead. Why would he ally with a necromancer?" He turned to Ravaella. "He spoke of resurrecting Margath. Of a group called the Rising Flame. Does that mean anything to you?"

"The Rising…"

Ravaella blinked. She seemed almost rattled by the name.

"You've heard of it?" said Trenloe.

The gnome took a sip of tea while she composed herself. "Maybe. Maybe." She set the cup back on the side table. "Loose talk amongst the faculty. Things I overhear from the students when they don't realize there's an invisible gnome nearby. Pamphlets I'll find occasionally in the private cloisters." She bit her bottom lip and looked again at Rendiel's drawing. "I need to study this in more detail and compare it to Rylan's notes. To confirm that it really is his work and what that might mean."

"I knew it!" Rendiel hissed suddenly. "I *knew* you'd kept Rylan's books after we turned his workshop over to the magistrates."

"I had to," Ravaella said quietly. "The things he'd achieved…"

The elf crossed his arms as though to physically prevent himself from going for his sword. "If I find that this is somehow on you, because you failed to destroy those books when you should have…"

"The answers will be in those books, you'll see." Seeing no forgiveness in Rendiel's glare, she turned instead to Trenloe. "You'll see. But I'll need time. The Magistrates have convened for a full session in the grand forum, and I need to be there."

"I thought mages weren't allowed in the forum," Rendiel muttered.

"I've been once before, but usually no, we're not."

"Then we should go with you," said Trenloe.

Ravaella shook her head vigorously. "That wouldn't be a good idea."

"If I could just speak with the Magistrates, I could convince them of the danger."

"*No,*" Ravaella snapped.

Rendiel raised an eyebrow.

The gnome took a deep breath. "Brother Augost is going to be there, too," she explained. "He'll have you both in chains before you can get inside the door, and you have no proof at all that he shouldn't. No. You and Rendiel should stay here for now."

"I'm not going to just sit here and drink tea while you head to the forum to chat with Augost," said Rendiel.

"I agree," said Trenloe. "Andira is in the Tower."

"There's nothing else for you to do until I can find real proof that the ironbound have been tampered with."

Rendiel shook his head, still pacing. "There's a mortuary, right here under the Academy, part of the library's lower vaults. It was used for research, mostly, but dangerous artefacts were often held there, too. It's where we interred Tristayne's remains after his brother's defeat. If he… if they should no longer be there…" He trailed off. "Well, by the time you get back from the forum we might have all the proof you need."

Ravaella looked as though she might protest, but then shrugged and gave them both a half-smile. Trenloe felt relieved. He understood that he could not simply barge into the Tower, but he was glad he had something more useful to do than sit in Ravaella's study and wait. "All right. I should warn you though that the mortuary has a permanent caretaker these days, to keep the likes of Tristayne from meddling in that sort of magic again. The library undercroft can be something of a labyrinth, too."

"I know my way around," said Rendiel.

"It would still be best if my student went with you." She leaned out of her seat and shouted towards the door. "Cabdal!" There was no answer. She leaned back and gave Trenloe an embarrassed smile. "He has a tendency to wander. I believe he thinks himself too good to be running errands for a gnomish sorcerer. He reminds me at least once a day that he's from quite the important family."

"I'll go and get him," said Rendiel, giving neither of them another look as he made for the door. "There's something about this room I don't like."

He opened the door and didn't shut it as he left. Trenloe heard him traipse down the otherwise deserted corridor.

Ravaella got up and moved to the desk Rendiel had left vacant. Placing Rendiel's drawing on top of the untidy heaps of paper already present, she proceeded to rummage through the drawers.

"Ahhh!" she said, locating the thing she had been searching for and whirling back around with a flat, imperfectly rounded white stone in her hand. She rubbed her thumb affectionately over the rune carved into its face, and then offered it to him.

Trenloe hesitated. He had never held a genuine runestone. Even after all this time, he was still wary of touching Andira's hand, lest he somehow activate it by mistake.

After a few seconds observing his indecision, Ravaella took his hand and popped the stone into his open palm.

He flinched, but nothing happened. It felt surprisingly ordinary. And small. He was more likely to misplace the stone and lose it through carelessness than accidentally command the ground to open up and swallow his friends.

"It's called the Dampener," said Ravaella. "It's not as powerful as the null-stones that the ironbound carry, you'll forgive me for not keeping one of *those* around, but it will help against any mage you encounter so long as you are holding onto it. Keep it against your skin, rune-side down. Like this." She took the runestone from his hand and slid it under his sleeve, where he had been keeping Rendiel's drawing. "It won't protect you, exactly, but any spell targeted at you will cause the caster to tire. It's unlikely they will get to cast a second. Just in case you do happen to run into Tristayne Olliven."

"Thank you," said Trenloe, pulling his sleeve down over the runestone.

The words seemed inadequate. The Dampener was, quite probably, the most valuable thing he had ever touched.

Ravaella caught his wrist as he turned to leave.

"Rendiel wasn't always like this," she said, suddenly urgent, as though there were things that needed to be said and little time in which to say them. "He was spirited, funny, youthful in spite of being ten times my age, his fingers never very far from that lute of his. He thinks I betrayed him, but I only did what the Magistrates wanted us to do. Orkell and Tinashi did the same by leaving. As Rendiel himself did by drinking himself to the bottom of the Snicks. And they were right, Trenloe. If the people of Nerekhall had known that the ironbound couldn't be trusted in the Church's hands, then the city would tear itself apart and the barons wouldn't be far behind to burn whatever was left. But Rendiel couldn't see it that way. He saw too much. We all did. He's just bitter that he couldn't even talk about it, except to me. There's a good heart in there, somewhere, but you can't go as deep into Nerekhall as he has, for as long as he has, without picking up more than just physical dirt. Just… just don't turn your back on him while you're down in the mortuaries."

Trenloe gave her a sad smile. "Funny, he told me something similar about you."

The gnome drew her hand from his. She looked older all of a sudden.

"Yes. I imagine he did."

# CHAPTER NINETEEN
## *Thaiden Mistspeak*

Thaiden swallowed a pang of guilt as he peered through the slot in the top of the cell door. The woman curled up on the stone floor inside bore only the slightest resemblance to the proud warrior he had found himself fighting alongside earlier that night, the hero he had pursued across the north of Terrinoth since long before that.

Her blonde hair was torn, bloodied where the ironbound had struck the blow that knocked her out, and matted with straw. The thin woolen undershirt she had been wearing under her armor was ringed with sweat and she was shivering as though in a delirium. She tossed and turned on the hard floor, muttering to herself as though to the figments of some terrible dream, but her eyes were wide open and staring.

Thaiden had the horrible feeling that she was staring at him.

His fee for finding Andira had come to more than a few pennies, and in his heart he knew that he would do it all again. The task he had been given was supposed to have ended with the delivery of the letter. Having her wind up in the Tower of Nerek was simply a bonus insofar as his employer was concerned. Andira was now in a place in which they could find her any time, unarmed and without wary companions always around her.

Thaiden drew a square of paper from his inside coat pocket, unfolding it one-handed and shaking it flat, holding it to one of the dozens of roaring braziers mounted along the wall in praise of Kellos.

It carried a small portrait of a woman, drawn using a charcoal stick by his employer. With half an eye on the drawing, he peered again at the woman in the cell. It was a more than fair resemblance, he had to admit, even if his employer had claimed not to have seen her in ten years. She had not aged a day. He looked back at the drawing. The eyes were the most striking feature. They *judged,* somehow appearing blue in a grayscale face. He was unsure if that was in the gift of the artist or of the subject, but he suspected he knew the answer.

With a grimace, he scrunched the portrait back into his pocket.

He wondered if anyone who had known his face ten years ago would recognize it now? They would probably be appalled. But they were dead. They had lost the right to judge him.

While he watched, the woman muttered something angry and rolled over as though to turn her back on someone. Thaiden felt a chill go through him as though, just for a moment, there really *had* been something in the cell there with her.

In the Forthyn highlands, high in the fastnesses of the Dunwarr where proud elementals and Dimora held sway, there had been rare places that made Thaiden experience something akin to this feeling. Deep in the mountains, beyond the claim of any chief, were grottos, caves, and ancient shrines that long predated humanity. Cursed places where those mortals who chanced upon them would flee and do their best to forget, living forever after in fear of the mark of the Fey upon their backs.

Thaiden had seen his share of things that could not be forgotten. Whatever danger Andira Runehand had involved herself in, he wanted no part of. He would have left Nerekhall already if not for this one last request on the part of his employer. They were still discussing matters with the Warden, but he expected them to join him soon.

A despairing wail from one of the cells pulled his attention from Andira's door and back down the corridor. One of the doors shook as the prisoner within threw himself at it before falling still. Another voice from further down the corridor picked up the cry, others rising to join it in a chorus while the torches lined up in their sockets danced.

This was not Thaiden's first visit to the Tower of Nerek. It was uncanny, the number of lost people that ended up there. It had always been an unpleasant place, corruption never far beneath the surface, but this was his first experience of the Tower's highest levels. There were more guards. More heat. More iron. This, he had been told, was the home of the recidivist, the unrepentant, and the irredeemably damned.

It was the home that Brother Augost had especially chosen for Andira Runehand.

The chaplain shuffled down the corridor from the guardroom beyond the portcullis. He was bare-chested, like a young warrior showing off his scars. And the priest had scars, as many as any clan fighter, young or old, that Thaiden could remember seeing. The torches flickered in the breeze of his passing, but then bent towards him, like pilgrims desperate to touch the holy man's feet. A short-handled mace, a ring of keys, and a bundle of burning candles swung from his golden belt. He smiled in welcome at Thaiden as he drew close. It was the falsest smile that Thaiden had ever seen, and he had once had the misfortune of standing beside a clear lake and catching sight of his own.

"This is not a good time to be visiting the Tower," Augost began. "The prisoners are ... more than usually disturbed."

"I noticed."

"It is nothing to concern yourself with, but it happens from time to time. They call out for the succor of Kellos' flames."

Thaiden ground his teeth. "I noticed that, too."

"It would be better if you and your companions returned tomorrow."

Thaiden had a vision of himself taking the priest's head by its prominent ears and headbutting it. It was so vivid that his face felt wet and his hands trembled. He took a long breath, and let the urge go.

He'd never laid hands on a priest before. The line had to be drawn somewhere.

"My employer is an esteemed knight in the court of Baron Zachareth. She would have Andira Runehand removed to her custody in Carthridge and has already secured the Warden's permission to speak with her. So stop pretending that any of us care and open the door."

Augost's smile tightened, but never wavered, staring hard into Thaiden's eyes as though trying to decide if he was someone he had met before. "Andira Runehand is dangerous and, as you can see, quite unsettled in spirit. She is a consort of demons and quite possibly possessed. I will know for certain once Daralyn and the Archpriest grant me permission to test her in fire. It took three ironbound to subdue her and, as a direct consequence, several innocent bystanders were injured in the process of bringing her in."

"What happened to the others?" Thaiden wasn't sure why he asked. Innocent people got themselves into harm's way every day. He knew that better than anyone. He hadn't the tears left for any of them. The words came out regardless.

"They are being held in a lower wing. They will be released in the fullness of time, but first the Chief Artificer and the Warden want to question them about the events surrounding Andira's capture and Trenloe's escape. A lot of people, a lot of questions. Priests and Magistrates and captains all needing pulling out of beds in the middle of the night to ask them. As I said," Augost added, his words a snarl. "This is not a good time." He gave Thaiden another probing look. "You will have to tell me how you knew to come here before any of them did."

Thaiden put a smile on his face and envisioned himself slamming the priest's head into the door until it opened. The door, that was.

"I'll see her now," he said.

"Andira remains chained and within her cell at all times."

Thaiden nodded in agreement. He suspected that his employer would have insisted on it even if Augost had not.

"And I will be present while you speak with her."

"You can eavesdrop from here and be grateful."

For a minute it looked as though the priest was determined to argue the point, but Thaiden had Carthridge nobility and the express permission of the Warden. Augost had nothing to argue and he knew it. With a scowl, he turned to the door, the implausible amount of time it took him to fumble through the ring of keys on his belt his last petty act of non-compliance.

He unlocked the door.

And Thaiden Mistspeak stepped inside.

# CHAPTER TWENTY
## *Trenloe the Strong*

Owl had told him that the Academy's library was the largest in Terrinoth. It was twice the size of the Daqan Collection in the Citadel of Archaut, and boasted rarer texts and more esoteric objects that had been the envy of Greyhaven's librarians for generations.

"Greyhaven," Owl had said, "is where a student goes to learn the basics of rune-magic. Nerekhall is where they realize how much more there is still to learn." Trenloe had no frame of reference to measure Owl's assertion. His experience went no further than the public library in Artrast, compared to which the Academy's library was practically a town in its own right.

The high shelves were streets, every bit as labyrinthine and clandestine as those of Nerekhall proper. Flameless torches burned at the end of every row, huge windows and skylights drew in every speck of starlight, and yet somehow there remained shadowed regions where light never quite touched, secluded areas hidden away behind high-backed chairs and tables laden with books. Robed librarians sat behind desks in spite of the hour, looking up from their own studies to keep a watchful eye on the unlikely trio of Trenloe, Rendiel, and Cabdal, monitoring the library's comings and goings as vigilantly as any town watch.

If it was a town, however, then to Trenloe's eye it was in the mold of Archaut rather than a living breathing home for real people.

Every sound was an event to be marked and recorded. The creak of a scholar's shoes on the lacquered floorboards. The crinkle of a turned page. The creasing of a leather spine. The air carried the mature odor of well-aged books and treated oak. The people, moving contemplatively along its book-lined avenues, had the feel of pilgrims rather than residents. Most wore the plain black robes of students or the more ornate versions worn by faculty and staff. Trenloe saw more than a few commoners about, too, men and women in simple homespun robes browsing the moonlit shelves with work-hardened fingers.

"Everyone is free to use the library," said Rendiel, keeping his voice low. "It's how the Academy shows the Magistrates that it has nothing to hide."

Trenloe picked up a book from a shelf at random.

The binding was hard and cracked, like an old shoe. A faded illustration adorned its cover alongside words he couldn't read. With a musty creak and a waft of scent, he opened it, flicking through page after page of inscrutable text while admiring the marginalia art. He recognized most of the alphabet, but that was the extent of his skill.

"The Academy doesn't teach as such," Rendiel went on. "Ravaella and her fellows give lectures from time to time on whatever they fancy, whenever they fancy, and anyone who can is free to attend. A determined, lucky, or talented few might convince a tutor to instruct them on a more formal basis, but most pick up what they can here in the library."

Trenloe glanced across to Cabdal. Ravaella's student mage was as tall and thin as a willow branch, with a scarred lower lip and eyes so dark a green they were almost black. He wore his dark hair in a topknot, in the manner of the more easterly Kellar, but had a face that was otherwise curiously forgettable. While quite obviously *young*, his age was similarly difficult to pin down. If Cabdal had told him he was anywhere between eighteen and fifty then Trenloe would have been unsurprised. The student himself had spoken little, however, responding to any personal question with a discouraging glare, while simply ignoring most others.

"How did you come to have Ravaella as a teacher?" Trenloe asked, returning the book to its place on the shelf.

Cabdal walked on without answering.

"We'll never find the mortuary caretaker in this maze," Trenloe muttered. "We should ask someone if they've seen him."

Rendiel laughed, earning himself a scathing look from a student carrying an armful of loose manuscripts. "This is just the upper gallery, Trenloe. The mortuary is downstairs."

"How many floors are there?"

"You'll see."

Cabdal took them to an ornate oak staircase and led them down.

Moonlight gave way to lamplight. Oak to stone. Bindings more esoteric than leather began to crop up on the shelves: wood, fur, dragon scale, glass, strange metals with locks on their hinges and chained together in rows. There were still plenty of young mages going about their studies, and even a few commoners engaged with more esoteric disciplines than could be found upstairs.

The stairs continued to descend through the floors. The library extended alongside it the way villages grew along the sides of a road, students and librarians becoming sparser as the books grew older and the shelves dustier.

How many books were there in the world? Trenloe wondered. What proportion of them were here in Nerekhall? He wondered if it was even possible to read them all in one lifetime. He saw how disciplines like necromancy might appeal to a mage with such a hoard of knowledge and but one lifetime to study it. With only the books he could see, Trenloe imagined he could fill the moat around Castle Artrast twice over and march an army across it. He could probably have taken the castle apart and rebuilt a perfect replica, brick by brick, out of the books he had left over.

His stomach began to growl. Having grown accustomed to simpler fare on the road west, it had been far from satisfied by the fruits and jams on Ravaella's tray. He ignored its grumbles. While his stomach fretted over its last meal, Andira and the others were languishing another hour in the Tower of Nerek.

He decided that he would do anything to hear Owl tell him one more time how large the Academy's library was. And this time, he'd believe him.

"Ahhh," said Rendiel, drawing a deep breath as Cabdal led them off the eighth flight of stairs into a crypt-like vault. The walls were braced with thick stone columns. The ceiling was low and crisscrossed with structural beams. "I know that smell. We're on the lowest level of the library now. This brings back memories." He coughed. The air was lousy with dust. "And not good ones."

There were fewer books here. This level of the library functioned more as a reliquary for magical artefacts. They were secured behind thick screens of glass that had themselves been finely cut with runes. Trenloe wondered if the runes were purely decorative or whether they strengthened the cases somehow, allowing them to retain the transparent qualities of glass whilst firmly containing whatever malign influence they held within.

Trenloe tried to peer through the first screen he came to, but the runes on the glass shifted under his eyes. While the glass was clear, the runes were deeply opaque and always seemed to be directly between Trenloe and whatever he was trying to look at.

Cabdal's robes stirred the thin patina of dust from the floor. It did not look as though anybody had descended to this level of the library in weeks. The air around him rippled like a liquid as he passed between the rows of locked cases. His skin took on a pale, purplish hue, his limbs lengthening, until he passed the end of the row and left the magical effect behind. The student snapped back into his own, scrawny body as he turned, looking impatiently at Trenloe and Rendiel to follow.

Trenloe felt no strange magicks distorting his limbs as he crossed, and noticed nothing untoward in Rendiel's appearance either.

It must have been a question of perspective.

With each level that the library had descended underground, the level in question had become sequentially smaller, and it did not take Cabdal long to find the entrance to the mortuary.

Trenloe had been expecting something akin to the entrance to a barrow: a great boulder or slab of stone across its opening, engraved with runes of power and excerpts from the holy books to command the dead to rest. Instead, Cabdal brought them to a sturdy but remarkably plain wooden door studded with iron rivets. A faded notice had been hung across the handle. Rendiel read it for him. It warned of severe consequences for anyone entering the mortuary without the permission of a faculty member.

Cabdal pulled the sign off the handle.

"We should find the librarian of this floor and let them know what we're doing here," said Trenloe, nervously.

"We have permission," said Rendiel. "Ravaella is faculty, remember?"

"Still..." Trenloe looked around the seemingly deserted vault. "I wouldn't want to cause trouble for anyone if we get caught down there."

The elf chuckled. "You're like the hero in a song for children."

A smirk pulled at the corners of Cabdal's lips as he opened the door, and Rendiel rounded on him with a triumphantly upraised finger. "I knew it! I knew you had to have a sense of humor. I can't wait to get back and tell Ravaella."

With a scowl, Cabdal walked through the open door.

Rendiel turned to Trenloe with a stage whisper. "I don't know where Ravaella found *him*."

Trenloe smiled in spite of everything and followed his two companions down to the mortuary.

The final descent was a short and narrow flight of stairs, dropping a few more feet but several degrees of warmth. Trenloe took his axe handle in a tight grip, more for the warmth he could generate than for any assurance he needed from the weapon. He drew the other hand to his mouth and blew into it. Air washed between his fingers as vapor. Rendiel pulled his collar up around his neck. Cabdal didn't seem to feel it.

The chamber at the bottom was frigid and unlit. The sizzling of runes cut into sarcophagus lids threw the entire thing into a blueish tableaux, giving off a low and steady creak reminiscent of ice at rest. The walls were undressed stone, literally chiseled out of the pale bedrock of the southern Carthmounts.

"I can barely make out a thing in this light," Rendiel complained, leaning across a tomb to squint his elven eyes at the engraved inscription. "It's enough to keep us from walking into each other in the dark, but it'll be no help at all if we want to find which of these caskets is supposed to be holding Tristayne."

"Perhaps you should wait here while I go back to the library for a torch," said Trenloe.

Rendiel made a face. "If you think I'm standing here on my own while you–"

"Wait." Trenloe held up a hand for quiet and peered into the unnatural gloom. The glow of the runes was making his eyes ache whilst offering little to actually help him see. They defined the chamber with contrast, painted it in block shades of runic blue, but offered so little in the way of detail that his eyes were in constant struggle with a mind that wanted to reject it all as unreal. He had fought some monstrous creatures in his travels, but still, the thought of being so deep underground, surrounded by the sleeping dead, unnerved him. He rubbed his eyes and saw it again.

A light.

A single candle flickered in the not-quite-dark ahead.

"There," he said, pointing towards it.

Rendiel frowned into the gloom. "It must be Ravaella's caretaker."

"If anyone can point us to Tristayne Olliven's tomb, it would be them."

"You know, now that we're down here I'm not sure that–"

"Come on." Hugging his chest for warmth, Trenloe led the way. Rendiel fell in reluctantly behind while Cabdal trailed quietly in the rear. Twenty stone caskets later, they came to the end of the chamber. A dark wooden desk stood there, like a tutor before a class of dormant dead. An ornately bound ledger had been chained to the top. A pewter bowl, still wet with ink, and a stamp with an ivory handle lay beside it. Beyond the desk, a corridor opened out of the pale stone like the mouth of a skull.

Trenloe shook off the urge to shiver and blamed it on the cold.

The light was coming from there.

"Err, Trenloe..." said Rendiel.

Swallowing his own unease, Trenloe ignored the elf and walked on.

Passages veered off in both directions to reveal additional chambers. Each of them was of a similar size to the first, holding twenty or so sarcophagi bathed in a runic glow and glittering under a protective rime of frost. The chambers were empty, and so Trenloe ignored them. Rendiel made the sign of a god with whom Trenloe was unfamiliar and kept close.

The light was ahead of them.

Trenloe stepped over the threshold into a small, circular anteroom.

A reading desk and chair stood on their own in a puddle of light. A skeletally thin man with a single sputtering candle sat over an open grimoire. He was garbed against the cold in a thick black robe trimmed with fur. The candlelight made his skin a waxy gray. Intricate tattoos covered his face. They looked like words or maybe one word, repeated over and over in dozens of languages both mortal and not. His forehead was pierced, long needles of thin bone holding sloughing flesh in an approximation of youth and keeping his black hair from his face. In one painfully wizened hand, he held a wand, a gnarled twist of bone filigreed with tiny writing that appeared to animate in the unsteady light of the candle.

Using the tip of his wand to hold his place on the page, the man looked up as Cabdal and Rendiel followed Trenloe inside. His eyes were the cloudy white of a blind man's. His teeth looked like stones exhumed from wet soil.

"That… doesn't look like the caretaker," the elf murmured.

"Is it Tristayne?" Trenloe hissed back.

"Do you think I'd still be standing here if it was?"

"She moves against me already." The robed figure calmly closed his book with a *creak* of moldering leather. His voice was the dry rattle of dead things moving. "Her plans must be nearer to realization than she had allowed me to see."

Trenloe's mouth worked for a moment.

He couldn't mean Ravaella. Could he? Trenloe hadn't even had the chance to speak yet. There was no way he could know who had sent them or why. He wondered what the chances could be that this mage and Trenloe had stumbled unwittingly into entirely unrelated plots. He could imagine Rendiel smiling, suggesting only half in jest that uncovering only conspiracies represented a good day in Nerekhall. Trenloe was unconvinced.

"She?" he asked.

"A rising flame consumes as it moves. The First among us seeks the power of the Burning Lord for herself, but Vorakesh is prepared. She thinks herself cunning, but she does not catch him unawares. If she wished him finally dead then she should have come herself."

With a sudden flick of his wand, the robed man pricked the paper-thin skin of his fingertip. He muttered a rapid string of syllables, each sounding like the *snap* of a tiny bone, and the blood smearing the end of his wand began to glow. The light grew in intensity until it was brighter than the candle and the chamber shrank as the darkness was consumed and the stonework soaked in red.

"Feel the power of Lord Vorakesh!"

The man rose from his chair and stabbed his wand towards Trenloe. A torrent of blood erupted from the tip, a howling swarm of semi-transparent shades spiraling around it like the spinning bit of a drill, honing its leading edge to a point.

Trenloe caught it full in the breastplate. The impact lifted him off his feet and hurled him back towards the corridor, arms and legs flailing at air. He screamed as he fell, not at the blow itself so much as the sudden heat of the Dampener burning into the skin of his wrist where Ravaella had hidden it. He hit the ground in a sticky clatter of blood-slicked plate and threw out an elbow to break his slide. He pushed himself up with a groan, feeling the bruised ribs under the fresh dent in his breastplate, and looked back.

The mage moaned, sagging into the table as the strength went out of his knees and knocked over the candle. He cursed and spun away. There was another exit on the other side of the table. Moving with surprising speed for someone so atrophied, he fled the room.

Rendiel drew his tarnished sword. "Not suspicious at all."

"After him," Cabdal hissed, the first words he had spoken

since leaving Ravaella's study. His eyes were intent on the fleeing necromancer.

"I'm guessing it's… not… the caretaker," Trenloe gasped as he got up, slipped on the blood-slicked floor, and ran after them.

The passage on the other side of the anteroom continued to branch, but the mage ignored every side-passage in favor of simply running. Trenloe saw the corridor's end. The necromancer, Vorakesh, banged between a set of doors and disappeared from sight. Trenloe growled out a last burst, more brute strength than genuine speed, and charged between the doors before they had a chance to close.

He slid onto his heels, Cabdal and Rendiel bursting in behind him.

The room was a dead end. The necromancer was trapped.

Vorakesh whirled. He gripped his wand so tightly that the fingerbones stuck out through the thinness of his skin. His smile could have been cut with a scalpel.

The room looked as though it had been used by the Academy for anatomical dissections. A wooden table large enough to hold an adult orc dominated the space. Bushels of dried herbs – sage, rosemary, and lavender – hung from the ceiling, peppering the sawdust on the floor with needles and sweetening the cool air with their scent. A number of large, open-topped barrels filled with body parts and rusty scraps of armor stood along the side walls.

"You think you have cornered Vorakesh," the wizard screamed, still panting and spraying his chin with spittle. "But you have only trapped yourselves." With his bloody wand, he traced the outline of a rune. It took less than a moment to complete and, when it was, the lines pulsed redly in the air before him.

He held out his free hand, palm turned upwards, and raised it towards the ceiling.

The nearest of the barrels trembled.

Trenloe spun towards it as a hand that looked to have been pieced together from the bones of twenty distinct individuals and five different species groped for the barrel's edge and drew a horrifically partial skeleton from its grave. The same red light as Vorakesh's rune flickered from the hollow sockets of its skull. A moment later, a second barrel disgorged a corpse of its own. Then a third, and a fourth, until they numbered more than thirty, their reserves of corpse-matter far from exhausted yet, drawing the cackling necromancer back into their still-growing ranks.

"I will send you all back to the First Flame as zombies!"

Trenloe heard the door close behind them.

Cabdal slid the bar across it and then, in a feat of strength that in other circumstances would have left Trenloe astounded, bent it back with a hard kick to the middle.

It would not open again.

The student turned, a smile breaking out across a face that was rapidly being drained of its color, taking instead the bloodless lilac hue of the Uthuk Y'llan. The smirk stretched into the cheek muscles until it accounted for half his face and all of its point-ended teeth. His limbs lengthened, strengthened, until he stood almost as tall as Trenloe, but wiry and lean like a dagger where Trenloe was broad. His robes became a form-fitting leather armor, red like the half-demon beasts of the Charg'r Wastes, and studded with what appeared to be human teeth.

Shrugging off the last layers of illusion like a snake loosening off its skin, he stepped the rest of the way inside. Only his venomous green eyes and his long topknot remained as they had been made to appear.

"I knew it!" Rendiel screamed. "I *knew* it!"

"Knew what?" Trenloe replied, but even as he spoke, he felt the blood draining away from his skin. Suddenly, he saw.

*Illusion…*

Ravaella!

He saw, but he didn't want to believe.

"What's happening?"

The man who had been Cabdal gave a tongue-flickering chuckle. "And to think that all this time I spent in my guise as a lowly student I was apprenticed to the First Flame of the Burning Lord herself. Her powers of deception are remarkable, would you not agree? Never once did I suspect. It is fortunate, though perhaps not for you, that I did not slit her throat as I wished when she woke me to serve you both tea."

"Boa," Vorakesh hissed.

"Skull." Cabdal dipped his head in greeting. "My true given name is Cabdal'aahi of the Viper Temple of Ynargal."

The Uthuk killer drew two wave-edged knives from the red slits that had been cut into the meat of his thighs to house them. Their hilts were snake-headed, a different colored gemstone for each eye. He sank into a fighting crouch and, remarkably, stretched his smile even wider. "A rising flame lifts all wings, and today the flame rises."

# CHAPTER TWENTY-ONE
## *Ravaella Lightfoot*

As Ravaella Lightfoot was being ushered into the grand forum for only the second time, and when Trenloe and Rendiel were entering the mortuary, Ravaella Lightfoot dismissed the illusory wall from the back of her room, turning the moonlit window into a door, and opened it. Ravaella Lightfoot, the real one, looked up from her work as she entered.

"How did it go?" she asked.

"I sent them to Vorakesh with Cabdal'aahi," she answered back.

Ravaella sighed and nodded, looking down into the pages of the open book in front of her. She rubbed her eyes, the words and illustrations blurring.

What was the true nature of illusion?

If you believed it, acted upon it as though it was real, then was it not real? If Vorakesh *assumed* that she had sent Trenloe and Rendiel to kill him and, in acting accordingly, forced her friends to do exactly that, then had she not, in fact, sent them to kill him? Was culpability for that murder his, hers, theirs, or was there blame enough to be shared amongst them all? She had managed to come this far without getting blood on her own hands. She looked down at them, ten slender digits and twice their number of rings.

Did that end tonight?

When Ravaella had been younger she had traveled around Trast with a troupe of gnomes (and an orc named Bragast who had been a surprisingly decent juggler) performing conjuring tricks she had taught herself. They had toured the villages for the holy festivals and feast days, building up to the Harvesthorn market in Artrast. They had not been especially good, looking back, but Trenloe had always been easy to impress.

She did not *want* to see him get hurt, or Rendiel. Perhaps that was the real reason she locked herself away in here while her proxies dealt with supposed friends on her behalf.

What was she supposed to have done differently?

Ravaella had felt the shadow that was rising in the east long before the baronies of Kell and Forthyn had fallen under it. She had seen the omens of the old power stirring anew in the Mistlands and found no one willing to heed a gnome's warnings of doom. Would the *right* thing to do have been to do nothing? No. She had power, and so she had used it.

Nerekhall was a city of mysteries and omissions, of sliding looks and secret handshakes, gentleman's agreements, backhanders, and outright corruption at every level of power. Magic was outlawed everywhere except the Academy itself, but everyone knew that it was practiced.

The city's underground was a crucible of arcane traditions from across the known world and from planes beyond it. They all made their pilgrimages to Nerekhall, sharing secrets, unintentionally enriching the esoteric lore of the city that would sooner cast them into a pit and burn them if it would only open its eyes and look. Terrinoth was at war and here, tangled in the web of rules and oversight that Nerekhall had spun around itself, existed the power to save it.

All she had ever wanted was to pull Nerekhall out of its self-flagellating malaise and let it stand again on its own two feet. Dark winds buffeted it from both the immediate north and the far east. With Kell and Forthyn fallen and Carthridge sure to topple next, it was Nerekhall where the storms would inevitably converge. It was Nerekhall where the fate of Terrinoth would be decided.

Ravaella had always known that people would get hurt. One did not overthrow a centuries-old regime and recall Margath the Unkind from his purgatory in the Aenlong without stepping on some toes. But, so long as it had all happened well outside of the Academy, to people with whom she would never come face to face, she had been happy to convince herself that their deaths were necessary tragedies in bringing about a greater good.

Lose herself in the work. That was the key. Focus on the larger picture.

But Trenloe…

She shook her head, angry at herself for doubting.

It was far, far too late to turn back now.

"What are you working on?" the other her asked.

Ravaella pinched the corners of her eyes and sat back, showing herself the enormous tome laid out across her desk. *Malrond the Elder's Compendium of Peerages, 999 to 1425.* It was so obscure a volume that the Academy library did not hold it and Ravaella had been forced to conjure a new simulacrum for the sole purpose of obtaining a copy from the courthouse library.

The title of the open page was *Baron Roland Dragonslayer, 1001–1029* accompanied by an elaborate illumination of a family tree in the form of a heraldic owl. Its feathered branches listed names, titles, and lands from hundreds of siblings, cousins, in-laws, and heirs. With half an eye on the page, she bent down to pick up the scabbarded sword she had left propped against the desk. It responded to her touch with a kind of hunger, and before she realized it her brushing fingertips had turned into a firm grip of the handle, the other hand migrating towards the middle of the ornate scabbard as though it had always been her intention to pull the blade free.

She let the sword go.

*Fascinating.*

Holding the page open, she compared the crosspiece design and pommel device to the illustrations of Roland's coat of arms. They were identical. She smiled to herself, excited enough by her discovery to forget about Trenloe and Rendiel and what must inevitably happen next.

"I knew there was something about you. From the moment you walked in here with Andira, I knew." With a brisk wave of the hand, she dismissed the simulacrum who had been watching with fascination from over her shoulder and looked up.

Baron Fredric of Kell was believed to have been slain at the Battle of Furnace Gate and had been succeeded by his daughter, Grace. The man who had been introduced to her as Owl sat in a plain wooden chair, restrained by shackles that only he could see or feel. A pair of small discs, exactly the size of his eyes and conjured from pure shadow, hovered directly over his eyes.

He could neither move, nor see – or at least he believed so

strongly that couldn't he had not even tried – but she knew that he could hear her. The tracks that his tears had left in the grime on his cheeks proved that. Having a foreign mind peeling away one's own delusions was a traumatic experience. Andira had intimated that the circumstances of his mental break had been exceptionally dark.

She regretted that, but it was necessary for him to remember.

It was *necessary.*

A piece of Margath the Unkind or a piece of the hero who slew him – that was all that the ritual to recall his spirit required. Of course, Margath and Roland had both died centuries ago and their remains were thought lost, but Roland's bloodline endured.

"The blood heir of Roland Dragonslayer, delivered to my very door. Do you wonder if Andira Runehand was perhaps right? It could only have been destiny."

*"Destiny is a lie."*

The voice from behind her was not her own. If old leather could have bent in such a way as to produce words, then this voice was how those words would have sounded.

Ravaella turned to look over her shoulder and dipped her head in acknowledgment of her master. She had been so absorbed in her studies, and he had been so cold-bloodedly patient, that she had not noticed his presence.

The white ragdoll cat stretched, and stretched, shedding the illusions that had permitted him to explore Nerekhall at will while she pursued their great work from this room. When the last of the magic was dispelled, the dragon hybrid stood three times her height, the spined back of his head scraping the room's high ceiling. His scales were a dark pink such as existed nowhere else in nature. His armor was the color of swamp water, but magnificently made, dragon-made, a gift from Margath the Unkind in the Elder Days, or so he claimed, to his most favored lieutenant. It was lighter, stronger, finer, than any armor ever worn by a hero of Terrinoth. The scythe in his man-like hand wept a poisonous pink cloud that stung Ravaella's eyes and induced Owl, Fredric, to toss his head and mutter the name *Acherax* over and over.

His name was Belthir, and he was ancient.

"This is not destiny," the hunched reptile croaked. "This is the reward of persistence after eight centuries of failure. Where the Dread crumbled, the Cult of the Rising Flame will succeed. *You* will succeed." He stepped closer, and placed a hard, scaled, and massively armored paw on her shoulder. His breath on the back of her neck felt like the open door of an oven. "They reject you. They doubt you. But my lord Margath will love you and lift you higher than all others."

Ravaella shivered in delight at the thought. "A rising flame lifts all wings."

The hybrid nodded its frill with a stiff creak of its muscular neck. A dry chirp vibrated from somewhere deep inside its throat. Ravaella thought it sounded like approval. "Yes. Yes, it will. Summon all of your ironbound, Ravaella. Send them to the place that Candlestick believes the door must be. I have spread word to my disciples. The time of Margath's return is now."

"What about Cabdal'aahi?"

"Leave him. With the loss of Acherax and Ne'krul's setback in Forthyn, he is no longer the friend of the Heath he once was. Hope only that he and Vorakesh kill each other."

And with Trenloe and Rendiel caught in between. Ravaella kept her doubts well hidden. She was *good* at hiding things.

She told herself that, even if they were able to deal with Vorakesh, and since she had unexpectedly gone and given Trenloe the Dampener there was a small chance they might, then they would still be far, far too late to interfere. That was all she wanted. That was enough.

Rising from her chair while Belthir watched on, unblinking, she hurried about collecting the arcane implements that would be needed to transport them to the Tower of Nerek, locate a stable portal to the Black Realm, fight their way through it, and recall the spirit of Margath the Unkind from the infinite dimensions of the Aenlong.

When everything was in hand, she returned to the last, most critical ingredient for the resurrection that she intended to accomplish.

"I'm sorry," she murmured softly in his ear.

It wasn't much, but she hoped it meant something.

With a snap of her fingers, she dispelled the restraints that had been holding him, leaving only the blinkers over his eyes. Belthir picked Fredric up and slung him over his shoulder as though the man weighed less than a child. He struggled, but against the hybrid's strength, he achieved nothing.

Ravaella snapped her fingers again.

And everything changed.

The time of Margath's return was now.

# CHAPTER TWENTY-TWO
## *Trenloe the Strong*

Cabdal'aahi had cut Trenloe three times before he had moved once.

His knives moved so precisely and with such speed that Trenloe hadn't even felt them break the skin. The belated sting yanked his shield up, but too slowly, as though he had attached weights to his limbs while the Viper had bound a spirit of air to his leather boots. Cabdal'aahi flowed backwards, laughing coldly as the hard, brittle fingers of the dead grabbed hold of Trenloe's axe-arm and pulled it back before he could answer the blows in kind.

The baleful red gaze of a chipped, age-browned skull glared over his shoulder. Trenloe yanked the arm free, the bare bone of the composite skeleton's fingers holding little purchase on the metal of his armor, and then threw the elbow back. The ramshackle skeleton's entire upper body collapsed under the blow.

"Kill him!" Vorakesh was shrieking from somewhere beyond his wall of undead. "Kill them all!"

Trenloe swung back towards Cabdal'aahi, but the assassin

had already slithered away from him. He and Rendiel had swept one another halfway across the chamber. The elf's much abused old rapier and the assassin's twin daggers clashed and parted with such blinding alacrity it looked more like a performance than a duel, spinning out shapes from colored metals to awe and dumbfound the skeletons that were trying, and hopelessly failing, to lay a finger upon either one.

Another skeleton groped for Trenloe. He beat it to pieces with a solid blow from his shield. A second made to grab him. He hacked through its wrist with his axe, then sent it flying into the shambling body of a third with a kick that shattered its ribcage and caused both of them to fall apart. The pieces twitched towards one another like the segments of a recently severed worm, drawn to one another by Vorakesh's necromancy. For some reason, they never quite came back together.

Trenloe felt the heat of the Dampener where it was pressed against his wrist.

He did not know what was going on here, or what he had unwittingly stumbled into. How had an Uthuk assassin managed to pose as Ravaella's student without her knowing about it? The things he had said about her being the First Flame of the Burning Lord made no sense but, from his and Vorakesh's talk of Margath it was clear they knew each other. And Augost. He did not understand how Ravaella had come to be tangled up in this plot. All he knew was that it was her stone holding Vorakesh at bay.

"Vorakesh is no one's minion!"

Bony hands groped Trenloe from all sides.

Trenloe struggled out of their grip, shaking a trickle of blood from his eyes, and pushed back against a sudden wave of dizziness. He had clearly lost more blood to the Viper's blades than he had realized. Either that, or the knives were tainted somehow. He had fought the Viper Legions of the Uthuk Y'llan before, and knew all too well their predilection for potions and poisons. The half-demonic creatures and tainted plant life of the Charg'r Wastes offered a near-limitless choice. The trio of cuts across his face and arms began to sting alarmingly.

With a roar that was as much fear as anger, Trenloe shrugged off the grasping attentions of Vorakesh's undead, and ran at the assassin.

Cabdal'aahi and Rendiel were fiercely engaged against the chamber's front wall, ignoring the mob of skeletons except to weave between and strike around. Trenloe did largely the same, smashing through the intervening corpses like a bull through a washing line. Cabdal'aahi snaked out of his path at the very last instant and Trenloe slammed headlong into the wall. He tore his head from the stone in a shower of mold-darkened bedrock as the Viper lunged back, turning the dagger thrust on a quickly raised shield and shoving the offending arm out wide.

The assassin's body was open.

Trenloe struck a blow that would have split the Viper from crown to groin had Cabdal'aahi not dropped to the ground as though there were no bones in his body, slithering around and delivering a backhand slash across the joint of Trenloe's knee. Trenloe gasped as the leg dropped from under him, plunging him straight onto the tip of the knife that Cabdal'aahi had sent to meet him. The blade slid neatly between two plates and deep into Trenloe's shoulder. Its wave-edge was designed for maximum cruelty and stuck fast.

Trenloe barked in pain, a split-second before an open fist to the chin staggered him backwards, putting him briefly onto the balls of his feet and into the path of a spinning roundhouse kick that smashed his head sideways through the nearest wall.

Trenloe pulled his head out of the stone. His eyes were on fire. The world was gray. He threw a blind swing that had his assassin bent near-horizontal to the ground and smirking as Trenloe's axe swept over him.

Pain, and in his terrified imagination something far more potent than just pain, pulsed from the knife in his shoulder. The arm hung limp at his side, the shield at the end of it a lump of metal, not really a part of him at all for all that it was attached to his body.

From the corner of his eye, he caught the dull red and gold of Rendiel's jacket as the bard was carried off in the tide of undead. There would be no help from there.

Cabdal'aahi bared his sharpened teeth, and drew another thin knife from yet another red slit in his flesh.

"I know all about you, Trenloe the Strong." The assassin emphasized the appellation with a sneer. "All the songs they sing of you. All the stories they tell. You hit like an Ynfernael grotesque, but the serpent is swift and hard to strike. Its bite is small. The death it brings unfelt."

Trenloe ran at him with a flurry of one-handed blows. Cabdal'aahi ducked, wove, danced, as though, instead of an axe, Trenloe had come to him with a skipping rope and a song. His expression never changed, the condescending smirk untroubled by the exertion. "My favorite tale of Trenloe the Strong is the Battle of Hernfar, how you single-handedly held the Lothan crossing against Blood Witch Ne'Krul." He delivered a swipe towards the jaw and this time Trenloe did not even try to avoid it.

The Viper was too fast. There was nothing to be gained by trying not to get hit.

He threw his shoulder into the knife and Cabdal'aahi hissed in annoyance as the weapon went spinning out of his hand, retaliating a split-second later with an uppercut that snapped Trenloe's jaw and his skull back onto his spine.

Trenloe staggered away, head spinning.

He made another lunge.

The Viper evaded it with contemptuous grace.

He swung back, missed by the width of the Cailn and stumbled, found the wall with his face and slid down it. His knees touched the ground and felt as if they might belong there.

With his axe still in his hand, he pressed it flat against his chest.

"Yes, Trenloe the Strong. Yes. Keep that giant heart of yours working. If you are lucky, the poison it is pushing to your muscles will kill you before I do."

Trenloe clutched at his heart and gasped for air. "Did… the songs… say how… the battle… at the Lothan… ended?"

"With Trenloe the Strong victorious, of course. With Terrinoth saved once again." Cabdal'aahi was close enough for Trenloe to taste the contempt on his breath. He pressed the point of his remaining knife against Trenloe's cheek. He leant in closer and hissed, "Is that not the way your songs always end?"

Trenloe gave his head an exhausted, almost imperceptible shake.

Cabdal'aahi tilted his head so as to better hear what song-worthy utterance Trenloe the Strong intended to make with his last breath.

"It ended… with everyone… who had believed in my legend… dead," Trenloe said. "And with… Trenloe the Strong… shot five times with Viper arrows."

His one good arm shot out.

Cabdal'aahi made a gristly, choking sound as Trenloe squeezed down on his throat, forcing the smirk from his face and turning it slowly white.

"The bards never sing that part."

Trenloe rose to his feet, effortlessly lifting the Viper one-handed and then, with a half-turn, all his frustrations rising out of him in one almighty roar of effort, he hurled Cabdal'aahi through the barred door. The doors buckled, tearing away from their hinges and crashing into the corridor beyond.

Breathing hard, still shrugging off skeletal fingers, Trenloe stumbled after him. He had been poisoned by the Uthuk Y'llan before and developed something of a tolerance to their toxins, but his exhaustion had not been entirely feigned.

Cabdal'aahi writhed on the fallen door like a serpent with a broken spine. At Trenloe's approach he went still, baring his bloodied teeth.

"I go willingly to death, Trenloe the Strong. I go with the knowledge that you were betrayed by one you trusted. Ravaella gave you the Dampener only so that you could kill Vorakesh, and so I could then kill you. That will please my masters in the Ynfernael. Enough, perhaps, that they will not immediately tear apart my soul."

He brought his knife to his own neck.

"No!" Trenloe yelled, as the Viper drew it across his throat.

Cabdal'aahi gurgled, still smiling, his eyes remaining on

Trenloe as they began to glaze. His head lolled to one side, eyes unblinking, and the assassin went forever still.

Trenloe slammed his fist into the floor.

What manner of upbringing did the Charg'r Wastes inflict on the Uthuk Y'llan that death and eternal damnation didn't seem so terrible? Andira would have walked away with a clear conscience, but he would never be Andira. The sheer waste of life infuriated him.

The click and rattle of bone drew his attention back to the room behind him.

A pair of skeletons had tottered after him through the remains of the door frame, making another handful of small strides before collapsing into a thousand different fragments and spilling across the floor. Trenloe coughed in the plume of grave dust and grit. As it slowly cleared, he saw that most of Vorakesh's skeletons had already fallen apart. A few were determinedly attempting to heed their animator's will and stagger on, swaying on feet that no longer possessed the strength to lift themselves up off the floor. One collapsed into a mound of osseous rubble as he watched.

Leaving Cabdal'aahi where he'd fallen, Trenloe got up and went back inside.

He found Vorakesh propped up against the dissection table, one hand on his heart and gulping for air. He looked even more pallid and drawn than he had before. He did not even look up as Trenloe approached, crunching over the litter of bone that had been strewn across the floor.

"He just… sat down." Rendiel stood over him. His bright clothing was gray with bone dust. He had his sword point held to Vorakesh's chest, though the necromancer showed no inclination to move.

It occurred to Trenloe that he hadn't told Rendiel about the Dampener. The elf had been out of the room when Ravaella had given it to him, which, in hindsight, may have been deliberate on her part. Explaining it now felt like more trouble than it would be worth.

"I'm not sure how to break this to you, Trenloe, but there appears to be an Uthuk sword in you."

Trenloe's good hand went to his left shoulder. He winced as it touched the golden snake-head of the knife sticking out of it. He wasn't looking forward to pulling that out.

"It's fine," he said.

"It looks nasty."

"It'll keep."

Trenloe crouched in front of Vorakesh.

The mage's eyes rose to follow him. "Had… Vorakesh… been at the full height of his… powers…" His gaze drifted inwards. "For centuries did Vorakesh seek the resurrection of Margath, a mighty ally with whom to drive his former master from the Thirteenth Barony and claim his rightful inheritance. Broken, diminished, he found his way to Nerekhall. It was the gnome who gave him this chance as caretaker of the Academy's mortuaries. He had no idea that she was the First Flame of the Burning Lord. If Vorakesh had only known…"

"I knew it," Rendiel muttered to himself. "I knew it all along. Rylan Olliven's books should've been burned when we had the chance."

"What about Tristayne?" said Trenloe.

"Tristayne was never here," Rendiel snapped. "It was my thought, and Ravaella encouraged it until we'd both agreed to come down here. It was Vorakesh all along." He shook his head bitterly. "This was all Ravaella's doing."

Trenloe wasn't ready to denounce his friend just yet. Not on the word of a Viper Legion assassin and a necromancer. Ravaella could have slain him herself if she had genuinely wanted him dead, or else turned him around in so much illusion he would never find his way back. Andira or Rendiel might have some defense against the sorceress but, without the runestone that Ravaella herself had given him, Trenloe would not have stood a chance.

There had to be another explanation. He refused to accept that there wasn't. He wanted to look her in the eye and have her explain to him what was going on.

"Let's go back. We need to talk to Ravaella."

"Wait," said Rendiel, gesturing to Vorakesh with his sword. "As good as that sounds, we can't just leave him here." He grimaced. "Just like Ravaella, leaving behind a mess to be cleared up."

Trenloe looked down at the beaten necromancer. He could not feel any anger towards him. Mostly, he felt tired and sad, a little lightheaded from the lingering effects of Cabdal'aahi's toxins in his blood. He didn't know if Vorakesh was technically still alive, but he was not about to just kill a man while he was helpless.

He rose with a grunt, another stab of pain shooting through him from the knife in his shoulder. "I don't think he's any threat to the city now. His own friends have seen to that."

The necromancer bared the rotten stumps of his teeth. "Vorakesh has no friends."

"Apparently," said Rendiel, and with a great show of reluctance slid his sword back into its sheath.

Trenloe turned to leave.

"Wait!" said Vorakesh.

He turned back. The necromancer looked up.

Trenloe wanted to believe that the look he saw in the mage's cold eyes was one of gratitude and, perhaps, of atonement. Trenloe had spared him where another might not and, so long as he was alive, could he not change for the better? "Vorakesh does not know the next stage of the others' plan. But he hopes it fails."

Trenloe nodded. It was equally possible that the only emotions the necromancer still felt were bitterness and envy and there was no hope left for him but vengeance.

But he refused to believe that.

"Come on, Trenloe," said Rendiel. Turning him by the shoulder, the elf guided him from the room. They stepped over Cabdal'aahi's pale corpse on their way out. "I know where we need to go from here."

# CHAPTER TWENTY-THREE
## *Andira Runehand*

"Do you know who I am?" said the voice.

*"Ask…"*

Andira did not know how long she had been left alone with her tormentor. It could have been minutes, hours, or days. As the voice had promised her when it had first welcomed her to the Tower of Nerek, it might as well have been forever.

The voice was different somehow.

"I asked you a question, Andira."

*"I can wait…"*

She shook her head and mumbled, "No," without opening her eyes. She did want to address the fact that she was speaking with an empty room. It was easier to be strong when she could entertain the notion that she had simply lost her mind. The demon of the Tower lost something of its power when Andira could confine it to her own madness. "No, I will not listen."

The very real sting of a slap across her cheek snapped her out of her determined denial.

Her eyelids leapt open, her hand going instinctively to the hurting cheek. The short chain between her ankle and wrist clanked taut. She grunted in pain, but not from the blow. Her eyes had been closed for so long that the light in the cell was like a gold ring, heated in a fire, pressed against each eye. They filled with water, blinding her as she looked up.

"You are going to listen to *me*," the watery figure in front of her snarled.

Andira blinked the tears away as her eyes adjusted. She had been expecting to be confronted by the demon of the Tower, a visual apparition to accompany the voice, and was shocked to find that the figure before her was not only real, but human.

The proud-looking woman knelt on one knee so as to examine Andira's face more closely. Her features were weathered. Her dark hair was turning to gray. The padded doublet she wore displayed the Grandmother Oak of Rhynn in Carthridge silver. To one who had learned enough obscure heraldries from many months traveling lonely backroads with Owl, the combination identified her as a lady of the unclaimed border regions of Roth's Vale. The ornate but well-worn silver hilt of a sword lay across her bent thigh, scabbarded in easy reach for the draw.

Andira listened for the voice. It was gone, or choosing to remain silent. She wondered if the imposition of the real world repelled it, forced it to withdraw until she was alone again, or whether it simply took this opportunity to watch, listen, learn.

It was patient. Or so it claimed.

She looked quickly aside, as if to catch its watching eyes from the corners of hers, and found that the gray-haired woman was not her only visitor.

Three children, two girls and a boy, stood against the wall behind her. The eldest of the two girls looked almost adult. The boy could not yet have been ten, but he looked as stern and unflinching as his mother. Andira intuitively considered all three to be the woman's children. They were all similarly attired, and there was a resemblance between them that went beyond the unfriendly expression they all held.

Watching from over the woman's other shoulder was Thaiden Mistspeak. He had lost his hat and his crossbow and was leaning against the door. It was shut behind him. The light from the corridor burnished his red hair with a kind of golden hue. He gave her a small, sorry smile before averting his eyes. As though nothing from this point on was any fault of his.

"Do you know who I am?" the woman said again.

Andira took a longer, steadier look into the woman's eyes. "No."

The woman looked disappointed, but it was the kind born of anger rather than sorrow. Her hand squeezed the grip of her sword as though in search of restraint. It seemed she found it, for she did not draw. Instead, she reached into a pocket in her doublet and withdrew a sealed envelope. It was bent, singed in one corner, but it was quite obviously the same one that Thaiden had delivered to her the previous evening. It must have been taken from her belongings with the rest of her weapons and armor.

"Perhaps if you had read my letter, you would, but no. The great Andira Runehand is driven by too high a purpose to trouble herself with that."

"I had intended to read it later, had we not been attacked."

"That is not what Thaiden tells me."

Andira glared across the woman's shoulder at the north-man. He appeared to be studying the crumbling stonework of the wall.

"Thaiden does not know everything," said Andira.

"He does not, and nor do I, but I know that you have not changed."

Andira brought her attention back to the woman. "Should I know you?"

The woman gave a bark of laughter. "I had heard you suffer from amnesia, but I would have thought you would remember that far. I am Dame Karol of Roth's Vale." She looked up, turning slightly in order to indicate the three children behind her. "These are my children. Isla. Izolde." She came last to the young boy. "And Hamma."

Andira felt as though she had been punched in the chest, a sudden inexplicable failure to breathe. Something that looked like grim satisfaction passed across the woman's face.

"I am Karol Brodun."

Sir Hamma Brodun had been Andira's first companion. She did not recall their meeting, for it was the earliest memory she had, surrounded by the fog of childhood. He had intended to kill her, she knew, for she had strayed into a crypt under his family's ward and he had assumed her to be a grave-witch intent on looting its treasures. It had been in that barrow, she had always presumed, where she had unearthed the rune, but why she had come to be there in the first place and how it had come to be bonded with her flesh were mysteries she had never resolved.

After her defeat of him, Hamma had bent the knee and sworn to serve her. He renounced his rank as a knight of Carthridge. He sold off his holdings to outfit Andira in arms and armor and gave his ancestral seat to the Church of Kellos. He had been a single-minded and ruthless warrior, but also a father-figure, a true believer, and a friend. Andira had always known that he had left behind a wife and family but he had spoken of them little, and Andira had thought of them less.

"Yes!" said Karol. "You remember *his* name even if you do not remember mine, the woman you left landless and impoverished when you stole her husband to join you on your *quest*." She hardened the final word, as though it was dirty and she was making a point by uttering it aloud in front of children.

"And so you join the Cult of the Rising Flame to punish me?" said Andira. "You brought me to the Tower to gloat over the destruction of Nerekhall while I am helpless?"

Karol leant back as though to examine the entirety of her. Her face was a curious mix of expressions, as though unsure whether to laugh out loud or hit her again. The elder girl, Isla, leant forward and whispered something in her mother's ear. Karol nodded.

"Yes. It would appear so."

"What did she say?" said Andira.

"She believes you have lost your mind. Warden Daralyn warned us that the Tower of Nerek can have that effect on some. She believes it to be the Tower's way of punishing those who cannot be properly judged for all the suffering they have caused to others. Seeing you now, I am inclined to agree."

"So, you are not with Augost?"

"The priest?" The woman looked insulted. "He did everything he could bar locking me in a cell to keep me from entering the Tower at all. As if he had the authority to stop me when Daralyn had already given her permission. I would have hauled him before the Archpriest of Vynelvale himself if he had tried to stop me at the gates. If the Cathedral was still standing."

Andira looked again at Thaiden, more purposefully this time, feeling her mind waking up to the urgency of the situation it found itself in. Something the priest had said to her on their way here, that she would see the light of the Rising Flame soon enough. Augost was part of something, and whatever it was planning, he clearly expected it to come to fruition here, and soon. That was why he had launched his attack on the Book Louse, and why Andira had been imprisoned so that she could not interfere.

The events surrounding her capture were still something of a blur, but she could only hope that Trenloe and Owl remained free. But Thaiden had been there, too. He had to know there was more at stake here than, what, a grudge? Because ten years ago Andira had taken this woman's husband and her wealth?

The northman was still not looking at her.

Andira tried again to raise her hand. When her shackles halted it, she tried to sit up. Karol held her down with a hand on her shoulder. In ordinary circumstances, Andira might have taken the woman by her wrist, thrown her through the wall, and then walked out through the hole she had made with her. Her strength was formidable, many times that of Trenloe's when the need called for it, but it was also passing and entirely beholden to her ability to command the rune she bore. Without it, she had nothing. Karol Brodun, meanwhile, had height, weight, and the lean power of a life spent battling the dead of the Vale in her favor.

"For ten hard years I thought you had simply disappeared

from the face of the world. In spite of this so-called destiny you claim to possess, there are almost no songs or stories of your deeds. It was only when I learned of Hamma's death in Kell that I realized that one of you, at least, was still alive." Karol shifted subtly to nod towards Thaiden. "So much has been lost in my part of the north. Thaiden and his gift are well known in the Vale. After ten years believing you dead, he found you in a month."

Andira wanted to laugh, but found it unforthcoming. "I fear you have chosen the worst possible time to visit the Tower of Nerek."

"The priest told me the same," Thaiden murmured. He still would not turn around.

Andira threw her back against the wall in frustration, making her chains clank.

"If you are not here with Augost then you are in danger."

Karol smiled down at her. "You really must be insane, if you think I could be convinced by such an obvious ploy."

"We are *all* in danger. If you are too bitter to care about your own life then so be it, but consider at least the lives of your children."

Thaiden finally looked up at that, but Karol flashed her teeth. She released Andira's shoulder, but only long enough to yank her sword from its scabbard. She pulled out an inch of gleaming, rune-inscribed metal before closing her eyes, muttering something under her breath, and sliding the steel reluctantly back into its sheath.

"Do you think my children are strangers to danger? Hamma may have given our lands to the Bishop of Rothfeld, but the Church needed someone to safeguard the barrows and to gather their taxes. So we were permitted to live in our own home, as long as we were prepared to fight. Every winter, the undead push further south and retreat a little less each spring. Baron Zachareth, at least, acknowledges the danger and sends us soldiers but we have little coin with which to pay them and few stay for long. Young Hamma here is eleven years old. He has wielded a sword to drive the dead from his home more than once. Isla has led the baron's counterattacks into the Vale many times."

The woman was practically screaming as she rose to her feet. Her knuckles were white around the grip of her sword, as though she was determined to draw it, only for some other force to counter her. "Where is this evil that is so much darker than that which my children have fought against since the day they could stand? Show it to me, Andira. I challenge you. Make me understand why you needed to take my husband all the way to Kell when Waiqar the Undying sits upon a throne not two hundred miles from the front door of my estate?"

Andira could only stare back at her, open-mouthed.

She had always known that Hamma Brodun had been a capable warrior and that men like him always had responsibilities. But she had never allowed herself to dwell on it. She had simply presumed that someone else would assume them when he left and that her purpose was the greater and naturally took precedence.

Andira rarely stayed in one place for longer than it took to crush whatever Ynfernael menace imperiled it and then move on. It tended to spare her the consequences of her actions, both good and ill. Defeating evil had always been of greater concern than simply doing good.

She wanted to tell Karol and her children of the creatures

that she and Hamma had slain together, the battles they had won and the lives that they had saved. She wished, too, to explain how Hamma had died, riddled with arrows but believing so firmly in her destiny that he had commanded her to leave him behind. Because he had believed that the Ynfernael was the one true evil that eclipsed all others.

Faced with the anger in Karol Brodun's expression, Andira found that those words would not come.

Instead, she found herself recalling the massacre of the villagers at Gwellan, shortly after she had left the town to pursue the suspected Daewyl, Greyfox. The leveling of Castle Kellar in her battle with the Dragonlord Acherax. The loss of Hamma and the rest of her followers. The scarring of Baron Fredric's mind and the destruction of his entire army when she had, against his protests, led them too soon into battle with Baelziffar. He had agreed to follow her to Furnace Gate only after she had coerced him, withheld the healing magic that would have allowed his wife to walk again until after the battle was won. After the battle, Castle Kellar had been ransacked by the Uthuk Y'llan and the Lady Renata, wheelchair-bound after the fight against Acherax, had fled the barony, while Owl had no recollection of any such bargain.

But she *had* won. Hadn't she?

Andira Runehand always won.

But what if Karol Brodun was right?

Had Andira really journeyed across Terrinoth to crush an evil in the east, only to allow another to flourish unchecked in the north? Was Carthridge crumbling before the legions of Waiqar and his lieutenants because *she* had left a crucial chink in its northern armor? She did not want to accept that it was possible, but why not? If she believed her actions to be a force for good, then why could they not be an equally potent source of calamity if applied without care? Did it matter that the Uthuk Y'llan had been denied Terrinoth if Waiqar was permitted to claim it in their stead?

She wanted to repudiate her doubts aloud but those words, too, refused to be found.

What did any of that say about her supposed destiny?

Karol was still looking at her, waiting for her to say something. Andira closed her mouth and looked away. She felt as though a stranger had come to show her that the rock her life was built upon was broken. It occurred to her that she could have listened more to Trenloe the Strong, and less to Hamma Brodun. Or, better yet, she could have thought harder for herself what kind of hero Andira Runehand was going to be.

Karol Brodun turned to Thaiden. "Summon the priest. Tell him that we will be taking Andira back with us to Roth's Vale to face the baron's judgment."

With a last look at Andira, Thaiden nodded. He turned and lifted the latch. The door rattled, but it did not open. The northman swore softly under his breath, and tried again. It did not budge.

"What are you waiting for?" said Karol.

"It's locked," Thaiden snarled, pulling ineffectually at the latch. "The priest has locked us in!" Giving up on the handle, he pressed his face to the hatch and yelled for Augost, threatening every physical hardship under the sun if he did not return to unlock the door.

He got no answer.

No, that was not entirely true.

If Andira closed her eyes and listened very intently then

she could just about make out the sounds of clashing swords and screams, and the mocking laughter of the demons that dwelled in the darkness behind a person's eyes.

It had begun.

# CHAPTER TWENTY-FOUR
## *Rendiel*

Rendiel had an appalling realization. He had not had a drink since last night.

He patted over his various empty pockets as he hurried out through the Academy's open gates and emerged, blinking, into the stabbing spots of light from the shop fronts across the way. It was impossible to judge exactly how much time they had wasted down in the library. The sun had risen, somewhere, but under heavy suspicion of cloud, while the previous night's drizzle had matured into a consistent rain that had drenched the city's skyline. Raising his lute above his head to shelter himself from the downpour, Rendiel squinted in what was still a discomforting level of brightness after the gloom of the mortuary.

He had not been this near to sobriety in years and he thought he saw why. The light was too bright. The colors were too sharp. His skull felt too big for his face. The smell of the river was making him ill.

"Hold it together, Rendiel," he muttered, and stepped fully into the rain.

To think: all this time, he had actually been right.

He had swallowed the lie that the shadow had passed without even realizing how it was poisoning his dignity. Rejecting it finally, after all these years, was almost as shocking as being sober. Tinashi the Wanderer who, much like him, had had nowhere in particular to go after the Ollivens' defeat, had pleaded with Rendiel to go with him when he left. Rendiel had refused. He had always believed it was because he had lost that spark that had sent him from Lithelin in the first place. He was no longer so sure. He was starting to wonder if he had stayed because of Ravaella. Because as long as she stayed, as long as Rylan Olliven's books had been unaccounted for, then their last adventure was unfinished.

The corruption was not over. The shadow had not passed.

He had stayed to keep an eye on Ravaella.

*Ravaella…*

He shook his head.

He had always known.

Trenloe emerged after him, bashing the door wide open with his broad shoulders and blowing like a warhorse after a battle. Rendiel had pulled the Uthuk knife out of his shoulder, over his protests. The hero had made a fuss of it and Rendiel had needed to play him the *Song of Elladan* just to make him calm enough to stand still. It had stopped bleeding now and looked almost as good as new. Following Trenloe out came a gaggle of servants, student mages, and library staff, all drawn by the disturbance in the undercroft and subsequently caught up in Trenloe's apparent sense of purpose.

*I'm just like them,* Rendiel thought, as Trenloe and his entourage stamped through puddles towards him.

"Why aren't we going back to Ravaella's study?" Trenloe shouted over the sound of the rain.

"If I'm right then she'll be long gone by now, and probably left an unpleasant surprise for us just in case we should come looking."

"We still don't know for certain that Ravaella knew Vorakesh was down there. Or that her student was an Uthuk assassin. I'm sure she can explain everything."

"Wake up, Trenloe." Rendiel was starting to get sick of this. "She deliberately sent us to kill off a rival mage and then sent her own student, an assassin disguised by *her* illusion, to deal with us afterwards. I don't disagree she has a lot to explain, but whatever she's involved in here, she's into it up to her neck."

Trenloe had a look that reminded Rendiel of an ox that was refusing to pass through the farmer's gate. "There must be other illusionists in the Academy."

Rendiel wasn't sure whether he pitied Trenloe's naivety or resented the kind of trust he had in his friends. He set off into the rain-slicked street and Trenloe, in spite of his protestations to the contrary, followed after him.

The shops around the Academy were open, but there was no sign of the usual crowds. In spite of the end of curfew, the streets were eerily empty. Rendiel had long ago observed that the average Nerekhall citizen had a sense for trouble that made the abilities of a Ghurish pathfinder or a Verdelam outrider seem amateurish in comparison.

Ten years was not nearly long enough a time in Nerekhall for Rendiel to develop his intuition to that same degree, but he knew enough to read the signs in the half-empty shops. He was seeing thousands of people conspicuous by their absence, sensing *something* about to happen and choosing to stay indoors and wait for whatever they could feel was about to happen, to happen.

Rendiel felt himself beginning to hurry.

"Where are we going?" Trenloe asked, struggling to keep up.

"To the Tower of Nerek."

"Why?"

"Do you remember how I told you that the Tower of Nerek had been built by the Daewyl?"

"Yes."

"Malcorne and his tribe, the Malcari, believed they could force their way back to the elves' ancestral homeland in the Empyrean, driving out and overthrowing the First who, they believed, had exiled them to the firma dracem under false pretenses. When the lords of the other ten elven factions failed to see things the same way, Malcorne decided he would need to find allies elsewhere and directed his followers to seek them in the Ynfernael. Thus the Malcari became the Daewyl. They carved out portals to the nether planes in dark places all over the world."

"Including here in Nerekhall," said Trenloe, rapt in spite of the beating rain and the hurried telling.

"According to legend. You've heard the tale of the damnation of Prince Farrengol, of course."

Trenloe looked at him blankly.

Human memories were so short.

"Farrengol was the son of Queen Riya and King Jerlon Penacor, better known these days as the King of Grief. One thing led to another, and the young prince eventually abandoned the Penacor court at Tamalir and found his amusement in outlawry, setting his camp in the region of Nerekhall which was largely swampland in those days. The Tower of Nerek was thought cursed and avoided even then.

On his eventual capture he was brought to the Tower by the Lord of Nerekhall, tried for murder and banditry and found guilty on all counts, but was spared punishment because there was no one willing to pass sentence on a Penacor. Farrengol spent that time in a garret cell where he and his fellows are said to have discovered the Daewyl portal to the Black Realm and made a bargain with the demon that dwelled there: freedom in exchange for the eternal fealty of Farrengol and his followers. When King Jerlon finally arrived to hang his son, the demon made good on his word. Farrengol, now Farrenghast, neither living nor dead, was soon back at his old crimes, raiding villages across Rhynn and Carthridge, and with even greater viciousness for having no fear of death or punishment."

Trenloe followed a step behind, silent for a moment. "Farrenghast, I've heard of."

"Well, before he became the Prince of Dread, he was one of the more usual kind, and it started here, in the Tower of Nerek."

"What's this got to do with Augost and Vorakesh and the others?"

*And Ravaella,* Rendiel thought, but chose not to add.

"If they're looking for the spirit of Margath then the Aenlong would be the place to find it. It's where the spirits of the dead roam before going to their rest, and if half of what is believed about Margath is true then he will have accepted no rest. The Aenlong is where he will be, and the easiest place in all the lands of the world to reach it is Nerekhall." Short of crossing the Charg'r Wastes and seeking out the Black Citadel of Llovar, of course, but Rendiel would not exactly call that easy. "How they intend to find him across the vastness of the spirit realm is another matter, but presumably they have found a way."

"But why the Tower?" said Trenloe. "Lidiya told me there are openings into the Black Realm all over Nerekhall."

"And we saw one. It was open for a minute, spawned a pair of demonic creatures that almost killed us both, and then disappeared. But think about it. The War of the Shadow Tear predates the Great Cataclysm and the coming of humanity to Terrinoth by thousands of years. If the portal that Farrengol is reputed to have found in the Tower of Nerek really *is* the one first opened by Malcorne then it would have been in place for at least two thousand years and is probably still there now."

"But no one knows where Farrenghast's cell was," one of the library students cut in, puppyishly following both Trenloe and their conversation. "I read that the entire wing was sealed off after his return from the dead. It's no more than a legend."

Rendiel gave the young mage a long look. After the incident with Cabdal, he was not feeling especially trusting. He turned back to Trenloe. "I'll wager Sanna's entire top shelf that Augost thinks he knows where to find it. Or, at least, that he's got a decent enough idea to point someone who can sniff out a Black Rift in the right direction."

"The modified ironbound!" Trenloe exclaimed.

*Rylan Olliven's books,* Rendiel thought, darkly.

"And this is the place they've taken Andira and the others?" Trenloe went on.

Rendiel nodded. "Whatever they have planned, you can guarantee it's happening soon if they've already started killing each other off and locking up heroes. That's why we're heading straight there now. Ravaella was always the sort to jump straight in and worry never. I'm afraid that she would not even have considered the possibility that Farrengol's demon is still there on the other–"

He came to a sudden stop, Trenloe and his collection of sodden-robed young mages piling in behind him.

"What–?" Trenloe began, but Rendiel shushed him.

His keen sense for the city's behavior was troubling him yet again.

They were at a crossroads. The rain drummed aggressively on slate roofs and canvas awnings but, as long as they avoided the very middle of the road, the tall, crooked shapes of the buildings kept them from being soaked. Wetness, like the city's Ynfernael taint, had become something they simply accepted. Rendiel shook the water from his hair with a vigorous rubbing of his hand.

But there was something else in the air besides rain. Something acrid and sharp. He could not place it. Rendiel bit his lip, feeling a trifle foolish with Trenloe and the others all watching him. He was about to tell them it was nothing and move on when the third story window directly above them burst out over the street.

A screaming woman went through it, plunging towards them in a deluge of glass.

One of the student mages, the one who had spoken earlier, brandished a runestone. Wrapping his tongue around the inhuman syllables of the Yrthwrights, he shouted the activating phrase that caused the stone to blaze with energy. The falling woman halted her descent immediately. Rendiel flung himself to one side as the shower of broken glass continued past her, crashing onto the path where he, and most of the young mages, had been.

What with the afterglow of the runestone, and the ringing

of falling glass, Rendiel barely registered the heavy thud of something *else* landing in amidst the broken glass.

It was as broad as Trenloe and almost as tall. Its muscles were sheathed in blue scales, its forehead swept back into a spined crest. Its huge body glistened in the wet, splinters of glass glittering amidst the scales like jewels in a suit of armor as it drove flailing students back from it with huge sweeps of a gigantic sword.

Rendiel was an elf, and purported to have an elf's reflexes, but the appearance of a small dragon in the middle of one of Nerekhall's wealthier districts was a shock. By the time he had his rapier quivering in hand, Trenloe had already split the creature's cranial plate with a crunching blow from his axe.

The brute slumped over the pavement, dead. Rendiel joined Trenloe in standing over it. It lay innocuously enough amidst the wreckage of the broken window as though, if enough rain were to fall on it, it might become just another thing that a passerby would not talk about.

For the first time in a long while, Rendiel could think of nothing to say.

"A dragon hybrid," the student with the runestone breathed, appearing between Trenloe and Rendiel and squatting down to poke interestedly at its wing. "I've seen illustrations, but I've never seen one in the flesh. A pity you couldn't stun it."

"You're not looking at an illustration now," Rendiel muttered.

"What's it doing in Nerekhall?" Trenloe asked.

"Everything turns up in Nerekhall sooner or later," said Rendiel.

"At least there's only–"

A screech, like that of a huge hunting bird, interrupted

whatever premature and ill-advised confidence that Trenloe had been about to express. Rendiel looked up to see a trio of muscular creatures flap across the sliver of sky before disappearing behind the rooftops. Each of them was as well armed, strikingly colored, and as massive as the one that Trenloe had just slain. Rendiel heard a scream from the street parallel to their own. And from further away still, the shiver of drawn steel, the shrill croak of what sounded like yet another draconic hunting call.

"This must be a…" Rendiel began, but Trenloe was already charging off in the direction of the nearest screams, yelling "*To me!*" and drawing the student mages willingly along after him. To Rendiel's gaping astonishment, even the nightgown-clad woman who had been thrown through her window, having just completed her magically slowed descent, had dusted herself off and was hurrying after the departing students. "… diversion," he finished miserably.

He turned to look over his shoulder.

It was not possible to *see* the Tower of Nerek, but he knew that it was there. You always knew it was there.

As terrible as Margath's return would be, it did not terrify him enough to seriously consider letting Trenloe head to the Tower alone. The Dragonlord could easily destroy Nerekhall and start another war, but it was the terror of Farrengol's demon that had sent him charging from the Academy the moment he had realized what Ravaella was about to do.

The demon had turned a dilettante like Farrengol into the Dread Prince. Rendiel did not want to see what would happen if it got its claws into Augost or Ravaella.

"Trenloe!" he screamed into the rain. "Wait!"

He was alone in the street. The creaks of the tenement rows

sounded like the patience of dragons. With a curse, he turned his back on the Tower and hurried after Trenloe.

If there was one thing that frightened him more than the demon, it was facing it alone.

## CHAPTER TWENTY-FIVE
### *Andira Runehand*

Thaiden Mistspeak had spent the last thirty minutes by the cell door, attempting to pick the lock using the lace from one of his boots.

Andira knew how long it had been because the zealots that had arrived to release their compatriots from the other cells had been able to sing the Hymn of Light twice through. The sound from the corridor was somewhere between a religious festival and a riot, a joyous smashing of anything wooden and breakable that could be found – chair legs, bedframes, slop buckets – all the while singing like celebrants at the Snowmelt equinox.

Karol Brodun stood warily over her with her rune sword drawn, but with half an eye on the door. Andira listened as the prisoners outside proceeded to stack wood up against their door. Thaiden grimaced and redoubled his efforts at the lock.

"What's happening?" said the younger of the Brodun girls, Izolde.

"It sounds as though they're building something," said Isla.

The girls were both unarmed, as was Thaiden and their

younger brother. Only Dame Karol, out of deference to her title, had been allowed into the Tower with a sword. Andira was determined to make use of that somehow.

"They are," she said.

Isla turned to her. "What?"

Andira gave her a cold smile. "They are zealots of Kellos. What do you think they are using all that firewood to build?"

Izolde moaned in fear. Her elder sister wrapped her arms around her and glared. Andira felt an unexpected pang of guilt. She had tried to be kinder since leaving Kell, but her nerves were frayed, and the old her was never far away.

There was a *snap* of boot lace.

Thaiden swore vehemently in a language Andira did not recognize as the metal aglet at the end of the lace sliced his fingertip. He stuffed the bleeding fingers in his mouth and gave voice to another, aggressively muffled, curse.

"You will watch your language," said Karol stiffly. "My children are present."

Thaiden drew his fingers from his mouth and spat out blood.

"This is a dwarf lock. Guild work. I can't pick this. Not with this anyway." He flapped the broken bootlace like a flag captured in battle. "If I still had my knives, it'd be another matter, but I don't."

Andira leant forward, shifting position in order to present her manacled left wrist. "Then let me take care of the door. The lock on my chains looks simpler."

Thaiden threw a cursory look her way. "I've only got one bootlace left."

"We are *not* setting her free," said Karol, firmly. She turned her attention to Andira, as though she might slip her chains if she was not watched constantly. "She will repay her debt to the Brodun family, or she will answer for it in the baron's court."

"You would rather die here with me just so you can watch me burn first?"

Karol licked her lips and looked uncertainly at her children.

Andira decided it was time to twist that knife. "I told you that you had chosen the worst of all times to visit the Tower of Nerek."

"After the door, what then?" said Thaiden, when Karol still failed to answer.

"Then I deal with the fools in the corridor."

"And then?"

Then, Andira intended to go after Augost, find out what he was up to and stop it. The demon that had been whispering poison into her ear since her arrival had clearly been long at work on the priest of Kellos. How else to explain his actions? Thwarting him, and it, was clearly the destiny that had drawn her to Nerekhall.

"If I remember correctly, there is a guard room at the end of the corridor."

Thaiden nodded.

"That is where they unfastened my armor and confiscated my weapons," said Andira.

"We are not going to rearm her with the equipment she stole from the Brodun family!" said Karol, but she sounded considerably less adamant now, as though hoping for someone to contradict her.

"You should be able to barricade yourself in there, or fight your own way to the main gate if you want. I will be going after Augost."

"We are not *leaving her*," Karol hissed, but so quietly now that even Andira barely heard it.

"Mother…" Isla began.

"I'll do it," said Thaiden.

The northman got up from the door.

"No!" Dame Karol swept up her sword.

There was too little room in the cell for a proper swing and Izolde and Hamma screamed as the sword struck sparks off the ceiling before sweeping back down. Somewhere, there was a part of Andira that had no wish to die and was afraid, but it was buried deep. Fear was a thing of the Ynfernael and permitting it only increased its power. She did not flinch as the blade came down, merely held the other woman's eyes as it hacked cleanly through the chain shackling her wrist to her ankle.

"No," Karol panted, as though she had already fought a lengthy battle and lost. "There is no time for that."

Andira brought her hand to her face. It was sleepy and stiff after being held still for so long. She wriggled the fingers, tested her grip with a fist and released it, enjoying the pins-and-needles sensation in the extremities as ice-blue runefire ignited across her palm.

She smiled coldly.

"I trust you will remember this," said Karol.

"Step back," said Andira.

She got to her feet, her focus narrowing on the door to the exclusion of everything else as she took the two short strides towards it and *punched*.

There was an explosion of force.

Her power had been shackled for so long. She had been beaten, bound, tormented by demons, and now she was free her frustrations boiled out of her in the form of far more power than the task demanded. The explosion obliterated the oak door and blew out a large portion of the wall alongside it. Unimpeded she stepped through into a corridor thick with dust and strewn with rubble.

A pair of coughing Kellosion zealots stumbled into view.

Their prisoners' rags had been dyed with the oranges, yellows, and reds of their new faith. Tattoos of dragons and flames encircled their bare arms. Augost's converts. They were both uniformly gray with dust. One of them had the wherewithal to swing his improvised wooden club at Andira.

She caught it in her left hand. The cultist snarled, straining his muscles, his expression turning to one of alarm as he realized that his weapon had not moved an inch in either direction.

The rune in her palm gave a sputter of force as she made a fist, crushing the club in her hand. With the same hand, she punched the man in the sternum. She heard his ribs crack. The man flew back from her, his body smacking into the stone wall behind him. And Andira was far from finished yet.

She drew more of the rune's power into herself until she shone like a new star at the heart of the pall, surrounded by a gleaming blue halo of flying dust.

The second zealot lunged at her. Thaiden roared from the ruined doorway and tackled him to the ground. Andira looked beyond them both. Dame Karol and her children were already advancing up the corridor as they had discussed. Andira could not see the woman clearly, but her runebound sword was an actinic flicker, like the first spasms of a storm in a cloud. Andira saw one fighter chopped down, then another. More surged towards the ghost shape of the knight from the distant end of the corridor. Beyond them, Andira could just make out the shape of the guardroom door.

With splayed fingers, Andira reached for it and focused. She pictured it overlain with her rune, mentally erasing lines and emphasizing others until it had the finished aspect that she intuitively knew that she required. She made a grasping gesture, wrenching the door from its hinges and then yanked back. The door flew down the corridor and slammed across the charging cultists' backs.

She marched on the guardroom.

Thaiden delivered another punch to the prone zealot's face and swayed up, kicking the man in the ribs for good measure before falling in behind Andira. She passed the Brodun children in the fog. They were searching the cultists' bodies for weapons. Izolde held up a ball-peen hammer and was testing its swing. They instinctively fell in, too.

Andira's power was in full blaze, destiny was on her, and even Dame Karol could not resist the singular authority of purpose it gave her. Sir Hamma had felt it, all those years ago, as many others had felt it since. As Trenloe and Owl had felt it.

The zealots pinned under the door groaned as Andira and the others walked across it and entered the guardroom.

The circular room was not large but, after being trapped in her cell with four others, it felt almost palatial. There was a lit hearth, a carpet, a rough wooden table surrounded by four upholstered chairs. There was even natural daylight and a window. The one guard gripped her sword and brought up her shield. The harsh glare of Andira's bound rune swam across the monstrous visage of her black iron mask.

"I will deal with this one," said Karol, stepping around her.

"No."

Gritting her teeth in effort, Andira pushed the power she had borrowed back towards the rune and punched it towards the guard. A ripple of force swept across the small room, smashing the table to splinters as though it had been hit by a cyclone. The soldier behind it was next. She intercepted the runic blast with her shield, but it was like trying to block a wave. It lifted her off the ground and smashed her into the shelving behind her. The various stored weapons rattled as the armored woman bounced off them and sprawled across the floor.

Thaiden planted his foot on her back. "I'd stay down if I were you."

Andira looked around, satisfying herself that there was nowhere for an unseen foe to hide themselves. There was only one other door, in addition to the one that Andira had destroyed, and that had been barred from this side. Presumably, Augost did not have the entirety of the Tower under his control. He needed to be certain that Andira and the Broduns would not be rescued before his plans were too far advanced to be stopped.

She smiled to herself as she spotted her armor and poleaxe. The former had been dismantled into segments and spread across a shelf. The latter was too large even for the spear-racks that the guards used for their own weapons and had been propped against a corner.

Now she was ready to make Augost pay.

She turned to see the Brodun children picking out weapons of their own and saw, with a twinge of conscience, that Dame Karol had not been overstating her family's situation in the north: even the young Hamma was evidently no stranger to the short sword he selected for himself. Izolde belted her hammer and took up a hand-axe. Isla took the longsword from the guard's hand to go alongside the small round shield she claimed from a rack.

"I trust you have taught your children how to armor a woman?" Andira asked.

Karol looked for a moment as though she was going to explode, then bared her teeth and nodded, gesturing for Hamma and Izolde to armor Andira as asked.

"What about this one?" said Thaiden. He jiggled his foot, rattling the mail coat of the woman under his boot.

The surest and most sensible course was to kill her and go, but in spite of that she found herself hesitating. If she really wanted to be better, to *do good* instead of simply destroying evil, then the only acceptable place to start was here, and now. She wondered what Trenloe would do, and sighed when it occurred to her how much extra work it was going to entail.

But it was right.

"Whoever released the prisoners from their cells must have had keys." Andira nodded towards the opening where the door she had destroyed had stood. "They will be back there with the others. Find them and lock them all in cells. This one, too."

The soldier laughed as Thaiden bent down, and pulled her back up. It was the hysterical, entirely humorless laugh of one who has been compelled to do so by a magic spell. "A rising flame lifts all wings!" she giggled, her voice made leaden by her mask. "The Burning Lord is coming and he will be *harsh* in his judgment of those who sought to prevent him."

Taking the soldier from Thaiden, Andira pulled the mask from her face.

Karol and Isla, who were standing behind her, both gasped.

The soldier's face was hideously burnt. From the appearance of it, and from the heat it was still giving off it had been done recently. "Brother Augost needed to test my loyalty and my faith!" she exclaimed. Her wide eyes stared from the blackened ruin of her face. "And he declared me worthy." Her voice rose in volume and pitch. "Worthy enough to stand before the Burning Lord!"

"What does Augost plan?" said Andira.

The woman laughed again. The sound gurgled in her throat. "You can't stop him. He seeks the Black Rift of Farrengol through which the Burning Lord will take wing and–"

Andira had heard enough. She knocked the guard out with a punch to the jaw. The woman went limp in Thaiden's arms who offered a nod of respect. One professional to another.

"Deal with her," said Andira. "It will take some time for me to get into my armor."

"And then?" said Thaiden.

Andira turned to glance over her shoulder. Dame Karol and her children stood armed and ready. She wondered what the right thing to do here was, and if there was such a thing when a corrupted priest with an army of zealots intended on opening a doorway to the Black Realm.

Andira knew all about the story of Farrenghast. She knew about his garret cell, and the demon that had supposedly granted him his unique form of unlife. She knew that it was as much myth as historical fact, that mages, historians, and custodians of the Tower had spent centuries in search of it, but none of that was to say that it *could not* exist. She thought of the voice.

She turned back to Thaiden.

"And then… I want you to find something for me."

# CHAPTER TWENTY-SIX
## *Ravaella Lightfoot*

The teleportation bubble popped, shedding the illusion of shelf-lined walls and depositing Ravaella, Fredric, Belthir, and five reptilian warriors in full plate armor on a patch of muddy ground. It was as close to the Tower of Nerek as she could get them. The castle was heavily warded. Ravaella could not even be sure *how* heavily. The churches of both Kellos and Pollux had worked hard to fortify it against any form of magical incursion or escape, and kept the nature of their defenses secret even from each other. Before setting herself the task of breaching them, she would have found the idea of a physical obstacle to her will laughable. It was simply a matter of imagination.

And yet here she was, and here they all were.

The Tower loomed over her, a castellated lump of stone hunched under a cloak of rain, lording over a field of weeds like a troll with no bridge to hide under. She had read that it had been raised in prehistory by the Daewyl. Indeed, much of what the Cult of the Rising Flame hoped to achieve was predicated on that thesis. But there was no elven beauty to the construction, only the stark, angular ugliness of a thing that had been built to defy her.

She had no idea what was going to greet her on the other side of those walls. Her ability to access the Turning would be compromised by the castle's defenses and she expected to be wholly dependent on Belthir and his warriors for protection. She had foreseen this and had thought to find the relative vulnerability thrilling. Now that the moment was here, however, she was terrified, her muscles refusing to participate in a single further step towards the Tower's gates.

Knowing full well what had become of Vorakesh and Cabdal'aahi once they became dispensable, she wondered if her anxiety was not well founded. She consoled herself with the knowledge that Belthir had thus far proven himself less ruthless than any human conspirator in his place.

She thought again of Vorakesh and Cabdal'aahi.

Of Trenloe and Rendiel.

Of Fredric.

Less ruthless than *her*.

Belthir craned his neck back to take in the full height of the Tower. Translucent membranes flickered back and forth across his golden eyes. Instantaneous travel made most people queasy. Something to do with fluids in the ear. But the dragon-hybrid seemed indifferent to the change of scene.

"For a city so fearful, it is complacent. It leans too much on its iron dolls." Stiff lips peeled back from gums into something approximating a smile. "Its soldiers chase my followers across Nerekhall. By the time they realize the danger is here, it will be too late. Margath will be arisen and a new Age will have begun."

Ravaella shielded her eyes against the rain and joined him in looking up at the Tower.

It rang like a tuning fork to the screams of the city all around them.

No, that was wrong: it had screams all of its own.

The hybrid warriors gave a warning chirrup, too low almost for Ravaella to register as sound, and gathered protectively around Belthir. A group of soldiers in the livery of the Tower had exited through the open gate and were charging down the dirt path towards them. They had an ironbound with them. It had a longer stride than any of the soldiers around it, walking as they ran. The runes engraved into its black armor smoldered like the ruinous marks left by demonic claws in metal. They hissed in the rain, stinging Ravaella's eyes even from afar.

She tensed instinctively, gripping Fredric's arm tightly and drawing him close so that he was standing between her and the war machine. He flinched at her touch, turned the shadowed discs of his magically blinkered eyes towards her, mumbled something she could not catch to someone who was not there, but did not attempt to pull away.

She may not have had her spells to rely on, but she still had the one means of summoning Margath in her power and she intended to keep it that way.

The Tower soldiers came to a halt a few strides short of the hybrid warriors. The ironbound steamed in the rain.

Brother Augost stepped out from their front rank with a look of rapture on his wide face before sinking to his knees before Belthir and his warriors. His bare flesh glistened in the wet, his red skirt sodden and clinging to the meat of his enormous thighs. The bunch of candles swinging from his belt, however, sputtered furiously in spite of the rain. As though a threat against which to rage was all that was needed for a fire to burn hottest.

"First Flame of the Burning Lord," he said, face upturned as if to the sun. "It is my honor to meet you in person at last."

Belthir chirped. He seemed amused. Ravaella had become somewhat adept at reading the reptile's moods.

"I am but a servant," he said.

"Then..." Augost took in the other hybrids, dismissing them at once before turning to Fredric. He lowered his gaze slowly until it was resting on Ravaella. "Surely not."

It would have been a simple matter for Ravaella to make herself appear other than she was. Literally a snap of the fingers, and she could be an elf, an orc, a man or a woman. Her life might have been easier if she had, but who wanted an easier life if that meant acquiescing to the stupidity of others? Where was the satisfaction in rubbing their noses in the wrongness of their collective thinking?

Her rejection from Greyhaven, for the disqualifying sin of being a gnome, had wounded her, but the experience had been formative. Being overlooked and underestimated had become her power. It was illusion, but without the effort.

Rylan Olliven had been the last person in Nerekhall to aspire to true greatness. He had been the Chief Artificer of Pollux and there was power in high status. Since then, however, there was also an unwelcome degree of scrutiny that anyone seeking real power in Nerekhall was wiser to eschew.

But oh, did she yearn for the day, the hour, the second, when she could stand tall as herself and *make* this city see her!

Ravaella. Their savior.

It would feel exactly like the look on Augost's face made her feel just then.

"Rise, Candlestick," she said, and smiled, feeling the fear loosen its grip on her as he obeyed without question. "Is the Tower under your control?"

"It is, First Flame. As you requested, I have done what I can to ensure that only your modified ironbound and guards loyal to the true cause were on duty."

"And all goes to plan?"

"It does, First Flame. We await only you…" He looked again at Fredric, his face caught between awe and contempt, as one would behold a relic that had been used to smite an avatar of their god. "… and the Dragonslayer's heir."

Ravaella gestured towards the open gate behind them.

At the perceived command, the ironbound that the soldiers had brought with them gave an acknowledging blast of steam and about-turned.

"Then let us not waste another moment, Candlestick. Let my ironbound guide us the rest of the way."

# CHAPTER TWENTY-SEVEN
## *Thaiden Mistspeak*

"Up the stairs," Thaiden barked, throwing an arm out to indicate the alcove concealing a small stairwell going upwards.

"Are you certain?" Andira asked.

Thaiden bit back his preferred response.

Yes, he was certain.

The only thing that he was presently *uncertain* about was why he was helping her at all when he could be helping himself to the way out. Ever since their departure from the guard room he had been able to feel himself leading them further and further into a corner. There were fewer and fewer decisions to take. Every staircase he took led up.

Andira had been held in one of the highest wings and eventually they were going to find themselves with nothing above them but the roof of the Tower. Where were they going to run then? Into the Black Rift? He told himself not to think about it. It was someone else's worry, like always.

"Get on the stairs before I change my mind," he snapped.

Karol Brodun poked her head into the stone cubby and

looked up. Satisfied it was clear, she ushered Isla, Izolde, and Hamma ahead of her, before following herself. Andira went next.

Thaiden halted halfway down the corridor, turning so suddenly that his green cloak snapped out as though determined to reach the stairs with or without him. The sense of something *out of its place* tingled down the back of his neck as he slotted a bolt into the crossbow he had 'borrowed' from the guards. The weapon was bigger than the one he was used to, demanding more strength and time in the draw.

It was meant for killing people.

Andira turned back and shouted, "Thaiden! I need you with us."

*Damn right, you do.*

"Right behind you."

Half a breath *before* the Tower soldier appeared under the arch at the end of the corridor, Thaiden loosed his bolt. He had not had time yet to get used to the bigger weapon's kick. It pulled his shot high and wide, drilling the steel bolt through the man's shoulder rather than into the big square target of the breastplate that he had been aiming at.

He cursed himself as the man cried out, the sound of his pain deadened by the iron mask he wore, and slumped to the ground across the archway. He was fully tempted to walk back down there and kick him until he was sure the message had gotten through: *this is what you get for locking children up in gaol cells and setting them on fire!* He shook off the urge, lowering the aim of his crossbow and backing away just as the rest of the squad clambered over their wounded comrade and came clattering into the corridor.

He bared his teeth. He could take them.

"Come on!" Andira yelled, her voice arriving like a slap to the face.

Thaiden spat on the floor and raced after her.

One and a half turns and he was at the top of the stairs. A darkened suit of armor greeted him at the landing. His heart lurched before he realized that the suit was an ordinary human-sized harness and not moving. It was an antique, not an ironbound. With a snarl, Thaiden pulled the suit off its stand. It clashed and clattered down the stairs behind him. Thaiden listened with considerable relish to the panicked cries of the soldiers it went through.

That should buy them a moment or two.

They had come to a small, circular chamber of gray-white stone with thick supporting columns and tall, arrow-slit windows situated high up in the walls. Weak morning sunlight and a thin rain spattered through. After the dash through the Tower, the freezing rain was welcome against his skin. It reminded him of home.

Then he did think of home, and he took no more pleasure in the rain.

"Which way?" Karol Brodun demanded, and Thaiden had to bite his tongue to keep himself from barking back.

Identical-looking doorways led off the landing to left and right. Another small staircase continued up. The stairs would be the obvious choice, but his intuition rejected them out of hand.

He could not have explained, even to himself, how he would go about locating a thing he had never seen and that no one could describe. It was a sense, that was all. A feeling. The conscious act of tuning his mind to the thing seemed to be enough. Like showing a scent to a dog, or releasing a messenger bird that intuitively knew its way home. Something in him just *knew*. And more, he had the distinct feeling that the closer he got to the portal Andira was looking for, the more it *wanted* him to find it.

What had he promised himself about not getting involved in Andira's mess?

"Left," he grunted.

Andira swung left and marched through the doorway, scuffing out the faint footprints in the dust. Karol followed a step behind, her shimmering runic sword held possessively over the other woman as though she was shepherding her through an angry crowd. It was obvious why the Broduns were still here. They were staying because Andira was. Thaiden wondered if that was why he was still here, too. For the Broduns' coin. He preferred it to the unsettling notion that he might just be here to save Nerekhall.

At full stride, the corridor lasted Thaiden a handful of seconds before throwing him out into yet another small chamber.

It was similar to the one before except for being semi-circular as opposed to a full circle. There were no doors except for the one that they had entered by and windows only along the curved outer wall. The spot where a flight of stairs might have been, assuming the layout corresponded to that of the previous room, would have been on the other side of the stone wall cutting diagonally across its middle.

A room that existed for absolutely no discernible reason was not inconceivable. This was a very old castle, after all, built millennia ago and rebuilt and repurposed many times since. Thaiden might even have been convinced, were it not for the huge, roughly human-shaped outline that had been knocked through that false diagonal. Dust hung thickly in the air around it and was still settling, suggesting that whatever had gone through had done so very recently.

"It must have been one of the ironbound," Karol breathed. "The size looks right."

"If they were created to fight the creatures of the Ynfernael plane then perhaps they are able to divine the same power emanating from the Black Rift," Andira mused. "That must be how Augost and his followers intend to find it."

"Why now?" said Karol. "If it really is this Black Rift that Augost's guard spoke of then it must have been here for centuries."

"I do not know," said Andira. "And I do not see that it matters. We are here now." Andira stepped through the breach in the wall.

Karol and her children followed after only a moment's hesitation, but Thaiden lingered. He was not sure where else he thought he might go, but the knowledge that there was at least one ironbound waiting for him on the other side made him uneasy. He cursed himself again for allowing himself to get caught up in this. He could have been halfway to Jendra's Harbor by now.

Taking a handful of cloak to mask his face from the dust, he stepped through.

The other half of the chamber was dusty and abandoned. Isla Brodun was coughing uncontrollably while her brother, Hamma, held her hand and thumped her back. Karol was wafting her hand to clear the air. The outlines of windows stood out from the wall. They corresponded exactly to where windows should have been, but had been bricked over. Whoever had ordered the work must have hired Latari masons and sourced the same strange, dark stone as the Tower of Nerek's oldest sections were built from. Thaiden could not imagine why anyone would go to such effort unless they had a portal to the Black Realm to hide. He wondered where they were in the castle and what it looked like from the ground.

The partition wall and the absence of windows made the room dark as well as close. The strongest source of light was coming from Andira's blueish aura. She held her hand up like a lantern to illuminate the entrance to another stairwell. It led upwards.

"What are you waiting for?" said Thaiden. "There's nowhere else to go."

"I know this stair," Andira murmured to herself. She extended her glowing hand into the stairwell, bathing a short flight of steps in blue light. "I have seen it a hundred times, but I have never climbed it."

"Is that some kind of riddle?"

Andira turned back to him. Thaiden recoiled. Her pupils had swollen to the point that they filled her eyes completely. There was a glazed look to them that told Thaiden that Andira Runehand was no longer entirely present. Her eyelids flickered occasionally as though she was dreaming, although her eyes remained open.

"No," she said, her voice husky and deep. "A vision."

"A vision of wh–"

A crossbow bolt shot through the breach in the partition wall before he could finish. It missed Thaiden by a hair and ricocheted off the stone wall behind his back. A second *thunked* into Isla's shield. Soldiers roared as they charged in through the pall, black iron masks and sparkling blue dust turning them into monsters. The clangor of wood and steel rang out as Dame Karol and Isla rushed to defend the breach.

Thaiden dropped to one knee to crank a bolt into his crossbow. They had a wall and a narrow point of entry: the Broduns should be able to hold off the Tower's soldiers and once they made the top of the stairs, they would have an even more defensible position to hold. At least until the ironbound arrived. He just hoped that Andira had a plan for them when they got there. Something better than escaping one of the most feared militias in Western Terrinoth by jumping into a Black Rift.

"Andira Runehand!" came a shout from the other side of the pall. Thaiden recognized it as belonging to Brother Augost. "Is that really you in there, Andira? When you first came to me to demand I release your friend, there was a part of me that admired you, but I fear that you are quite irredeemable. You have no idea how bad you are making me look to my partners in the Rising Flame."

Thaiden glanced back to the stairwell and cursed. He was not sure whether it was Augost and his army of zealots or Andira Runehand that was currently worrying him more.

"What is my name?" Andira murmured, in a voice that was no longer her own, and promptly collapsed on the stairs, unconscious.

# CHAPTER TWENTY-EIGHT
## *Trenloe the Strong*

Two dozen Tower guards and former prisoners stood in front of the Tower's gates. The prisoners were decorated with flaming tattoos and the brand of Kellos. The soldiers had orange ribbons tied around their arms. They had to be the Cult of the Rising Flame. Trenloe still could not make himself think of it as *Ravaella's* Cult of the Rising Flame.

At the sight of Trenloe, and the mass of bodies charging up the dirt path behind him, they started running back to the gates.

The citizens of Nerekhall brandished their poles, pitchforks, hammers, and knives and roared as they surged ahead of Trenloe, running through the tall grass either side of the path.

Stopping at every other junction to save another group or family from a dragon hybrid attack had made the long trek across Nerekhall ten times as hard as it might have been, but if the alternative had been leaving them to the Cult's soldiers, then he knew he had chosen right. It had not escaped his notice that the attacks were a ploy to delay them.

Rendiel had pointed that out once or twice. But he was here

now, and the more he had begged the people of Nerekhall to go back to their homes and leave the Tower to him, the more determined they had been to follow him.

Deyan, the self-appointed leader of the Academy students, made a fist and pointed it towards the startled Cult soldier. It flashed as he uttered a mystic phrase and a bolt of lightning leapt from the runestone in his hand. The bolt struck a soldier in the chest and hurled her back.

Brost, a milliner that Trenloe had pulled from a housefire, clubbed the woman unconscious as he ran past. The old woman, Paleese, leapt over the body and swung a stolen dragon's battle-axe at an orange-robed prisoner. The spectacularly unwieldy weapon thudded into the turf a yard shy of its mark, but several dozen of her fellow citizens were already rushing in, dragging the cultist down and clubbing him senseless.

"Trenloe!" they cried as they clubbed, stabbed, and bludgeoned their way through the routed cultists. "Trenloe the Strong!" or occasionally, "Companions of Trenloe!" all to the fevered accompaniment of Rendiel's lute.

"Only you could take Ravaella's attempt at a delay and somehow use it to build yourself an army," the elf marveled as he followed in Trenloe's wake.

Trenloe strode towards the gates. He was big and slow, encumbered by armor, tiredness, and a not-insignificant dose of Viper Legion poison. The charge of his citizen militia had cleared a path most of the way to the gate by the time he arrived.

The gates were closed but the postern door was still open. A pair of heavily armed and serious-looking soldiers were holding the opening for their cultist brethren streaming past.

Trenloe was a human battering ram. He knocked both soldiers down with a shoulder barge, leaving them flat and dazed as he forced his way into the courtyard.

Half a dozen cult soldiers held it, reinforced by frothing prisoners too rabidly in thrall to Augost's promise of a fiery redemption to surrender. The guards had turned over a table which two crossbowmen were sheltering behind. The moment Trenloe bracketed himself inside the postern, they loosed.

Trenloe was too big a target to miss. Both bolts slammed into his big metal shield and punched through. Trenloe jerked back as one flattened point erupted an inch from his face.

He lowered his shield.

There was a moment's lull as both sides appeared to consider the other. Trenloe could almost see the guards across from him dwelling on the choices that had brought them here, reliving them, ruing them, concluding that their faith in a fallen priest had left them with little option but to fight and pray.

Trenloe roared as he started across the courtyard, in no way *fast* but with an inevitability that said he was going to get there regardless of what any cultist had to do or say about it.

A swing of his shield demolished the upturned table without him breaking stride. The crossbowmen fell back with cries of panic as though a giant had been released into their midst. Cultists rushed in from both flanks to swamp him, only to find themselves pulled away in turn as Trenloe's allies, exhorted on by Rendiel, came screaming through the undefended door. The courtyard descended into a score of desperate melees.

A soldier threw himself at Trenloe with a wild, overhead lunge. Trenloe bashed the sword aside with his shield.

The soldier retreated behind his own shield like a tortoise. Trenloe snapped it in two with a kick that left the man flat on the ground and six yards back from where he had been standing.

A second rushed him from the side before he could catch a breath. Trenloe ducked behind his shield as she thrust over the top with her polearm. The wooden pole scraped across the metal as he braced his shoulder and shoved, lifting the woman and slamming her into the wall of the Tower. Ancient Daewyl masonry rattled off the angle of his shield as the soldier slid off.

A blood-curdling yell from behind caused him to crane his neck around. A cultist zealot was half a stride away from him, a kitchen cleaver poised to sink into the back of Trenloe's head. It never fell.

The man coughed up a welter of blood and collapsed where he was standing. Rendiel drew his sword from the zealot's back, looking around for something to wipe it on before eventually settling for the dead man's orange rags.

Trenloe did not want to thank someone for taking a person's life, but he nodded his gratitude, nonetheless.

"On your feet, Trenloe," Rendiel said. "We're still only halfway there."

Trenloe looked up and nodded wearily. He could scarcely believe how the elf had changed since their first meeting in this very place. Was it really the same Rendiel who had wanted so little part in this that he'd allowed a rogue ironbound to escape rather than get involved? Or was it the bard who'd helped save Nerekhall from the Black Realm all those years ago?

Trenloe could believe it.

Accepting Rendiel's helping hand, he pushed himself back off the courtyard wall.

The last of the cult soldiers was fleeing the courtyard. The crossbowmen disappeared through a doorway into the castle and pulled the door shut behind them. Trenloe heard a lock being drawn into place, moments before the pursuing mob slammed uselessly into the iron-banded wood.

Trenloe took a deep breath and let it go in a sigh. He had lost track of the number of doors, walls, and people he had knocked through since arriving in Nerekhall. He prayed to every minor deity and spirit he could name by heart that this would be the last.

He drew back a pace, then one more, giving the sturdy-looking door the acknowledgment of an extra yard's run-up, and then charged.

The civilian militia scattered like chickens before a runaway cart. Trenloe dropped his shoulder for the final stride, slamming into the door at full tilt and tearing it clear off its hinges.

The sound of it crashing to the floor at his feet echoed down the narrow corridor.

The fleeing crossbowman was halfway to the end. He turned at the crash and screamed. He threw his crossbow to the ground and fled down the corridor. Trenloe let him go. His shoulder ached. His calves were burning. If the man didn't want to fight anymore then Trenloe certainly wasn't minded to make him.

The corridor he found himself in was narrow and low-ceilinged with half an eye on defense. Rusted grates covered murder holes that no longer appeared in use. Crumbling arrow loops bloomed with mosses. Guard rooms from which soldiers would have once sallied to fall on an intruder's flanks had been converted into gaol cells, their narrow doorways fitted with iron bars.

"Thank Pollux!"

A tall elven woman appeared at the other side of the bars. She was dressed in the black doublet and mail vest of a Tower guard, but with golden thread worked into the doublet and more elaborate heraldry on the surcoat. She wore no mask, her anger perfectly captured by the abundance of torchlight in the corridor.

"Whoever you are, you have my thanks for running off those traitors."

"Who are you?" said Trenloe.

The elf struggled to remain patient. "I am Warden Daralyn, the commander of the Tower of Nerek, so if you could hurry up and let me out of this cell I would very much like to retake my Tower."

Trenloe looked past the warden. There were no torches on the inside of the cell, but Daralyn's shadow concealed several dark shapes.

"Trenloe!" one of them exclaimed, rushing the bars at Daralyn's side and pushing thin arms through the gaps between. Lidiya's pale face appeared in the torchlight as she beamed up at him. "I told Sanna you'd come for us."

"She did," came the orc's low grunt from somewhere in the shadows.

Wincing at the tired ache in his thigh, Trenloe lowered himself to one knee. The space between the bars was too narrow for him to give the girl the hug she wanted, so he wrapped his massive fists around her hands and gave them a reassuring squeeze.

"I was here with Chief Artificer Ermhilt to interrogate

the prisoners from the Book Louse disturbance," Daralyn explained. "Then Brother Augost locked us both inside and set the guards to releasing all the prisoners. I think he's gone mad, started hearing voices. The same thing happened to my predecessor."

"Have you come to get us out?" Lidiya asked.

The question broke Trenloe's heart. It tore him up to even consider leaving her and the others in their cell, but Andira would have wanted him to go on. Somehow, he knew that she *needed* him to go on. He took a hold of the bars and tensed his arms and shoulders, testing how their strength fared against his. They did not give even a little. He let go and shook his head. Deep down, he knew that they were safer here behind a locked door than they would be anywhere else in Nerekhall just then.

"Wait here." He gave her hand a parting squeeze. "I'll be back for you soon, I promise." Getting back up to his feet, he turned to Daralyn. "There are more people behind us. Talk to them. One of them will be able to find the key to this door." It would be better for everyone if his citizen militia remained with the warden while Trenloe and Rendiel went on. Securing the gate and ensuring no more cultists got in or out would be useful enough. "I need to go after Brother Augost."

Warden Daralyn set her jaw but, to Trenloe's surprise, nodded her understanding. "He returned shortly after locking us in here, told me he had found Farrenghast's cell and was going to use the Black Rift there to speak to someone he called the Burning Lord. There was…" Here, she paused, glancing over her shoulder to someone that Trenloe could not see. On the basis of what she said next, Trenloe assumed it was Chief Artificer Ermhilt. "There was an ironbound with him. And a gnome woman, dressed as a mage. An older human man who looked like one of those landless knights from the eastern baronies you see around Nerekhall these days. And… and some kind of dragon."

"More hybrid soldiers," Rendiel murmured softly.

Trenloe didn't know how long the elf had been behind him but he had chosen, apparently, to make no further comment on the apparent complicity between Ravaella and the rest of the Cult of the Rising Flame.

"We've seen them," said Trenloe.

"Not like this one, I assure you." Daralyn shuddered. "I didn't start my career as Warden of the Tower. I've fought hybrids in the sewers, and in the elven ruins in the marshes. This one was some kind of leader, and the largest I've ever seen by far. Be careful if you plan on pursuing him any further into the Tower."

# CHAPTER TWENTY-NINE
## *Andira Runehand*

*"What is my name, Andira?"*

She felt her way in the dark. There were other objects and people around her, bumping into her, calling for her attention, but they felt unreal to her. It was as though she had woken from a dream in the dead of night and could not now find her way to her bedchamber door. Her hand touched the corner of the stairwell. She grasped hold of it, heartened by its solidity as she looked up. A patient gulf of blackness breathed across her face. The air was cold. It smelled of old stone and evil. She felt an overwhelming urge to climb.

*"That's right, Andira. Come to me."*

With one hand running against the wall, she left the dream behind her and stepped onto the stair.

Round and round it took her, on and on, forever. What little light there had been fell away behind her. She held her open hand out like a lantern, but the rune in her palm had become dim. It illuminated nothing beyond the skin around the bones. She felt the beginnings of panic. The darkness was getting thicker. The walls of the stair felt closer, pressing against her chest and forcing her breaths to come short and shallow. How much further did they go?

*"What is given can be taken away."*

Andira turned to identify the source of the voice. It was impossible to find amidst its chuckling echoes. "My power does not come from you."

*"Maybe it does and maybe it does not. You are too ignorant to speak with such conviction."*

"I know."

Laughter rang through the stairs. "*You are a receiver of gifts that do not belong to you, Andira, a hero who asks no questions. A servant of destiny is but a slave ignorant of its master.*"

After what seemed like centuries, she emerged at the top of the stairs. Her heart was hammering so hard it was as though she was being stabbed repeatedly in her chest. She felt lightheaded. Her breaths came so quickly they were hardly pulling in air at all. A corridor stretched ahead of her. A horribly familiar corridor. It was low and narrow and so very, very old that only the cobwebs and mold kept it from crumbling outright.

Someone was screaming in her ear, a presence pulling on her sleeve, but she ignored them both.

At the end of the corridor, there was a door.

It was already slightly ajar, but as she stared it drifted wider, as if pushed on a breeze that had nothing to do with the whim of the evil thing that dwelled within. There was a small amount of light coming from inside.

Andira's heart lurched as she saw the awful shadow it cast across the threshold of the door: it was cold and horned and terrible, and existed until she found the strength to breathe again before fading from the floor and returning to Andira's mind.

It made itself comfortable there, laughing at her.

*"Just a little further now, Andira."*

Unable to prevent herself, she walked towards the door. It was as though the corridor was on a downward slope. She opened it fully and stepped inside.

She had to duck her head to go any further. The ceiling was as low as the corridor preceding it and crisscrossed with age-darkened beams that creaked in protest of every change in the wind outside. The single window was a grubby slit in the ancient stone. It admitted a feeble shaft of light for the dust of ages to dance in, carefree and old without the troubles of human attention.

Taking up most of the tiny garret, five ironbound stood with their heads bowed as though commanded to stand there and sleep. They stood motionless, gathered in a circle facing into what looked almost like a doorway. It hung a foot off the floor, defined only by the absence of substance or color within a frame of wind-blown dust and restless light.

Andira closed her eyes tightly. No, that was not right. She opened them again. Yes. That was how it should be. The five moribund ironbound became five corpses, skeletons clad in the moldering green and brown jerkins of marshland bandits. Their articulated bones were bent in supplication around a thing that was no longer a door. She gasped. It was an eye, the dark pupil of which was another eye, and so on, and so on, until Andira felt as though she was standing over a drop into infinity and was about to fall.

She threw her hand out for something to hold onto. A part of her was certain there was someone there although the garret was empty but for the five corpses and herself, and her hand passed through nothing.

The infinity of eyes turned their attention towards her.

Andira's head spun with vertigo.

"*I offered you the world,*" it said, the voice she had been hearing all this time rumbling from deep within this bottomless space, not a sound so much as an Ynfernael vibration to which her bones were specifically attuned. "*You denied me before, but only because you cannot understand the fullness of what I offer. Farrengol was a brat, but at least he had imagination. You, on the other hand… Maybe you need to be shown.*"

There was a barrage of clicks as the five dead men suddenly stirred. Andira backed away from them, still dizzy, as they found their feet and shambled around to face her. The demon wanted her. It wanted her fealty as it had once claimed that of the Dread Prince, Farrenghast. She did not know whether it was deluded to believe that it could have it, or whether that belief betrayed the delusional in *her* sense of moral rectitude. The worst part was that she did not know anymore. She shook her head, trying to blink the skeletons away, but they shuffled on towards her.

Remembering that she was still carrying her poleaxe, she took it two-handed and sent the heavy blade crashing through the chest of the closest skeleton. Its ribcage shattered under the blow, the rest of its frail corpse collapsing into a mound of brittle bones and decomposing rags. The remaining four drew notched and rusted swords from scabbards that were little more than scraps of leather.

She screamed with relief.

"*You still think like a mortal. Is that really the best that you can do?*"

A fierce pain in her hand forced her to look down. Her rune was glowing so spectacularly that it was making her entire arm shake, as though she had taken hold of a Star of Timmoran and could not let it go. She turned from it with a grunt, unable to bear the brightness, and thrust her hand towards the tottering skeletons. The explosion from her fingertips blasted the room to white. Andira screamed, but could not hear it for the burning in her ears. As the explosion faded, she blinked her eyes.

The dead men were all gone, nothing in front of her but mangled scraps of metal that might once have been swords. She brought her hand to her face, palm inwards. The rune's brilliance had faded to a more tolerable intensity, but it was still burning and spitting, eager to break from her flesh and mete its power on an enemy worthy of their righteousness.

*"Better. But now for a real challenge."*

She sensed a presence behind her.

The shape of her deepest nightmares towered over her. *Baelziffar*. The demon king was an inversion of light and shade, the antithesis of what a physical entity was meant to be and yet harder than stone. His muscular torso was a monstrous corruption of the heroic ideal, his black eyes empty voids that threatened to pull out Andira's soul through her skin. He was utterly still, a statue sculpted from the deepest malice of the Ynfernael, and yet, in his stillness, vibrated with a sense of menace, *the threat of motion,* that left Andira's eyes burning lest she blink and miss her own death.

Even so, she sensed that her great rival was the lesser of the evils in this room.

*"I am the one who summoned you to the Tower of Nerek. I am the master of your destiny."*

Suddenly, Baelziffar skipped the half-dozen strides to be right in front of her, his huge, twin-pronged sword overhead, poised for a downward stroke. For another agonizing split-second he remained there, still. There was no movement. He shifted from one pose to the next, the way images in a picture book advance a story without needing the stages in between. There was no way to predict or counter what the demon might do next. Andira's skin crawled as her brain fed it the premonitory feeling of the demon's sword appearing next inside her. She stumbled backwards with a scream, throwing out her hand on a reflex, and the next move that the demon king made was to crumble like a statue that had been aged ten thousand years in the blink of an eye. His collapse sounded like laughter.

The dissolution spread to encompass the garret cell around her. Andira threw her feet out wide to brace herself as the walls fell away around her, but somehow the floor she was standing on remained stable even as the rest of the Tower crashed to earth.

*"You do not even have to ask me for the power. I will give it to you. All you need do is not refuse. Do not ask yourself where it came from. Is that really so different from the power you already possess?"*

The collapse of the Tower left her standing not over a ninety-foot drop, as it should have, but on solid ground in the middle of Nerekhall common. The city stretched all around her, held at a remove beyond the borders of the common and the reach of its Ynfernael resident. It was burning. The air was thick with smoke and noise. The sound of screams came from all around. She turned a full circle. The same scene greeted her from every side.

"What is happening?"

*"You did this, Andira. Don't you remember?"*

Andira looked down at her hand. The fierce brilliance it had exhibited before had softened. It put her in mind of a feral dragon after it had feasted. It repulsed her to look at it.

*"Nerekhall is a magnet for evil. Its rulers ignore it. Its people deny it. But you and I know that it is true. They compete and they collaborate and in the face of your oppression they become stronger. They share their knowledge of the arcane and they perfect their plots for the overthrow of all you hold dear. And so this is what you did to them in return, Andira. With the power that I granted you."*

Andira shook her head. "No."

*"And this is merely the beginning."*

The view around her blurred and swam.

She saw herself.

Standing at the foot of Llovar's Black Citadel as she reached for it with her blazing hand and pulled it down. The Charg'r Wastes burned for a hundred days and nights as, by her will alone, the landscape purged itself of its Ynfernael taint. Sitting in judgment over the Undying King as his fortress at Zorgas sank into the swamps of the Mistlands. There could be only one verdict for one whose evil stretched back through the ages. *Guilty.* Only one sentence that Andira would countenance. *Death.* Driving the goblins and the Daewyl from the halls of the Dunwarr and banishing the spiteful elementals to the Aenlong. Halting the march of the Tangle and banishing it to the Aethealwyl. Banishing the spawn of Syraskil and Marnn to the deepest trenches of the Kerdosan Devide where they could but dream of the fury they had once wrought on human shores.

Her power had made her a force for good in Terrinoth. Was this vision what she could achieve if she only had more? Would that not be worth any price?

In one kaleidoscope of blood and fire, the visions carried her from Last Berth to Last Haven, from Dawnsmoor to Lorim and to cities beyond the sea. She saw them burning, evildoers begging her for a mercy she would not grant whilst innocents forewarned of her coming gathered their families and fled lest she, in her great power, judge them guilty.

"No."

She pulled back, resisting the fevered rush of judgment and sentence, of people blasted to dust where they stood, of children's faces turned up to her in terror, because who needed the distant, imagined wrath of the Stormlords when death incarnate walked amongst you.

"No!" she yelled again. "This is not the world I want."

*"I have lived inside your heart, Andira. I have dwelled amongst your thoughts. This is the world you would create if you only had the power to do so."*

"Then I am glad I do not, and no one should. I would not trade a world of small and petty evils for the rule of a tyrant."

Against the constant swirl of Andira's nightmare vision for Terrinoth, the endless procession of the guilty coalesced around a single abject figure in its foreground. It was Brother Augost. He knelt before her, his head bowed in either supplication or resignation so that Andira could see the whipping scars on his bald head.

*"Punish me,"* he said, in the resonant base tones of the nameless demon. Even as Andira hesitated, he transformed again, pulled out of shape by the forces of change to become taller, thinner; an evil-looking crone with lilac skin, red eyes and a misshapen skeleton that left her hunched and in pain but bestowed with the talons and horns to alleviate that pain in the suffering of others.

*"Am I not deserving?"*

The blood sister, Ne'Krul, looked up and smiled, and in the process of moving, melted into the more familiar likeness of Hamma Brodun.

The sight of the grizzled old knight who had followed her, molded her, believed in her, only to fall in ignominy to bandits in the forests of Kell made Andira gasp. It brought an ache to her heart, even knowing that the vision was false.

*"Is it because you fear what I would be getting in exchange? Well, fear not. As with the Prince of Dread before you, I seek only the joy of creation, of giving birth to something magnificent and releasing it upon the firma dracem to enjoy that which I will never have for myself."*

Andira shook her head vehemently as she backed away. She quenched the baleful light of her rune in her fist and hid it firmly away behind her back, lowering her poleaxe so that its blade lay by Sir Brodun's bent knee. If the woman that the demon had just shown to her really was *her* then she already owed it a debt.

It had shown Andira that she was not the person she had set out to be.

"You say that Nerekhall is a nest of evil and you are not wrong. But it is free. You say that every creature of cruel intention is drawn here to practice their dark arts and you are not wrong. It is a city of knowledge and of learning, where all are welcome so long as they can follow its rules. Trenloe and I walked into this city with refugees. *Refugees*. There are cities in Terrinoth that would have welcomed us with crossbows and shuttered gates, but not Nerekhall. *That* is the Nerekhall I choose to see. That is the Nerekhall I would fight to preserve from the likes of you."

Sir Brodun looked at her with disappointment. It was a look she had seen only seldom, but one that she had clearly never forgotten, for the demon rendered it perfectly from her mind.

*"So be it, Andira, but know that the loss is solely yours. I already have another in mind."*

The years fell away from the old knight as she watched. The lines faded from his forehead. His gray hair darkened until it was black, spreading from a severe widow's peak to the blood-spattered mop of young Hamma, the son. He was garbed in a padded jerkin rather than his father's heavy mail, and was looking up at her with a kind of willing desperation as though expecting her to do something.

One last ploy of the demon to tempt her.

But she had seen through it and it would not succeed. Brushing the young Brodun aside, she looked up.

She was back in the garret cell. It was standing and whole once again, much as it had been when she had entered. It had seen fighting, however. The bodies of Tower soldiers lay strewn across the floorboards around her. One lay with a shattered breastplate, consistent with a blow from Andira's poleaxe. Four more close by had been blasted to ash and armor fragments by runic magic. Andira shook her head.

*More lies.*

The demonic eye in the middle of the room was gone. The five skeletal bandits who had been knelt around it were again five ironbound, slump-shouldered and gazing listlessly into the wavering doorway. Thaiden Mistspeak and Karol Brodun stood protectively in front of it, side by side, brandishing their weapons and snarling at the thicket of spearpoints presented to them by a dozen Tower soldiers. Izolde was fetched up against one of the motionless ironbound, trying to stem the bleeding from a shallow wound to her bicep. Isla, meanwhile, had been separated from the others. She had been fought back into a wall by an unusually large and powerfully built dragon hybrid in dark green armor.

Whatever fighting had been going on, seemed to have stopped. Andira looked around, disoriented. She wondered why.

"Lower your hand, Andira. You should know that trinket of yours is no match for me. And while we're making demands, you can throw down your weapon as well."

Now Andira knew that this had to be one last trick.

Ravaella Lightfoot half-smiled at her as she came into the room, ushering Owl through the crowd of Tower soldiers at sword-point. The sword had been shrunk to fit the gnome's hand by some kind of magic, but Andira recognized the sword as Owl's own.

"I have told you already, no!" Andira turned her face to the ceiling and screamed. "There is nothing you can offer me, so stop playing your games."

She waited. The voice gave her no answer.

Ravaella cleared her throat.

"If you could just lower your rune, Andira, I think that really would be for the best." The gnome gestured absentmindedly towards the floor with the tip of her sword before realizing that it was supposed to be elsewhere. She swung it back towards Owl's neck. Andira flinched despite herself, but the gnome's careless swing halted just short of the skin.

Ravaella grinned, willingly owning up to her lack of experience with bladed weapons. Owl did not react at all. He had been incapacitated somehow. Black discs shadowed the movements of his face so that they hung over his eyes like the blinkers of a horse.

Andira had the terrible feeling that this might not be a trick after all. What was the last thing she remembered before her encounter with the demon behind the portal? She had been climbing the stair when– No, before that. She and the Broduns had been running ahead of the Tower's guards and then– No, *after* that.

Brother Augost smiled triumphantly at her from over the gnome's tiny shoulders. There was a sixth ironbound with him and a second, larger, group of soldiers. His arms were crossed, elbows perched across his enormous belly. His heavy mace swung from his chasuble, unused.

"Lower your weapons and have your friends step away from the rift. Let us pass unhindered, or Ravaella will have no choice but to kill your companion here and rob him of his chance of judgment." Ravaella looked unhappy about the priest's proclamation, but dutifully brandished the sword over Owl's neck. Augost went on, "And my lord, Belthir, will undoubtedly do the same to the girl."

Isla struggled to break out from the corner she had been driven into, but the enormous hybrid was immovable. Karol Brodun screamed something furious, but without words, looking as though she did not know what to do. She had not followed Andira to the very top of the Tower of Nerek because she wanted to fight Nerekhall's battle. And yet this was where Andira had brought her, just as she had her late husband before her.

Andira turned back to Ravaella. The realization that this could be real was as heart-wrenching as any vision that the demon of the Tower had been able to throw against her. How could it be that Ravaella Lightfoot had been behind this plot all along? Trenloe was trusting to a fault, it was true, but not her. How had Andira allowed herself to be fooled?

Her hand made itself into a fist. Her rune shook with such a fury that beams of light lanced through the clenched fingers. The most expedient course would be to strike at Ravaella with everything she had, blast her to ash for her betrayal and accept whatever harm befell Owl as a consequence. Even thinking it, she felt the Andira Runehand shown to her by the demon of the Tower appearing in her thoughts like a devil on her shoulder.

She unmade her fist and let it fall to her side.

She could not do it. She would not.

With a grunt of acquiescence, she dropped her poleaxe to the floor. Following her lead, Thaiden Mistspeak reluctantly backed away from the Black Rift. Karol Brodun called her children over to her and joined him in retreat.

Ravaella smiled and allowed her sword to drop from Owl's neck. "Oh, Andira. If you had only come to me sooner, you might have joined me. The power that Margath will give me is the power to free Nerekhall from its mediocrity, to show all of Terrinoth that *I* can save it from the Uthuk Y'llan and the Undying King. Tell Trenloe that I–"

The dragon hybrid, Belthir, issued a low, threatening chirp.

Ravaella smiled weakly. "Yes, of course." She turned back to Andira. "Just tell him I'm sorry." Leading Owl ahead of her, she stepped into the rift.

Andira watched it swallow them both whole, one after the other, thinking of what Farrengol's demon had told her last: that it already had another in mind.

# CHAPTER THIRTY
## *Trenloe the Strong*

Trenloe charged up the stairs. His armored shoulders bashed into the sides and scraped sparks off the stone, his body feeling as though it had assumed a perpetual lean from the right-hand spiral of all the stairs. Everything Trenloe hated about running, he decided, could count double for running upstairs.

Warden Daralyn had known less of Augost's plans than Trenloe and Rendiel had already figured out for themselves. Nor had she been able to tell them where Andira was being held or the location of Farrenghast's cell, except that it must be somewhere near the roof. At first, he had followed the signs of fighting: the gouges struck into wooden doors by swords and axes, the crossbow bolts sticking out of furniture, always climbing. Then, he'd come across the partially demolished false wall and the room full of still-warm bodies and known he was close.

He paused at the landing, standing with his hands on his hips and wheezing.

A group of about a dozen Tower soldiers emblazoned with

the orange ribbons of the Cult of the Rising Flame packed the far end of the corridor. They were trying to push through the small attic door beyond. There were some bizarre sounds coming from the other side. The two soldiers at the rear of the group turned, alerted no doubt by the wheezing clatter of Trenloe's breath as it pulled his breastplate in and out, and called an alarm to the others. They raised loaded crossbows. Trenloe gave a sigh of weary resignation and lifted his shield.

He heard the twinned *BANG* as both bolts hit the metal shield, but didn't flinch as he advanced up the corridor. A shield to the face took out the first soldier. The second hurriedly swung his crossbow to defend himself, and Trenloe struck the wooden stock in half with his axe. The man stumbled backwards, but only as far as the soldier directly behind him as Trenloe's elbow struck him in the chest. He dropped to the floor, gasping, as Trenloe stepped over him. The remaining soldiers turned around, bunched up, and closed ranks. They did not last for very long.

Trenloe became a far more effective fighter the longer the fight wore on, as though restraint was a muscle that could be exhausted with overuse.

Leaving Rendiel with little to do but avoid falling bodies and make appreciative noises, Trenloe stepped into the attic.

The room was crowded with more soldiers. Andira was to his left. Trenloe's relief at seeing her alive was cut short by the realization that she was unarmed, facing off with Brother Augost and surrounded by cultists. Thaiden Mistspeak, meanwhile, was present and in similar straits. He was standing alongside an older woman that Trenloe did not recognize and shielding a trio of children. For all the lethal looks and sharp edges on display, however, there didn't seem to be any actual fighting going on. Trenloe wasn't sure why. Something must have happened, but Trenloe could not figure out what it was.

An ironbound that seemed content to ignore everyone walked slowly through the crowd before assuming position alongside five others. They were stooped around what looked like a doorway except that Trenloe could see right through it and it was hovering six inches above the floor.

Trenloe's breath caught in his throat as he realized that he was looking at the Black Rift that the Cult of the Rising Flame had been seeking.

It looked different to the portal that he, Lidiya and Rendiel had found in the Snicks. It was older somehow, as though it had taken on something of the firma dracem's character as it matured, assuming the appearance of a door and losing its awful reek. Nor did it look as though anything monstrous was about to fight its way through. Trenloe wondered why that was, and whether it boded good or ill. Rendiel would call him a foolish optimist, but he decided to hope for the former.

For a brief moment, everyone in the attic but the ironbound had turned to look at Trenloe.

With a menacing creak, a large dragon hybrid crossed the room towards Trenloe. It had to be the leader Daralyn had warned him of, the prophet that Augost had been following. The creature was taller than Trenloe. Clad in rough pink scales, Trenloe suspected it was significantly heavier, too. Glossy green plates of glowing metal encased its barrel torso. Wings hung from its back like a pair of ragged nets, but Trenloe reassured himself that they would be more of an encumbrance than an advantage in the tiny attic. It was carrying a large scythe that wept a poisonous green cloud.

Trenloe grimaced. Another opponent with a taste for poisoned weapons.

In spite of it all, however, Trenloe felt curiously relieved. Andira was here, Lidiya was safe and with no suspicion of illegal magic to be held against her, and Ravaella was nowhere to be seen. He allowed himself to hope that there really could be a good explanation for the business with Vorakesh and Cabdal'aahi and that she had no part in Augost's insurrection.

The hybrid's eyes shone red, smoke leaking from its jaws and nostrils as it ducked a low beam in order to plant itself between Trenloe and the portal.

"We take him together," Rendiel muttered.

"No." Trenloe jerked the side of his head towards the group of children with Thaiden and their mother. "They look like they could use one of your healing songs."

Trenloe swung his head under a ceiling beam and started towards the hybrid. It was beneath him to look forward to this, but after fighting his way through cultists and soldiers he was keen to fight something that looked capable of fighting back.

It would be more than just the children in need of healing soon enough.

He rolled a crick from his thick neck. "I'll deal with the dragon."

# CHAPTER THIRTY-ONE
## *Andira Runehand*

Taking advantage of the distraction caused by Trenloe and Rendiel's entrance, Andira threw a left hook towards Augost's head. Her poleaxe was on the ground by her feet, but there was no time to pick it up without Augost being able to draw his weapon first. In any case: one punch would be enough.

Her fist smashed across the Brother's temple.

Andira was not as strong as Trenloe, but she could put enough behind a single punch to knock down a wall. Ordinarily. She cursed as Augost simply shook his head and staggered upright.

It was the six ironbound gathered around the Black Rift. They weren't doing anything to interfere with either side, but their armor was sapping her rune of its powers. She was just an ordinary woman.

Augost grinned and raised his fists into a boxing guard.

He could have gone for the mace swinging from his chasuble, but had evidently arrived at the same conclusion as Andira. It would afford her too much of an opening, and with Andira's rune nullified, he clearly felt he did not need it.

She raised her hands to mirror his as they circled one another warily.

With Ravaella and Owl having departed through the rift, fighting raged again throughout the attic. Out of the corner of her eye, Andira could see Trenloe and Belthir battling one another, seemingly taking it in turns to duck around intervening beams to strike at the other. Belthir appeared to hold a slight advantage, but she had no time to worry about Trenloe.

"You have no idea what is waiting for you on the other side of that door," she said, although she was under no illusions of her ability to persuade Augost to let her pass. She had encountered zealots like him all over Terrinoth. They were rarely susceptible to common sense.

He threw a quick jab towards her ribs. His heavy arms were slow, but she did not doubt that they would pack a punch. He smiled as she ducked back, ceding the ground rather than counter head-on.

"I know what awaits me." He returned his fists to their floating guards. "The Burning Lord and the great renewal of Terrinoth before the trials ahead of it. Praise Margath." The Brother bared his teeth. "Praise Kellos!" He threw a punch and Andira gasped as the fist burst into flame.

She leant backwards, flames rippling out behind the Brother's looping punch like the tail of a comet as it swung across the sky. She felt its heat as it singed her skin, crisping the ends of her hair as it whooshed across her face.

"My power is Kellos'," he went on, delivering a quick left and then a flaming right that forced Andira ever more quickly back. "It is a sign of his faith in me. His reward for my unwavering faith in him."

Andira raised her left hand to shield her face.

The rune had proven itself indestructible on countless occasions before now, but Augost's fist hit the open palm like a mangonel stone hitting a castle wall.

The explosion of flames shredded her sleeve down to the shoulder and burnt the skin from her face. She cried out, half-blinded, smoke curling from her fingertips as she hit the ground.

Augost laughed as he stood over her. "Runebound shards can be defiled or broken. The powers doled out to a profane chosen by the lords of the Ynfernael wax and wane with their place in the Turning. Even sorcery is nullified by the artifice of Pollux. Faith, Andira. Only faith holds primacy over all."

He raised his fist. It burned like the sun above his head. Blinding.

"Andira!" Rendiel the bard threw out a splay-fingered hand, muttering a sing-song Latari verse about a fire dimora and her unrequited passion for the waters of Mehras. As he sang, the flames wreathing Augost's fist guttered and perished.

Smoke hissed from his cooling knuckles as Augost stared at them in shock.

Andira kicked up from the ground while he was distracted. Her steel boot met his groin with a satisfying *crunch* and the Brother folded over, face red with agony and outrage. Andira pushed herself back along the floor and then rolled onto her chest, crawling quickly to where her poleaxe lay abandoned.

She dragged it to her and rose to her feet.

Augost stood in a tender hunch where she had left him, sucking in delicate breaths through his teeth. He had drawn his mace. He muttered furiously under his breath and the spiked metal began to flicker like kindling. Rendiel quickly hummed a somber tune in response and the flames shrank back into the metal, not dying out completely, but not fully catching either. Augost looked furious.

"The ironbound aren't affecting your magic," said Andira.

"Were you even *at* the Book Louse?" said Rendiel.

Andira did not have the time. "The priest is yours!"

"But, the injured–"

Andira threw a quick glance to where Thaiden Mistspeak and Dame Karol were fighting furiously to keep Augost's soldiers from the Brodun children.

"–will live," she concluded.

"Trenloe wanted me to help them."

Andira smiled. Of course he did.

But this was the time to forget about right and wrong. Their enemies were on the brink of realizing their ambition to summon their Burning Lord from across the Aenlong and it was impossible to know how terrible the consequences of that might be. All that mattered now was catching Ravaella and Owl before the Cult of the Rising Flame could complete their resurrection or the demon of the Black Realm got to them first.

With an unspoken apology, she shoved Rendiel towards Augost.

And sprinted for the portal.

# CHAPTER THIRTY-TWO
## *Rendiel*

The push in the back sent him stumbling. He cursed Andira as he threw out an arm to balance himself, thrusting forwards with his rapier before he simply ran headlong into Brother Augost. The priest was red-faced and moving gingerly, but still managed to beat the clumsy stroke aside with the fury of a demon.

Face twisted by rage, Augost took the heavy mace two-handed as though intending to throttle the handle and brought it crashing back around. Rendiel wondered what he had ever done to offend Augost besides consorting with Andira Runehand. For his part, he had always been rather fond of the priest.

Rendiel twirled neatly aside. The spiked mace-head thumped through his flaring coat-tails. He came back with a stinging riposte that clanged across the shaft of Augost's mace. The blade missed the Brother's little finger by half an inch, striking sparks that Augost, with a snarl of triumph, blew into Rendiel's eyes.

The spell was too fast, and too close, for Rendiel to counter.

He recoiled backwards, parrying blindly as Augost pressed his advantage.

Andira and Ravaella were so alike. She always thought she knew what was best for everyone. Throwing him on the priest like this would have been a typically *Ravaella* move.

"You should have drunk yourself stupid and stayed out of trouble for a week like you always do when I let you out," said Augost. "Now I'm going to have to kill you, and then I will do the same to Andira."

If Rendiel was to die here then, to be honest, Augost was welcome to her.

Wiping the last stinging mote of fire from his eye, he glimpsed Augost's smoldering mace as it burned across his vision. He reacted on instinct, meeting the incoming mace with a belated parry that sent numbness jangling down his arm. He grunted, turning the blow with a twist of the wrist, and then punched the pommel into Augost's gut. The mass of fat that the priest carried cushioned the blow. Augost simply swore and brought the butt of his shaft down onto Rendiel's head. The priest was as tough as a boar, but Rendiel was still faster. He leant into the blow at the last moment, allowing the priest's mace to slide painfully, but harmlessly, down his back. He slashed his rapier up and spun away with the rising stroke, carrying him all the way back to his feet and several paces clear as a thin red line opened across the priest's side.

Augost pressed his hand to the cut, then took it away to inspect the blood. He snorted in rage. Rendiel was no less surprised.

He had not realized his sword was still that sharp.

"You are nothing, elf. Less than nothing. You are a worthless fop and a drunkard that would spurn a hundred second chances in jest. Win or lose today, tomorrow you will find your way to whichever inn is now the worst in Nerekhall after I burned down the Book Louse, because you will have nothing better to do. I do you and this city a mercy by simply killing you now. You are beyond my powers of redemption."

A week ago, Rendiel would have taken such insults with a shrug. He would have laughed blithely and agreed, perhaps only half-listening anyway and muttering something about sticks and stones before offering to buy Augost a drink. For some reason, they stoked a fury in him now. Not at Augost for being the bearer of them, but at himself for knowing that they were true.

He thrust sharply at Augost who parried quickly, but a mace was not a weapon designed for dueling. It was for bashing knights off the backs of horses and crushing their helmets while they were down. It had been adopted by the Church of Kellos because it was just as good at smashing skeletons and pulverizing zombies: two breeds of enemies not exactly known for fighting back.

Driven by fury, Rendiel's sword slipped around Augost's mace faster than the human eye could follow, faster certainly than Augost could have ever moved. The priest bled from a hundred blunt-edged cuts as he struggled to block the stroke that had already sliced and gone, slowing every time as Rendiel only became faster.

Rendiel felt the years falling off him like a too-heavy coat that he was only now realizing he did not have to wear.

"I needed the right person to bring me back," he said. "And it wasn't you."

He thrust forwards.

The priest looked down at the sword sticking out of his

chest in disbelief. Rendiel put his hand on Augost's shoulder. The priest looked up at him, as though unable to comprehend how his god could allow such a thing as his death to happen.

Rendiel did not think that Augost had been truly evil. He had just been so certain of his own righteousness that he could overlook his cruelty to others.

There were tears in his eyes as, hand braced against the priest's shoulder, he pulled his sword from the man's heart.

# CHAPTER THIRTY-THREE
## *Trenloe the Strong*

Augost's blood-curdling shriek rang from the rafters, but Trenloe did not get the opportunity to dwell on what it meant for the battle. He was losing. However hard he hit, the dragon hybrid hit harder.

His armor felt like a cracked papier-mâché shell over a body that would probably collapse if it was taken off. It was the duel with Cabdal'aahi, the subsequent run across Nerekhall and then the fight into the Tower. That was what he told himself. If it wasn't for that then he was certain he would have been the hybrid's match, or at the very least made a more impressive fist of it than he was managing.

He ducked under a beam, bobbing sideways like a crab, and swung his axe for the dragon's legs. The dragon blocked it easily on the pole of its scythe. It gave a low chirp of amusement. The low ceiling was restricting Trenloe to blows that were too easy for the dragon to avoid. On the other hand, they allowed for free sweeping motions of the dragon's scythe.

Trenloe's shoulders ached from trying to fight whilst

hunched double, his thighs burned from shuffling sideways, his axe-hand felt as though he was wearing metal rings around each finger.

The dragon hybrid opened its jaws wide and hissed, throwing its shoulder through the intervening beam and showering Trenloe in sawdust. He coughed, surprised, thumping the dragon hard with his shield as it bore into him. His shield buckled around the shape of the dragon's head, doing more damage to itself than to the hybrid's scales. They grappled for a moment. Trenloe bashed it several more times over the head, thumping his axe handle into the dragon's armpit where there was a gap in its armor.

The dragon bore the punishment with irritation.

It beat its wings once, hard enough to lift Trenloe a foot off the ground, hover for a second, and then threw him down with the force of a collapsing building. The floorboards split under Trenloe's body. With a shudder that Trenloe felt through the broken floorboards, the dragon thumped back to the floor. It put its clawed foot on his breastplate and issued a death-rattle purr from somewhere deep inside its throat.

"You served with courage, Trenloe the Strong. I see why Ravaella could not bring herself to kill you. Die now with honor."

There was no space for it to swing its scythe.

The dragon simply raised its foot as though to stamp his face into the ground.

Trenloe tilted his head back. He didn't want the underside of the dragon's foot to be his last sight. He would much rather make the journey across the Aenlong, or wherever the spirits of people like him went when they died, with the knowledge that his friends were still alive and fighting.

It was with an unexpected splurge of relief that he saw Andira sprinting across the attic towards him…

And then hurtling on past.

He rolled his head so that it was facing forwards again, watching as Andira barreled between the handful of unengaged cultists towards the Black Rift.

No sooner was his sense of relief turning to one of bewildered upset than the dragon hybrid issued an incredulous shout of its own. Leaving Trenloe for dead, it turned after her to give chase.

Trenloe hurt in every place it was conceivable for a human body to feel pain. With a groan, he pushed himself back up.

Rendiel was cradling the stricken body of Brother Augost, tears streaming down his face and singing what sounded like a Latari hymn. Thaiden and the stranger were fighting furiously, hemmed in on all sides by soldiers. Augost's death and the sudden flight of their leader didn't seem to have dampened their zeal.

Andira threw herself at the Black Rift.

It resembled a door, but it didn't function as one. It did not open. It simply wobbled as Andira passed through and swallowed her whole, as though she had leapt into a body of black water that happened to be lying at a right angle to the ground and disappeared. The dragon hybrid followed a yard behind.

It sank without trace after her.

Trenloe thought again of how Rendiel had described the Black Realm to him: a sort of border realm between the Ynfernael and the Aenlong but belonging to neither, a place of half-formed ideas and restless spirits. It was not a place he wanted to be, but even if he would not trust Andira with his life, he would never doubt her judgment on what was necessary. If the Black Realm was where she had gone, then it was where they needed to go. There was no one left to help her but him.

With a resigned scowl, he drew himself up and strode towards the door.

# CHAPTER THIRTY-FOUR
## *Thaiden Mistspeak*

Karol Brodun slid her sword out of the soldier's side. He flopped to the floor at Thaiden's feet. He was dead. Thaiden kicked him several times for good measure, not because he expected the misguided fool to get back up, but because it felt too good to stop.

The Cult of the Rising Flame were not the same band of murderers who had slain his family and created the shell of a man he occupied now, alive in his own skin only when he had someone to hate, but they were cut from the same cloth. They slunk around the dark corners of Terrinoth, feeding off each other's delusions of righteousness, hurting people because they were under the mistaken impression that they had special license to do it without Thaiden Mistspeak tracking them down and breaking their ribs.

"Well, you're wrong!" Screaming at no one but himself, he swung the small hammer that Izolde had given him after he had broken another crossbow, staving in a soldier's helmet.

More pressed in.

Thaiden hoped they never stopped.

Dame Karol parried an overhead swing, straining to hold the sword in place long enough for Isla to stab between them. Her sword slid into the soldier's groin. His legs turned to jelly and he dropped with the most pathetic of sounds.

Thaiden screamed into the soldier's face. "Not so special now!" he yelled each time his hammer went in, over and over and over.

"Mistspeak!" Karol barked. "Focus!"

He ignored her.

He wasn't thinking about running away now. He couldn't believe he ever had. *And miss all this?* He wondered if his family would be proud of him: protecting people like them, saving Nerekhall from a dead Dragonlord alongside a band of real heroes. But that was a stupid question to ask. They were all dead and he was the one who still had to be here. Like the gullible fools with the orange ribbons, they'd take what he was damn well giving.

A figure in a blood-red coat darted in from the corner of his eye.

Thaiden swung around with a furious shout, hammer poised, but he hesitated just long enough to heed the nagging voice in his head that said he recognized the person. It was the in-house drunk from the Book Louse. Rendiel. The elf slid courteously in between Thaiden and Dame Karol. Thaiden gave a wet snort in what was meant as a welcome.

A zealot armed with a pole stabbed low for where young Hamma was defending his older sisters. Rendiel nudged it along with an elaborate parry, sending the offending fighter spinning back into the crowd with a stinging flesh wound on his cheek. It looked like trick-fighting in a circus. Thaiden rather liked it. It made them all look like fools.

"Augost is dead," said Rendiel.

"Pity." Thaiden would have done a more thorough job of it himself.

"Trenloe and Andira have gone into the Black Realm."

Thaiden snorted again. What did he care?

"We should go after them," Dame Karol shouted over the numbing clamor of steel. "We have followed Andira this far and, loath as I am to admit it, she was right."

"This *was* a bad day to visit the Tower," said Isla.

Thaiden laughed.

"I admire your vim, my lady," said Rendiel. "But I fear we're not going anywhere."

Thaiden looked up and saw what Rendiel meant. A fresh wave of cult soldiers was already pouring into the attic. An ironbound clanked in from the corridor, followed by yet more soldiers. With a crash of glass, a dragon hybrid with nightshade-blue scales and a light metallic coat drove its fist through the attic's solitary window, beating its wings hard to maintain its unlikely position high up against the Tower wall. The frame was too narrow even for Izolde, the smallest of them, to crawl through, never mind a bulky dragon hybrid, but Thaiden did not expect the old stone to hold the creature out for long.

The small group of warriors drew themselves into a circle. Karol and her runesword faced off against the dragon hybrid. Thaiden and Rendiel, the soldiers and their ironbound. The Brodun children in the middle. The portal to the Black Realm and its six iron sentinels anchored their backs. The surface of the uncanny doorway seemed to waver, as though fully aware that the coming slaughter was for its benefit.

"We hold the Black Rift for as long as Andira and Trenloe need to finish this from the other side," said Rendiel.

"Yes!" Thaiden roared, overcome with anticipation.

"For Terrinoth and for the Vale!" cried Dame Karol.

Thaiden gripped his hammer tightly.

He wished he could say that he was unhappy.

# CHAPTER THIRTY-FIVE
## *Ravaella Lightfoot*

Green fields stretched out before Ravaella, neatly tended parcels of land divided up by hedgerows, the landscape dotted with barns and windmills. The sun was warm against her face. Insects hummed in meandering clouds. The air was sweet with cut grass and wildflowers and the faraway tinkling of cowbells, the creak of a windmill's sails carried over the breeze. It was home.

Shielding her eyes and squinting against the brightness, Ravaella peered across the wide valley. The Barony of Trast was famously flat and arable. Stand anywhere you liked and you could see for hundreds of miles over picturesque villages and twinkling streams, uninterrupted by even the gentlest hill. On a clear day from the top of Castle Artrast you could see all the way to Brightvale in Allerfeldt.

Her own village was out there somewhere. It did nothing to stand out. Her family owned a small bakery there. They had been prosperous, by local standards, and respected within the tight-knit community they were part of. They had been poor, Ravaella knew now, but she had not at the time and had rarely known genuine hunger. They had all been poor. But Ravaella had always wanted something different, even if she could not explain what that something was.

Her childhood had not been as idyllic as it looked. She had grown to despise the bakery. There was nothing worse than a pre-dawn start to a young gnome that had been out all night causing mischief. She had been twenty, practically an adult by gnome standards, when she saw her first book. She still remembered the wheat blight of 1799 that had turned the fields barren and shuttered the bakery for the year.

And when kobolds had come down from the Lorim's Gate Mountains, the village had been defenseless, dependent on faraway garrisons in Castle Artrast and Summersong who could do nothing but help pick through the wreckage. Even in that, Ravaella did not know then how fortunate she had been. In Carthridge or Kell, midnight raids tended to result in scorched villages, corpses mounted on sacrificial spikes or reanimated to menace distant relatives in neighboring counties. Kobolds were thieves and vandals, and all Ravaella's family had lost were their livelihoods.

Ravaella was already gone in spirit by that point, traveling the barony with her anarchic little circus of friends, imagining a life for herself further afield even than Haverford or Dawnsmoor.

She had been tempted by the old-world splendor of Lorim, the exoticism of the Latari enclave at Therial, but in the end her dreams of studying magic had taken her further, to Greyhaven. Knowledge was power. It was the one thing that she and her family had never had.

She never wanted to be weak again. She would never be dependent on others again.

The wind ruffled through her long, red hair and she closed her eyes, feeling it on her face, softening the warmth of the day. She shook her head slowly.

She had not been back to Trast in twenty years. Her parents were both still alive, her brothers and sisters. She wrote to them regularly though they wrote back less and less. The bakery had never been rebuilt after the kobolds destroyed it. They had been taken in by cousins in Summersong and employed by a guild baker with connections to Baron Rault.

None of this was right. None of this was real.

The wind fell away.

She opened her eyes.

She was in the faculty room of the Academy. Portraits of distinguished former magisters looked down from the walls. Ravaella had always dreamed of filling one of those golden frames one day. A fire roared in the stone hearth. Curios crowded the mantelpiece. Nerekhall was the home she had never known she never had. It had accepted her when Greyhaven had spurned her. It had not cared that she was poor, untrained, or chronically undisciplined: they had seen her ambition and they had nurtured it. It did not matter to her that it was dark and wet and always cold. Those things could be fixed by good, solid walls and a well-fed hearth. She loved it. Everything she was and had she owed to Nerekhall, and she would give it all to protect it.

"Where are we?" said Fredric.

The baron of Kell was standing beside her. His battered armor looked burnished in the gloom, the gray in his hair coming out for the firelight like worms from the soil after a heavy rain. The blinkers had fallen from his eyes and he was looking around in confusion. For a moment, Ravaella was confused, too. This room and Fredric did not belong together. Then it came to her.

She snapped her fingers.

*Of course.*

The Tower of Nerek. Candlestick's welcome. The fight. The stand-off with Andira and her friends.

Entering the portal.

She stared at the trinkets on the mantelpiece, examining them with newly critical eyes. She was in the Black Realm. The Aenlong. This must be how a mind unequipped for a realm of unbound potential dealt with a landscape without form. The mind was adept at filling gaps in its perception from its own experiences. Most of the time the results were woefully inaccurate. That was how the most basic illusions worked – which cup is the ball under? It was behind your ear all along! – but in creating the seamless impression of a world where no world existed, Ravaella had to marvel. She wondered if this was why those who had flirted with death and come back always spoke of familiar scenes and reunions with loved ones.

A tingle of excitement ran through her. She was *this* close to the resurrection of the Dragonlord. Soon, all the power she ever dreamed of would be hers.

With that in mind, she raised her hand and wriggled her fingers, smiling as she performed the cantrip that caused her fingers to shift in and out of visibility and to change color. It was the first spell she had ever mastered. Her ability to access the Turning seemed to have returned now that the ironbound were behind her. Indeed, she felt stronger than ever.

She concentrated. The world fell away and a new one arose in its place. A castle assembled itself around her, stone by rugged stone, the walls of the Academy tumbling to reveal a landscape that plunged away from her and stretched on from there. It was rural and rugged, as different from the fields of Trast as two landscapes from the same plane of existence could be.

The forest to the south was a sea of sibilant greenery that ran from horizon to horizon. A wide river sparkled in the distance and beyond it a range of great mountains made a wall of snow-capped rock between this world and the next. She was standing on the high tower of a sprawling castle that was perched on a rocky hill. Purple and gold banners bearing heraldic owls snapped in the fierce, icy wind.

"Where do you think we are..." She made a series of arcane passes with her hands, layering herself with another spell. "Father?"

Fredric turned from the view, looking at her for a moment, before tears welled up in his eyes and he dropped to his knees with a cry of grief. He cupped her face in his large, human hand, staring at her as though part of his mind was consciously willing him to reject the illusion but could not shout loud enough to make him do so.

"Grace," he said, choked with emotion. "My girl." Giving in to it at last, he threw his arms around her. "I had a terrible dream where I had forgotten you. I tried and I tried, but I could not remember."

It almost broke Ravaella's heart to perform this last, awful trick on the poor man, but it was necessary. She told herself that it was necessary. She needed him present if he was going to help her reach Margath's spirit. "It's all right, Father. It was just a dream. I'm here now."

Fredric shook his head, still holding her. She felt him shudder in her embrace. "It felt so real."

"Where are we, Father? It's important."

Drawing his hand from her hair, Fredric stood up, leading her by the hand to the parapet. He stared out. "Why, this is Kezian Tor, of course, the highest point in Castle Kellar. You can see right across to the northern reaches of the Barony from here."

"Do you see Margath?"

Owl opened his mouth as if to answer, but then paused, head cocked. "Margath… But Margath the Unkind died eight hundred years before you were born."

"I need you to call him, Father."

"I don't understand."

"Please."

Ravaella unbuckled her sword belt and passed it to Fredric. The moment it left her hands and returned to his, it reassumed its proper human proportions. He looked at it for a time, doing nothing but remembering.

That blade, if the stories of Kell's recent battles had not been exaggerated, had tasted the blood of the Dragonlord Acherax, Margath's own living kin. Fredric himself was the distant heir of Roland Dragonslayer. Simply being there in that place with her, holding that sword, thinking the name *Margath* was like a clarion. It was a summons that rippled across the infinite ether of the Aenlong.

The banners flying over the castle's walls suddenly caught and fluttered, as if in a stiff wind. The trees of the great wood sighed.

Ravaella gripped the rampart and looked out eagerly. There was a part of her that was terrified. Margath was the monster of eight centuries of folk nightmares, the calamity from the Heath who had brought down the Elder Kings. But she was excited, too. Ravaella had always been the child who would decide what she wanted and take it, uncaring of the consequences.

"Margath the Unkind!" she called, adding her own voice to Fredric's blood call. "Burning Lord of the Dread and the Cult of the Rising Flame! On behalf of your loyal servant, Belthir, I call you back to Mennara!"

She waited, listening.

Her fingers danced impatiently on the stone. Although the Aenlong had boundaries, most theologians believed it to be infinite. That circle was squared by the theory that the concept of distance, at least insofar as most residents of the firma dracem would reckon them, did not truly exist there. She had been expecting some kind of sign that Margath had heard her almost immediately.

Could it be that the theories on which the arcane community's understanding of the planes rested were flawed?

"Fascinating…"

*No.*

The Dragonlord should have answered her by now. Perhaps the problem was not with the order of the planes, but with her tools. She turned to Fredric.

While her focus had been elsewhere, the baron had turned away and was now looking bemusedly around himself. "I thought Acherax destroyed this part of the castle. I remember…" He closed his eyes and winced as though whatever it was pained him. "Gods, I remember."

Ravaella whirled back to the ramparts, sensing that something was very wrong indeed and that it was not her understanding of the planes. She looked down. A number of ant-like figures were now moving across the hills towards the castle. They looked like Uthuk Y'llan, raiders running towards the castle. She shook her head violently. She was in the Black Realm, a misplaced thought away from the edges of the Ynfernael. Whatever she thought she saw in this place, it was not going to be Uthuk Y'llan.

"Margath!" she screamed, and received no answer.

Only a crushing sense of emptiness.

There was only one explanation for it. Her hands were trembling as she considered it. She drew them uncertainly from the battlements. "Gods help me."

Margath the Unkind was not here.

Which could only mean…

"Margath the Unkind isn't dead."

# CHAPTER THIRTY-SIX
## *Belthir*

Something was wrong. Belthir could taste it on his tongue.

He flew on tattered wings over a landscape of boiling lakes and scorched yellow forests. It was an amalgam of features from the Molten Heath, which he dimly recalled, the Weeping Basin, and the wooded hills between Pelgate and Otrin that humans called the Gardens of Tarn. He had spent so much of the past eight centuries there, in service to his dead master, that it was as close to a home as anywhere. He beat his wings, catching the sulfurous thermals rising from the cracks in the earth. All that was hard, cold-blooded, and good in him told him that nothing in this place could be fully trusted. The dragon in him perceived the Aenlong on its own terms, as it truly was, but that abject part that the Dragonlords had made human overcompensated with the familiar, creating an anarchic amalgam of disjointed scenes.

He did not know whether the anxiety he felt belonged to the man or the dragon, but it was troubling both. Something was *wrong*. He knew his master's taste, had held it in his thoughts for close to a millennium, and if he could be certain of one thing then it was that Margath the Unkind was not here.

"Master!" he shrieked in desperation as he arrowed through sulfurous clouds.

There was no answer.

For eight hundred years, he had striven to continue Margath's unfinished work, insofar as the great Dragonlord had seen fit to reveal it to him. He had raided human settlements and plundered them of their magicians and lore. He had fomented unrest. He had made alliances. He had undermined the successors to the Soulstone legacy in every small way he could. After its possibility had been made clear to him, he had followed others with the dream of bringing about Margath's resurrection. Even as his scales had splintered and faded to gray, as his once-great host had dwindled for want of the draconic art to reproduce, Belthir had continued.

For Margath.

Margath, who had combined the elements of Belthir's being and breathed first life into his spawning pool. Margath, who had instructed him. Margath, who had trusted him. Margath, who had rewarded the razing of Kedrun and the rout of the Jourgar orcs by lifting Belthir to his right claw. Margath, whom he had praised as a god and a father until a weakling warm-blood named Dragonslayer had taken him from this world.

In the cold stillness of his heart, Belthir yearned to see his master again.

He lived only to serve.

"Master!" The clouds parted as he swooped low.

Demons that his eyes refused to perceive as demons crawled over the volcanic plains. His keen, reptilian eyes picked out Ravaella and her human catspaw, Fredric, though he could not fully make out what they were doing. He marked, as well, the position of Andira Runehand, swamped by half-formed beasts as she struggled through her own mistaken impressions of the Black Realm. Belthir had followed her across the rift to give chase, but had soon left her behind.

Hard, unfeeling skin prickled with a sense of disquiet.

Ravaella had entered the Black Rift well ahead of him. He understood the nature of the Aenlong better than most and doubted himself less than any. If the gnome was going to be successful, then she should have been successful by now.

*"Margath is not here."*

The voice came to him as a dry whisper in the back of his skull. It was the voice of human weakness, of sensory confusions and doubt. He rejected it with the dispassion of a lizard ignoring the buzzing of a fly.

*"Your master has abandoned you."*

Belthir knew that was untrue. He had served loyally for twelve human lifetimes. He was so much nearer to victory, to kneeling before his master again, than he had ever been before. He bared his fangs and exhaled a plume of smoke. But that was not to say his concerns were unfounded. Ravaella should have achieved something by now.

*"When will you realize that it is you who has to lead?"*

Belthir was a servant. It was the purpose for which he had been spawned. Obedience was in his bones. Pride was the emotional offspring of ambition: human foibles all that Belthir did not possess.

This had to be Andira's doing. The human woman with the arrogance to carry the mark of the dragons in her flesh. She had spent several slow heartbeats in the Black Realm before Belthir had arrived to pursue her. She must have done something to thwart his master's return. It was the only explanation.

*"It is not."*

An anger he would not acknowledge kindled in his breast. This was *her* fault.

*"Ravaella should have killed her. And Trenloe the Strong."*

Yes, he thought. She should. He wondered why she had not.

Belthir split the air with a fierce, predatory shriek, tucked in his wings, and plunged. The false landscape rushed towards him. He felt its heat, smelled its pleasantly sulfuric reek. Andira Runehand turned and looked up, alerted by the ruffling of wings, but for a warm-blood she moved far too slowly. His clawed feet slammed into her back, throwing her to the ground and sending her skidding across the rocks. He thumped his wings to soften his own landing, setting his feet on the false ground with an enraged hiss and stalked after her. One of the demonic things that the woman had been battling reared up at him. It had too many limbs and not enough waxen flesh to cover them all. Belthir cut it down with a snarl.

"Where is my lord, Margath? What have you done?"

The woman gave him a look of disdain that would not have been out of place on a dragon. Belthir reached her just as she had climbed back on her feet. He cast his scythe aside, struck by the need to tear the life from this woman with his own teeth and claws. He grabbed her by the shoulders, untroubled in the least by the weight of her armor, and lifted. His breath blasted her face.

"Give him to me!"

"I do not know what you are talking about."

Andira thrust out her hand.

A blue flash filled his eyes. A freezing burn skewered his

chest. For a moment it felt as though he was flying again, only backwards and without the aid of his wings. He thumped the ground with his tail and blinked the membranes across his eyes until they cleared. Andira was now two wingspans ahead of him, her open palm held out to him. The rune traced into it glowed balefully like ensorcelled ice, shriveling the illusion around her to reveal the fog of the Black Realm as an eerie, unsettled blue. Feeling an ache in his chest, Belthir looked down. There was a scorched handprint on his breastplate. He exhaled wrath. The metalcraft of Margath himself, defiled.

*"He does not deserve such loyalty."*

With a growl, he picked up his scythe and rushed at her, ignoring the unformed things that tottered out of the Heath towards them both, drawn by their life and shape and the *definition* of their emotion. He swung his scythe, a reaping action from right to left that would have cut her at the stem had she not blocked it on her weapon's metal pole. The vibrations shuddered through both weapons, but Belthir's hands were unresponsive and cold. While Andira staggered, he delivered a headbutt with the hard, scaly end of his snout. He tasted burnt flesh on his lips. The woman stumbled with a cry, impulsively retaliating with an open-handed punch that buckled his shoulder plate and almost spun him to his knees. Belthir gnashed his fangs in fury.

"Do you find me a different proposition now, without your ironbound to shackle me?" She was breathless, but still proud. "This hand slew a monarch of the Heath over Castle Kell. His fall leveled most of the keep. What are you compared to him?"

Her invocation of the Dragonlord's name was almost enough to make him waver, but his anger was too intense. Even inbred obedience was unequal to the task of smothering it.

She spoke of Acherax, of course. Belthir had heard the reports of his death, but they had all attributed the killing to Baron Fredric. Was that the reason that Ravaella's summons had proven ineffective? If it was then he would devour the gnome himself. Was the direct lineage from Roland Dragonslayer not strong enough without the blood of Margath's kin on his hands?

*"That is not it. You know it. A direct heir of the Dragonslayer is more than adequate. There is only one explanation for Margath's failure to heed his cherished lieutenant's call."*

With an outraged shriek, Belthir drew his scythe back.

Something behind him caught it.

He craned his head back, confronted by the unexpected sight of Trenloe the Strong. The man should have been dead. He was battered, bruised, bloody, clad in armor that was hanging off him in pieces but held onto Belthir's scythe with his strength undiminished.

Belthir had a moment to peel his lips back over his teeth, before Trenloe buried his axe in his neck. The heavy blade blunted itself on Belthir's scales, but retained enough weight and sharpness to sink deep into the muscle. Belthir howled with the first real pain he had felt in centuries, but even that paled in comparison to the anguish he felt at finding that his master was not here to receive him.

He had failed. Somehow, he had failed again.

*"No. It is Margath who has failed you."*

Belthir shook his head. He grunted as Trenloe wrenched the axe out of his neck, and slumped to his knees as though all the blood had just run out of his head.

"The master cannot fail the servant."

*"He is not here. Ravaella will tell you herself that it is true."*

Belthir closed his eyes. He had been there at the Battle of Weeping Basin. He had seen Margath fall, his body entwined with that of the human hero, his runic sword driven deep into the Dragonlord's throat. He had seen that lake turned to steam as it broke his fall, and had guarded his mortal remains from relic-hunters and pilgrims ever since. Margath the Unkind was dead.

"*He is dead. But he found his own way back. I saw it all.*" The voice in his mind chuckled. Neither the sound nor the feeling behind it was one that Belthir's lips were capable of reproducing. He was beginning to question whether the voice really was that of his human weakness. "*For decades now, Margath the Unkind has been at large in the firma dracem, and he never even told his most faithful servant.*"

Belthir jerked as Trenloe fought to lever his axe out of his neck. He should have felt cold as the life left him, but he felt *hot*. A true dragon did not feel rage. A good servant did not expect a master's loyalty.

He told himself both of these things.

"*Who are you*?" he thought to the voice in his mind.

He felt it smile. "*I was hoping you would ask.*"

# CHAPTER THIRTY-SEVEN
## *Trenloe the Strong*

Trenloe planted his boot into the dragon hybrid's back and levered his axe until it came loose. It wrenched free with a spurt of iridescent blood and a waft of grass seed that made Trenloe want to sneeze. He pinched his nose and held it back. It was hard to keep reminding himself that he was in the Black Realm, and not his father's farm in Artrast. That it was not Rusticar he could hear stamping his hooves and demanding his morning apple, or his father calling out to him from behind the hay bales. Even knowing that none of it was real, there was a part of him that wanted to leave the hybrid and help the old man with the hay, introduce him to Andira Runehand, feed his horse one last time.

He turned back to the hybrid. Trenloe was of half a mind to hit it again, just to be sure, but he found defiling a body as distasteful as attacking a person from behind. After the fight the hybrid had given him, though, he had chosen to make an exception. Just this once.

"Is it done?" he asked Andira. "Is it over?"

"I do not know."

Andira was leaning into her poleaxe. She looked decidedly

less fearsome in the middle of a Trastan hayfield as opposed to a Daewyl ruin or a sewer. Her hair was as yellow as freshly baled straw. The rune in her hand shimmered like water in an ornamental pool, as though it understood somehow that there was no need for such destructive magic here. It was the Harvesthorn sun, he thought – it showed everyone in their best light. He gave his head a deliberate shake. *Not real.* He focused instead on the dead hybrid. That was the one thing all his senses could agree on.

"Ravaella is still out here." Still leaning against her weapon, Andira turned away from the direction Trenloe was vaguely thinking of as *back*, peering over the endless field of nodding grain. Trenloe wondered what she saw. Did she see the childhood home she didn't remember, or were dungeons and battlefields all she allowed herself, even in her own mind? For some reason, the effort of putting himself into Andira's head made taking a firm line with his own that little bit easier. *Not real.* "Until we find and stop her, I am not certain that the danger to Nerekhall is passed. I am certainly not leaving Owl here with her."

"Owl is here?" said Trenloe, surprised. "I thought he was taken to the Tower with you. What's he doing with Ravaella?"

"I neglected to ask her while she had his own sword to his throat. Maybe you can ask when we find him. She's *your* good friend after all."

Trenloe coughed. Even that made his chest muscles ache. "It sounds as though we both have stories to share once we're out of here." He looked up, frowning across the hayfield as what looked like a man and a child hurried towards them, the latter being dragged by the arm by the former. The man was tall and clad in gold where the sun brushed his armor. The child, or what had appeared at first to be a child, was shorter than the wheat stalks the man was pulling her through. She had long red hair and was robed in black. They were both periodically looking back over their shoulders and seemed to be in some haste.

Trenloe pointed. "Ravaella," he said.

Andira turned, just as Owl pulled Ravaella out of the tall grain and onto the swath of freshly scythed ankle-length stalks where she and Trenloe were standing.

"He's not here…" Ravaella muttered to herself, apparently only dimly aware that she was even moving. "How can he not be here? Belthir always said there was something calling him to Nerekhall. If it wasn't Margath, then who was it?"

She stopped talking when she saw Trenloe and Andira waiting for her. She looked from one to the other as though uncertain what to say or think, or what to expect. Then she noticed the dead hybrid and seemed to shrink even further. Trenloe was relieved that she was not going to make them fight her.

"It's over," he said, finally.

"It is about to be." Andira lifted her poleaxe out of the ground and started towards the distraught gnome.

Trenloe found himself between them. He dwarfed Andira. He could have lifted her like a child if he dared. The stare she turned on him terrified him more than any dragon or rune-powered war machine. It took all his stubbornness to stand up to it.

"She's beaten, Andira. It's over."

"Let us assume that Ravaella did whatever she did out of good intentions," Andira said. "She allied herself with the Dread, and stole lore she claimed to have destroyed in order to corrupt the Nerekhall ironbound to her cause. People have died, Trenloe. More would have, if not for you."

"I know, but..."

Andira gestured angrily to the hybrid, on the ground behind her. Trenloe was almost certain that he saw the half-severed neck twitch.

Just his imagination.

"We don't have time for this," said Owl.

Andira looked taken aback. She was not used to her companion voicing opinions of his own. Now that Trenloe properly looked at him, there was something different about the old knight, a worldliness and a weariness that he wasn't sure had been there before.

"Do not tell me that you are going to defend her, too?" said Andira.

"I'm saying that we need to get back to the door," said Owl, checking back over his shoulder once more. "There is... *something* behind us."

"And I am saying that a person who thinks they have done no wrong can never be redeemed."

"Fortunately, the place we're running to is the most notorious prison in the world."

"Trenloe!"

Trenloe jerked awake when Andira shouted his name. He had been staring at the hybrid's body. As such, he was about as ready as a person could be when the corpse gave a sudden lurch for Andira. The woman cried out in surprise as Trenloe pushed her out of harm's way and sank his axe into the hybrid's skull.

To his astonishment and rapidly mounting horror, the hybrid issued a sibilant hiss that Trenloe took as laughter. It wrenched the axe out of its brow ridge and tossed it aside. Trenloe watched as the two sides of the gaping axe-wound reached out for one another and pulled themselves closed.

Trenloe backed away as the hybrid stood. It grew in height as its spine straightened and elongated, bulking out, limbs thickening, until Trenloe could barely recognize the creature he had fought in the Tower of Nerek.

This went beyond mere necromancy. This was Ynfernael magic. A hideous red glow shone from its eyes. Smoke gouted from its nostrils. Liquid fire leaked between its teeth in myriad weird and otherworldly hues. It looked down its lengthening snout at Trenloe as though it was smiling.

"Belthir..." said Ravaella, staring up at her former ally, open-mouthed. Owl had let go of her arm in order to properly handle his tainted sword, but it had either not yet occurred to her to escape, or she had chosen not to.

"No," said Andira. "Not anymore. It is Farrenghast's demon."

Trenloe looked sharply at Andira. Rendiel had warned him of something similar.

"What?" said Ravaella, confused.

"Oh, I am still Belthir," the possessed hybrid hissed, continuing to pack on new muscle at an alarming rate. "I have only found myself a new master. One who rewards loyalty with power instead of lies and neglect. As he might still reward you, Ravaella, if it is still power and acclaim you hunger for."

The gnome looked ill.

"We need to run!" Owl yelled.

A motley assortment of drudge-like creatures came shambling in from the field. They were long-limbed, and uncertainly jointed, like monsters made of wet clay. Some looked vaguely like Uthuk Y'llan, or Kellar knights, or Trastan farmhands. One neighed like Rusticar. One grumbled like Trenloe's father. Seeing them up close filled Trenloe with horror.

"My freedom from Margath and the Dragonlords is

complete!" Belthir shrieked, and his elation shook the ground and the sky around them. "I do not even need them to make more of my kind."

A summons passed out from the possessed hybrid. Trenloe felt it go through him as though all the bones in his body were being oriented in the Turning. With each step they took, the Black Realm beasts became more sure of themselves and the shape that Belthir wished them to hold, as though they had been set into molds. A handful of increasingly certain steps later and the transformation was almost complete: the first wave of a horde of hissing dragon hybrids marched aggressively towards Trenloe and his friends. Far too many to fight, even assuming that Belthir could not simply fashion more.

He stared at them in horror.

"Back to the Tower!"

He tugged on Andira's arm, but she resisted. The woman glared up at the now-building-sized Belthir. The halo of flames that wreathed the possessed hybrid danced across her face with every variation of color.

"It is the enemy that called me to Nerekhall. I will not leave here with him unslain."

"He's in the Black Realm where he belongs," said Trenloe. "Close the door behind us and make sure he never leaves."

Andira scowled, but gave up resisting as Trenloe pulled her away. Ravaella and Owl were already ahead of them, tearing through the hayfields towards the rift.

"You cannot run from me!" Fire roared from Belthir's jaws.

# CHAPTER THIRTY-EIGHT
## *Andira Runehand*

Andira screamed as the flames swallowed Trenloe. She did not know if the possessed hybrid remembered the one who had struck the killing blow on its mortal flesh, or if it attacked Trenloe rather than her purely by chance. He screamed, arms flailing, but the flames shriveled back almost immediately, all except for his left sleeve which caught suddenly ablaze. Andira thumped at it but the fire would not go out. It felt as though there was a hot coal against his wrist.

Groping under his sleeve, Trenloe pulled something out. Andira stared in astonishment. It was a runestone. How long had Trenloe been hiding a runestone? Trenloe yelped as the white heat of the runestone forced him to drop it. It fell to the cracked flagstones of the tomb complex and sputtered. Belthir gave a shuddering moan and sagged. His new-grown form rippled and even shrank a little as the Ynfernael magic that sustained it ran instead to the stone.

Trenloe bent to pick it up only to hiss as it scalded his fingers.

"Come on, Trenloe." Andira flung his arm over her shoulder,

turning hand out-stretched, to blast a loping demon-hybrid's head from its shoulders.

"You waited for me," Trenloe said.

Andira was hurt that he could sound so surprised. She had not defied Farrengol's demon just to damn her friends. To her shock she found she meant it. They were her *friends.* They mattered more to her than the evil she fought. "I would never leave you."

Leaving the precious runestone to lie in the grass, she hauled Trenloe up and ran.

Trenloe hated running, she knew, but he would live.

They closed on Ravaella, the gnome's shorter legs drawing her further and further back towards Andira and Trenloe. Andira caught the arcane words she was uttering, each sound accompanied by a pass of her wand as though she was accumulating energy with every stroke.

"Belthir wants to play that game, does he?" The gnome's outline began to blur into the gloom of her surroundings until Andira felt the need to blink because she was seeing double. There were *two* Ravaellas running ahead of Belthir now. Each one continued to wave their wands albeit to a slightly different pattern, weaving together a subtly different string of words. Two Ravaellas became four. Four, sixteen. "His demon will rue the day it thought it could make a fool out of Ravaella Lightfoot!"

All but two of the Ravaellas turned and started running back towards the slavering hybrids that Belthir had fashioned from the Black Realm beasts. Fourteen pairs of hands sent fourteen variations of lightning bolts, fireballs, and hails of ice raining down on the demonic hybrids. Giant beasts bounded out of the nothingness of the Black Realm at her command, apparently illusory until they started ripping into the hybrids' necks. Clouds of chromatic bees swarmed their faces. Spitting images of Trenloe, Owl, and even Andira split off from their original likenesses and turned, yelling in their own voices as they charged back into the fray.

Watching herself hacking into demon hybrids was a forceful reminder of the *her* that Farrengol's demon had tried to show her. The bleak but familiar illusion of a Roth's Vale crypt wobbled around her, like a curtain in a breeze, as the gnome unleashed her power across it. Andira wanted to scream at her to stop.

She gritted her teeth and ran.

"I see the rift," Owl shouted.

The floating doorway looked even more ominous under a sealed tomb than it had in the Tower of Nerek, and yet its appearance was identical. Owl leapt through. His passage left no effect on the door at all. It was as though he had fallen into a hole. Next through were the Ravaellas. Andira felt a lump in her throat. She had taken her first jump through the Black Rift without stopping to consider it.

Trenloe squeezed her arm, and she nodded.

She took a last look back. The Brodun's family crypt was as dark and dimly remembered here as it was in her memory. She wondered whether it was the demon's cruelty or her own that made the Aenlong appear to her in this fashion. It had always been a part of her, she supposed, a burden of guilt that she sought to lighten with greater and greater quests rather than acknowledge.

Dame Karol was right.

That was a mistake that she now had the chance to set right. The demon had shown her that she needed to.

But she had to get out of here first.

She brought up her arm, as though to shield her face from the surface of the rift, and leapt herself and Trenloe across with a yell.

She felt a brief tightening across her skin, like a piece of leather being stretched taut before being let go, and then she was through. The sights, smells, and sounds of the firma dracem hit her as though the real world had slapped her awake and revealed the entire experience as a dream.

Rendiel, a grinning Thaiden Mistspeak, and the Broduns leant on each other and their weapons. They were stood in the aftermath of what looked to have been an extraordinary final stand holding the Cult of the Rising Flame from the Black Rift. The bodies of rag-wearing cultists and soldiers lay around them. A shattered mass of armor, formerly an ironbound, was particularly conspicuous under Thaiden's boot.

An elven woman in elaborate gold-filigreed armor, Warden Daralyn she presumed, was busy directing loyal soldiers to restrain the survivors. One overzealous soldier attempted to put manacles on Rendiel's wrist before a few stinging words from Dame Karol of Carthridge sent him fleeing back to the warden.

An older woman with short gray hair and sleeveless work robes tinkered with the modified ironbound that were standing still around the Black Rift exactly as they had been. Andira assumed that she must be the Chief Artificer of Pollux. Andira had never heard the woman's name. The Artificer was taking measurements with a set of golden calipers, comparing them to a set of schematic drawings she had in her hand, and scratching her head while she muttered sums under her breath.

Andira turned to Trenloe with a weary smile. They had made it.

Then a draconic demon hybrid burst through the rift behind them.

Andira cursed, letting go of Trenloe who hobbled a few short steps before crumpling to the floor. The man was exhausted, but still tried to push himself back up. His axe lay somewhere in the Black Realm, a relic to be unearthed by some other hero in the days far from now. She stepped between the hybrid and her fallen comrade and punched with an open hand.

And nothing happened. There was not even the tingle of power flowing from the rune into her hand.

Andira drew her hand back and snarled.

She should have stayed and fought Belthir in the Black Realm. Here in the Tower of Nerek, her powers were worthless.

Trenloe raised his arm from the ground and called a warning as two more demon hybrids emerged through the rift. She had expected the portal to prevent Belthir's creations from crossing over. They were creatures of the Aenlong and should not have been able to survive for long in a warded environment such as the Tower of Nerek. Whatever Belthir had wrought on them, molding them into facsimiles of his own kind, must have hardened them to the painful realities of the firma dracem.

They could not fight an army of corrupted hybrids without the Tower's ironbound. Nor did she relish the prospect of testing Belthir's newfound powers without recourse to her own.

The first of the hybrid soldiers gurgled and collapsed into the formless putty from which Belthir had made it, catching a crossbow bolt from a startled soldier in the mouth. The other two hissed and ducked to either side, the portal behind them already wobbling and straining as it threatened to disgorge still more. Owl accounted for the second with a looping, overhead stroke of his sword. The cursed weapon smoked as it took the demon's head and greedily immolated it, the metal reddening like a hot iron in the taint leaking out of the rift. The knight followed up, stepping over the dissolving body, and struck through the last. The cherry-red blade shrieked in delight as it devoured the monster's Ynfernael essence.

Owl's sword spun, his grip reversing in a display of swordsmanship that Andira had rarely seen matched so that the smoldering tip angled down towards the Black Rift itself.

In that moment, Andira saw what he meant to do. She wondered how Owl knew to do it, but the awareness of his actions was there in the weight of his eyes. At the last he hesitated, as though reluctant to give up this last part of who he was.

"Do it," Andira yelled.

With a grimace, Owl plunged his sword into the Black Rift.

A scream from the other side blasted a gale through the garret cell. Andira felt the shockwave as it lifted all of those stood nearest off their feet and hurled them into the milling ranks of Tower soldiers behind them.

After a moment or two waiting for her head to clear, Andira sat up with a groan.

The door stood exactly as it had been, but Owl's sword was now struck through it, hanging there in midair like a magician's trick. The blade glowed an unwholesome red, sated finally by all of the demonic energy it could ever consume, and was slowly filling the attic with brimstone-scented smoke. Trenloe covered his mouth and coughed out a sigh of relief.

The Black Rift was sealed. There would be no more hybrids coming through. Belthir and all the might he had been given were firmly trapped on the other side. Warden Daralyn could reseal this wing of the Tower and let Nerekhall forget about it for another thousand years.

Trenloe lay back down. "Thank the gods. It's over."

Leaving him, Andira picked her way around dazed soldiers and Brodun children towards Ravaella. The gnome was sitting on the ground near to where the blast had thrown her. She gave Andira a resigned smile. She made no attempt to escape. "Now it is over." Andira reached out for Ravaella, only to scowl as her hand passed straight through her. The gnome winked up at her.

From his spot on the floor, Trenloe began to shake with laughter. Andira remembered that there had been *two* Ravaellas escaping the rift with them.

Now there was only one.

# CHAPTER THIRTY-NINE
## *Ravaella Lightfoot*

Ravaella looked up from her desk as the door to her study burst open.

She had spent a magnificently underwhelming few hours in the company of the city magistrates in the Grand Forum and had only just made it back to her desk. With the rest of the Academy in uproar about dragon hybrid attacks and rogue ironbound, she saw an excellent opportunity to get ahead on some of her peers.

It made these kinds of interruptions all the more vexatious.

Her counterpart stumbled in through the open door, looking tousle-haired and anxious. There was mud on the hem of her robes and blood on one of her sleeves. Her wand was glowing like a faded coal in her hand. She looked as though she had intended to magic herself directly here but had not had the strength and so had been forced to run halfway across the city on foot. She shut the door behind her and leant on it while she gulped down her breaths. Ravaella took a wild stab that she had not brought herself good news.

"So... how did it go?"

"You don't want to know."

Ravaella sighed. Marking her page with the feather quill of a dry pen, she closed her book. That was disappointing. Belthir had made her some grand promises, but this was Nerekhall: there would always be other cults, other plotters, other willing and not-so-willing partners who could open the right doors to the power and status she craved. She just needed to put herself out there, to be in all of the right places at just the right times.

For Nerekhall, of course. Always for Nerekhall.

She rocked back and forth on the edge of her seat, steepling her fingers and wiggling them while she thought. Her counterpart fidgeted impatiently.

"Can you not keep still for a second?" she said. "It's very distracting."

"I was about to say the same."

Ravaella frowned. She kept the worst company.

"We should leave. Trenloe and Andira and half the Tower's ironbound are probably on their way here now."

Ravaella looked around sadly, wondering how many gnomes it would take to carry all of her books and possessions safely out of the Academy in the next half hour or so. She sighed again. It sounded like the opening line of one of Rendiel's jokes.

Springing out of her seat, she cracked her knuckles. She whipped the wand from her belt.

Yes, quite the pity indeed.

She had rather enjoyed her position in the Academy, but every setback was an opportunity. A change was just a chance to learn something new. And she did not want to be here when Trenloe and Andira arrived. Next time, she supposed, she would really have to find it in herself to deal with him properly.

For Nerekhall.

Of course.

"Yes," she said, raising her wand. "I suppose we'd better."

## CHAPTER FORTY
*Owl*

Owl sat on a pile of netting in the barge's prow, watching the sun set on the fields of Cailn. Most were yet unplanted, barren and brown and twinkling with a late frost like heralds of the stars to come. The acolytes of Pollux were out lighting lamps along the wharf. The barge's boatswain hung a lantern from the wheelhouse, muttered a prayer to the Artificer God and leant over the side to hawk a gob of spit into the water.

The river was technically exempt from the laws of the city, curfew included, but it was a rare captain who wanted to risk a night moored in Nerekhall. Owl could hear the woman's rough voice yelling over the commotion of the docks. Andira was still arguing with her over the fare for their passage, even as Trenloe single-handedly carried the Broduns' considerable belongings up the gangplank. Rendiel had turned the aft-deck into an impromptu dance floor for the crew, much to the exasperation of the cockswain in charge of poling them off. Owl could hear Lidiya giggling as she clapped along to the elf's jig. He smiled. How long had it been since he could just sit and close his eyes and listen to children playing?

Borne away by the strains of the Aymhelin lute, Owl wondered at Andira's change of heart. What had convinced her to abandon her long quest for Baelziffar, or to call off the search for Vorakesh and Ravaella in order to join Karol Brodun on her journey to Roth's Vale?

"There are other evils imperiling Terrinoth beyond the Ynfernael," she had said. "Perhaps we will find them in Carthridge."

Trenloe had seemed pleased. He had looked particularly happy to be making the journey by river and had requested Owl wake him when they passed Castle Talon in six or seven days.

Owl wondered if there was a part of Andira that was not also tempted by a return to the Vale, where this quest had all begun for her. It was Ravaella, he remembered, who had put the idea into her head. She had told Andira that there was more to her power than she had questioned yet, and that there was another in Terrinoth, sitting on the throne in Carthridge coincidentally enough, who possessed a similar power.

At the thought of Ravaella, Owl fingered the hilt of the long knife buckled at his hip. He knew better than anyone else how strong the appeal of the past could be.

The prow rocked as someone sat down beside him.

Thaiden Mistspeak leant over the gunwale rail, letting his feet hang over the side. He had taken his boots off and the cold water lapped eagerly at his toes. He had a bottle of something in his hand. He took a swig and offered the bottle to Owl, who demurred. Thaiden shrugged and took another pull. He scratched his short beard, looking across the river.

"I always liked the water," he muttered reluctantly, as though his own fare for traveling with Andira and her companions was to give up this one small, precious account of himself.

"Not me. My wife was born to it, though. I had to dig her a lake so she would not take our daughter back with her to Dallak." Owl smiled at the memory. He and Litiana Renata had spent half their words together arguing over one petty thing or another, but they had grown into their roles as political spouses and had loved each other in their own way. He missed her. He wondered if she missed him. He smiled again, but it hurt. Knowing Anna, she had not yet forgiven him for dying.

He saw Thaiden looking at him, perceptively, and realized he had given away more than he had meant to. Trenloe clearly suspected that there was something different about Owl since his capture at the Book Louse, but he did not know what. Andira, however, as lost with the complexities of her fellow human beings as Trenloe would be with a book, had not noticed. Owl intended for it to stay that way.

Yes, he yearned to see Kell again. It felt like another life. Not one he had lost, but one that had been cruelly taken away. He would give anything to feel its cold wind and freezing rain on his face, to wake up to the smell of the ice on the Dunwarr before glimpsing the sun, to hold his daughter and never let go, to somehow make his absence over the past year right again.

*Almost* anything.

From what he had heard on his travels, Grace had proven a surprise to many with her swift maturity into the leader the embattled province needed. Alliances had been struck. Hernfar Island had been retaken. Castle Kellar had been reoccupied and, though still largely in ruins, the great horde of the Uthuk Y'llan had been held there, their leader, Ne'Krul, drawn north to Forthyn and killed in battle. Kell did not yet prosper, but under his daughter's stewardship it had found its feet again. He could not threaten all she had achieved by returning from the dead now. If his experience with Augost and Ravaella had taught him anything, it was that the title of *Dragonslayer* was his burden to carry now.

Better to take the name with him into the wilderness of the far north and lose it there.

His heart would always be in Kellar, with Grace and Anna. He would always feel it pulling. But he could not go back.

It was as Andira had said.

There were other evils, other ways to serve Kellar and keep his family from harm. He would find them with her.

"Have you noticed how all the boats are heading the other way?" Thaiden gestured towards them with his bottle.

Owl nodded, deciding it was safer to stick to saying as little as possible.

He had noticed.

It was how he knew they were going in the right direction.

## ABOUT THE AUTHOR

David Guymer is a scientist-turned science fiction and fantasy author from the north of England. His work includes many novels in the *Warhammer*, *Warhammer 40,000*, and Marvel universes, notably *Dark Avengers: The Patriot List*, the bestselling audio production *Realmslayer*, and *Hamilcar: Champion of the Gods*, which has since been adapted into an animated TV series. He has also contributed to fantastical worlds in video games, tabletop RPGs, and board games.

*bobinwood.wixsite.com/thirteenthbell*
*twitter.com/warlordguymer*

ARKHAM HORROR™
Riveting pulp adventure as unknowable horrors threaten to tear our reality apart!
LAIR OF THE CRYSTAL FANG
S.A. SIDOR
SECRETS IN SCARLET
EDITED BY CHARLOTTE LLEWELYN-WELLS
IN THE COILS OF THE LABYRINTH
DAVID ANNANDALE
THE DEADLY GRIMOIRE
ROSEMARY JONES
GRIM INVESTIGATIONS
DARK ORIGINS
THE COLLECTED NOVELLAS VOLUME 1
DAVE GROSS • GRAEME DAVIS
RICHARD LEE BYERS
CHRIS A JACKSON
CULT OF THE SPIDER QUEEN
S.A. SIDOR
THE DEVOURER BELOW
LITANY OF DREAMS
ARI MARMELL
MASK OF SILVER
ROSEMARY JONES
THE LAST RITUAL
S.A. SIDOR
WRATH OF N'KAI
JOSH REYNOLDS
ACONYTEBOOKS.COM